"Elizabeth Crowens takes aim at what we've found familiar and adds a twist of surreal adventure that is fun, entertaining and delightfully different from what is expected. SILENT MERIDIAN is a rollercoaster ride with a side of the sublime. Highly recommended!" **James A. Moore, best selling author of the *Seven Forges Series*, *Aliens: Sea of Sorrows* and the *Serenity Falls Trilogy*.**

*   *   *

"This is one of the most unusual and offbeat novels that I've read in years. It bridges several genres in a seamless and cohesive fashion. Devotees of Conan Doyle, H.G. Wells, Freud, Jung, Harry Potter, Ninjas and Samurai, and the Edwardian Era will all find something of great interest here. The book constantly turns in unexpected directions and holds the interest from start to finish. Be prepared for a rollicking journey down a complicated and fascinating route, beginning with the surprising, ending with the unexpected and leaving all wanting a sequel." **Robert S Katz, MD, BSI Sherlockian and Co-Editor of *Nerve and Knowledge: Doctors, Medicine and the Sherlockian Canon***

*   *   *

"A magical mystery tour of early twentieth century Europe that blends time travel, psychoanalysis and the occult. It's a rare first novel that succeeds on every level, but Crowens pulls it off with panache. An intriguing and original debut!" **Alan Smale, Sidewise Award-winning author of *Clash of Eagles***

*   *   *

"A case of mistaken identity (or was it?), a secret society and a mysterious red book propel a young music student and Arthur Conan Doyle into an adventure through time and the paranormal. "Silent Meridian" is the first-rate first novel in a new series by Elizabeth Crowens. I can't wait for the next installment!" **S. P. Hendrick, author of *The Glastonbury Chronicles* and Tales of the *Dearg-Sidhe* series and *Raven's Daughter*.**

*   *

"In his lifetime Conan Doyle seriously investigated spiritualism and ... things that go bump in the night... In *Silent Meridian* Crowens extrapolates what might have happened if he had joined forces (quite literally!) with a paranormal investigator with unusual powers of his own - a psychic archaeologist who travels in time! What they uncover about the past - and a possible future - will leave you wondering what karma you unknowingly carry with you. It's a fine romp through time and space and the infinite dimensions of the mind."
Robert Stek, PhD, Transpersonal psychologist, Baker Street Irregular, lecturer on Conan Doyle, *I Hear of Sherlock* contributor

*   *   *

"The mind is truly infinite in what we can achieve!!! For anyone interested in history, time travel and progression into the future this book is a fascinating read."
Heather Holman, Reiki Master, Member of the Past Life Therapists Association, www.regressiontherapywales.co.uk

*   *   *

"Just when you thought time travel has been exploited so often, Elizabeth Crowens takes you to totally new places with a mash-up novel worthy to place beside Nicholas Meyer's works (including *The Seven Percent Solution* and *Time After Time*) with a with a soupcon of Tim Powers. Take all your favorite Victorians and mix them in a TARDIS-like cocktail shaker, and you'll be in a time loop -- revisiting this wonderful debut of the Time Traveler professor series until the next installment comes out. A wild, engrossing book that will delight you as it takes you to worlds and events unexplored, until now."
Jim Freund, Producer/host of *Hour of the Wolf* over WBAI-FM in NYC since 1972.

*   *   *

To Sir Arthur Conan Doyle
Then, now
and in the future

Edinburgh, 1898

Scotland was just barely crawling its way out of the nineteenth century. I was a naïve, but ambitious student studying music at the University of Edinburgh hurrying over to meet Arthur Conan Doyle, the man who would change my life forever.

"John Patrick Scott, sir," I said as I approached Mr. Doyle, who was already seated at a back corner table where he hoped he wouldn't be recognized. He had picked the Deacon Brodie, the pub that inspired the *Strange Case of Dr. Jekyll and Mr. Hyde*.

I extended my hand to greet him and removed my rain-soaked hat, while my overcoat slipped out of my hands and fell on the floor by accident. It was still hard to believe that good fortune had finally brought us together, but we were both nervous.

"The pleasure is all mine." Doyle responded like a father to his son.

"Mr. Conan Doyle, or should I call you Doctor Doyle?" I said unsure how to address him.

Doyle scrutinized me from top to bottom as he signaled the waiter. "John, call me Arthur," he said casually, ignoring the tension I couldn't control.

"Sir, I'm so honored that you agreed to discuss this matter. Perhaps you can enlighten me in a way that I've failed to comprehend."

I wanted to ask him about my unusual turn of events straight away but he caught me off guard and was dead set on pulling me into the swift current of an unexpected conversation.

"Can I assume you believe in the transmigration of souls?" he asked.

"Until now, I haven't given it a lot of thought," I said, unsure as to which direction he was leading.

"Did you ever read those books about that Swiss doctor who felt his body and soul had been taken over by a Benedictine monk? That presented a curious case. He claims that he was approached by the spirit of an elderly monk before he died, and that the monk needed to *rent* his body to continue his spiritual mission."

"Rent?" I choked in disbelief.

"We truly don't take anything with us when we pass on, do we? This monk knew that he was dying, and therefore had to replace his physical body with something more youthful and vital."

"That's incredible. It debunks the theory that you have to die and be reborn as an infant to carry on your spirit," I said.

Mr. Doyle had the tinge of excitement in his voice.

"John, here's another instance. I've had my suspicions about a famous musician who had an obsession about a notorious and controversial mystic. You'd surmise by his overwhelming attraction to that person that he might've been him in a previous lifetime, but facts were clear that he was born three years before the mystic died. My understanding is that the mystic knew he didn't have long in his present incarnation. Therefore he made plans for some sort of partial soul transference while he was still alive to imprint his essence upon the child. That would've allowed him to carry on and accomplish unfinished business that couldn't have been executed otherwise. Essentially he had the ability of being two places at once."

"Sounds more like Spiritualism," I replied.

"Honestly, John, I don't think there are any steadfast rules when it comes to this matter. That's what makes it so intriguing."

I sensed he had a secret agenda.

Doyle reloaded his churchwarden pipe with fresh tobacco and continued, "This is not at all like anything you've ever read from H.G. Wells or Jules Verne. We're poking holes in every treatise written on the subject— the idea of being able to reincarnate a part of yourself while you are still alive into another soul."

Our conversation was quickly becoming like a speeding train ready to jump the tracks. Realizing this, Doyle slowed down the pace and took a deep breath. He carefully composed his next statement.

"Fiction it may seem to be but it's not hocus pocus. Don't you also find it strange that you somehow found yourself initiated into a mystical order on a commuter train bound from London to Edinburgh when the instigators kept on mistaking you for me? There are no accidents."

I became silent for a moment, stalling for time as I slowly raised my glass of ale to my lips. As soon as I fished a small red book out of my coat pocket and placed it on the table in front of us Arthur eyed it intently. It had been the source of intrigue that led me to Doyle in the first place and had piqued his curiosity as much as it did mine.

"Could I have done something terrible in my youth that caused this to happen?"

"You have no recollections, John?"

I bit my lip as internal chaos wrested with memories. "I remember so little of my childhood. I wish that I could."

"You're a smart young man. I'm sure you'll come up with a clever deduction."

Mr. Doyle paused to relight his pipe. He had an unnerving look in his eye, which I vainly tried to read into, but he took me for a spin when he brought up the next topic.

"On another note, John, have you ever considered that people have the capability of communicating without speech, and I'm not talking about writing letters?"

"Pardon me?"

3

"Imagine communicating by mere thoughts. I've always wanted to experiment with someone open to these concepts. God knows—my brothers at the Society for Psychical Research certainly talk enough about it. My wife, Touie, has been an unwilling subject and is not the most objective choice."

I looked at him, somewhat perplexed. "Are you asking me to accurately guess what you're thinking?"

"Come now. We'll play a game. I'll form an image in my mind, and for the next minute I will try to project it into yours. Clear your thoughts of any distractions and be as receptive as possible," he explained.

As much as I tried, I couldn't have been more preoccupied. Images of that fateful event flashed through my brain. Once again, my recollections revealed my rain-soaked train ticket in hand. I kept arguing with the steward that I thought he was putting me in the wrong cabin. An erroneous judgment had been made when three strangers insisted that I was Arthur. He and I couldn't have been more different in physical appearance. He was a large, athletic man with a distinguished moustache. On the other hand, I had baby smooth skin and couldn't grow facial hair to save my life. I was nearly twenty years younger and much shorter with wild auburn hair that resembled Maestro Beethoven's with the exception of premature strands of gray.

It was impossible that I could've been mistaken for him, so why was I singled out? Was there laudanum in my brandy? Details spun like a whirlwind. I must've been in a drug-induced stupor but I was initiated into some secret Masonic-like society, and when it was all over those mysterious men were gone. What remained were an engraved silver ring on my finger and an ominous red book on the seat beside me.

"Looks like you've seen a ghost," Arthur said breaking my trance. He realized my thoughts had been elsewhere.

4

"I felt like I had," I said, barely able to articulate. I tried to tame my wild mane in place. Visions faded in and out. Timelines jumped. So I gulped down another swig of ale to focus on the present.

Arthur leaned in closer. "I can see you're still worried about that event on the train. Those men have been after me for some time. Why? It's hard to fathom. I'll dilly-dally with notions here and there about Sherlock Holmes and his partner, Watson, who fancy themselves as detectives. Me? I'm just a simple doctor and writer with interests in Spiritualism trying to find scientific explanations for the unknown."

"Arthur, what would anyone want with an unassuming music student like me?"

"Personally, I don't think this was *A Case of Identity*," Arthur replied with a smile.

Obviously he meant to say that my dilemma was not a case of *mistaken identity*, not the name of one of his famous Sherlock stories. He was pleased that I caught the humor of his play on words.

"Perhaps it has something to do with that book," he said pointing to the one I had brought.

"I'm concerned that it's dangerous, that it's a curse. I wish I had never found it," I replied as I shoved it back into my pocket and drained my glass.

*   *   *

One week later as I was returning home from school, my landlady, Lydia Campbell, yelled from the kitchen as I trudged my muddied shoes through the front door of her boarding house. "John, a letter from Undershaw arrived for you today! I wonder whom it could be from? You don't know anyone from Undershaw, do you?"

Oh, yes I did. I snatched the letter and ran upstairs so fast that I nearly tripped on my muffler and fell on my face. I poured myself a glass of port to calm my nerves, doffed my wet garments and sank into my most comfortable brass-studded leather chair that I affectionately called my *thinking chair*, where I had created many a melody in my head, could think deep thoughts, and drift off to dreamland.

*　　　*　　　*

Dear John,

I wholeheartedly enjoyed our conversation at the Deacon Brodie and kept my promise of a prompt reply. By now, you are well aware of the fact that my passion to explore the realms of Spiritualism and related paranormal phenomena far surpasses any personal interests involved with Sherlock Holmes. Public demand for my writing, however, exerts a strain on how much I can overtly reveal to even my most trusted colleagues. Whenever I indulge in any activity, be it a simple séance, investigating a revered medium or attending a meeting of the British Society for Psychical Research, it never fails to raise the eyebrows of my wary publishers and critics. I truly believe in many of these inexplicable accounts. Even my father painted beautiful renditions of fairies, which I trust that he witnessed with his own eyes. The betterment of mankind rests on embracing such theories once they are proven to exist by the scientific community. Thus, I suspect I'll have to continue more controversial and debatable endeavors in utmost secrecy, or at least for the time being until more evidence can be brought to light.

Since you seem to be an open-minded young man who has already experienced some effects of the preternatural, this is my proposal: At midnight every night, we should conduct a variety of remote operations with the primary purpose of communicating through means of telepathy. Since I have a tendency to travel, we'll have to make some sort of adjustment to take into account the different time zones. Of course, you must share this secret with nobody. Besides us, only my wife will know, although she will not participate.

When you shared the account of the strange incident onboard that commuter train that was enough to convince me that you would be the perfect partner for this private undertaking. Most assuredly, there was something you had done in the past in the realm of the arcane to warrant that chain of events. That was not mere happenstance, and now since you possess that enigmatic red book, I'm sure it will affect your life in ways that you've never imagined.

My intentions have been to also perform similar trial and error enterprises with Harry Houdini, a rising star whose stage performances have been astounding audiences, but his busy schedule has made it nearly impossible so far to coordinate such engagements with any sort of regularity. One of these days we'll catch up. Meanwhile, I collect whatever news comes from across the herring-pond. I suspect that at one point, he and I will develop a special relationship based on mutual interests.

Regarding the two of us, however, we'll back up our observations with letters or telegrams as often as possible as proof of results, but those must be destroyed as soon as they are read. Once again, I cannot overemphasize the importance of confidentiality. Whenever we know that we will be otherwise engaged, we should attempt to communicate with each other in spirit to apprise the other of that fact. Regardless, we must keep a faithful agreement, as skill will come with practice.

If you are willing to put aside any apprehensions regarding trains, I'll pay for you to travel down to Undershaw and visit me on weekends whenever possible. My driver can meet you in London at a pre-arranged time. You'll stay in one of our guest bedrooms, and as long as you don't mind the children and can tolerate what our kitchen staff provides, you'll be well taken care of. That'll give us the opportunity to expand our repertoire and commence further psychical experimentation with ectoplasm, spirit photography and astral projection. And bring that book. I'd like a chance to look at it.

I've also desired a partner to accompany me for ghost sightings and occult investigations. For all we know, with the knowledge gained, we might even break through the barriers of time. That would certainly give Bertie (H.G. Wells) a shock to the senses, proving that his imagination does not merely dwell in the realm of fiction. He and I have been at odds on this topic for years.

Regarding telepathic technique, I can only suggest that you conduct yourself in a way as you see fit. Personally, I don't believe in things like magical amulets, but if it helps to have an etheric link with me, use this letter you hold in your hand, as it contains my heart, soul and signature with a drop of blood, which I have added to the ink. You might wish to reciprocate.

Let's raise our glasses to honor the quest of conquering the unknown.

Arthur Conan Doyle

*   *   *

Arthur apparently was serious when he first brought up the subject. When he and I left the pub, I really didn't know what to think. After all, he was a famous author, and I was merely a student. What possessed him to choose me for such an engagement?

I shuffled through my schoolwork to find my pen and ink and a fresh sheet of paper. Blood, I needed blood. Ah, my razor! That would work. I fetched my shaving kit and winced as I drew a few drops. I scribbled a swift, affirmative reply with the blood-tainted ink, mailed the letter the following day, and looked forward to our first otherworldly encounter.

*   *   *

Conscious Sleepwalking

Since Arthur firmly believed that death was not the ultimate finality, who was to say that the two of us hadn't experienced a significant encounter in a previous existence, and this wasn't the first conscious time we had set foot on earth? Time travel became a never-ending fascination. I was unstoppable. My curiosity was limitless, and I desperately sought ways to find proof. Considering the fact that one of my favorite stories was H.G. Wells' *The Time Machine*, I took it upon my own initiative and built my own construction, which was no easy undertaking. There were many thwarted attempts before I could confidently say that I had achieved any success, whatsoever.

How this time machine worked was another mystery. What I never expected was that in my pursuit of perfecting this invention, I got more than I bargained for. Metaphorically speaking, it was like saying that I was attending the university to get a degree, but I unwittingly learned how to sprout wings and fly to the moon in the process. Once enough magic doors were opened, whether I liked it or not things changed. I began to transform into something unexpected, which I was assured was for the better, although often I begged to differ. Personal ambitions unraveled. Friendships and associations fell apart or felt shallow and worthless. Nightmares appeared more real than they had before and manifested in physical form on my doorsteps. Many times I'd venture either into the past or the future, and I'd bring back a souvenir. Sometimes it was a tangible object. Other times it was merely unlocking a long obscured memory, and often it wasn't welcome.

The recently discovered Neptune was considered the planet of dreams. Whether or not you believed in astrology, it induced many prominent Victorian scholars to explore new frontiers. Darwin's theory of evolution toppled religious dogma, but in reaction to the Industrial Age, that mysterious planet also influenced an interest in exploring the depths of the human mind and the realm of the unknown, challenging the limits of scientific knowledge.

Tables were tipped. It was like having a clever stage magician swiftly yanking off the tablecloth of perceptual reality, but leaving the candelabra intact with all observers wondering how it was done.

Discovering facts about the past was amusing, but even more exciting was being able to capture glimpses of events to come. The future was never absolute. It could be changed with the blink of an eye. It was mutable and quite dependent on volition and free will. Nonetheless, it was an obsession, and I'd conduct test runs in any which way possible using a variety of techniques, some benign and others not, but regardless I was always treading into dangerous waters to see what the future might bring.

I hurried back to my flat after class and dumped my book bag atop my cluttered worktable causing a haphazardly stacked pile of books to tumble to the floor. These books were atypical of a student aspiring to become a composer and concert pianist—ones on elementary physics, astronomy, earth science, and, of course, a brand new copy of H. G. Wells' *The Time Machine*.

With my motley assortment of research material, sundry gears and machine parts, lamp fixtures and the guts from broken clocks, I meticulously set up my own version of a time machine fashioned from an old hand-cranked electroshock device. I had jerry-rigged together a mechanism consisting of an old leather belt with magnets running alongside both lobes of my brain facing their polar opposites. However I wanted the magnets to move and not simply bolted or glued, so I inlaid small grooves with a set of gears that would move them side by side almost like a tiny train going down its own track. To power that motion I would drop in special mineral pellets. I really had no clue what they were, but the man in the shop who sold them to me said that once I tossed enough of them into water that they would instantly cause the water to boil and create steam, and that's what would cause those tiny gears to move the magnets along their course.

I must've forgotten to refill its canister from the last time, but all was well as my timepiece indicated that I had spent way too long dallying in *extracurricular* activities, and it was time to head off to my next class. It wasn't really vital that I utilized such an elaborate construct, but if it was theorized that it could give a boost to my currently developing psychic abilities, I was all for the chance to test it.

In fact, my flat was beginning to look more like an alchemist's den. Of course, I still had my upright piano in the corner with its metronome perched on top, as well as, scores of sheet music and books on music theory. How could I not? But now I was gradually collecting a strange assortment of rare books, mostly procured from back alley establishments as well as trinkets found in curio shops. There was also unconventional laboratory equipment, as well as herbs and minerals that I'd acquire from the medical and science colleges, often bribing the lab assistants for their discards. Alas, I continued to curse the day when I elected not to take a chemistry class. It would be reassuring if I fully understood the nature of the elements I'd be working with and not feel like I was groping blindly in the dark.

Lydia, my landlady, was beginning to wonder if I was becoming an eccentric. I finally requested that she knock first before bringing tea, rather than barging in without warning. This put me in the habit of locking my door more often, something I hadn't thought about previously.

The very first time *it* happened, it was like watching a novice weightlifter struggling with barbells way beyond his capacity. I looked to see how long, if at all, it would take for my time travel experiment to work, and the first thing I noticed was that the second hand of my timepiece started wobbling like the needle of a compass near a lodestone. Almost like Atlas shouldering the burdens of the world (and very similar to the experience I had when I encountered a strong headwind the other day, catching me dead in my tracks unable to advance forward), my watch's second hand, against all odds, started trudging backwards. Its minute hand followed suit using leaden baby steps, eventually pulling the hour hand in tandem.

My lungs were barely able to function. At first I drew a few quick breaths through my nostrils and choked down a few gulps of air, fighting against suffocation. Instinctively I dispelled my panic, slowed down my heart rate and took very long, slow, controlled breaths deep from my abdomen. Although everything around me seemed to be spinning out of control, I needed to be operating in slow motion. Houdini knew this technique. I was certain of it. This was one of those magician's secrets whereby slowing your vitals and heart rate you could survive the odds of extreme heat, severe cold or being buried alive. I think the Hindu mystics even performed this when averting pain while lying on a bed of nails.

Perhaps, one day I wouldn't need an elaborate or expensive scientific contraption to catapult myself beyond conceivable physics. Wouldn't it be great to prove H.G. Wells wrong and that traveling through time was more of a mental journey? Maybe he just romanticized it as a physical machine in order to make it more believable. It was reassuring, yet scary nonetheless, to know it was a lot easier than depending upon an elaborate assemblage.

Not to say that I didn't love science. I loved science, but I was never a man of science like Arthur who was impressively trained as a physician. I understood music theory, tempo and a scientific explanation behind sounds. I was also willing to accept ideas that tonal vibrations had their intrinsic metaphysical qualities linked with planetary rhythms that scientists failed to understand or find proof. It might've been an act of faith on my part combined with so much arcane material handed down by the ancients, but time travel defied all rationale. Deep down inside I knew that the possibility of it existed on some level or another. In that effect, one might have accused me of being as mad as Arthur was in his quest for proof that there was life after death, that spirit photographs could be made of the dearly departed, and ectoplasm could be documented spewing forth from mediums' mouths.

Even Houdini's head would turn if he were able to experience what was happening to me now. My first results took me back only five minutes, which didn't seem all that significant except for the physical sensations of fighting an enormous force of gravity. Each successive exercise became a little bit easier, and as long as I was able to achieve the proper state of mind, projecting into alternate dimensions became as easy as slipping on a fresh change of clothing. Eventually, I was able to develop a semblance of procedural consistency.

Was I finally prying open the door to my past that wished to remain shut? My subconscious had unlocked a vault pointing to another institution of knowledge, not the University of Edinburgh, but one arcane and forbidden, but as much a part of my soul as the blood coursing through my veins. Finally, I was remembering.

Not too long ago, I was having a fitful and sleepless night. My landlady's cat woke me hours before sunrise. Drowsiness caused rationality to fly right out the window. But as I reached for my diary to jot down an account of the perplexing dream I had woken from my attention was diverted to that peculiar red book that I had acquired after that unsettling *incident*. Something about that book transcended the barriers of time, but left a permanent impression that I'd carry back with me to the present.

In my dream I had stepped back into the past. No longer did I look like a redheaded Scotsman. Instead, I appeared slightly older as an employee of the Imperial Palace in ancient China named Jiang Pan Sheng.

"Jiang, you were supposed to have attended the arrival ceremonies of the Emperor's third cousin from Nanjing!" Li Zhi Wen shouted as he stormed into the room.

Calmly, Jiang Pan Sheng, a revered scribe of the court, placed his brush and bottle of ink aside. He had been fastidiously working on a lengthy book, one of many for the collection of the Imperial family. This book, quite different from most, was an elaborate anthology of fables. Some were about mythical creatures. Others were about people from foreign lands. This one told the story of a young explorer, and he titled it in Japanese, not in his native

13

tongue. It was called *Shokunin, The Thief of Tales—the same name of the book that I had back in Scotland*!

Undaunted, Jiang quietly went over to a washbasin to remove excess ink that had spilled on his fingers, then returned to sit upon his silk cushion.

"She was the fifth cousin to his grandmother on his mother's side, not the Emperor's third cousin. Besides, no one informed me about it, so I remained here and continued my writing," Jiang replied.

"All Imperial affairs demand your presence no matter who they're for!" said Gao Xun An, the other man from the welcoming party.

"I was never notified. Therefore, I'm blameless. Perhaps, one of you should take the fall if questioned?" Jiang suggested.

His two associates looked at each other in horror. Such an indiscretion, depending on the Emperor's mood, or one of his aides acting in his behalf, could come with the penalty of death.

Li spoke first. "Jiang, your apathy may one day cost you your life."

"I do not fear I will die from an insult to the Imperial court. I fear that I might die of a broken heart, instead," Jiang replied as he smiled and carefully folded his hands in his lap.

His two colleagues looked at each other, rather disturbed. Imperial court servants were always under the watchful eye of someone above them who monitored and observed their personal affairs down to the very last detail. Being part of the court carried way more privileges than merely being a simple farmer or a town merchant, but restrictions came hand in hand.

Li Zhi Wen took out his fan, a hand-painted one edged in gold with a long red tassel dangling from the end. He whipped it around and angrily struck Jiang across his forehead.

"Ouch!" cried Jiang. "What's that all about?" He rubbed his head. A stinging red mark remained.

"Next time it could be worse!" his friend warned him, but suddenly all three of them were interrupted by a fairly large group of

14

children that ran into the room chasing a small monkey with a ball. Li and Gao promptly exited and left Jiang to contend with this unexpected surprise.

Amused, Jiang arose from his comfortable seat as the children filled the room following the monkey that had stolen one of their toys. He quickly gathered his brushes and his ink to prevent the children from knocking them over and proceeded to carefully take his manuscript with its ink still wet and place it out of harm's way. Like a lively circus parade, the children circled his study several times before they chased the monkey out of the room. Just as Jiang reached over for his workbook and was ready to return to his tasks, another uninvited and quite peculiar group of youngsters wandered into his room.

Immediately, Jiang noticed a remarkable contrast in their attire, and that they were not Chinese, but foreigners from different lands, ones that he had never been to and didn't know much about. Their garments were made from cotton and wool, not silk, and it was clear to him they were neither acquaintances nor members of the Imperial court. They looked more like peasants or villagers, but certainly not from anywhere nearby.

The children, on the other hand, eyed Jiang Pan Sheng as strangely as he must have looked at them. They entered his chambers and examined all of the novel objects and surfaces while boldly running their fingers over the unknown textures of silk, porcelain, carved cinnabar and jade, and of cherry wood and imported teak. They spoke in languages that he failed to comprehend. Some had dark hair, but nowhere near as black and silky as his, and they all wore it significantly shorter in a variety of coifs but in hues of chestnut, red and even gold—colors he had never seen before and never knew that hair could be.

Spellbound, Jiang returned to his cushion and observed them in quietude unsure if these were ghosts, or perhaps fantastic human-like creatures, which had stepped from the pages of folktales and legends—the characters of dreams and of flights of fancy.

15

"Come, we should go," the oldest boy called out as he gathered the group together from exploring Jiang's private quarters. "We shouldn't be here, and we don't want trouble."

As the other children rallied to his side, Jiang silently put his finger to his lips indicating that he wouldn't breathe a word about them to anyone else, but before they parted, one last boy, a precocious little lad, who was a bit shorter than the rest and had a head of curls like Jiang had never seen, approached Jiang. He pulled a strange coin from his pocket. It appeared that the child was trying to offer him the coin, but as soon as Jiang reached for it, it disappeared.

Jiang was confused and shook his head. He looked down on the floor to see if it had slipped out of his fingers, yet he never heard it drop. Then the curly-haired boy held out his closed hand. Slowly, he opened his fingers to reveal the missing coin. This completely surprised Jiang who looked up and saw a huge grin on the child's face. Once more, the boy handed him the coin but somehow magically, the coin would disappear and then reappear again in the boy's hand.

Finally, the oldest boy called out, "Erik, come!"

Erik ignored him, intent on tricking Jiang one last time.

"Erik Weisz, come here at once!" the oldest boy shouted, angrily. Finally the small lad ran off to join his friends, and they all scampered from the room. Jiang was now alone and unsure of what had transpired and where those foreign youngsters came from. Then an Imperial messenger arrived and spoke with a sense of urgency.

"Jiang, a captive has arrived from Japan. You've been summoned to assist the prison wardens. They suspect he was involved in a shipwreck."

"Very well," Jiang replied, as he reached for his hat and heavy silk outer garment. Japan was one of the very few countries Jiang was familiar with, as he had traveled there several times with the court as a goodwill ambassador. He was also the only member of the Imperial court who had studied and learned their language, which

16

looked similar when written, but sounded very different on the tongue. With that, Jiang reached for a scroll bound with colorful red string and followed the court messenger out the door.

*   *   *

After I was done entering these accounts in my diary, I stared at that ominous red book once again, but this time it bothered me so much that I put it away and hid it in a drawer. My mirror revealed that not only had my auburn hair had grayed prematurely, but I must have appeared twenty years older than my actual age. The cat hopped onto the credenza and pawed at it wildly, as if trying to tell me I was supposed to turn my mirror around facing the wall. I eased back into my favorite chair, the one I called my *thinking chair*, and became lost in my thoughts thinking about all of the strange dreams I had for more years than I could remember.

Soon I began to feel the soft, warm fur of Lydia's cat rubbing up against my side, but she started to scratch and dig her claws into my left pants pocket. I threw her off, but she insisted on jumping back on my lap. There was no food inside; so what could she have wanted?

Something, which I didn't recall being there before, dug into my thigh. I reached in and felt a smooth, round metallic object— a coin, but not one I'd normally be carrying. United States of America was engraved upon it, a place I had never been, and on its face was the head of one of the American Presidents. I soon learned that often, when I traveled in time, I'd bring back a physical memento to prove that I actually had gone elsewhere or elsewhen.

"Erik Weisz, that curly-headed child from the dream? Wasn't that Harry Houdini's real name?"

Dreams? Dreams powered my time machine, or so I was beginning to suspect. There was an etheric alchemical power that tied into the workings of the universe. Not steam, not interlocking gears, clock mechanisms or bizarre sundry gadgets I'd construct. This limitless force was way beyond that.

*   *   *

Partners in Crime

It was way past midnight, cold and damp with the fog so thick I could barely see my feet, and I felt like the village idiot. While all the sensible and sane residents of Edinburgh had crawled under their covers to go to sleep, I was shivering in front of *Bluidy* George Mackenzie's mausoleum at Greyfriars Cemetery. I had thrown my waistcoat over my nightshirt, donned my overcoat, wrapped my muffler tight around my neck and done a miserable job of hiding the pieces of my homemade time travel device under my tatty top hat. Popular rumors were that his angry spirit haunted the kirkyard. I closed my eyes, took out my grandfather's heirloom silver timepiece and focused my concentration to make the second, minute and hour hands of my watch go backwards against all odds, as I was determined to find this ghost, jump back in the past, and meet him when he was still alive.

That plan backfired.

"John, open your eyes!"

I must have leapt three feet in the air.

"You're not *Bluidy* Mackenzie!" I shouted, realizing at once I had to tone it down not to alert any of those amongst the living.

"Who do you think you are? Some kind of Time Traveler Professor?" Finn laughed. "Don't you think you ought to be in bed at this hour?"

Quickly, I tore off my miniature brain launcher and stuffed it into my threadbare overcoat pocket.

"Do you always have to follow me around?" I argued.

"You're quite aware that you can't go anywhere without me," Finn quipped and casually hopped off the adjacent headstone. He was so tall and lanky compared to me, I felt like I was standing next to a skeleton.

"John, I honestly don't know why you're wasting you time trying to contact Mackenzie. You have no debts to pay off to that man. Why don't you plan your travels where they may better serve you?"

"Come again?"

He wiped his filthy hand on my shoulder. It was full of damp moss and mud from the rain-soaked tombstone he'd been sitting on. "You were meant to break the barriers of time, and your success was not meant to be for entertainment. Otherwise, I would've never permitted you to continue."

I shoved my mechanical apparatus a bit further into my pocket as it kept inching out.

"You mean to tell me it wasn't pure ingenuity that helped me discover the secrets of time travel?"

"There are smarter men and women than you are out there, and they've never managed to do it," Finn replied.

"Then why was I one of the lucky ones?"

"I'm not saying the task is easy, John. It's not, and in your case, you certainly weren't an easy specimen. You had to return quite a few times after death."

"Specimen? Now I sound like I'm a science experiment! How many times have I lived before?"

"More than you've realized," Finn replied. "Oh, and one more thing. Do yourself a favor. Next time you're ready to meet your Maker, don't have any regrets. If you entertain any thought whatsoever that you never had time to do this, or you wish you would've done that instead, that'll almost guarantee that you'll transmigrate and have to play the game of life with all its suffering once again."

I was completely perplexed. Finn made a hasty exit.

So, who was this intruder, and why the bloody hell was I sitting in a graveyard attempting to contact an infamous man known throughout Scottish history for witch trials and persecutions? My ungovernable meddler was Finneas Fertle. Some could've called him my invisible friend, but he claimed he was assigned to me from the beginning of time. Yes, and that meant long before I remember taking my first baby steps upon the cobblestone streets of Edinburgh. I was supposed to believe that I had lived many lives before this one, and he apparently was some sort of trustee—someone responsible for keeping me on the straight and narrow whatever that was supposed to be. Every person had one, although most weren't aware of it. My memoirs would never be complete without introducing my other partners in crime. Besides Arthur Conan Doyle and Finneas Fertle, I had to include Whit and Wendell Mackenzie, not to be confused with the ghost I just tried to contact.

*   *   *

Allegro non Troppo
Frost bit my hands and nose as I cut across the University of Edinburgh's misty grounds seeking refuge in the library. My course load was overwhelming, not only with academics, but I was also diving head first into my musical studies as I was vying for several coveted scholarships. Anxiously, I looked at my timepiece knowing that I had precious little time to dwell on my impending literature assignment.

"Can I be of assistance?" said a head of brown curls hidden between two stacks of books.

"As a matter of fact, I do need some help, but I didn't realize books could talk," I replied not sure where the voice was coming from.

A male university student, who was about three fingers shorter than I with a distinguishingly high forehead and glasses that couldn't get any rounder, emerged with his shirtsleeves rolled up, waistcoat unbuttoned on the bottom three rows, and tie askew.

"You look lost in the modern literature section," he said.

"I'm afraid I'm lost in any literature section," I replied.

"Ah, John Patrick Scott!" He struggled to balance the stack of books he was carrying so he could shake my hand.

"And whom should I have the pleasure of meeting?" I asked.

"Charles St. Andrews Whitcomb, III," he replied.

"Do you ever go by an abbreviated version?"

"My friends call me Whit, for short."

"Then Whit it is. I don't recall ever seeing you in the music department before. How do you know me?"

"From our Great Britons of Literature class with Professor McKnight. I sit three chairs behind you. When I first noticed you, I suspected you must have been one of the professors."

"Oh, that class." I sighed and pointed to my head beginning to blush. "It's hard not to notice the only student in the class who has a few gray hairs on his head, am I correct?"

"Oh, I hope you didn't take any offense," he said taking pause. "You don't like that class?"

"You must have the power of reading my mind."

"Not exactly," he laughed, "McKnight is brilliant and extremely knowledgeable in more subjects than you can possibly imagine. How can you not like his class?"

"Well," I replied, "I'm a music major, and my mind is on other things."

"Ah, I understand. You see, my interest is in literature, so for me this is all fascinating. He also teaches history—another passion of mine."

"As long as he doesn't have you chasing dragons from lost continents, I guess you'll be fine. There are quite a few rumors on campus about him including ones where he engages in falconry in the Highlands, but those hawks have been known to fetch more than game."

"Fair maidens and a wee bit of Robin Hood derring do, so I've been told. Can I help you find anything?" Whit asked. "I work here part-time and know this place fairly well."

"How about finding my soul and my salvation?"

My witty remark sent both of us laughing in unison.

"The best I could offer is help as a study partner," Whit replied. "Unfortunately I'm not a theology major."

"I might take you up on that offer. All right, let's see how smart you are. I need to do an assignment on mythology in modern literature." I shook my head in dismay. "I honestly don't know where to start."

Eagerly seizing the opportunity, he pulled a book off the shelf and led me over to a table where we could both sit down. "Try *The Picture of Dorian Gray* by Oscar Wilde. It's a variation of *Faust* and rather entertaining. Wilde has a promising career as a modern writer."

I paged through the book, mostly paying attention to its illustrations.

"*Faust*, you say?"

"Yes, a fascinating interpretation of a mythological concept—very well done!"

"I'll take your word for it," I replied taking the book from his hand.

"You don't care for other suggestions?" he asked, a bit surprised that I was going to take his word at face value.

"No, that will suffice. Let's make this as simple as possible. As it is, I have to learn both German and Italian this semester. I have enough dialogue prancing around in my head."

Whit was eager to engage in conversation. "By the way, John, what instrument do you play?"

"Pianoforte, mainly. Although I've had some training in violin, I don't take it too seriously beyond helping me with original compositions. I wouldn't dream of playing violin in public. Why?"

Whit took the Oscar Wilde book from my hand and led me to the back of the library.

"Excuse me momentarily," he said as he unfastened a latch on one of the bookcases, which revealed a hidden doorway. He quickly slipped through it.

"What on earth is in there?" I asked, but the door instantly slid shut. As his voice was silenced, a feminine one replaced it.

"You won't learn a thing by simply staring at books."

I spun on my heels and turned around. "I beg your pardon?"

That's when I came face to face with a freckle faced lady student who had red hair almost as crazy as mine. Hers, however, was much longer and pinned up, but curls fell down all over.

"Oh, I know you," I said, recognizing her from Professor McKnight's class, "you're..."

"Sarah Elizabeth Chandler! You really don't know my name, do you? I overheard you're looking for a help with a book report?"

"Whit just volunteered," I replied, oblivious to the fact that she was flirting with me and tried to catch my attention.

"And you'd refuse a lovely lady's generous offer?" she asked.

The hidden door reopened and Whit emerged, who was covered with dust all over his ridiculously curly hair and impishly round glasses.

She gave him a mean stare and turned back towards me. "Shame on you! Perhaps you're as heartless as a piano without its player."

Then she stormed off in a huff.

"What was she upset about?" Whit asked, trying not to laugh.

"I have no idea," I said shrugging my shoulders. "Where did you go?"

"You'd be surprised what's hidden there. There are all sorts of depositories, secret passageways and cubbyholes hidden in the Edinburgh University library," he confided.

"Really?"

"John, beware of strange books. You never know where they'll take you."

We continued advancing towards the checkout desk.

"So, John, as I was about to say, I belong to an extracurricular club, consisting mostly of literature majors, called the Bookworm Society. We engage in lively debates and literary criticism once a week and are sponsoring an upcoming fundraiser, but we are at a loss for entertainment. We meet in a basement

23

recreation hall at one of the local churches. They have a piano and..."

"Are you requesting my assistance?" I asked, cutting him off and raising my eyebrows in suspicion.

"That would be much appreciated."

"I don't think I'd be much of a contribution otherwise. I doubt if I could hold my ground in the presence of a group of literary scholars."

"That's not necessary. Please do us a favor. Time is short, and we are running out of options."

"And what would I get out of it?"

"Perhaps an English tutor for the rest of the semester. I can guarantee you will get a respectable grade for that class. That's, of course, as long as you're compliant."

I held out my hand to shake on it. "You have a deal. Tell me where and when."

"You won't let me down?"

"No, I will honor my word. Just curious, but what do you plan on doing after graduation?"

"Oh, I don't plan on remaining in Edinburgh. I'll be going to London. I suspect there will be opportunities to work as an editor at a publishing house. And you? What do you plan on doing afterwards?" he asked as he began processing my paperwork.

"Ideally, I'd like to establish myself as a concert pianist, compose original scores, and one day conduct a symphony orchestra," I said.

"You have high hopes and noble plans. I wish you luck."

As I began to leave, Whit stopped me.

"Give me your address. You'll need the details about our party. Maybe you should invite that girl. I think she likes you."

"What girl?" I said, trying to play the innocent. Whit gave be a funny look, and I winked back as I scribbled the information on a scrap of paper and handed it to him.

"I'm counting on you, John."

"And I'll be counting on you to get me through my literature class!" I replied as I left the library.

At full gallop, I cut across the Quadrangle to meet my friend, Wendell at our favorite tea and pastry shop around the corner from the University of Edinburgh campus. He was already seated with lunch and waiting for me. I was famished, but my student's stipend only allowed me to indulge in a cup of tea with an extra lump of sugar.

"John, *The Scotsman* has commissioned me to do an article on H.G. Wells, and he's agreed to meet me in London. Last year *The War of the Worlds* was serialized in *Pearson's Magazine*, and the entire story will be released in a book this year. If I depart Friday afternoon I'll be free the whole weekend before I commence my assignment on Monday. You're always pleasant company, so I'd like to extend my invitation."

It was hard to hide my jealousy regarding my friend's accomplishments. Wendell had been a medical student and studied under the famous Doctor Joseph Bell, Arthur's former professor and inspiration for Sherlock, before taking a detour in his studies to explore other options with journalism. By now, he had already published at least a dozen articles in various professional newspapers and journals in addition to being on staff on the university's paper.

My credentials were paltry in comparison. I'd been featured in several local concerts, including the venue at St. Cecilia's Hall and placed third at the University of St. Andrews Composition Competition. Hesitant to answer, I pulled out my timepiece to make sure I hadn't lost track of time, as I couldn't be late for my next class. That particular instructor had a nasty reputation of locking the door and banning students from entering his classroom if they were a mere two minutes late.

"John, it'll be great fun, and I can cover your train and lodging." Then he bit into a fresh bun that dribbled crumbs all over the place.

"I'm assuming that means we're rooming together?" I asked. My colleagues already had too many suspicions about me regarding women, and I hated getting teased. On the contrary, with Wendell plans would often be brushed aside if a lassie entered the picture. I just couldn't seem to be interested and preferred the intellectual engagement of male conversation, instead.

The bell by the front door sounded as a fair young lady entered. Her intoxicating perfume of fresh garden lilacs overwhelmed the aroma of freshly baked scones the second she stepped over the threshold. With Puckish acumen, Wendell dropped his bun on its saucer and whirled around, hypnotized by the presence of an attractive female and potential bedmate. I never could understand how Wendell, who was a reasonably handsome man, but certainly no Casanova, could amiably capture the heart of nearly any woman he had set his mind to. I, on the other hand, seemed to be married to the keyboards of my pianofortes and harpsichords in order to arouse the finer sensibilities of my emotional constitution.

Her chestnut eyes peered around the shop to find an empty seat. She had soft brown hair with a slight wave, pinned and upswept in the current fashion. She was wearing a delicate cameo on her high-necked blouse, which was demurely trimmed with tiny bands of lace. Before I could comprehend the subsequent events, Wendell had already leapt to his feet and was pulling out the chair at the table next to us for her to sit down, all with a chivalrous bow and a gentleman's smile. He captured hearts despite the fact that he only had a few more pence in his pocket than I did at any given time. What was even worse was that Wendell would routinely taunt me and inquire whether or not my lack of conquests revealed a secret attraction towards men.

"Posing as a potential suitor, I presume?" I asked, wiping my upper lip with a crisp linen napkin while noticing that my feeble attempt to grow a moustache was going awry. Whiskers sprouted in an orange-red color and were offset by my auburn hair, which had started turning gray when I was a mere child. When the sunlight struck them with a sideways glance, they glistened like shards of amber.

"And why not?" he asked.

"She's probably way above your social station," I said, fighting not to stare at the uneaten half of his bun although I was starving.

"Why should that stop me?" he asked, settling back into his seat.

His air of overconfidence intrigued me. He glanced over to the lady beside us with a flirtatious smile and then resumed our conversation. "*Tu conciliandos sexualem subactam?*"

My face flushed, cognizant that my noble friend's passion for controversy was equal to his love of conquest.

"And where would I stay?" I asked skeptically knowing his manner of behavior from previous excursions.

"In my room, of course."

I cut him off before he went any further. "Perhaps you forgot what happened the last time you and I shared a room in London?"

"Yes, I know, I put you out to entertain a lady friend. You had to sleep on a bench in Soho Park overnight. A constable mistook you for a vagrant, whereby I had to pick you up from jail the next morning."

Wendell grabbed my right forearm assuring me he was a man of his word.

"You won't have to sleep in the park again. I promise."

Something even more important had happened the last time we traveled to London together, making my distaste regarding Wendell's sexual proclivities trivial in comparison. Wendell decided to remain in London for a few extra days but I had to return to the university so I hurried to make my train connection at Kings Cross. Affording another night's lodging was out of the question. Had I missed my train, I would've wound up sleeping on a bench in the station overnight, and I was not eager to repeat history.

I dropped my ticket on the pavement by accident, so it had gotten a bit soggy from the rain. The ink bled, and it was hard to make out the number of my reserved seat. After I misinterpreted it twice, a uniformed attendant took the ticket and led me to a cabin, insisting that it was my assigned seat. So, I took off my overcoat, hung up my umbrella, and tried to make myself comfortable for the long ride.

Exhausted, I sat back in my seat, closing my eyes, thinking about events from the last few days. Then the doors to my cabin opened and three other men joined me. I tried to ignore them, but they created such a ruckus banging about their luggage. One of them leaned over and pulled shut the curtains, blocking the sunlight. I was looking forward to a much-needed nap except that a rude gentleman seemed to be hell-bent on disturbing such repose. He was a queer fellow with distinguishing muttonchops, wearing a houndstooth plaid waistcoat with a ticking pocket watch that was much louder than usual.

"So, Arthur, we finally caught up with you," he said bending over me so close that his foul-smelling saliva dripped onto my eyelids.

"I'm not Arthur," I mumbled, semi-conscious and dog-tired from my long weekend with Wendell. I wiped off that disgusting spittle and turned my head away to resume my sleep.

Well, I suspected I had been in the wrong seat to begin with, but now these three strangers had mistaken me for the fourth man in their party. So much was happening so quickly that it was difficult to comprehend the events that followed. They might've offered me a drink, but it felt more like I'd been drugged. They donned costumes reminiscent, perhaps, of Freemasonry and began to perform an ancient rite based on Egyptian magic. The details were a bit hazy, but somehow I felt like I was being wrapped in a shroud and placed inside a tomb. I don't know how they had managed to drag a coffin on to a train, so I suspected it must've been one of their steamer trunks, but for the life of me I couldn't tell. Then, once the ceremony

28

was underway, I felt like I had died and had been reborn to become an initiate in some sort of secret order. All I could recall was that when I finally came to, the men appeared to be dressed in their original garments, were ensconced in a lively game of cards, and offered me a glass of brandy.

When I was able to focus my eyes, I noticed an engraved silver ring on my left hand. I darted silent glances at each party in the room, mentally questioning them where it came from, and the man with the muttonchops smiled. Numb and speechless, I drifted off to sleep, possibly, this time aided by laudanum in the drink I had accepted.

As the train finally arrived in Edinburgh, I woke up and looked around, but those three strangers were gone, and a red book had been left behind on the leather seat beside me. As I gathered my belongings together, I caught the brief attention a train attendant mentioning that someone might've forgotten that book by accident, but he seemed busy clearing out the passengers rather than attending to my concerns. So I stuffed it into my coat pocket, disembarked, and headed back to my flat.

*   *   *

Many are Called, Few are Chosen

"John, are you all right?" Whit asked as he tugged at my shoulder.

My thoughts bounced over stacks of books and papers then drifted away on the sunbeams right out the library windows.

"Absolutely crapulous!" I said, rubbing my bloodshot eyes and unconsciously twirling the hairs of my brows, a ridiculous habit that my friends would tease me about. I was unenthusiastic and sore in the head from highballs and hijinks with Wendell last night. Partnered like Watson to Sherlock, we made our rounds about Old Town. Whit attempted to tutor me for my English exams, but my attention was absent.

Besides, I already performed my obligation for Whit's soirée at the Bookworm Society. I was prepared to play Chopin's Etudes,

Opus 10, when Whit was struck by Cupid's arrows chasing a feminine ideal as fleeting as fairy dust. A young lassie by the name of Isabelle made her appearance at the event and captivated the hearts of every man with a pulse. It would've been in error to say she didn't make mine beat a little faster, as well. The moment I placed my hands on the keyboard, Whit, overzealous in wanting to impress the lady, insisted that I play her choice, which to my regret consisted of frivolous popular ballads more fitting for dance halls and cotillions, and when I was requested to play a polka, it would have been enough to make even Gilbert and Sullivan writhe in agony.

Whit was surprised that I was unfamiliar with many of the melodies, so he hummed the songs—miserably off key—while she feebly sang along. I hammered away on the sharps and flats, but the thought of replacing the music of a maestro with fashionable nonsense was like bitter medicine to my esthete sensibilities. Obligation fulfilled, I chose not to back myself into a corner like that again, but now Whit insisted on upholding his end of the bargain and scolded me for my inattentiveness and lack of enthusiasm. With my musical studies, extracurricular ventures in time travel and countless thoughts about my forthcoming studies with Arthur, I was caught in a barrelful of distractions.

*   *   *

Recently Arthur put me on the spot about my lack of childhood recollections. So I put on my own deerstalker cap and become a detective. However, my methods of deduction and reasoning involved magic and odd science, ones that Sherlock Holmes would have considered utter nonsense and balderdash. Nonetheless, they worked for me.

Once again, I dared to travel back in time. One of the frightening results of time travel was that I was rarely just an observer. Every so often, Finneas, my ever-persistent sidekick, would lead me by the hand to what appeared as a theater, but by and large I would almost always find myself wearing a different costume and pair of shoes, so to speak. Needless to say, this could prove to be disturbing. The mere thought of becoming a small child again made me feel vulnerable, but I was compelled to summon the courage to find out the truth.

*   *   *

Edinburgh, Scotland 1886

Suddenly, the deep well of lost memories brought forth highlights from that forgotten childhood I had been striving to recapture.

"I cannot believe John hasn't listened to us again," my mother lamented with worry carved upon her forehead.

My father rushed over to the mantelpiece where he seized my metronome.

"Edward, don't! He needs it for his musical studies!"

"It's an instrument of evil, I say," Father retorted as he put it back in its comfortable, usual spot. He had all the intentions in the world of destroying it, but he backed away following Mother's advice.

"You must keep an eye on the boy. He cannot continue to play in the graveyard. That's where all the trouble started! That, and those damned time travel ideas he's had in his head. What's gotten into him?"

Then my parents both grabbed me under my arms dragging me into the other room, and as soon as they lowered me into the tub of scalding water, I shattered their eardrums with piercing wails, as my skin turned beet red with burns. Mother then poured a pitcher full of icy cold water over my head, which made me scream in agony even more. When the steam penetrated my lungs, I almost forgot how to breathe.

"Edward, you need to keep a better eye on him. He could have died!" my mother, Maud cried, distressed and completely unnerved. "May I remind you of when John nearly poisoned himself by eating those mushrooms he found at Princes Street? We were lucky the doctor was available to rush over on Sabbath day."

31

I had a secret place where I'd climb one of the hillsides leading up to Edinburgh Castle. There was an overgrown root, which reminded me of forks and tributaries of a river but almost with an animated human quality. Under that root, I always imagined that there lived a small family of trolls; good trolls of course, underground workers who would keep the grounds and protect the castle. Hidden by some of those roots were magic mushrooms, pale white ones, tinged with red, which had tiny purple dots. I collected some and hid them in my bedroom, allowing them to dry. Then, I took a mortar and pestle, created a fine powder and mixed them with a shot of my father's brandy.

Immersed in the world of phantasmagoria, I climbed a wall in my back garden, spread out my arms like wings, gazed up at the dancing clouds overhead and, with visions of grandeur leapt into a clump of rosebushes below. I screamed in dire pain. Father extracted me from their thorny embrace and rushed me into the house, immediately administering some evil tasting syrup which made me vomit violently, forcing me out of my euphoric dreams.

He pushed my head under the unbearably hot water and held it under for a few seconds. I struggled against his strength and surfaced, coughing and sputtering.

"That should bring him to his senses," my father concluded and stormed out of the room.

Mother cradled my head in her arms, as I nearly fainted. After being enveloped by hazy dreams of water spirits and otherworldly beings, I woke several hours later, naked and wrapped up in blankets, not exactly sure how I had managed to get from the bath to my bed. I was famished and dragged trails of bed covers with me as I made my way to the kitchen to get something to eat.

"Welcome back to the realm of the living," Father said, as he saw me gulping down some leftover cold porridge.

I didn't answer. I was more interested in filling my aching belly. Mother entered and straightened my blankets, as I was stark naked underneath. Father began pacing the room.

"Maybe we should consider sending him to a stricter school with more discipline. I thought piano lessons would keep him on a straight path. Maybe he should take up violin instruction, as well."

"When will he have time for his regular studies?" my mother asked. "He already practices the piano here and at St. Martins several hours a day."

Yes, I had talent. One could say I was a child prodigy. I started giving public piano recitals at the age of six. My instructor would always tell my parents that God's angels gave me their special blessing. I believed something more otherworldly beyond that. I had already known how to do all of this before.

I was only eight years old. How else was I going to describe it? It wouldn't be until years later that I would understand words such as *déjà vu* or reincarnation, and that mastering the art of music wasn't new to me. There must have been a map within my memories that I took with me from some far away, unknown place. I wasn't sure where it was or what it was, but I knew I had been there, previously. I also suspected that access to this special realm would allow me to converse with angels—although my father considered them demons—and therefore they would help me find out why I was so special. However, that path was not without its risks or dangers.

These exploits of trial and error would consist of mixing chemicals and herbs and ingesting them, or breathing in the vapors until I would faint or lie near death. Other times I would try to visualize spirits dancing in the flames of fire. This time I almost killed myself by jumping into the river and holding my breath as long as I could in order to communicate with water spirits. What nearly did me in was the coldness of the water, and that's why my parents threw me in that tub of boiling water to ward off the chill.

I didn't dare tell them about the spell book I found left behind the organ at church, nor did I tell them of my own journal, which I created with details of those spells I would try for myself. Oh, should I mention the times I got caught sneaking into the

33

cemetery behind St. Martin's trying to raise the spirits of the dead? My parents didn't take kindly to those incidents, either.

"John Patrick Scott," he raved in anger, "what do you have to say for yourself this time?"

Mother intervened, "Edward, leave your son alone. Let him eat and regain his strength. We'll deal with it tomorrow morning. Yelling will only give him more gray hairs!"

That's right. Gray hairs. I was an eight-year-old child already sprouting gray hairs, and that was another reason why my father was convinced I was conversing with fallen angels.

Well, the next morning, when I awoke and scrambled straight for the kitchen, starving as usual, we had a strange visitor sitting at the table with two traveling bags by his side. I stood in my nightshirt, staring at him from the bottom of the stairs, hesitant to approach nearer.

"John, meet Professor Mockingbird. Your mother has already packed your bags. After breakfast he will accompany you to your new school."

"New school?" I asked, surprised, "I don't want to go anywhere. I like my old one. I don't want to leave my friends or my music lessons."

"You'll continue your musical studies at your new school," Mother assured me, "and I'm sure you'll have no trouble making new friends."

"When will I be able to come home to see everyone? Not until Christmas?" I asked between mouthfuls.

"You won't," Father interrupted. "You'll be staying at your Uncle Thomas and Aunt Maggie's place from now on. Your mother, brother, sister and I will be moving to Ireland."

That news came as a shock. I ate breakfast with apprehension while Professor Mockingbird went into the other room to discuss arrangements with my parents. Back in my bedroom was a set of street clothes laid out on a bench, which my mother must have prepared. Then I looked under my mattress for my secret spell book, but it was gone! One of my parents must have found it since I remembered a burning smell near the oven this morning. What about my journal, which was my personal spell book? This had my private recipes and accounts of experiments gone right or gone wrong. I removed a loose brick from the wall near my fireplace, and there it was safe and sound. I placed it in a leather satchel with several stacks of sheet music, grabbed my hat and coat and scampered downstairs. If my parents were going to sell this old house, there was no way that I wanted the new owners to discover the journal.

By the time I returned to the kitchen, I could already hear the horse whinnying outside. I asked my parents as to why they were moving to Ireland, but they refused to give me any answers.

Both of my parents bid their final farewells, but as Professor Mockingbird began to lead me outside, Father shouted, "Son, wait! Your mother forgot to pack this."

He placed a smooth metal object with a chain attached in my hand and then closed my fingers tightly over it. I separated them a wee bit to see what was inside. It was my grandfather's silver pocket watch on a well-crafted chain.

"Take good care of it, son. It will serve you well."

"I will, Father," I replied with a tear in my eye, "I remember it gave me good luck at my first public recital," but before I could say another word, the professor whisked me out the door.

I bit my lip and tried with all my might to hold back more tears as the carriage trotted away. I found myself alone with a strange older man, who was neither friendly nor conversable. As our driver took us to the outskirts of town, several graveyards dotted the landscape, and sleepy residential neighborhoods gave way to verdant pastures filled with cows, sheep and goats. After humming Beethoven's *Pastoral*, or what I could remember of it, I dropped off the sleep. Once again, I entered into the land of dreams and witches, goblins and monsters from kingdoms unimaginable.

*   *   *

When I took Wendell up on his offer and accompanied him to London, he seemed to be more interested in mimicking H.G. Wells' free love ideology rather than interviewing him for a newspaper. At least I didn't wind up sleeping in the park again. Although debatable, I did indulge in one too many drinks at the closest public house while unable to enter our hotel room. Yet, while I bided my time, I felt the distinct impression that another patron was watching me.

Saturday morning, Wendell must have slipped out of our room for another manly pursuit while I was still sleeping off my brandy. Since Arthur's driver wasn't due to meet me at the hotel until 2:30, I set forth in search of a moderately priced café for tea and the morning news, breathing in the atmosphere of the waking city. Sounds from local shops on Shaftesbury Street were amplified like a smooth crescendo. A puddle below showed my reflection rippling against the sky, distorting the image of me wearing my heavy wool overcoat, top hat and customary gentleman's walking stick like a carnival mirror or a storybook hero. What other characters would pop from the pages of novels and join me on my afternoon stroll? Doctor Watson and Sherlock Holmes?

After the restaurant patron next to me left their seat, I swallowed my pride and quickly snatched an uneaten muffin from his plate and plopped it onto mine. When would the day come when I would be beyond such petty thievery to assuage my growling stomach? This wasn't stealing, I thought to myself. It was going to be tossed to the dogs, anyway. Ah, to be a successful concert pianist in London! My wishes rode on fantasies, but I was certainly determined.

*   *   *

"Arthur, do you ever wish you could predict the future?" I asked.

It was way too soon in our relationship to share the secret about my working time machine. Wendell knew, and of course there

36

was no hiding anything I did from Finn. Arthur was busy going through papers on his desk, while I tried to be as patient as possible.

"Why should I be concerned?" he replied, "Spiritualists believe that death is not the end for us."

"Sir, I wasn't referring to looking that far into the future. Did it ever pique your interest as to whom your children will marry, or whether or not certain books of yours would be published?"

"Not as much as what will happen in the afterlife, John. It's much easier to deduce the other outcomes. What happens to us after we die is a greater mystery."

Careful not to reveal too many secrets, I interjected, "I've had glimpses of the future where I was much older and, instead of being an internationally famous concert pianist, I was stuck as a professor back in Edinburgh. The thought of that sounds dreadful. Don't you agree?"

Arthur ignored my comment and began to read over a letter. I was getting fidgety, and continued to jabber away.

"Speaking of enigmas, I had the strangest occurrence the other day. I borrowed a book from the university library, which I needed for a report. I knew for a fact that I deliberately put it on the table, which was always next to my *thinking chair*. That night, I must've had too much wine, as I nodded off in that chair instead of my bed. The front door to my flat was always locked. God forbid Lydia or the other lodgers become too inquisitive. However, despite the fact that there was no possible way that anyone else besides me could have entered that room, when I awoke the next morning the book was missing.

"I was frantic. I couldn't afford to replace that book, but what was I going to do? I scrounged about my flat for spare change, assuming that I might have to skip lunches the next week, but maybe I'd be lucky to find a used copy at Dalrymple's Rare Books, and none would be the wiser if I replaced it. Dalrymple didn't have a copy. I had to spend a good part of the next afternoon, which I needed for piano practice, scouting for the book in several other secondhand bookstores and found a copy over on Victoria Street. I hurried home, placed it on the same table where the other one should've been and then had to catch up on my studies.

"The next morning when Lydia knocked with biscuits and tea and I opened my door to the outside world, I was shocked to find two identical books lying side by side on the table top."

"I suppose that at some point you stepped out to use the lavatory down the hall," Arthur said. "Someone could have borrowed and returned it when your back was turned."

"Impossible. I always locked my door even to go there," I replied. "Arthur, what I suspect was more of a paranormal affair, as if there was a crack that opened up into another space or hidden world where something could slip through. Does that make sense?"

Arthur sat back in his chair and laughed, "That happens to me all the time. My wife is always complaining that some sort of imp or fairy is stealing her hats, and they turn up in the strangest places. Several times we found her hats perched up in trees far away from the house or in our garden. Another time we found one under our bed. Our children swore they weren't up to pranks, and our house staff denied every bit. Not that any of them would be scolded, mind you, but I find it amusing, nonetheless."

"You don't think that's out of the ordinary?" I asked.

He shook his head.

"Arthur, that was an abnormal experience. It was as if the book slipped through a mysterious and invisible mouse hole that was hidden between two walls inside my house. Then that hole reappeared, and the book returned on its own accord without warning."

I was surprised that Arthur wasn't in agreement. Finally, I reached into my jacket pocket, pulled out a red book and placed it on Arthur's desk.

"What's this?" he asked, quite curious as he leaned in closer to examine it. "Is that the book that disappeared and reappeared inside your flat?"

"No, it's that bizarre book that I found that was left behind on the *train*."

"*Shokunin, the Thief of Tales*?" Arthur asked.

"Odd title, right? All I can say is that extraordinary events have been chasing after me like iron filings to a magnet since I found it. Of course, that's not to say that my life wasn't a wee bit unusual before it entered the picture," I added, while putting the book back in my jacket pocket.

"The world as we know it is out of the ordinary. So much of it is beyond our wildest perceptions," Arthur said as he sighed, looking like a disappointed dog being teased with a bone that he would never catch. I sensed that he was fascinated by that book and was well aware that I was withholding information on purpose. The problem was that I knew little more than he did about it, and I didn't want to bear the responsibility if something terrible were to happen.

"John, I'm a doctor and a sportsman, quite athletically fit. I'm confident that I can look after myself and a simple book wouldn't pose a threat."

Every time the subject was brought up, I knew that his tension was mounting. He rose from his seat and began leading me out of his study and into another room.

"Come, I apologize for any delays. We have so much to do with so little time left in the weekend. Later after supper, several others will be joining us for a séance. Accompanying them will be a medium from France, whom they say is amazing and very accurate. John, have you ever been to a séance?"

"I can't say that I have," I replied trying to hide a yawn. It had already been a long day, especially since the previous night had been spent drinking in excess while waiting for Wendell to let me back into our room.

Arthur's spirits perked up, and his enthusiasm began to return. "Then consider it your first encounter in speaking with the dead. Let's see what news they have to share."

*   *   *

What Book?

After returning to Edinburgh, my obsession with time travel continued with little concern for the consequences. There was always a new gadget to try with many hit-and-miss attempts on the road to perfection. I didn't know whether or not I was poisoning my perception by daring to traverse the forbidden and unknown depths of improbable science, but I began encountering the oddest occurrences. Beyond temporal astral projection in the present, or dipping my toes into the inviting waters of the recent past, I began a series of enterprises projecting myself into a context of events and circumstances which had not yet occurred—ones more like scenarios from the creative imaginations of writers such as Wells or Jules Verne. From all appearances, it seemed like I was traveling into the future.

One would think that such an accomplishment would be exciting, to say the least however; in my case it was disconcerting. When I'd take that leap, I'd appear as someone of the opposite sex. Yes, that is correct. I appeared the same age, but in the guise of a woman—a woman who called herself by the unusual name of Aliskiya Lleullne. This was inexplicable, and I kept this secret from Arthur fearing he'd think I was two-bricks-short-of-a-load and terminate our friendship. Yet, my curiosity outweighed my trepidations. So again, I strapped on my equipment, drained the last drop of brandy and succumbed to the nickelodeon-like visions that penetrated my consciousness.

*   *   *

September 2228

"What do you mean you can't find my luggage?"

Aliskiya slammed her backpack on the counter refusing to take no for an answer. Sheayank Spaceport officials called security, insisting she move aside so they could help the next distressed passenger in line.

Worried about making her flight back to college on time, she hurried from the diner where she worked that summer. She wasn't thinking clearly when she stuffed all her valuables in her check-in bags, where they could get stolen. What was lost? Her warm clothing, her Peregrine Academy Student ID, textbooks on investigative journalism and film history, and the Ouija board she used to play psychic games with her best friend, Wanda, amongst other things. All that was replaceable, but she couldn't believe she was so stupid as to put her *tip chip* in her baggage. Now, all her money was gone.

As soon as she took a moment to assess what to do next, I did the same. After all, now I was inadvertently wearing her shoes at the same time. The surroundings looked like nothing I had ever encountered. Wherever she was it was freezing this time of year. Gone were the commonplace Victorian appurtenances, diurnal trivialities, *occurrences quotidiennes, die tagesordnung* that I had taken for granted—horses and carriages, engineering inspired by Playfair, customary walking sticks for every gentleman with parasols for the ladies, and the familiar aromas, both pleasant and disagreeable from the heart of Edinburgh.

There were foreign metals, polished white for the most part, instead of lush, rich wood finishes or the scent of cool, damp stone masonry fresh after a morning's rain. In fact there seemed to be metal everywhere—even objects resembling birds, only because they

41

flew through the air. Although they were not at all like familiar balloon-like airships, people did seem to be getting into and out of them. My five senses were overwhelmed with so much novelty that it was a challenge to concentrate on the dilemma at hand. Suddenly, I realized this young lady was using terminology and language quite different from what I was used to, and yet I was able to understand each and every word she was saying. If I didn't, then I had to pick up whatever I needed and didn't have a lot of time to do it. Her problems became my challenges. How was she going to pay for her tuition and college expenses? What remained? She rummaged through her pack. There were heavy, old dusty volumes of the Sherlock Holmes stories, *The Final Problem* and *The Hound of the Baskervilles*, which she had picked up in an antique shop. I suppose the volumes were antique for her from her *punctum visus* or futuristic point of view. Then she pulled out an unidentified flat metallic object with the symbol of an apple embossed on its surface, which seemed pretty useless as far as I was concerned. She said something or another that it had a dead power supply, as she kept stroking her fingers over it. *Honestly, I had no idea what she was doing, or what this contraption was, but I had been thrust into the thick of it, and she fretted over it as if it was important enough to have resolved her predicament.*

Also included were a few candy bars, something that was labeled as a meditation recording, although I wouldn't have recognized it as such, and two toy magic wands she had purchased from Apollonius's Astral Emporium. She was surprised she hadn't been stopped by interspace security for such odd looking objects except that one of them was in its original packaging so it looked like a gift. Lastly, she uncovered an ominous, rumpled booklet. Buying those wands made her eligible to win a Mearden Scholarship to the Underground University of Magic and Alchemical Science, and that was the receipt for her purchase.

"Stranded with no money at Sheayank Spaceport. A sweepstakes ticket isn't going to bail me out of this jam!" she said, all upset.

She looked around the bustling spaceport to see if she could recognize any students arriving on other flights. Happy families were picking up students from other universities, but her homecoming was met with emotional pain. Where was her family when she needed them? Suddenly, she was grasped from behind.

"Sister Sylvania, you scared me. What are you doing at the spaceport?"

It was reassuring to recognize the familiar fashion of a Sister of the Academy, the starkness of the blacks, whites and grays, the long flowing frocking capped with a hooded cowl.

"Can you use a lift?" she asked.

"Back to the Academy?"

"Follow me," Sister Sylvania said as she picked up what was left of the girl's belongings.

A cruiser pulled up alongside the curb, piloted by yet another *Bon*, or instructor from Peregrine Academy. Although relieved to get a ride back to school, she couldn't get a straight answer as to how Sister Sylvania showed up to bail her out. She kept inquiring as to how were her roommates? How was her best friend, Wanda? She realized she was wasting her breath on unanswered questions. Her suspicions became an itch in a place that couldn't be scratched.

Autumn hadn't quite fallen. The red roninalia and wild strawberries still sprinkled the valley like a case of prickly heat with a good deal of snow on the mountaintops. She was definitely not in Edinburgh, but in a place called Kscandria. A damp chill crept through the thin fibers of Aliskiya's clothing, which was adapted for San Scientia's dry, warm climate where she had recently spent her summer vacation. Peregrine had a strict policy regarding students

43

arriving on campus out of uniform. Since her luggage had been stolen, there was no doubt that she'd be reprimanded upon return.

Physically nothing had changed. All the antiquated buildings looked the same in their fortress-like stone grandeur, hidden away from the rest of the civilized world by the guardian Mountains of Mekura, which were about a mile above sea level. Mechanization and renovation had not yet destroyed the local landscape. Peregrine still had its traces of untouched and pristine paradise, cathedral-like auditoriums, and the architectural renderings of a gothic monastic community hallmarking many years of tradition.

After passing security checkpoints, their vehicle stopped in front of a building which centuries before had been an old brewery. She was instructed to get out and ask no questions. Before them was a massive oaken door secured by three strong wrought iron bolts of divers designs and surrounded by a stone brick arch. Atop the door, bricks formed a triangular design enclosing sculptures, which resembled drunken brew masters frozen in stone.

Between the weight of her heavy backpack and her seasonally inappropriate clothing, words couldn't begin to describe how uncomfortable she was. After Sister Sylvania unlocked the door, the girl followed her inside.

"Wait there," Sister Sylvania commanded in a harsh tone pointing to a threadbare couch outside of Sister Anna's office.

All of the Peregrine students had a *Bon Consilium*, or counselor, assigned to them, and Sister Anna was hers. Aliskiya feared there would be serious repercussions for showing up on campus without her Fourth-year uniform. It was always complicated to get a new one quickly. However, Aliskiya was so drained from her long flight and disheartening ordeal at the spaceport that she slumped into the sagging couch and passed out. Slipping into a world of her own, she had the most peculiar dream.

Strangely enough, this dream seemed to take place in *my* present time, 1898, or three hundred and thirty years earlier. Even more shocking was that it touched upon real events in *my* life that had, in fact, happened, as if now I was going to be watching actors on a stage playing the roles that both Arthur and I had already lived through. Once again, both of us were back inside the Deacon Brodie the day we first met, but this time I was reliving it in this young woman's subconscious mind.

"John Patrick Scott, sir." I extended my hand to greet Arthur.

"The pleasure is all mine," he replied.

"How should I address you, sir?"

He signaled the waiter for drinks. "John, call me Arthur. I prefer being informal."

"It's quite fortuitous you happened to be back in Edinburgh on business. I'm honored that you would meet and discuss this matter, which I find so disturbing."

Arthur put fresh tobacco in his churchwarden pipe. "Can I assume you believe in the transmigration of souls?" he asked.

"I suppose that I do," I said.

Our waiter placed two glasses of ale on the table.

"My publisher forwarded your letter, and I read it at least three times before deciding that it was best to meet in person. Don't you also find it strange that you somehow found yourself initiated into a secret society on a train heading to Edinburgh? Regardless of your theories on a case of mistaken identity, there are no accidents. Can you think of anything that you did in the past, which could've been of keen interest to these gentlemen?"

Details were elusive. I had boarded a train with a rain-soaked ticket, so wet that the print bled, and I couldn't find my correct seat. Then I was caught up in a soporific course of events, as if tossed to the winds. What remained were an engraved silver ring on my finger and a mysterious red book on the seat beside me.

*　　*　　*

Aliskiya woke when an armful of new Fourth-year student clothing was thrust into her face.

"Get changed!" Sister Anna demanded as she pointed towards the nearest restroom.

She staggered getting up; noticing the sister still had her backpack. It was unzipped and obvious that someone inspected its contents. When she returned properly dressed and resumed a seat on her couch, the sister threw the pack into her lap. Attendants were all around, and the door shut. Fear formed a stone in her throat. Sister Anna glared right at her with pale blue eyes as hard as bullets, almost hidden in the flesh of her face. Her stare was razor sharp and cutting.

"Where is your book?" Sister Anna asked.

"What book? The Sherlock Holmes books?"

Outside of being reprimanded for the loss of her school uniform, Aliskiya wasn't aware that she was supposed to be carrying special books. What book?

Sister Anna arose from her chair, approaching her with an outstretched arm.

"Aliskiya, your book!"

Aliskiya thought to herself, "My best friend, Wanda, was a *Bosch2* book and film fan. I bought both of us toy magic wands on the Connection making us eligible to attend a special school of alchemical science. Could she have been referring to the receipt I had in my backpack to enter a contest for a Mearden Scholarship?"

46

Then, Sister Anna leaned over so close that her breath flushed the girl's face. "Aliskiya, do you pledge to transmute your soul into that of an ultimate spiritual warrior?"

"I do... Wait! What are you talking about?"

One of her attendants thrust a book into Aliskiya's arms. Pulling a knife from under her frocking, Sister Anna sliced the girl's finger while three drops of her blood tumbled on to a page. She shoved a ring on one of the poor girl's fingers—a silver engraved ring identical to the one I received when three strangers accosted me on the Edinburgh-bound train from London.

Aliskiya swallowed hard and shouted defiantly, "The spaceport authorities lost everything I brought from San Scientia. The Ussurian government and Mugrayanian insurgents took my parents from me, and you confiscated my backpack. I have nothing. All I have left is myself!"

Sister Anna kept talking to herself and shaking her head in dismay as she rummaged through her backpack discovering her *Bosch2* wands. She examined them, and then handed them back, but she clearly gave the impression that she couldn't find what she was looking for. Finally she found that the souvenir receipt for the Meardon Scholarship. Meanwhile, Aliskiya clutched her wounded hand trying to stop the bleeding.

The sister took in a deep breath with her sight fixed on the horizon as she gazed out the window. "There are people and powers who control the destiny of the universe, and sometimes they force us to re-evaluate what we envisioned as our original plans. Being given the gift of life is an initiation, and what we do with it is what counts."

She kept the booklet and handed the girl an admission pass with rapidly fading disappearing ink. "There's been a slight change to your schedule this semester."

Puzzled, Aliskiya took it from her hand and examined it, thinking to herself, "Is this a joke? The only writing, which remained reveals that I won the Meardon Scholarship."

"Sister Anna, I'm not sure this was part of my curriculum."

"All of us sign up for this course, whether we like it or not. Education never ends. It is a series of lessons, with the greatest for the last."

Sister Anna had quoted a line from Sherlock Holmes with impeccable timing. Then she handed the girl a strange object that looked like a crystalline seashell.

"Consider this amulet your library card. It's also a passkey that will admit you to commuter transportation necessary for travel. Meet me at Hermann Willington's engine room tomorrow at three."

"I have a class then. Can't we make it another time?"

"That class is not important. This is. Cancel the other," she replied as she began to focus her attention on work piled up on her desk. "One last thing, if your classmates get too curious as to your whereabouts, inform them that this is an *extracurricular activity*, and leave it at that. Aliskiya Lleullne, welcome back to Peregrine Academy."

*   *   *

I yanked off my time travel apparatus, making a beeline for my washbasin while breathing so fast that I thought my lungs were going to leap out of my chest and run down the street. Cold water helped me snap to my senses. Who was Aliskiya Lleullne? What was this mystifying book that Sister Anna was looking for? Where was she from, and why was I barging in on her life in this futuristic theater?

It was as if my brain was a decrepit old mattress and my memories were poking through the surface like worn out springs.

48

Had I suppressed that much of my past and was I forced to travel to the future in order to see the consequences of my actions? Behold the comparisons! Why was I being told that this woman had undergone some sort of initiation similar to what I went through before I met Arthur?

"What is this all about?" I shouted loud enough to alert my meddlesome landlady downstairs.

Exasperated, I ran my hands through my disheveled, gray-streaked auburn hair. A knock came from the door. Oh horrors! My time travel equipment was all over the place. A neighbor must have called the police.

"Who's there?"

My visitor made an unconventional entrance passing through the door and materializing on the nearer side, like an apparition.

"Sherlock?" My breath was taken away.

The ghostly man increased in solidity.

"John, I wish you'd stop calling me Sherlock. I am not Sherlock Holmes."

"Finneas Fertle, you scared the Dickens out of me!" I cried.

"As usual, I presume."

"So, what's the nature of this unexpected visit?" I asked, trying to calm myself down by slowing my breathing to a steady beat.

"Poking your noggin into the future, aren't ye lad?"

"And what's that to you?" I asked, defensively.

"Don't you think you should be excavating the past, instead? Why on earth did you want to jump into the 23rd century?"

"23rd century? Is that where *she's* from? How come there are so many odd similarities?"

"Consider the fact that maybe you did something in your past that brought you to the situation you're in now?"

I rose to my feet, but Finn had disappeared as quickly as he had entered. Finn seemed more spirit than human, and somehow I was stuck with him—forever! Yes, I did say forever. He'd give me hints that he had been assigned to me, by a secret council, to make sure I stayed out of trouble, but he'd never explain as to who they were or where they'd come from. What I could never comprehend was when he told me he had been by my side since the beginning of time, way longer than merely my childhood. He called himself some sort of guardian angel. However, I begged to differ. If I had been born Irish instead of Scottish, I would have thought him to be some sort of ridiculous leprechaun, but much taller. Since he always had to dissect and analyze every bloody move I made, I gave him the moniker of Sherlock, named after that famous character.

*   *   *

The Future Revisited

First in order was to get a grasp on being able to control where and when I'd travel in time, since I felt that time had the upper hand with my fate being cast to chance. For reasons unknown, I found myself, once again, filling the shoes of Aliskiya Lleullne. As soon as I arrived in that somewhat familiar future, I found myself fighting cold and blustery headwinds while cutting across the Peregrine Academy campus. When I struggled to stuff my books and supplies into my pack, blowing gusts nearly took my special admission pass from my grasp, the one connected with the Meardon Scholarship to attend the Underground University of Magic and Alchemical Science.

Oddly enough, I, assuming the role of the young collegiate woman, was supposed to present my scholarship document to Hermann Willington, the custodian of the campus engine room. His engine room comprised Peregrine's power center. Part of it was a museum of old brass and copper turbines and generators that used to the run the school back in the late 1800s, combined with solar and modern energy-generating technology. Although this must've looked strange to her, to me, its nineteenth century portions appeared quite normal.

Hermann and his wife, Winnie, had set up private living quarters in the back of the engine complex. Being animal lovers, they somehow acquired a menagerie of at least twenty-five cats, five armadillos, four raccoons, six dogs, ten rabbits, five xpurrtins, seven aardfunkles, and several other species of small furry animals. Steam and oil mixed with the antiseptic aromas of futuristic machinery. Most Peregrine students were aware of the rumors about the existence of underground tunnels built under the school with one of those entrances located somewhere near there.

Three people greeted me upon arrival. In addition to Hermann, Sister Anna introduced me to Professor Morgan Santana, the Underground University's headmaster. He was a tall, fatherly gentleman with a dark complexion with a resonant and reassuring tone to his voice. Both he and Sister Anna were dressed in ceremonial robes. I was handed a similar, but plainer robe. As I was slipping it on over my Peregrine student uniform, I overheard Sister Anna and the Professor having a private conversation.

"You never found the book?" he asked.

"No. I looked everywhere. She said she lost her luggage at the spaceport. All she had was the sweepstakes ticket."

"That's unfortunate," he replied. "That means someone else has got their hands on it. All I can say is that I hope they're aware of its unpredictability. In a sense, the book needs to be tamed...like a wild animal."

They stopped whispering amongst themselves when they caught me eavesdropping. Then Sister they explained to me that I would have to undergo a test in order to prove that I was worthy to study in this special school. Merely winning the Meardon Scholarship was no guarantee for admission, although it helped. I was led to a long, flat sturdy wooden table cluttered with an assortment of oddities, smoking beakers, and a leather-bound book, which looked well worn but familiar. Upon closer examination, I realized why. Its title, oddly enough, said that it was *The Spell Book of Charms and Incantations*, by J.P. Scott—my personal grimoire, but now centuries older. However, that couldn't possibly have been the book that they were referring to earlier. Hmmm, beware of strange books...

"Aliskiya," Professor Morgan called my attention.

Once again, I had to remind myself that I was supposed to answer to that name. "Yes, sir," I replied.

"Go to page seventy-two and follow all the instructions to the letter. On the table before you, you will find all the items you need to perform your test, but a lot of them are unnecessary and have been placed there on purpose. Part of your job is to sort out what is indispensable and place the rest aside. Wrong choices can waste valuable time."

Then he pulled out a stopwatch, dangling on a chain from underneath the generous folds in his robe.

"You have exactly one hour to complete this task," he said eyeballing the hands of his watch as they went *tick-tick-tick*, "Starting now!"

Oh, how I hated timed examinations no matter what century I was living in! My fingers were inexplicably drawn one page further to seventy-three with an illustration of a spirit prefacing a new chapter on how to summon it. Then, I turned back the page to seventy-two. Meanwhile, everyone else left the room while I struggled through the assignment. Page seventy-two had a spell to conjure the hidden entrance to all matters unknown. Beyond its title, were instructions for a formula but components were missing. I flipped the page forward to page seventy-three. Then, I glanced back at page seventy-one, which dwelt on a different subject altogether. I continued flipping the pages back and forth, probably three times, convinced that there should've been an additional page or insert when slowly, these following words appeared in the air inches above page seventy-two:

.05 grams of The Apple's Poison in a tincture of alcohol

Three ounces of Pimwing mensurs

.25 grams of Lavenda

One-quarter ounce tincture of Brandy Florentine

.01 grams powdered Mandrake root

One ounce Wormwood leaves (Artemisia absinthium)

One-third ounce Hyssop (whole plant)

A sprig of Mint

This eye-opener warned me to expect a surprise or two along the way. Identifying the sprig of mint was easy, and mandrake was mentioned in one of my Sherlock Holmes books. It looked like it had legs, almost like ginseng, so I sifted through the assortment of herbs on the table and put the mandrake next to the mint. Hyssop? I wasn't sure what that looked like. Some of the items had hand-written labels, but of course, they were difficult to read.

Wormwood was readily recognizable. That one I could detect by its smell, since it was one of the primary ingredients of absinthe. Lavender should've been easy to spot by both its smell and its color, but it seemed to be hiding. However, while I was rummaging through the mess, I noticed that objects began to have an animated life of their own. The stir stick jumped three inches out of my grasp. When I'd reach for a test tube, it would float away like a butterfly. Finally, I checked the recipe and noticed its spelling. It wasn't lavender, but lavenda. That's why I couldn't find it, and every time I reached for the wrong object, everything on the table would escape from me. What was lavenda? Each passing moment had time slipping through my fingers like quicksilver.

Other ingredients were going to be more difficult than I imagined, so I took a deep breath and prayed, and prayed really hard that the powers of the universe guide me to find them. I stood there for a moment in silence. Too many items on the table, the choice was overwhelming. This time, I took a deep breath and felt the sounds of my heart beating loudly in my chest cavity with the words speaking in resonance:

"A man should keep his little brain attic stocked with all the furniture that he is likely to use, and the rest he can put away in the lumber-room of his library where he can get at it if he wants."

What an appropriate and comforting Sherlockian quote for the moment!

"Aliskiya—over there, three over from the top left, that's the lavenda. Grab the scale."

What did I have to lose except precious minutes? I followed the lead from the voice in my head and continued.

"The hyssop is that beautiful purple flower you mistook for the lavender. Measure it out according to the formula, and do so quickly."

Suddenly I remembered how my mother warned me when eating an apple not to eat the seeds because they contained a very powerful poison—cyanide.

"The Apple's Poison," I thought to myself.

Thus, I found an apple on the table and sliced into quarters. Although there seemed to be additional preparations with a tincture of alcohol, at least I hadn't been prevented from taking the seeds by having the apple run away from me, so I figured I must've been on the right track.

Gathering the remaining items, I was still at a loss, because instructions were incomplete as to what to do after I mixed them all together. So, I closed my eyes, and I saw a movie screen across my forehead—a vision or second sight, like jumping into a waking dream. I was in an ancient classroom, perhaps one built around the time of *my* century. A professor with white hair and notable aquiline features was conducting a demonstration.

"Class," he announced, "it's important to be able to distinguish substances by their tastes and smells."

He held up a vial of amber-colored fluid, dipped his finger into it and tasted the substance.

"This particular solution is exceptionally bitter," he grimaced. "I'll pass this around for everyone to try for themselves."

While the medicine was being passed around, the students' reactions were much to be expected.

"Tastes dreadful, agreed?" he asked.

The entire class nodded. Most of the students continued to make faces and spit into their handkerchiefs.

He continued, "The point that every one of you failed to understand was the most important part of the lesson. If you paid full attention, you would've noticed that I used one finger to dip into the liquid. What you overlooked was that I placed a different one in my mouth to taste it. My reactions were deliberately faked to fool you.

Therefore, the point that none of you grasped was that you hadn't truly observed me throughout the process."

Then it occurred to me that Wendell told me that story before. It was about his professor, Doctor Joseph Bell, the man who also inspired Arthur to create the character of Sherlock Holmes. Then, a voice in my ear urged me to leave Doctor Bell's classroom in search of a wall.

With my eyes still closed, my ethereal substitute paced about the room, but realized there wasn't anything resembling a wall. Then I turned my attention back to my spell book waving my physical hands over it to see if any special vibrations from within would lead me there.

After opening my real eyes, there was a sketch of a brick wall inside that book that hadn't been there previously. I flipped its pages back and forth several times again, but it still remained intact convincing me that I wasn't imagining things. Therefore, I touched my corporeal fingertips to the drawing. A brick wall appeared a short distance away with a small note tacked on it.

"Are you sure you want to go through with this?" A voice rang in my head, as my astral form sprinted over to open the envelope.

It gave specific mixing instructions. Just like the scene in *Alice in Wonderland*, it said to *drink it*.

"Heavens no! Not the potion I have been making!" I thought.

It was poisonous, but here I was standing in front of that brick wall and running out of time. So, I painstakingly combined everything. Was this a warning? Was I being given a choice? Why would I have received an insight about Doctor Bell if there weren't an important lesson in all of this?

I gave the noxious mixture one last shake, dipped a finger into the solution and put it in my mouth, but instead I switched my

56

fingers, giving the impression that I had tasted the solution but I hadn't. That's when the solid wall gave way to reveal a hidden passageway. I cautiously crossed the threshold with my physical body, whereby I greeted Professor Morgan and Sister Anna on the other side.

"Congratulations, Aliskiya, you've passed," Professor Morgan said as he praised me with applause. "Its objective was to see if you were capable of realizing that you had the power to manipulate your environment. You possess a variety of senses, many of which reach beyond the physical plane. You paid heed to your intuition, utilized an active form of dreaming, and you also connected to other realms using a willful form of visual projection. Very good! We're proud of you. Many candidates don't get this far."

I, of course, was relieved that I didn't have to taste that dreadful substance that Doctor Bell's students had to and wondered whether or not Doctor Bell, or perhaps a future reincarnation of him, was secretly a professor at this institution.

"By the way," Professor Morgan added, "rest assured, no potential students died in the process, although a few did have to get their stomachs pumped out."

My equilibrium was way off kilter. Not only was I being jerked back and forth while popping in and out of illogical realms, but I also had to constantly remind myself that now I looked and acted like a young woman, complete with silly girl-like speech and mannerisms.

"You've successfully demonstrated your resourcefulness," Sister Anna said, "and that's what this trial was all about." One of Hermann Willington's armadillos was curled up on her shoulder.

"Do I get to attend the University now?" I asked, still unconvinced.

57

Professor Morgan replied, "Yes, your admission to the Underground University is now assured. I just have to figure out where to place you. You did get into this game rather late."

He explained that on some levels I was quite advanced, but as far as the educational curriculum at the Underground was concerned, he told me that I really was a novice practitioner. Since I hadn't learned any of their methods or disciplines, I'd be lost if he put me in classes with students closer to my own age.

The headmaster introduced me to a young boy, who appeared to be only five years old and was wearing the appropriate Underground University robe and school uniform. His shocking red hair was on par with mine from the nineteenth century. For some unknown reason, as soon as I gazed upon the color of his hair, I had the shivers. After all, it wasn't like I was the only redhead in the world. Regardless, he looked out of place to be my escort but I was assured that he would show me the way to class.

"Wait, Aliskiya, one more thing," Professor Morgan called out as I was leaving, "you did bring your amulet, I hope. I see you're already wearing your silver ring."

I nodded.

"You'll need both of them to gain access to the Underground, and of course, make sure to present your admission pass. Good luck." As he walked away, he said under his breath, *"You'll need it."*

Hermann led us over to a large archway supporting an ominous dark wooden door. Next to it was a control box to punch in a series of codes. The door rapidly dematerialized, and the redheaded boy and I were able to pass through it. Right afterwards, the door returned back to its original state. After the little boy dragged me by the arm down several tunnels, we came to another barricade where he asked me to pull out my crystalline shell and explained how to use it in the future when traveling by myself. Once we reached the other side, I felt we stepped into an entirely different world from Peregrine Academy.

We were in the midst of a hectic commuter rail station with people of all ages and from all planetary destinations. Specialized vendors had stalls and kiosks off to the side selling everything from various technological periodicals, umbrellas and essential accessories, to merchandising ceremonial robes, books and accouterments that appeared to be related to my studies. Electronic advertisements and monitors were posted all over the place showing the schedules for departing and incoming trains. Left to my own devices, I would've never arrived at the Underground University in a timely fashion. Being on time was imperative.

He rushed me over to an electronic gate, but an alarm went off blocking my entry.

"Oh, you need a *topper*," he said in his high-pitched pre-pubescent voice, and with that he took my *communicator*, activated my *monetary unit card*, and placed it in contact with some machine posted on the wall near the gate.

"There's an entrance fee to get in, you know," he said without much more ado.

He took my crystalline shell and placed it on the turnstile. Its red alarm light turned off, and we entered, continuing at a swift pace. We must've traversed at least a half dozen more staircases, and the longest escalator I had ever been on in my life, which left me with a slight case of vertigo. We finally arrived at a platform where he said we would catch the next train. It seemed that upon approaching each level, we had to get past another security checkpoint where I either had to show my admission pass or my crystalline shell amulet in order to proceed further. At one point the boy and I had to run our belongings through a scanner, and another time I got frisked by an adult woman, who was half my size, but placed her larger than

59

average hands right on my crotch to see if I was either smuggling contraband or carrying weapons!

We boarded our train, and when we arrived at our station, we still had to go through a maze of exits. The boy pointed out which staircase was the closest exit.

Now topside, he led me through an alley to a nondescript building. A uniformed attendant asked for my admission pass and scanned it. Then he accompanied me over to a red slatted wooden door with a brass bolt and unlatched it. It led down a dark corridor with crumbling staircases, smelling dusty and musty but with a hint of cinnamon. One minute I felt like we entered a world of some time to come, and the next minute I felt like I had stepped back into my time machine into the past and all the futuristic earmarks had disappeared. Sparks sprang forth from my guess pass. My pass would change colors—red, if I was on the right path and blue, with a shock-like sensation, if I was going astray. Ultimately, the illuminating effect served as a beacon leading me to another wooden door at the end of a convoluted, cave-like tunnel.

Without warning, my pass burned to a crisp, leaving behind one large smoldering ash. I suspected this meant I finally found my class. When I opened the nearest door, it appeared as if I were entering a world conjured from a medieval wizard's imagination. Racks appeared to be filled with laboratory distillation devices, beakers and flasks, test tubes and vials of chemicals of every color imaginable.

"Ah, perfect timing. One minute more and you would've been locked out," the professor said looking at his pocket watch. "Do we have a new assistant instructor for our Historical Initiations class? Magister Wigdom's my name, and yours?"

His question threw me off guard. "I'm not an instructor. I'm actually a student."

The class was comprised of tiny five-year olds, except one much larger person around my age sitting in the back of the room.

"Let me have a look at your pass," the professor asked.

"There isn't much of it left," I replied handing him the giant cinder, crumbling in my hand.

He put on his gargantuan, oversized reading glasses, which had all sorts of telescopic magnifying lenses clipped on to them. Magister Wigdom gave a miniature hand crank a few twists and turns, and these spectacular appendages doubled as a music box. *Ping!* A melody, originally a tune from Bach composed for a harpsichord, sounded like it was played on musical triangles. Clockwork gears were set in motion, automatically adjusting their focus, pulling the component lenses in and out, closer and then retracting them back so everything was clear and easy to examine the ash residue. Pulling a tiny notepad from his pocket, he made several calculations then put it back. It was mystifying as to how he could see anything special, but he analyzed it as if it contained a secret code. Finally, he looked back up and handed me the remaining pile of dust.

"Odd, but according to this, you seem to be in the right place. Have you had any alchemical training or formal study in the mystical arts?"

"No, not really, but I have been known to have very strange dreams. Does that count?"

Without warning, the room grew cold. A beam of *astral* light hit a prism and split me (as Aliskiya) into three people at once. I saw myself as a mature woman of middle age looking at the present-time version of myself, a youthful woman in her prime, and then as a third person, a mere child, the same age as the other young students in the room. The conversations of the other children sounded like echoes underwater with the volume of their voices *slow-w-w-ly* being

61

silenced. Everything seemed in the right place, but in the wrong order at the wrong time. It was then that I returned to the nineteenth century.

Realizing that my enterprises hadn't quite gone as planned I removed my brain launcher, which is what I nicknamed my time travel machine. I took two shots of Scotland's best to kill the frustration, practiced one of Chopin's nocturnes one last time, and retired for the evening hoping that by the time Wendell came over to test my device, that he would find more successful results.

                           *   *   *

Future Perfect

"How's my friend, the mad scientist?" Wendell asked after greeting me with a firm manly slap on the back so hard it almost knocked the wind out of me.

He sank into my *thinking chair* throwing his coat on top of my worktable. Several displaced pages of sheet music slid on to the floor.

"Some kind of fire or explosion created a commotion nearby. Rumors seemed to fly with the wind," he explained trying to catch his breath, coughing and breathing heavily. "I was walking by Spittal Street Lane on the way over to your place, and it looked like it was happening near your friend, Whit's flat. Whatever occurred created a crowd on the street eager to watch the spectacle. Didn't think I'd ever make it over here in time to squeeze in one of your excursions before my next class. So, John, show me this time machine you built."

I could barely hear our conversation over the racket I was making assembling all the components for his trip. He was eager to see if my device would successfully work on him and that I wasn't just playing him for a fool.

Wendell preened his feathers in my mirror while I took out a tool kit and began tightening a few screws.

"Wendell, backwards or forwards? Your choice."

"Come again?"

"Do you want to explore the past or the future?" I explained, forgetting he wasn't used to time travel phraseology.

"The future, of course. How could one resist discovering what lies ahead and that which has never been recorded in any way, shape or form?"

"The future it is, then. However, Wendell, I must give you a fair warning. So far, every time I've traveled into the future I've turned into a woman."

"Ha! A lady! You must be pulling my leg!"

"*C'est vrai mon ami*. You might not even speak the same language any more. This could be quite a shock."

"John, I started out in medical school. After handling corpses and performing plenty of surgeries, there's very little that can rattle my nerves."

"I'll take your word on that."

He loosened his tie. "John, let's get started. I can't wait to see whom I'm going to wind up as in the future. For the life of me, I fail to comprehend why we cannot stay the same."

"Don't be upset if you look in the mirror and don't recognize the person staring back at you. I'm still learning this process and can't guarantee results. For all I know, you might wind up back in the past, instead. Promise me, that whatever you encounter, you won't blame me for it."

"Very well," Wendell sighed as I began securing the leather straps to his head while he wrinkled his brow with suspicion. "Is there any chance you could also hook yourself up to this device so we can travel through time together? I'd hate to venture into any strange, unknown land without my best friend by my side."

I laughed, "You've traveled the world more than I have. The farthest I've gotten out of Scotland is to London. I've never even once had the chance to cross the Channel."

"Yes, but I've never gone back or forth in time," he replied with concern.

"Golly, I don't own two of them. I've been working on a spare but haven't finished yet. Let me think of something."

If the two of us traveled together, then we could keep an eye on each other to make sure neither one of us got into trouble, so that sounded like a good idea. Thus, I pulled up a second chair beside him and applied final touches to assure his apparatus was secure. My connecting wires took several attempts before they stayed put. Next, I started hand-cranking the gears and dropping my mystery mineral pellets into that special steam canister. Quickly, I sat down and strapped on my headgear from a spare I had constructed, causing enough sparks to fly to fear being electrocuted.

Once everything was under control, I grabbed my decanter of port and took a swig. I put a soothing record on my gramophone to drown out the barking dog outside, adjusted the leather straps on my time travel device and eased back into my chair so we could get underway. At first, the whirring of the gears and the hissing of the steam was distracting, and I could see that Wendell must have had an itch in his pants by the way he squirmed in his chair.

"Take this, my friend," I whispered as I passed him the wine and insisted that he drink, like I did, straight from the bottle.

After gulping at least five times without taking a breath, Wendell wiped his hand on his jacket sleeve.

"Much better," he said, "Promise me, John, we won't encounter Morlocks." He was referring to the creatures in Wells' *The Time Machine* and was apprehensive.

"Sorry, brother, I cannot promise anything. Get ready for the ride!"

Steam began to fill the room making it look like a foggy dawn. Wendell gave my hand a firm squeeze for one final goodbye. Between the two of us consuming almost all of the wine, we finally floated into a new realm of reality as smoothly as a tightly fitting glove and as simply as changing one's socks.

Although it hadn't been planned, Wendell and I had split up and lost contact. I was praying that he hadn't been transported to a different year than I, otherwise that could've been disastrous. When I looked around and discovered that I appeared to be inside an engine room run by steam turbines, I didn't think I had gone too far into the future at all. In fact, I felt like I might've jumped in space or moved a distance rather than fallen into a far off time, since this machinery looked like modern fixtures that I could, perchance, come across in the here and now.

Next, I looked at my hands, then feet. Much to my dismay, they didn't look a stitch like mine. The first reflective surface showed that, once again, I appeared as a strange young woman, who must have been around my age, but she wore such absurd and peculiar clothing, like none I'd ever seen. I also found myself holding a strange shell-like object and entered a series of underground tunnels.

These led to a main rail station, resembling nothing like Victoria, Paddington or any other train station I was familiar with. Surfaces gleamed of polished white metal, and rainbow colored lights flashed from panels announcing arrivals. Vendors sold objects clearly from a different century, but nothing was notable that could pinpoint a date. This most unusual thoroughfare was more reminiscent of a three-ring circus or carnival than a railway depot.

The station was under lockdown with a high security alert. I asked one of the vendors what the commotion was about, and he told me that guards suspected that political firebrands were on the loose and feared trouble. Extra personnel were posted at various checkpoints to select random passengers for baggage inspection and interrogation. Unexpected time delays created an air of nervousness amongst all passengers. I was relieved that I hadn't been stopped and questioned, because the school bag I was carrying contained vials with herbs and potions that could've aroused suspicions.

Instinctively, I knew that I was taking the correct route, although nothing looked familiar. My final destination appeared to be a special school—it was the only place, which looked somewhat recognizable, but for the life of me I had no idea why. I sprinted down a few corridors and cautiously entered one of the classrooms.

"Ah, you must be Aliskiya," the professor called out looking at her attendance ledger.

"Aliskiya? That's her name, isn't it?" I thought while testing my memory from previous time travels when I'd appeared as her.

Each time that would happen, I'd be similarly surprised as if it were the first encounter.

"I'm Professor Emma Kipling, and today's class involves the customization of your magic wand. Please, take a seat. You should find room in the back. I hope you remembered to bring your wand."

Negative. I gave the teacher a blank stare.

"In that case, go back to the wooden cabinet on the left and pick out one from our leave behinds. It's surprising how many students from each semester leave anything from desiccated rats, to wands and even explosive compounds behind in our classrooms," she complained while shaking her head, unable to believe she accumulated such a variety of forgotten treasures.

After picking up the sturdiest stick in the cracked jar of leave behinds, I looked towards the rear and saw an empty spot next to the only person in the class who looked anywhere close to my age, so I joined up with her. I had seen her the last time I traveled to the future. Everyone else appeared half my age or younger, which made me even more self-conscious and out of place.

"Aliskiya Lleullne," the words forcibly came out of my mouth as I took my place beside her, "and yours?"

"Wanda, Wanda MacDowell," she introduced herself looking equally stunned as I.

Wanda MacDowell? Wendell Mackenzie? Our eyes locked and unspoken thoughts confirmed my suspicions. I knew *he* felt the same.

"Owning a wand is a very serious matter and a grave responsibility not to be taken lightly," the professor admonished. "Some schools like ours discourage children receiving their first wand under the age of eleven or twelve. At the Underground University, we advise and instruct our students of those dangers, as they can turn into deadly weapons if the proper discipline isn't exercised. So, students, please use caution and also, please make sure you take them with you and *don't* leave them behind."

We were all instructed to go over to very long tables on the other side of the room. The teacher called our attention after everyone settled in.

"Students, I want you all to take your wands out of their protective casings and place them on the table in front of you. By now, I'm sure you are aware that there's an assortment of objects near your individual workspaces. Please note that everything is grouped and organized according to categories, so you *must* take care not to return any unused supplies to the wrong place, otherwise not only would my assistants have a huge task cleaning up but it would also be unfair to the next class of students who also have to find things for their projects."

She began articulating the details of our assignment using grand gestures and her own wand as a pointer.

"Your wand is your extension of your personal power. It will help you focus and direct your energy. Many of you purchased yours

67

over the counter. Some of you cut your own from a special bush or tree, and others like our newcomers, Wanda and Aliskiya, didn't listen to instructions and had to fish one out from our leftovers jar. Regardless of where it came from, you still need to put your special signature or mark upon it and make it your own."

In front of every place setting were folded pieces of parchment. If we picked up our placards and folded them in the opposite direction, on the inside were riddles. Upon answering the riddles, each would reveal the individual ingredients with which we were to adorn our wands. It was useless to discuss this with our neighbors in order to speed up the process since each one was different.

Gemstones, amulets, paints made of herbs and ground minerals, fossils and rare oils were at our disposal. Once we instinctively chose our correct objects, we were to glue, solder, carve, paint or bind these trinkets in various ways in order to individualize our wands, taking care that whatever we'd fasten to them needed to be made secure and not break off with repetitive use. Finding a particular affinity with some glue and copper wire, which I suspected would be a great conductor for energy, I sanded down my secondhand wand and dipped it in a variety of mineral-infused oils turning it into something quite unique. These extra elements balanced the wand very well in my hand, whereas it had felt light and awkward before.

Once we were all done, we were to hold our new wands in our hands and begin to transfer some of our essence or personality into it, since it was supposed to be an extension of ourselves. Afterwards while I was tidying up my workstation for the next group of students, Professor Morgan, the headmaster, who was present when I was tested for admission to the Underground University, entered the back of the classroom. When class was dismissed I tried to hurry over to the door to ask him a few questions but, in the scuffle with all the students packing up their belongings, he

68

disappeared into the hallway and I never got the chance. I rejoined Wanda and both of us assessed each other with equally confounded looks. We held up our wands, slowly vanished from that classroom and found ourselves back at my flat in Edinburgh.

Coarse hair began to regrow on my knuckles, and my hands appeared larger, stronger and more masculine. My brain felt swollen, perhaps because it grew slightly. So, I rubbed my bleary eyes and loosened my collar and the leather straps of my half-finished time device. Wendell, on the other hand, let out three short, embarrassing hiccoughs from the port he guzzled down. When he stripped off his headgear, static electricity made his hair stand on end. Both of us dropped our jaws in disbelief, noticing that each of us was holding a funny looking stick adorned with an assortment of trinkets held together with glue and wire—souvenirs brought back from our excursion in time travel.

"John, have you ever experienced anything that outrageous? You said I might wind up as a woman—and I did!"

"This is what I encounter every time, *Wanda...*" I smirked with glee watching his face turn red.

A quick flash of doubt seared through his icy blue eyes as he patted down his chest to make sure he hadn't grown breasts. Then, he sprang from his chair, dashing to the mirror, making sure that not only his hair was still the same color as the sharps and flats from my pianoforte, but his neatly trimmed beard and moustache were still intact, as well.

Smells of smoke and steam from my time machine alerted Lydia downstairs. She thought her pots were boiling over and a disaster was about to erupt in the kitchen. Both Wendell and I barricaded the door as she went against my previous requests never to barge in. Much to our dismay, we began to hear the clinking of a skeleton key being inserted in my keyhole.

"Everything's under control!" Wendell shouted, "Something accidentally fell into the fireplace!"

Both of us were exhausted and bewildered, but also elated and eager, nonetheless, to attempt this experiment once again. Wendell reached for his coat and hat but couldn't help make one last remark.

"John, didn't that class remind you a bit of our old school?" I raised one eyebrow and was completely mystified.

"You forgot almost everything, didn't you?" Wendell laughed as he took his wand and shoved it into his pocket.

Meanwhile, my head was still spinning from so much excitement. Once he left, I finished off the last of the port and examined my new wand once more before putting it away in a safe place, one which would be particularly hidden from my landlady, whom I feared would be way too inquisitive.

Without any warning whatsoever, Finn made another grand entrance into my flat.

"The future is never absolute!" Finn shouted. He was displeased with the fact that I had ventured off into the future once more without his permission. I guess being a discarnate individual of a higher-than-human vibration, who had the ability to break the rules of the physical universe, had its advantages. His antics never failed to amaze me.

"How many times do I have to tell you that every little word, action and deed you perform now will change and affect your future?" Finn yelled as he snatched my timepiece and began winding it backwards.

"You'll break it! Be careful!" I cried.

"I won't," he replied. "Didn't I warn you to stop going there? Does the phrase, *Clavem ad futurum ex clues in praeterito fuit*, mean anything to you?"

He tossed the timepiece across the room. "The key to the future lies in clues from the past?" I dived, head first to catch it before it hit the floor, barely having time to translate the Latin in my head. Then I wondered if there were ways and means of finding out the futuristic fate of Arthur, and if so, whom did he wind up as?

*   *   *

A Lesson in Magic

"Arthur, this is ludicrous. It's not working," I said as I began to get a stiff neck from concentrating too hard.

I rushed over to my piano, slammed my fingers down on the keyboard, playing several loud discordant, frustrating sounds of nonsense, downed a shot of brandy and plunged back into my chair, loosening my tie. Thank God, the entire boarding house was empty. My landlady took the train to London to attend a play that her niece, Florence, was starring in. She'd be gone the entire weekend, which afforded me the luxury of peace and quiet without the possibility of interruptions.

"John, for some the ability to move objects with the mind comes right away. For others, it could take hundreds of attempts before experiencing any perceivable results," Arthur elaborated.

"That's encouraging," I said with a hint of sarcasm, "I'm beginning to think this is all rubbish."

Our trial and error attempts at telekinesis were stretching the limits of my imagination. First of all, Arthur and I were not in the same room when they took place. We were communicating telepathically and agreed to try these tests while I remained in Edinburgh, and he was wherever he would be that weekend. By sheer persistence, we established a telepathic link so strong that we might've been using Morse code or speaking over a telephone line with little distinction. We had started this correspondence when we first met and continued no matter where we'd be at any given time, and Arthur was quite a man for travel.

We might've made some progress communicating but had a long way to go in regards to moving solid objects using self-generated psychic energy. In front of me I had a crystal paperweight, a candle, a brazier full of church incense, a photo of Arthur and my journal open to a blank page so that I could take notes documenting our progress. Our first tests involved "pulling the flame" which meant that we'd try to manipulate each other's candles from afar. By projecting psychic energy, we'd make the candles flicker and change shapes but that seemed too difficult to prove whether the results were successful or not.

My aim was to move one of the denser, heavier objects I had selected on the table. I was losing my patience. So far those attempts had been futile.

"Don't tell me you are giving up the ghost?" Arthur inquired.

Even from a distance, he could sense my frustration.

"If you really take telekinesis down to its lowest common denominator, all movement, whether it is turning on the engine of a motor car and traveling out to the countryside, or overcoming your inertia to get out of your chair to walk across the room is telekinesis, as you have utilized thoughts to complete and accomplish both actions," he explained.

He had a valid point.

Arthur continued, "If everything boils down to energy—that we are made of energy like the paperweight on your table. If the hay I feed my horses gives them energy to move their muscles and pull my cart, that steam can turn all the mechanisms to make a locomotive move down a track at remarkable speed, that lighting a candle will not only provide light, but also warmth, then there has to be something said that when we meditate we can create a tingling sensation in our fingers and have our entire hands feel warm. There's a science behind this."

I drank the last drop of brandy from my glass and then closed my eyes. My clairvoyant sight honed in on Arthur, as I could visualize him in his favorite chair lighting his pipe.

"Perhaps, we'll have more success after I've had a good night's sleep. Sorry to be such a disappointment," I said, somewhat embarrassed.

"John, life is infinitely stranger than anything which the mind of man could invent. We would not dare to conceive the things which are really mere commonplaces of existence."

He couldn't have re-quoted a better line from Sherlock Holmes. He rose, walked over to his study window and continued quoting from his stories.

"If we could fly out of that window hand in hand, hover over this great city, gently remove the roofs, and peep in at the queer things which are going on, the strange coincidences, the planning, the cross-purposes, the wonderful chains of events, working through generations, and leading to the most outré results, it would make all fiction with its conventionalities and foreseen conclusions most stale and unprofitable."

"Besides a good memory of some of your famous lines from *A Case of Identity*, what are you insinuating, Arthur?"

"That one's imagination creates one's own game. John, was there something else you wanted to explore with our preternatural undertakings this evening?"

I paused a second. "This must sound absurd but, I'd like to play a trick on Professor Lorraine Smith from the medical school. Close to a year ago I was walking across campus. I fell right into his path after stumbling on wet cobblestones and was quite surprised that he kept on walking as if I were invisible, despite the fact that I was covered with mud from head to toe. In fact, since he was a doctor, I was surprised that he didn't stop and ask whether or not I'd been hurt. For months afterward, when I'd pass him every day going to classes, I was embarrassed to make eye contact with him, wondering if he still remembered that I was that clumsy music student who nearly knocked him down. As testimony to our telekinetic exercises really working, I'd love to have the ability to make the professor drop his brief case or umbrella forcing him to pick it up and realize that I had something to do with it. That would be significant proof of my ability to impose mind over matter."

Arthur strained to control his laughter. "You'd like to play a trick on him?"

"That would be a lot more significant than making my paperweight fall off the table. Besides, no harm will be done. Isn't it true that all those medical professors are two-bricks-short-of-a-load? I've heard rumors that they'd experiment on themselves by injecting viruses thereby exposing themselves to all sorts of ailments. Didn't you tell me that Doctor Bell, the man who was your mentor and inspiration for Sherlock Holmes, was notorious for research like that?"

"Very well, we will use Doctor Lorraine Smith as our test subject. Oh, John, one last thing."

"What's that?"

"I've been so proud that you've been so dedicated and faithful with these attempts, so I'm going to leave you with a little token of my appreciation."

Arthur's ghostly astral body extended its hand and reached towards mine with a hardy handshake. Thinking nothing of it at first, as his apparition began to fade and disappear from my room, I winced in disgust at the sticky, honey-like residue coating my hand, wrist and extending to drench the cuff of my starched and pressed dress shirt.

"Damn it! He loves his ectoplasm."

It was repulsive and disgusting, and I was covered with slime.

* * *

Right Turn From the Far Left Lane

A note was left on my door. Whit said he needed to see me right away at the university library. It sounded urgent.

"Thank you for rushing over," Whit said as he handed me my book titled, *The Spell Book of Charms and Incantations* by J.P. Scott.

74

"I should thank you," I said as I took the forbidden book from his grasp and stuffed it in my book bag, glad that he didn't have it in his possession a moment longer.

Although my nose shouldn't have been attuned to such things, I couldn't help noticing that it was tainted by a distinctive scent reminiscent of the soap and aftershave that Whit always used. Two quick sniffs were enough to make me raise an eyebrow.

"Oh, by the way, some redheaded girl from our English class keeps pestering me and asking questions about you." There was more he wasn't telling me.

"That's strange," I replied. "I can't understand why she keeps following me like a hound. We've barely exchanged a few words until now."

"Maybe she likes you," Whit said, cracking a smile.

"If she does she has a funny way of showing it." My attention was drawn back to my spell book. I clutched my satchel with a sigh of relief that it was finally back in the right hands.

"It's a rather private book, somewhat like a diary," I hinted with a slight edge of warning. "I hope you weren't inclined to read it."

"Oh no, not in the least."

He denied the suggestion, shaking his head so hard that his curls whipped back and forth, and his glasses nearly flew off his nose. Considering the bizarre events that followed, I suspected otherwise.

The lack of sleep was taking its toll. Night after night Arthur and I persisted with our outlandish and controversial psychical ventures. The next morning my landlady called upstairs at least five times to wake me. I skipped breakfast, donned yesterday's clothing, and barely had the luxury of splashing cold water on my face before running off to class. Professor Niecks, the head of the music department taught this one and if I were to impress him for any scholarships whatsoever, I had to be attentive and I had to be on time. My heart was set on attending the Royal College of Music in

75

London, not only for its prestige, but Wendell would be interning at a publishing company in London, and I was looking forward to exploring the city together as friends. I stepped up my pace in order to get to class and decided to take the road that cut behind Greyfriars Church. It always gave me the itchies and the woolies, but that route was cleaner, smelled better and was more pleasant than taking the steep back alleys or stairways off of Cowgate. Cutting across Chambers Street under the bridge that connected two buildings in the Quadrangle, I sprinted past McEwan Hall to get over to the Reid Concert Hall where I arrived seconds before the professor closed the doors. I nearly slid off the slick polished surface of my piano bench, still wearing my muffler and overcoat. Vigorously, I shook out my fingers and wrists and then waited for my cue. The violins and cellos had already finished their warm ups, but the French horns bellowed so loudly that my seat vibrated.

The sheet music for today's lesson focused on Bach's *Brandenburg Concertos*. My advanced abilities allowed me to pluck out any melody without much forethought, despite the fact that today instead of the usual pianoforte I was to be playing my part on a harpsichord. However, my attention was torn in two. Finn materialized and scooted up alongside me. The heated discussion that went on in my head nearly drowned out the music I was supposed to be playing along with the rest of my class.

"Yes, Finn, what is it now?"

His exposition and criticism would rip through me like a dagger dipped in poison.

"Your stupid friend, Whit, did exactly what you didn't want him to do."

"And what's that?"

"He took your spell book and used it."

"He didn't?"

"Oh, I'm afraid so. He should've known better, but he didn't pay heed to your warning."

76

"The inscription I have at the very beginning?"

"Not discouraging enough."

"For God's sake, what will become of him? I'm not sure what demons he might've let loose. Do you?"

Ah yes, Finn, my old comrade and friend. His manners were questionable, and he had this horrible habit of intruding at awkward moments. Yet, at other times his sudden appearance was like a godsend. He said that my friend Whit had borrowed my spell book, the one I compiled with excerpts from the famous mage, Eliphas Levi, complete with Celtic runes, snippets from rare manuscripts ranging from Simon Magus to Doctor John Dee, and also the same one that somehow survived through the centuries and wound up in the future. It also contained my hodgepodge of herbal formulae and, of course, sketches and notes on the construction of my time machine. I created this collection on my own, and perhaps Whit had visions of days to come when he, himself, gave me the warning, "Beware of strange books!"

But Jesus Christ and the Ghost of Christmas Future! No one was supposed to set eyes on *that* book, not even Wendell or Arthur. What possessed him to take that risk? Curiosity, I guess, but where an idiot dares to dream, stupid people will follow, or I think the quote goes like that.

Didn't Wendell mention something the other day when he came over to test out my time machine that there was nearly a riot with a fire or explosion near Whit's flat? God, have mercy! I hoped he was okay, and no one else was injured.

After class I ran over to see if Whit was working at the campus library, but either something did happen, or it was his day off. So I left and figured that Whit would eventually turn up at Professor McKnight's history class.

*   *   *

Wanderings Beyond Spiritualism

"The power of words? An author can take words and create double meanings. Words will entertain, pass the time, and yet, interject views of politics, of religion, of morality, and still get away with calling themselves fiction. Words are teachers, and the novels they find themselves in are their classrooms.

"Take the story we're reading, *Sybil: or, the Two Nations*, for example, by Disraeli..."

Professor McKnight roused one sleeping student with a tap on the shoulder while pacing up and down the aisles.

"At the end of Book 2, Chapter 5, Egremont says, 'Our Queen reins over the greatest nation that ever existed,' but a young stranger interrupts him asking, 'Which nation? For she reins over two.' Of course, he was referring to the disparate factions of the rich and the poor.

"We all should be aware, especially for those of you also taking my history class, that Benjamin Disraeli is a key player in our modern political drama. Yet, he also wrote notable fiction, which he was able to use as a platform for his viewpoints no matter how debatable they were.

"In comparison, think of one of our most modern writers, H.G. Wells. Having an entirely different outlook altogether, he's used fiction to create allusions towards a perfect world, a utopia in his mind, forecasting the future with warnings implied. Often, it's simpler for an author's audience to accept a controversial point of view if the mysterious veil of fiction is used versus explaining one's theories in such a clear-cut or literal manner.

"And that's the magic of literature," Professor McKnight concluded, "Your homework assignment is to finish the rest of the story. I'd be particularly interested in your opinions of Sybil's character and personality as an emerging feminine ideal. Therefore, be prepared for a discussion on that at our next class and a short examination, as well. Class dismissed."

Throughout the professor's oration, I kept glancing back at Whit. Burns graced his arms. Telltale scorch marks were on his favorite waistcoat, and the ends of his curls were singed. Meanwhile I didn't need a well-tuned sixth sense to know that Sarah Elizabeth, that haughty girl whose advances I ignored when I chose Whit as my tutor, also had me under observation. Goosebumps formed and the hairs sprang from the back of my neck picking up on her projected thoughts, which kept me from paying the proper attention to the lecture. Whit managed to tiptoe out of English class early to avoid confrontation. Afterwards, I rushed over to the university library to catch up with him and to avoid her, but I was still out of luck. Anticipating my plan, he must have disappeared through one of the secret passageways inside the bookcases. Guess who showed up, instead?

"Sherlock?"

"Would you quit calling me Sherlock?" Finn was annoyed. "If you've forgotten already, my name's Finn, but if you'll listen to my advice as long as you call me Sherlock, then I'm doing a splendid job. John, did you really expect to address Whit about your spell book?"

"Yes, I did, but…"

"Perhaps, I'm expecting too much of you."

"Nonsense! Sherlock—Finn, whatever you want to be called, I must warn him that he has to undo what's been done. He won't confess anything. You're supposed to know everything. What did he do, and how do I find out?"

"John, do I have to remind you?" Finn yawned and rolled his eyes.

"Go to the Library? You always make me work for my answers, don't you?"

*   *   *

Finn was not referring to the University of Edinburgh Library. No, he meant the Secret Library, the archive of everything and every incident that ever happened since the beginning of time, and it would continue keeping records of everything *ad infinitum*. Often while engaging in time travel, there were still unanswered questions afterwards, and the records stored there often could provide objective reports as to what was really going on.

79

What was amazing was that it not only kept detailed accounts in the present that I was aware of, but also everyone else's developments simultaneously. Therefore, if I wanted to know what Arthur, Wendell, or anyone I knew or didn't know was doing right now, I could find that out, as well. This was one of the many explanations as to why phenomena such as telepathy or astral projection were supposed to work, or so I was told. The one thing the Secret Library could not do was to predict the future. That was because the future was still malleable and affected by actions done by people in the present. To get a glimpse of the future, even though it could always take a turn on a five-cent piece, one had to resort to time travel.

Reigniting memories from the Library or via time travel could create a similar experience. Generally, one accessed the Secret Library through a portal, although that portal could be within one's dream state or meditation. Portals could also be symbols, objects or locations of power. Objects could manifest as nearly anything, and often had a psychic connection from a former owner. Other times objects had no logical connection, but they just worked, such as finding a strange book. However, locations could be special trees, ruins, abandoned churches, statuary, and yes, even gravestones or burial mounds.

After I had successfully gained access to the Library, I'd follow my intuition and hunt for a special book, and that's where I'd find my answer. Sometimes, Finn would take me to a theater to watch a film. In ancient times, long before the days of written words, there was the possibility that one entered the Secret Library through cave paintings or images similar to Egyptian hieroglyphics. Yet, I was only able to speculate on that. Finn made it clear that one also needed a guide, like him, as an escort, and often the first few attempts entailed passing by checkpoints and security guards of some sort. This was not an idle playground for curiosity seekers. Occasionally, someone bypassed all those precautions, but odds were against them doing it again, or those visits would become less frequent with possible repercussions.

However, I'll never forgot the first time I discovered a new way of accessing the Secret Library by making a special visit to Ding Dalrymple's Rare Books hidden off one of the closes in Old Town. At the crack of dawn, I woke and went out for a walk. Strangely enough, I was surprised to have stumbled upon an antiquarian bookstore open at that hour. I peered though the front window, noticing there were lights on inside, reached for the doorknob, and was lucky as I made a half turn that it was open. The store's proprietor was aware of my presence, but paid it no mind. Trying to be as inconspicuous as possible, I reached for a book of travel, but was disappointed that despite its well-worn appearance it had only been published last year.

"Need assistance?" he asked. He was a balding, thin man with dark curly hair, or what was left of it. His wire-rimmed glasses perched on his nose. He wore a white, wrinkled shirt open at the collar and without a tie, but his oversized waistcoat was impeccably buttoned and adorned with his requisite timepiece. He reminded me of my friend, Whit, but looked old enough to be his grandfather. I didn't bother asking whether or not they were related, but the resemblance was remarkable.

"I was searching for something a lot older," I said.

He pointed to a shelf in the rear left of the store. "I have books over there dating back almost as far as the Gutenberg Bible," he said, "older, handwritten ones in the basement."

Before I took my next step, the book I was holding began initiating a magical effect. Some unknown and indescribable force was disintegrating my right hand, which started fading away, transparently being displaced by the space around it. Molecules danced in the air like fireflies.

"Great Caesar's Ghost! I'm losing ground," I cried.

I discovered a portal—a crack in the wall of the fabric of time and was now in the dilemma of betwixt and between. My

81

molecular structure was too unstable, and once again I felt myself rapidly dissolving. I was merely a novice practitioner, botching the attempt with improper entry. What I hoped to accomplish was merely to enter the portal to find the information I needed, but I ethereally atomized and wound up over by St. Cuthbert's cemetery, instead.

Eventually, when I became a bit more adept, I realized that Dalrymple had both new and antiquarian books, manuscripts, maps, and a variety of diagrams and illustrations that could all serve as gateways to vast depositories of information. His small and cluttered bookshop would transform into a library of incomprehensible size merely by the act of performing the lost art of psychometry or bibliomancy. By opening the right book at the right place and time, the long sought-after answer to one of my questions about someone or a particular event in history would be magically revealed.

"Ghost stories and mysteries on sale today," Ding shouted out, hidden somewhere in the midst.

"Not today, sir," I called out, not sure which direction I should be shouting.

Ding knew who I was by now and could recognize me by the sound of my voice. However, I was surprised that he'd never get annoyed with my frequent visits, since I rarely had more than a few pence to spend at any given time compared to some of his more affluent customers.

"Looking for anything in particular, son?" he called out, still invisible to the eye and hiding somewhere in his store.

I saw the trap door to the basement open way in the back, so I suspected he was down there.

"I'll know what I want when I find it," I replied, and that was what I'd always say when I had no intention of making a legitimate purchase, but was scouting out a gateway, instead.

For some unknown reason, I was drawn towards a shelf with illustrated books on science—natural science, botany, zoology and marine life. I even found a used medical book, notably one with medical illustrations, drawn by H.G. Wells, which he did for a living before he became a famous writer. I started to thumb through it. Instantly, I felt a queer sensation in my solar plexus, and my brain began to tingle. Ding seemed to be off on his merry little way still rummaging through whatever he had stored down below in the cellar, so I began to get to work reciting a few incantations to prepare my mind for the journey that was about to follow. Then, as if the book I held in my hand turned into a crystal ball, the fated tale of Whit's misadventures began to unfold.

*　　*　　*

"Whit, would you mind going though all the stacks in the corner and make sure that they are put away in their proper places?" the head librarian pointed as he continued walking forward kicking up puffs of dust as he left the room.

Without question, Whit rolled up his sleeves, straightened his tie and sauntered over to the back of the work room eyeing his task for the afternoon, thinking to himself that instead of shelving books he would've much rather been ensconced in a political discourse by Disraeli or even better yet, a juicy novel about a bawdy and forbidden affair between clandestine lovers during eighteenth century France.

Years of accumulated dust forced poor Whit to sneeze so hard that his glasses hit the floor. As he groped for his handkerchief, he realized he must've left it at home and was forced to wipe his nose on his sleeve. After rummaging through the first pile of long-forgotten returns, Whit moved on to the next stack. However, what was expected to be a long, drawn out dreary afternoon took a sudden twist. In the middle of that second stack one particular book caught his attention. It looked hand-engraved, not the standard from most print shops he could recall. His inquisitive fingers carefully extracted that book without causing the other books to fall in its wake.

"Beware of strange books!"

Who said that? Where did that come from? He looked over both shoulders. Whit ignored the omen, as he continued to skim through its pages. Naturally, he missed the first page with its hand-inscribed caveat warning stray onlookers to proceed no further. Finally his attention became affixed upon Chapter 57: How To Win The Love Of Another. Then another book caught his attention, a red one with an odd title. Since he had no extra time to spare he hid both. However when his work shift ended, he took only the spell book, in haste, which he smuggled out of the university library and then made a few detours to pick up the necessary ingredients for that spell that he had come upon earlier. For reasons unknown, the red book he was also interested in had been left behind.

When he arrived back at his flat, he rushed to light a candle, placed a hunk of cheese and stale bread on the table, poured a large helping of beer, and returned his attention to his newly acquired treasure.

"Garlic? Sawdust? Nitric acid (ooh, sounds dangerous), black powder (don't like the sound of that), oil of red roses (might quell the garlic smell), seven drops of mercury (poisonous?) three handfuls of grave yard dirt (sounds macabre) and sodium carbonate—I guess being an expert in English literature isn't going to help me one bit," Whit said to himself.

He went to work, busy as an ant. Once he was finished, he took the baneful mixture and stirred a spoonful or two into the icing of a small cake from a local bakery. His plan was to offer the potion-laced confection to his lady friend, Isabelle, while courting her on a carefully planned picnic the following Sunday afternoon. There was a lovely lake with boats for hire right outside of Edinburgh, and he was eager to exercise his romantic charms on the girl.

Before Whit tested his potion on his unknowing subject, another terrible event occurred. Somehow in the midst of the hustle and bustle, Whit was so clumsy that he knocked over the candle on his table littered with those pernicious and flammable ingredients. The spilled sawdust ignited. Flames spread resulting in a minor explosion, which filled his entire boarding house, and fire authorities were summoned immediately. Lucky to be alive and still have the

84

house standing afterwards, he had to conjure up a fantastic yarn to cover his tracks and save face with the local community.

*   *   *

"Garlic? I never could understand why a love potion would include garlic as one of its ingredients?" I asked, holding the book with the portal in my hand and calling out for Finn, wherever he was hiding.

"Turn around, you imbecile."

He had the air of a master magician, and I was merely the victim of his illusions. I found him as he appeared in a reflection from the front window of Ding's bookshop.

"Thanks for the compliments, Finn. You're predictably condescending," I said.

"Just doing my job, John. By the way, it wasn't my doing to create those recipes, spells or whatever you wish to call them."

"I know, and by the way, I haven't tested out that love elixir." I looked back to confirm he was still there.

"Perhaps you should, John."

I gave Finn a quick glance of disapproval and kept watch to make sure Ding wasn't spying on me.

"By now you should know that I'm aware of all your actions, including the fact that you carelessly returned that grimoire along with your other borrowed books to the library a few weeks ago," he said, scolding me.

"Then why didn't you tell me? We could've stopped the crime before it happened—Sherlock!"

"You do fancy calling me Sherlock, don't you?" Finn laughed. "Should I start calling you Watson? You really aren't very observant, by the way."

"Care to explain?"

"When you retrieved your spell book from Whit, outside of its scent, you didn't notice anything else different?"

"Such as?"

85

"For one, I found sawdust inside which you should've be aware of. Secondly, on page forty-six you failed to spot the cartoon your friend, Whit, must've drawn. For what reason I have no clue, but I'm quite surprised you didn't inspect that book thoroughly," Finn explained. "But that's not the only item you overlooked."

I scratched my head. "What else could I be missing?"

"Perhaps you returned two books by accident?"

Testing my memory, I closed my eyes trying to picture every single book I owned and where I stowed them away in my flat. "The red book!" I cried out. "The one that had been left behind on the train. It's gone!"

I was angry, frustrated and nervous since I was never quite sure what was so special about that book except that strange events revolved around it. Besides, I was waiting for him to reprimand me and ask what on earth was I doing carrying it around on campus where it could so easily be mislaid.

"Finn, I wish you'd you shut your mouth and stop calling me unobservant and idiotic, or should my fist tell you otherwise?"

Any threat from me was harmless. Besides, I was talking to an apparition trapped within window glass.

"Yes, as I was saying, I suspect your little friend, Whit has been captivated by the fair, young Isabelle and was possessed to conjure up a little help. God knows why, he's charming enough left to his own devices. Regardless, the result is going to spell nothing but trouble. I'd suggest you talk to him."

I checked my timepiece. Soon I'd have to leave for class.

"Finn, how am I going to speak to him if I'm not even supposed to know he actually read and tried something from it?"

Finn raised an eyebrow. "If you don't finish what you were meant to do on this round, I'll simply have to continue to haunt you until you do get it correct," he replied cynically.

He laughed at the quizzical look on my face.

"In other words, John, if you don't get it right this lifetime, I'll be responsible for trying to straighten you out once again."

Lifetime? He and I did have an occasional conversation about heaven and hell and the possibility of reincarnation after death, but I was unsure of my beliefs. However, coming back and not actually dying a real death didn't sound all that terrible.

"Well, I hope you won't be as loathsome as you are now," I said with sarcasm while walking forward, but looking the other way.

Like an idiot, I walked right into a freestanding bookcase. It toppled over, and I had to get down on my hands and knees to pick up the mess. Ding came back upstairs wondering what I had done. Thus, I closed the science book I used as a portal and shoved it back on the shelf with the others.

"Don't think I found what I was looking for today," I said, a bit embarrassed, "Do you expect more deliveries?"

"They arrive all the time," he replied, standing there slightly upset with his hands on his hips.

*   *   *

The Wrong Destination

One of the dangers of being a neophyte of the arcane was that occult manuals were deliberately encrypted to ward off meddlers and mischief-makers and were probably that way for very wise reasons. Those of us with special permission to enter such unknown realms were still wandering around wearing blindfolds most of the time. Since the Secret Library was located beyond the physical plane, only a non-corporeal guide could assist you to get there, and the impression I got was that this guide was invisible to everyone else in the physical, every-day universe, but was discernable in supernal realms. In one sense, I could almost define Finn as an *anthropomorphic imprint* that I more or less carried around in my back pocket. Even with a chaperone like him, I subjected myself to many blunders in order to perfect difficult techniques. This applied to my expeditions in time travel, and it certainly affected my excursions in astral projection, as well. In my case, often I would project automatically and subconsciously while sleeping, which was the hardest time to exert control over my actions.

One evening, the Society for Psychical Research concluded a séance at the private residence of Sir Oliver Lodge, a prominent physicist and mathematician. Afterwards, Arthur commenced a lively discussion with Lodge and Frederic William Henry Meyers, a classical philosopher and scholar who was one of the society's founding members. Goodbyes were exchanged as the other attending parties either parted for the evening or split off into separate conversations throughout the house.

"So, what did you think?" Lodge asked Arthur as the three of them entered the library.

One of Lodge's house servants entered with a tray of refreshments, set it down and left the three men in privacy.

"I'm glad our medium was able to dispense with any props or gimmicks," Myers said.

"I agree," Arthur added, "Humans might be dependent on using technology such as the telegraph to communicate with each other for the most part unless they've developed powers of telepathy, but since our departed friends in the spirit world no longer have the need for such physical things, they should be as easy to contact using non-physical techniques."

Myers interrupted, "When one uses a Ouija board, I'm convinced that the planchettes are moved by humans and not by spirits. Back in the '50s, scientists such as Michael Faraday and William Benjamin Carpenter conducted experiments saying that even table tipping was created as a result of an *ideometer* effect, or automatic human muscular movements without conscious volition. But, before we move on, tea anyone?"

Arthur barely took a sip of his beverage before he opened another topic of conversation straightaway on theories and principles about apparitions and hauntings.

"Gentlemen, earlier this evening we were discussing dreams and their importance in psychic investigations. I'd like to present another authentic dream case. On February 8, 1840, Edmund Norway, the chief officer of the ship called the *Orient*, had a dream

88

between the hours of 10 p.m. and 4 a.m. in which he saw his brother Nevell, a Cornish gentleman, murdered by two men. In that dream, Nevell appeared on horseback. One of the assailants caught the horse's bridle and then shot him twice. The two thugs proceeded to beat him and dragged him to the side of the road, where they left him to die. As soon as Edmund woke up from this terrible nightmare, he promptly recorded it in writing and shared the event with the other officers of the ship. One thing that he made special note of was that in the dream, the road in Cornwall appeared as he had always remembered it, but the house, which should've been on the right, appeared on the left side of the road, which he found most unusual.

"As time passed he discovered that this murder actually occurred, and the assassins, two brothers named Lightfoot, were executed a few months later. In their final confession, they confirmed that they killed Nevell during the time of his brother's dream."

"I do remember that," Myers said while relighting his pipe. "It was written up in one of the prominent occult review magazines."

"These are actual facts, although they cannot be explained," Arthur said, once again capturing his colleagues' full attention. "During sleep there is a part of us, which can detach itself and visit distant scenes, though the demarcation between waking and sleeping is so complete that it's rare that the memory of the night's experience is carried through. Some people call it the etheric body. Others call it the subconscious self. I could give you additional accounts, but..."

All three were distracted as books started falling off the library shelves behind them.

"John, what are you doing?" Arthur said under his breath so none of his friends could hear him.

Unaware of my own actions, I ignored him and continued tossing more books about.

Lodge rose to his feet and pointed at the commotion. "Gentleman, don't you find that strange? Books have been tumbling on to the floor."

Myers looked perplexed. Arthur tried to play dumb.

Arthur interrupted, eager to divert their attention, "It's psychic residue left over from our session. I'm sure whatever activity is going on, it'll fade away in a few minutes."

Believe it or not, what was really happening was that I had been astrally sleepwalking and inadvertently producing telekinetic activity. I had no control over when these paranormal movements would start or stop.

Relieved, Arthur continued his story and pretended as if nothing out of the ordinary happened, "In the dream of his brother, Norway used a technique, which I call *traveling clairvoyance*. Similar events can also occur in the delirium of high fever. Thus, it can be conceived that the consciousness of the sleeping man, drawn by love and sympathy, was able to link with the spirit of his brother and witness his murder and still be able to carry that experience through to his normal memory."

Later that same evening during our midnight *tête-à-tête*, Arthur was upset.

"John, what possessed you to spy on us?"

"Pardon me? I was exhausted from all of my studies and fell asleep earlier in the evening. It was only in the past hour that I woke up because of our little *arrangement*."

"You interfered with our discussion and started throwing books off the shelves like a fractious child!" he exclaimed. "Don't you find that behavior inappropriate?"

I was completely baffled as to what he was insinuating. "I don't believe that I did anything like that, and if I did, I was unaware of it," I protested in my defense. "Why would I deliberately sabotage your meeting? Did any of the others see me?"

"I don't suspect they saw you," Arthur explained, "but they definitely witnessed the results."

"If that's the case, sir, I apologize and will try to find out a way to be more cognizant of my actions when I'm sleeping, but spying? Arthur, I wouldn't *dream* of it."

*   *   *

"Wisdom is a gift given to the Wise"
–Florence Farr, motto from the Golden Dawn

I'd been writing a letter to Arthur to back up some of our findings. He had impending travel plans, but we still made a pact that at midnight that we would continue faithfully with our undertakings. Meanwhile Mackenzie, who also studied medicine and the macabre at the University of Edinburgh, was on his way over.

"An intruder approaches!" I coughed, as I heard footsteps.

"My niece, Florence Farr, is a famous actress," my landlady said, bragging to Wendell as she escorted him upstairs to my flat. "John tells me that you frequent London. Next time you're in town, you should look her up."

"I'd be delighted," Wendell replied with his coy and captivating smile.

Lydia knocked on my door. "John, you have company."

"The door's unlocked," I shouted. That was rare, but I was expecting him.

Wendell swung it open wide and was a bit surprised. "With God as my witness, don't you look like a pathetic soul!"

My thick, uncombed, reddish hair looked like a tangle of brambles. I was shivering and sitting by the fireside sipping medicinal tea while wearing my muffler and coat trying to brave the chill. It was a strange concoction my landlady insisted would cure my ague. However, it tasted vile, and it took incredible fortitude to get each swallow down. The ink was still uncapped and several pages of Arthur's letter were drying on top of my desk. Recently, he urged me to travel up to Loch Ness to investigate a haunting in his absence. It was unfortunate that I encountered nothing more than the beginnings of influenza and my place was in shambles.

"Since you're halfway dressed," he said sarcastically, "all you need to do is grab your umbrella and hat. Come, join me at the Kenilworth."

We made a hasty jaunt over to the local pub, dodging puddles along with the sudden downpour, and spoke over fish, chips and locally brewed ale.

"So my dear friend, what were you writing when I disrupted your thoughts?" Wendell asked in his usual jovial manner.

"Nothing really," I replied. I still wanted to keep my relationship with Doyle a secret.

"Such a creative man as yourself? You're probably a brilliant writer," he suggested.

"I'm really a writer, not a mus-i-c-i-an..." I stammered, reversing my words.

Mackenzie raised his eyebrows. I shook my head, taking a sip of ale a bit too strong for my taste. Excess foam from its head clung to my lips.

"I meant to say that I'm not a writer, just a musician."

"We're all writers," Wendell said with confidence.

With my two closest friends being professional writers, I was the exception. My history of dreams was so vivid that if I wrote them down, I probably could've published them.

Promptly, he changed the subject. "Doctor Bell took our surgical class for a tour at the Autopsy Museum on Friday."

"Are you still in medical school or are you focusing more on your writing?" I asked. "What about that internship with that London newspaper?"

"It's impossible to quit my classes with Doctor Bell. After all, he's the person that Conan Doyle claimed was his inspiration for the character of Sherlock Holmes. Yet, I pay more attention to the doctor's quirks and idiosyncrasies than his lessons. Regarding my major, I'm still undecided. That's why I'm continuing to take classes in both disciplines. It's also impossible to turn down any chance to write an interesting story.

"But I must tell you about our museum trip. The curator said the tour wasn't for the faint of heart. Only one nurse and I had the courage to go through with it. Everyone else bowed out. He kept opening oaken drawers with glass containers with mysterious remains of corpses. They were so decomposed that many resembled slime and ooze. We continued our tour and passed walls filled with multicolored glass jars containing mummified body parts."

"Wendell, you better stop," I said burping up some phlegm.

"John, specimens like that would be enough to make anyone quit the medical profession."

"I agree wholeheartedly, so please change the subject," I replied, coughing to clear my throat. I was beginning to turn paler than I had been earlier, but took another sip, assuming that it was hard to feel any worse.

"Well, at least that trip to the museum wasn't as bad as the time when Doctor Bell had us sampling those terrible tasting medicines," he said.

Wendell went on to remind me about what I experienced during my recent trip in time travel into the far future. "John, the point was to illustrate the fact that we hadn't been paying attention to his demonstration. Doctor Bell mentioned that in order to identify certain substances a physician, when in doubt, might have to taste them. This, of course, was all a sleight of hand trick to distract us from the fact that he didn't actually taste that horrible substance but he dipped a different finger into the chemical mixture, instead. None of us noticed, and we all fell for the gag. I must've been sick to my stomach for days afterward. Remember? I couldn't even join you at McLaughlin's for a drink after exams.

"But you must accompany me on my next trip," Wendell insisted. "We'll go to the Eagle and the Child in Oxford. There are some budding young novelists, Tolkien and C.S. Lewis to name two, who are frequent patrons. Just to overhear their conversations over cognac and cigars would be pure ecstasy. Besides, you're always fun to have around. It's a long train ride to London, and you've always entertained me with the best stories. Except now, I'm beginning to wonder if there was something more to them than I was aware of.

"John, every time you've shared accounts of those unusual dreams you've had, I've also had disturbing dreams and sometimes nightmares as a result. Recently I had one where I was a Chinese courtier from centuries ago with an odd name—Li Zhi Wen, if I recall correctly. There was a monkey on the loose inside the Imperial palace. It stole something of mine, and I found myself running after it like a fool! You haven't been slipping anything into my drinks, have you? No magic powders or anything like that, I hope?"

"How could you say such a thing?" I replied in my defense, shaking my head and trying not to laugh. Then I looked down at my beer to make sure that it didn't look cloudy or out of the ordinary. Wendell was known to be a practical joker at times. Maybe he slipped a potion into mine. Instead, he insisted that I share his enthusiasm and quickly forgot that I might've crossed the line.

"Then we'll head to London. We'll join the intellectuals, artists and writers at Bedford Park—discuss politics and philosophy—meet your landlady's niece, Florence Farr. Catch a Gilbert and Sullivan!"

With that Wendell got up, saluted me and sang the famous line from *The Pirates of Penzance*, "But still, in matters vegetable, animal and mineral, I am the very model of a modern Major-General."

It was impossible not to laugh when he made a complete spectacle of himself. He always knew the spell to break my tone of seriousness.

"Wendell, if I keep on trotting down to London with you, how am I ever going to find time to practice for my upcoming scholarship competitions? It would be one thing if I played the piccolo, but I can't stuff a piano in my suitcase."

* * *

London, 1899

Once again, Wendell dragged me to London during a university holiday. Instead of catching a glimpse of *The Pirates of Penzance*, he procured tickets to a premier at the Avenue Theatre, located in the West End, where my landlady's niece, the incomparable, Florence Farr, was cast as the leading lady. If I had developed more psychic acumen, I would've been more prepared to encounter the illustrious crowd and the events thereafter.

For close to three weeks, I skipped meals in order to purchase a brand new suit. I also had taken special care to polish my grandfather's heirloom silver pocket watch so it gleamed as bright as the moon. Wendell, on the other hand, wore a traditional Scottish kilt, which stood out and attracted undue attention. Unfortunately, it didn't come close to upstaging his inappropriate behavior that evening. The theater lobby was filled with the dim roar of a gala fête and crowded with a spirited cast of actors, writers, producers, admirers and prominent London critics. Drinks and hors d'oeuvres were being served to the jubilant guests celebrating a successful opening performance with live music in the background.

"My dear brother, our starlet, Florence has captured my heart," Wendell cooed.

Most likely on his fourth drink, Wendell lost his balance and spilled whisky on my lapel. Abruptly, I seized him by his collar.

95

"You ruined my jacket," I complained, bitterly.

"At least it wasn't port," Wendell replied without sympathy.

Our attention turned towards the famous playwright, George Bernard Shaw, conversing with a group of other critics and playwrights. Florence Farr, the star of *The Dionysian Chronicles*, went over to join them in celebration, shocking all when she flung her arm around Shaw's neck and kissed him right on the lips. One of the other critics took up her hand and gave her a kiss in the traditional gentlemanly fashion. William Butler Yeats, wanting to monopolize her attention, wedged himself between Farr and Shaw.

Wendell's self-confidence was disconcerting. "How can she resist my animal magnetism, my *savoir-faire,* and irresistible charms? All this hocus pocus we learned at the Underground University couldn't have been in vain."

"The Underground University?" I asked.

"John Patrick Scott, is your memory of our youthful days that absent? Don't you ever get the itchies and the woolies when you pass those vaults by Cowgate and Nidry? You must have been sprinkled with fairy dust and have forgotten everything."

"What does that have to do with you casting a spell to win the heart of our fair young thespian?" I asked.

"Because I summoned up Enochian spirits last night, and in my handkerchief is a Venusian talisman. Indeed, there is no way she can resist me."

Perhaps it was from the effect of my drink, but of all things, my response was a quote from *The Picture of Dorian Gray*:

"You do anything in the world to gain a reputation. As soon as you have one, you seem to want to throw it away. It is silly of you, for there is only one thing in the world worse than being talked about, and that is not being talked about."

Wendell whispered into my ear, "We're spending way too much time in each other's company. Others will begin to assume things, especially if you're shamelessly quoting Oscar Wilde."

Unnerved, I spotted from across the room someone I wanted to talk to. I dolorously examined my drenched lapel, put my drink down on a ledge and worked my way through the crowd. Meanwhile, Wendell finished *my* drink.

"Annie Horniman, I presume?" I asked, greeting her.

"Yes, and who do I have the pleasure of meeting?" she replied.

"John Patrick Scott, composer from Edinburgh. I want to compliment you on your fabulous production. Miss Farr's performance was beyond compare."

"Why thank you, Mr. Scott. Have you composed any theatrical scores?"

"I've focused primarily on classical orchestration and music theory, but I'm interested in branching out into scores for the theater. I've toyed with the thought of creating a work based on *Scheherazade*. Arthur keeps insisting that I can outdo Gilbert and Sullivan."

"Arthur Sullivan?" she asked.

"Pardon me, I was referring to my friend, Arthur Conan Doyle," I explained.

"Is that so? See that gentleman over there, the diminutive one with the…" She pointed discreetly.

"J.M. Barrie?"

"Indeed it is. I know him well. Quite successful in the London theater scene and very close with Doyle, but it appears from the crowd that your friend must have missed the performance," she

97

said, while craning her neck to see over the sea of pates. Being six foot five and heads above everyone else, Arthur was hard to miss.

While Annie and I continued our conversation, on the far side of the room our leading lady was surrounded by a bevy of admirers. Shaw took a whiff of her mesmerizing perfume, nuzzling his nose close to her neck. Florence was giddy with delight with all the attention, as she answered questions to the press and signed several playbills.

"Mr. Scott, I'm developing a project based on Neo-classicism in the Pre-Raphaelite vein where Florence will play one of the Muses. I could use a composer, who has astute classical training, and the teams I've been using are starting to ask way more than I can compensate. I know this is a business of making a profit, but often the risks involved make it more of an effort for love than money. Do you live in London?"

"No, in Edinburgh. I'd love to be in London."

"Did any specific business bring you here?" she asked.

I peered over her head. Wendell was off in another corner, continuing to play the fool.

"I came with my friend, who's been looking for opportunities in publishing. Personally, I've been looking to sell original compositions to music publishing companies, as well as recording that music."

"You must be very dedicated to your craft to travel here all the way from Scotland. Here, take my card. Please, stay in touch."

Before I had a chance to thank her, I found myself chasing after Wendell once more. He was about to cause trouble with a pretty, young cellist.

"Wendell Mackenzie, Mademoiselle." He introduced himself making a grand bow and spilling more of his drink.

98

"Sir, please don't disturb me. This is not a social call," she replied.

"Pardon me if my dear friend has caused you discomfort. It's too bad he insists on making an ass of himself," I interjected, rushing to her assistance.

When I pulled my friend aside, the lady cellist was relieved and resumed playing with perfection. Meanwhile, cognac was served, corks popped and celebrants smoked cigars. I examined the room to identify anyone else noteworthy.

"Wendell, look," I pointed out, "There's H. Greenhough Smith, the man behind *The Strand*, the magazine serializing Arthur's Sherlock Holmes' stories, and William Butler Yeats, and also Bram Stoker, who is huge in the London theater scene. Next to that pillar is Sax Rohmer. It's interesting that Miss Farr invited some of her friends from the Golden Dawn.*"

Whispers were heard as others recognized Arthur making his entrance.

Miss Farr said, leaning over to Yeats, "That's Conan Doyle. I hear he has also tried his hand at writing for theater."

"Ah, yes, the acclaimed *spookist* of London and a member of a society called, of all things, the Ghost Club," Yeats added. "He's been dabbling with Spiritualism, not the stuff we've been interested in at the Golden Dawn, but it's known that he's visited quite a few famous mediums and has written articles about them. Doyle's convinced that he can successfully speak with the dead. If you desire my opinion, most of it is pure stage magic."

Playwright J.M. Barrie, very short in contrast to Arthur, pushed his way through the crowd, grabbing an extra glass of champagne. Arthur spotted me and nodded his head in acknowledgement. I still was within earshot, but I kept my distance since I knew that the two of them were close friends.

"Keeping busy, I hope?" Arthur asked Barrie initiating the conversation.

"Same old, same old," Barrie replied, "but tell me Arthur, if you're not writing about Sherlock, please tell me that you're not wasting time on those *spooky* affairs."

"My friend, you know I'd drop everything in a heartbeat to get a good lead on a real live poltergeist. Why the other day I received a call..."

Barrie stopped his train of thought. "Didn't you also write me at one point about a mysterious book you've been trying to get ahold of?"

"Indeed, I did," Arthur, whispered with an edge of paranoia in his voice. "I've spent an inordinate time seeing what I can dig up over at the British Library. It's a legendary book, but the myths surrounding it are as diverse as there are fish in the sea. One popular rumor is that it could rewrite its own stories."

"As in creating new endings?" Barrie asked.

"That and so much more, but no two sources are in agreement, which is even more intriguing."

"That sounds rather confusing," Barrie interjected. "What's the attraction for you?"

"It's Holmes. I'm fed up with him and am really forcing myself to continue writing about him in order to keep my publishers content," Arthur said, worried in case the wrong ears were burning. "If the rumors about this mystical book are true, then I could use it to write these bothersome tales, but keep that a secret."

"But of course," Barrie replied in disbelief realizing that their conversation was getting too farfetched. "Arthur, come with me. Let me introduce you to Miss Farr."

Barrie began to lead him across the room. When I followed, trying to intercept him, Wendell carelessly bumped me into someone who also spilled their drink on my brand-new suit, so now there were two embarrassing stains. I continued in Arthur's direction hoping to catch him first. Concurrently, Wendell split off and sprinted over to Bram Stoker, who was engrossed in conversation with Shaw, Farr and Henry Irving.

Arthur greeted me with a manly hug like a father who hadn't seen his son in a long time.

"Arthur, I owe you an apology."

"What on earth for?"

"For intruding on your recent séance. Gaining control on astral projection while unconsciously dreaming is not that easy. It's like being two places at once but with two minds acting independently."

Arthur laughed, "Oh, that? Yes, that did give some of my psychical colleagues a chill. Think nothing of it. By the way, I see you didn't come alone. Is that your friend you've been talking about? Didn't you say that he has also shown an interest in metaphysical and Spiritualist studies?"

Wendell managed to wander off chasing more ladies and booze. It was impossible to keep an eye on him.

"Regretfully, he is not in his best behavior at the moment," I replied.

"That aside, how are you doing, son?"

"Still wrestling with Chopin," I said.

"I am quite confident of your talents in the musical realm. From your letters, you said that now you're also dabbling in amateur photography?"

"That, and trying my hand at writing. For some strange reason, perhaps our psychical tests have opened up creative inspiration I never knew I had inside me. Thoughts have been flowing freely, and I've been writing them down."

Once again, I spotted a glimmer in Arthur's eye, one that would surface every time I'd make even the remotest reference to that arcane text. But that special moment was soon to be replaced by another upset. The room was packed. A waiter rushed past us with a tray full of discarded champagne glasses. One toppled off and soiled my suit.

"Heavens!" Arthur exclaimed as he jumped back, "Did I cause that?"

Now, I had three wet spots on my brand new suit. Arthur reached for a napkin to blot it out.

"Sir, I think it was from that waiter's tray. Bad luck, I guess. Tonight it seems to be running in spades."

"At least I didn't do it from uncontrollable telekinesis, right?" he said, attempting to at least put a smile on my face.

Then he stuffed a wad of pound notes in my hand. "Here, buy yourself a new one."

"A new suit? Arthur, you're too generous."

"Think nothing of it. So, getting back to our conversation, what have you been writing about?"

"Stray thoughts in my diary more than anything else, but I'd like to try my hand at mysteries. I suppose it's impossible not to be inspired by Sherlock Holmes, but you can't compare the stories," I said, modestly. I continued to smooth down my jacket, which began puckering from all the dampness.

"To be honest, John, I've been getting a bit tired of Holmes, and that's why I had Professor Moriarty kill him off in *The Final*

Problem. I'd much rather work on *Brigadier Gerard* and focus more on historical novels, as well as, non-fiction. The folks at *The Strand* have been after me to miraculously bring him back and continue writing the series despite the fact I'd rather have him remain dead and gone. If it gets to that point, maybe we can arrange for you to help me finish some of my manuscripts? I'll pay you handsomely, of course."

"You'd ask me to write for you?"

"Ghostwrite. Why not? You're a bright and creative young man. I can't see how you couldn't do it. Besides, I would do the final editing so the style would resemble mine," he replied.

"Well, I guess that would be amenable."

I was a bit tongue-tied, both scared and excited at the same time. What I didn't realize then was that Arthur's choice in selecting me involved other considerations. Who was I? I was a young, unknown pianist, still a student and not even living in the hubbub of London, therefore out of the public eye. I'd be a perfect choice. Plus, he had designs on that book—the one no longer in my possession. Then I posed several bold questions. I had to play dumb about his conversation with Barrie, but I knew exactly which book he'd been talking about. He dropped a few hints in several recent letters asking me all sorts of abstruse questions, but little did he know I no longer had it. But suddenly I thought of an alternative strategy. Instead of Arthur always prying into my mind to get information, I was going to play the role of the instigator.

"Arthur, suppose I become competent at this. Would you be willing to influence a few of your friends to publish stories under my own name?"

Arthur hoped that no one had overheard.

"We can't talk about this here," he said in a hushed tone.

"Then what about introducing me to some of these people here tonight? After all, it's no secret that I'm a musician. My friend and I spotted Arthur Sullivan a bit earlier."

Once again, Doyle was evasive, but commended my persistence and willful ambition. It was much better to change the subject after my inquiries proved counterproductive.

"Arthur, do you still want to continue our *psychic experiments?*"

"I plan on going to South Africa soon, but yes, we can still conduct them at midnight."

"You're going to serve in the Boer War?"

"I'd prefer to be a soldier," he replied, "but I suspect I'll be commissioned as a doctor. Why?"

I leaned in closer and whispered in Arthur's ear. "You know that peculiar book you keep asking me about?"

"What about it, John?"

"I first came across that book while traveling to ancient China."

Arthur's eyes grew wide and beads of sweat popped out all over his forehead like a sudden rash. He took out his handkerchief and wiped them off.

"John, how and when did you travel to China? I thought you said you never left Scotland."

"Technically, I haven't," I replied, smugly maintaining my secret and keeping him on edge. "But we'll have to discuss this in private."

Arthur anxiously peered across the room. "Excuse me, but I must discuss some rather urgent matters with Barrie."

Afterwards, when I spotted Wendell, he was flaunting his intellect and engaged in debate with Shaw and Stoker.

"In his defense, Rudolf Steiner is another one of those metaphysical pioneers influenced by Goethe's phenomenological approach to science who believes that spiritual experiences combined with discipline and moral acumen can help one become a more powerful and creative individual," he stated with conviction.

"Since when are you the expert?" asked Shaw.

"Name's Mackenzie," Wendell replied. "I'm a writer and editor from David Balfour's publishing office."

After all, he rudely interrupted their conversation and had to come up with something expedient that at least sounded brilliant.

Bram Stoker called his bluff. "David Balfour was a character in Robert Louis Stevenson's *Kidnapped*. Since this is a private affair by invitation only, I suppose your name-dropping and false credentials got you past security. Maybe I should summon them."

Sax Rohmer, restrained Stoker, who was obviously upset, and he began laughing.

"Mackenzie? Maybe he's related to Mackenzie in the Golden Dawn, that coroner on his spiritual high horse?" Rohmer suggested.

Farr interrupted, "That was Wynn Westcott."

Convinced of a conquest, Wendell leaned over to Florence while gesturing in Shaw's direction.

"Fair lady, why do you waste your time with a stuffy old playwright who never has anything nice to say about anybody?"

She shrank back from the smell of alcohol on his breath.

"Would someone remove this buffoon?" Shaw shouted.

Two burly gents heeded his call and picked up Wendell by each arm, escorting him out of the room.

"We'll be together. It's predestined, I tell you!" Wendell protested, struggling against brute strength.

He was drunk, obnoxious and creating a scene. I approached the imposing men, told them that I'd assume responsibility from there and taking the lead, grabbed my friend.

"Wendell, why do I feel like troubles and woe are stuck to your toes?"

That silly rhyme expressed my sentiments completely, and this wasn't the first time he spoiled our plans. However, it was time to call it a night, and I unhappily escorted Wendell back to our hotel.

*   *   *

Otherworldly Pursuits

My recent jaunt to London proved to be a pyrrhic victory as far as self-promotion was concerned. Mackenzie's insobriety ended the night earlier than anticipated. Annie Horniman was only interested in engaging my services if I were a London resident, and Arthur was apprehensive to allow me to step out from behind his shadow. This also raised my concern about possible ulterior motives. However, Arthur would soon be leaving for South Africa. Thus any notions of picking up on those issues where we had left off were on hold. Not that I was jealous that he was heading off to war, but part of me was green-eyed that he had the opportunity to explore the world. Be that as it may, we agreed to continue our telepathic tests. Besides, I had neglected way too much of my studies and obligations by dedicating that much time to our paranormal pursuits, although I had to admit I enjoyed every minute.

However, the Underground University was an issue that persisted like a pesky fly. I suspected there had to be an involvement in my past and something inside of me was suppressing that knowledge. The notion of a special school came up when Wendell came over to test out my time machine, although that was a trip to the future. Meanwhile, I had an overwhelming desire to rekindle memories of my childhood, which for the most part was like vainly trying to capture bubbles rising to the surface from carbonated soda water. Every so often, I'd experience a dream or a flash of insight that would unlock those vaults, and it was synchronistic how I came up with the term, *vaults*. For some reason, I wanted to think that I'd sneak around those seedy damp side streets near Cowgate and Nidry right around the corner from St. Cecilia's Hall, and slip into one of those notorious catacomb-like passageways.

I couldn't recall too much about the time I spent there or what kind of studies I would engage in but I do remember that as I progressed and absorbed some of the knowledge the professors were attempting to drum into my head that I was assigned a mentor, or a guide. He called himself Finn and was painfully thin, with a quirky personality as eccentric as he was slim. With a Jack-be-nimble air, he dogged me like a hungry stray nudging me oftentimes in opposite directions.

It was Saturday afternoon, and I had the whole boarding house to myself. My landlady went to visit friends in York, and her other tenants had either gone home for the weekend or skipped off to London. Thus, there was no better time to conduct a series of time travel excursions without being disturbed. Painstaking preparations were well underway. I was all set to make several trips to both the past and the future if I had to. With all that taken into account, after taking inventory of all the mechanical components of my time machine, I realized that I was all out of my special mineral pellets. It was already late in the day, and the shop where I procured them had already closed. Utterly distressed, I fell back into my *thinking chair*, and ran my fingers through my thick hair making it even more of a mess. That's when Finn slid right through my locked door.

"There go my time travel plans!" I threw up my hands and shouted.

107

Finn started rummaging through all my instruments, taking random components here and there, and began either stuffing them in his pockets or going over to my open window and throwing them out.

"What in God's name are you doing?" I cried out, confiscating some of the items from him before they met their demise. "You're disassembling my time machine!"

"All these parts aren't necessary. You're already capable of dispensing with them," he replied and continued destroying my marvelous invention. "Besides, you won't be able to haul all that garbage with you when you go to Germany."

"Since when am I going to Germany?"

I was completely beside myself when he had all the answers to my future, and I knew absolutely nothing. Was he referring to my continued studies? I wanted to go to London, not to Germany despite the excellent music schools there.

"It's not trash," I affirmed while on my hands and knees cleaning up the springs and gears he was tossing about with wild abandon. "How do you expect me to travel in time without my machine?"

Finn grabbed hold of my shoulder and pulled me up to my feet.

"It's all in your mind," he said pointing his finger and digging his fingernail into my skull until it hurt. "Good riddance with all this mess. You are way beyond that."

"I beg to differ," I protested.

I broke away from his grasp, refusing to believe such nonsense. I continued cleaning up the debris, which was strewn everywhere.

"John, what do you think you've been doing in your sleep when you seem to be traveling in time?" he asked, putting me on the hot seat.

"That's my imagination, I guess. Besides, I always sleep with my timepiece under my pillow. I suppose that contributes to wandering about like I'm traveling somewhere."

"You're wrong," he corrected me, "plus, it's imperative that you hone your abilities to be able to make the leap at a moment's notice from anywhere—the lavatory or bath tub, if necessary."

Finn must have been pulling my leg once again. He looked at me straight in the eyes.

"How do you expect to survive the war otherwise?"

I shook my head. "Here we go again, Finn, talking about events I know nothing about that haven't occurred yet."

Meanwhile my study looked like disaster struck. Finn told me that I was on my own to figure it out and left the same way he had entered. I scooped up the broken remnants of my time machine off the floor and examined its main headpiece. He purposely disconnected a whole bunch of wires, and it was going to take me hours I didn't have to figure out how to put them back together. What was I going to do? I had planned my whole weekend around this.

A shot of brandy would be a temporary solution, albeit not the answer. I poured myself a glass, battened down the hatches, and sank into my favorite chair in order to sort out my thoughts. All was quiet except the loud ticking of my grandfather's silver pocket watch. The watch? Was that it? I pulled it out. I dangled it back and forth—self-hypnosis, perhaps?

Then, I held it up to my eyes and began concentrating on the face of the watch making its hands go backwards, exactly like I did the first time when I jumped through time, and guess what? It worked! Once again, I transcended into a space in between my study room and a completely different world.

*　　*　　*

It was 1886, and I was only eight years old riding in a carriage beyond the outskirts of Edinburgh and sitting next to a strange older man named Professor Mockingbird. My parents had sent me away to boarding school.

"Where are we going?" I asked with bleary eyes and tear-streaked cheeks. "I'm hungry."

"You'll have to wait," he answered, sternly.

The ride to my new school seemed to last forever, and my stomach growled even more loudly as the minutes trickled by. We rode past verdant meadows and hundreds of grazing sheep in an otherwise monotonous countryside. Our willful horse was perpetually hungry and wanted to stop every few minutes. He must've found a particularly scrumptious patch of clover near a railroad crossing and finally refused to trot any further.

"Professor, I hear a train. Shouldn't we alert the driver?" I asked. There was a distinct rumbling in the ground below us.

"Nonsense, his horse is stubborn—eating all the time," he replied.

The driver dismounted. He gave the horse an affectionate pat and began to stretch his legs.

"I thought I heard a whistle blowing in the distance," I told my escort, this time taking out my grandfather's silver pocket watch in my tiny little hand and checking to see how long we had been on the road.

"Quit worrying," he said curtly and checked his own watch. "We're making very good time. When the horse is done, we'll be going."

However, I swore I heard an approaching locomotive, and the horse kept grazing dangerously closer to the tracks.

"But, sir..." I interrupted.

He reached into his satchel and pulled out a red book.

"Here," he said thrusting the book in my lap, "if you're that bored, read this!"

Its title was *Shokunin, The Thief of Tales*. I began to read the first page, then the second and flipped to the next.

"It's blank," I told the professor who had pulled out a bible and was reading a passage out loud.

"Hush! Read it anyway!" he shouted, upset that I disturbed his prayers.

Going back to the beginning, I started sounding out the words one syllable at a time. However, my angry, empty stomach upstaged the prose—but it still wasn't as loud as the impact.

As I crawled through the grass, I tried to assess how long I had been asleep. Dirt and cuts were all over my face and legs. That strange storybook was on the ground beside me, and so was one of my suitcases. I quickly locked it inside. My head pounded, and the ground was moving like a boat rocked back and forth by big, strong waves.

My other suitcase had splintered into many pieces, and whatever was inside was strewn about. Two feet poked out from under the carriage that was lying on its side. They belonged to Professor Mockingbird. One shoe was missing. The rest of his body was hidden and crushed by the overturned carriage. The dead horse was already swarming with flies and attracted crows. I had been hungry earlier, but vomited in reaction to the horror.

Where was our driver? I found more blood, mush and a severed arm hidden in the grass. I recognized the ring on a finger and clutched my stomach again, wanting to vomit, but nothing was left to come out. In shock, I picked up the one suitcase that I found intact and tried to locate the nearest farmhouse.

A light gray wooden door with peeling paint and squeaky hinges opened, and a plump lady inspected me from head to toe. She wore an oversized apron, stained from cooking and had reddish hair almost as crazy as mine peeping out from under a print kerchief tied around her head.

"Look what the stork brought in! The angels answered our prayers and sent us one of their own. Quick, draw him a bath."

The big woman grasped the lapel of my tattered jacket and pulled me inside.

"But, I don't want a bath. Where am I?"

"Poor child, you're completely covered with dirt. Looks like you had a rough tumble from heaven. Better clean you up before giving you supper. Are you hungry?"

I nodded, looking around her kitchen. I was hesitant to accept such hospitality from strangers, but it smelled terrific. "Ma'am, I didn't come from heaven. I'm not sure what happened except there was an accident." My tongue was sore. I must've bitten it when I fell.

"That red hair? He's an angel, I tell ya!" she said ecstatically as she ran her fat fingers through my hair.

Her husband came and joined us.

"But, the gray?" he asked. "Are you sure he hasn't the Devil's curse?"

He bent over and began plucking blades of grass from my hair. His wife ladled hot stew into a bowl and set it on the table with a giant spoon. Immediately I began eating.

"Where were you going, son?" he asked.

"My parents sent me away to boarding school, but there was an accident and everyone died."

"Your parents died?"

"No sir, just the professor, the horse and our driver. Where am I?"

"You're over in Scottish Borders territory. Lots of sheep farms here and local textile mills. The nearest town is Galashiels. Where did you come from?"

I slurped the stew. It was piping hot, and I didn't want to burn my tongue.

"Edinburgh," I replied.

"You're too far to walk home," his wife called out. "Do ya know where they were taking you?"

"To school, but they didn't say where," I said, still engrossed in my supper.

"Well, ya can't stay here," the farmer said, "Fiona, he's got parents back in town."

"No, I don't," I replied.

"What da ya mean ya don't?" his wife asked, kissing my forehead and pinching me on the cheek so hard that I nearly spit out my stew.

"They're leaving Scotland. I'm supposed to be staying with my aunt and uncle, instead."

The woman began tidying up around the kitchen, sliced a piece of bread for me and put it on a plate. She looked at her husband and asked, "Let's keep him. He's a sign from God. We've wanted a child of our own for so long."

113

"Dearest, we can't. Someone's going to be out looking for him when they find out he hasn't shown up at school. It's too late to do anything now, but I'll go into town early tomorrow morning and alert the local authorities. Perhaps, one of them can reunite the lad with his family. Meanwhile, I guess he'll have to spend the night."

The woman made me take that bath and gave me one of her husband's shirts to serve as a nightshirt. She read me a few bedtime stories, and I must have fallen asleep during the last one because I couldn't remember the ending. The next morning, she woke me for breakfast and had me join her when she fed the chickens outside. Her husband had already ridden into town.

I was still shaken up, and didn't want to have to deal with the police or whoever was going to show up. I took a fresh set of clothes from my suitcase and tried to find the right opportunity to escape. Escape where? My plans went awry when the officer arrived.

"Little angel, someone's here to see you."

Hesitant, I made my way into the kitchen where I could hear all the excitement was coming from.

"I'm Officer Finneas Fertle," he said as he rubbed my head full of curls. "What's your name, son?"

He was very tall and thin and wore a brand new uniform with shiny brass buttons.

"John Patrick Scott," I responded.

"Where are you from?" he asked as he circled around and made an inspection.

"Edinburgh, sir."

"Well, I guess that's where I'm taking you."

"I don't think my school is in Edinburgh, sir."

He countered my remark. "It is now and, from this point on, you'll call me Officer Finn. Time to go!"

What I didn't expect was how he had planned on transporting me back to town. I wrongly assumed that he had a horse or a dogcart, but instead he had a velocipede, which was a version of a bicycle powered by steam. He strapped my suitcase to a tiny seat behind his, and when I asked him where I was supposed to sit, he told me that the only other place where I could go was in his lap. Therefore we pitter-pattered all the way to Auld Reeky.

"Hop off," he said, waking me up from my nap.

I yawned so wide that I thought my mouth would get stuck in place. Then, I rubbed my eyes. We were at the crossroads of Cowgate and Nidry.

"Why are we stopping here?" I asked, yawning once more.

"You're going to school," he replied.

"Where?" All I could see was a run down tavern on the corner, a few shops, and some doors that I knew led to the Edinburgh vaults.

"Over there," Officer Finn said as he pointed to the third vault door on the left heading up the hill. An old sign was swinging in the wind up above it. Most of its paint had come off.

"I'm not going in there. Inside are ghosts, beggars and thieves." I protested, shaking my head. Maybe they were all gone by now, but I didn't want to take any chances. I had heard all the rumors.

"No angry spirits in that one," Officer Finn assured me and took something that looked like a shell out of his pocket along with a few coins. "Take these, you'll need them for your fare. Knock on the door three times. When someone lets you inside, show him the shell, but pocket it afterwards. But give him the coins."

115

Perplexed, I began walking away eyeing the unusual crystalline shell he gave me.

"Don't forget your suitcase," he shouted. "But wait, there's more. After you give him the coins, I want you to run. Run as fast as you can, as if your life depended on it. Do you understand?"

I retrieved my suitcase and nodded anyway even though I had no idea what he was talking about.

"It will be dark, but you'll see a light, probably a lantern. Don't trust what you see, which won't be much at all, because you'll probably start imagining things—things that will scare you so much you'll turn tail and head back for the street. Ignore those. They are meant to scare off intruders.

"After you reach that light, someone will be there to meet you and lead you to your new school. Show him the shell, but don't give it to him. Return it to your pocket where it will be safe. Are you following what I'm saying?" he asked.

I nodded skeptically. This was a lot for an eight-year-old brain to follow.

"Now go!" he said, mounting his steam-powered contraption while I ran off. "And good luck!"

*   *   *

A Gift for the Past

"What's the Mad Scientist got in store this time?" Wendell asked as he burst into my flat full of enthusiasm.

Previously, Finn had done a splendid job of disassembling my time machine. What he didn't realize was that there was a possibility that someone else might need to use it. I went completely mad piecing together the components that he casually tossed out my window during his demonstration insisting that I no longer needed them. This also didn't take into account the cost of replacement.

116

"I can't tell you what I went through to prepare for this," I sighed, wiping the sweat off my forehead and loosening my tie. "To be honest with you, I didn't think I'd get this far."

My study room was in complete disarray. I didn't even bother looking in the mirror, but I'm sure I looked just as muddled and disordered. Wendell started picking up anything that wasn't screwed on or nailed into something else and examined it until he moved along to the next object of interest.

"John, your flat looks like a junk shop. What happened?"

Instead of wasting valuable time with an explanation, I handed him a tatty old suitcase with an assemblage of machinery stuffed inside.

"What's this?" he asked.

"*Pour vous.* Your very own time machine," I replied, rubbing my wild hair in place as if that would do anything to make it lie down.

"You're giving me this? Then, John, where's yours?"

"I don't need one, anymore," I explained while taking my grandfather's timepiece out of my waistcoat pocket. "All I need is this."

"Are you sure?"

Surprised, Wendell began poking around inside the suitcase.

"Absolutely," I replied, "I've even tested it out already. But, you must promise me one thing. This time machine can be very dangerous in the wrong hands. Can I trust you with it?"

Wendell gave me a look that needed no explanation.

"Very well, but from now on, I'd strongly suggest sticking to only exploring the past and forgetting about jaunts into the future."

"Your choice, John. Lead the way."

Wendell helped himself to my brandy and poured both of us a glass. I pulled up a chair and began hooking him up. I dropped in the mystery pellets, got the steam going and sat back in my chair for a few sips, until I felt that everything on his end was running like clockwork. Then I took out my timepiece, squinted until my eyes weren't much more than slits and began swinging it back and forth.

"John, you said we were going to the past, but you didn't say when," Wendell interrupted.

"You're right, I didn't. Since you're always giving me a hard time about my poor memory, we're going back to our childhoods," I replied. "This time I can also guarantee you won't wind up as a woman."

"That's reassuring, but your idea doesn't sound too exciting."

"It's important. Now, be quiet."

Wendell's awkward machinery hissed, clicked and once in a while made a resonant boom, like a tympani drum. Meanwhile, I felt carefree and unencumbered. Once more, this crazy and complex device filled my room with steam, while I eased into my chair like taking a nap. Time travel with another person, besides Finn, was still a novel undertaking with much to learn.

Back in 1886 we would've been eight years old. Even back then, time travel was my obsession. That's how I got into the trouble that sent me away from home to begin with. I never understood my parents, and neither did they understand me. They'd tell their friends that I must've been dropped into our household by a wayward stork that had stolen whisky from my father's liquor cabinet, because something was never quite right about me.

I had been sent to a special school called the Underground University, although I don't think that was the original school that my parents intended. On holidays, I stayed with my aunt and uncle. However, when I scurried back and forth from my aunt's and uncle's domicile, I'd traverse many tunnels starting from one of the infamous vaults located nearby Cowgate and Nidry. They were sandwiched between two seedy public houses, which were always packed with rowdy sailors, soused farmers and local merchants after a hard day's work. No wonder I always got spells of nervousness every time I'd perform or take classes right around the corner at St. Cecilia's Hall.

Mackenzie was my best friend then, as well, and he and I were always ones to stir up mischief. We knew that there was a trap door behind the specimen shelf in our biology classroom. Supposedly somewhere beyond that was the infamous broom closet of Professor Horus C. Aetas, which we suspected was really a secret time machine in disguise.

"Did you bring your wand?" Wendell asked me.

"Of course, do you think I would go anywhere without it?" I replied with a good hardy sneeze.

"You have to take care of yourself, John. You cannot always be getting sick."

"I'm not sick. It's from the dust and ashes all over the place. This school is hundreds of years old, and too big to keep clean."

"Come, let's go back there before we get caught," Wendell warned me.

By the rear wall specimen case, there was a secret lever behind a pile of skulls that we had seen our teacher operate. The shelf gave way to the hidden passageway we were looking for. We made sure to light our lanterns as we snuck into the tunnel and slid the shelf back into place behind us. Now, we were on our own without our teacher as a guide. I stumbled and was lucky not to skin my knees as I got up and continued down the low-ceilinged corridor.

Finally, we reached a secluded classroom on the other side. Wendell and I looked around to reorient our bearings. He whipped out a compass, which I wasn't sure was necessary but he insisted on lining up the needle so it pointed north. I antagonized him by pulling a lodestone out of my pocket, making the needle rock back and forth.

"Do you want to get lost? This is serious, John. We could get into a lot of trouble, or worse."

Our mission was to find that notorious broom closet and check it out for ourselves. Did it really have the magical ability to travel through time? We were soon to find out.

Shortly, we discovered that the classroom seemed to be arranged differently. Although we thought we were in an underground passage, the room still had windows that seemed to be on the right instead of the left. The examination table in the front of the classroom was now clearly located in the back, and there were distinct differences as to where certain items were located on various shelves.

"Look, Wendell, I found it!" I cried, as I pointed to what appeared to be a glass display case full of fossils, but was on wheels. When both of us pushed it aside, behind it was the tall dark wooden door to a hidden closet.

Wendell and I climbed over each other and tumbled inside.

"Wait! Don't close the door. We're forgetting the most important rule!" I shouted so loud, but oblivious as to whether or not anyone, including the mice or termites in the walls, could hear me. "We have to leave something of ours outside. Otherwise, either it might not work, or we might not come back!"

What if our experiment went terribly wrong? He brought a letter that his mother had written him, dated 1886. That date was very important, because it anchored us to the present. Since this was only the second instance where we had traveled in time, or at least one that either one of us was consciously aware of; we wanted to make sure that nothing was left to chance.

"What did you bring, John?"

I tugged on the chain and pulled my grandfather's pocket watch out of my waistcoat pocket and checked the time.

"You're not leaving that," he cried, "How will we know the time without it?"

"No, of course not." Underneath it in my waistcoat pocket I had a brand new shiny ha' pence coin that I found on the sidewalk. "That's my anchor piece," I explained. "Nothing better. It says 1886."

"Good. Now, get out your magic book."

"Shouldn't we be reading the spell once we're inside?" I asked, snatching it and my satchel and joining Wendell back inside the cabinet.

He began to shut its door, leaving it open a smidgen. "Hey, it's dark in here!"

"Don't worry, I came prepared," I said lighting up a match. Not even thinking, we had extinguished our lanterns and left them outside.

"Hurry up." Wendell was impatient. "Its like a coffin in here."

Yes, it was confining. I took the match and lit a candle I had stashed in my pocket, handing it to my friend.

"Wendell, get out your wand. I can use the extra fire power."

We both took out our wands, which added extra illumination as we chanted a few incantations. Then, I thumbed through my spell book for instructions. Together we quickly recited the spell but came to a dead stop when we were supposed to state where we wanted to go.

"John, wait. We never discussed where we were going?"

"We also didn't discuss what year we wanted to travel back in time to," I added.

"I'd like to see real dinosaurs," Wendell replied.

"I'd like to see dinosaurs, too, but for the first time we better play it safe especially since we are doing this on our own without our professor nearby."

Wendell agreed.

"Let's go back right here, say by nine years," I remarked. "Students from then would've graduated by now. It's unlikely we would be running into them at school when we returned."

"Okay, the Underground University, back to 1879—no harm in that, I think."

"Ohm adlfallfg...Trin papaloo qalphigious swit!" we called out in unison.

We recited the rest of the charm and waited. Candle wax started dripping on Wendell's hand burning him on his wrist. Then it happened. I'm not sure about my friend, but as for myself, I began to feel lightheaded and faint. I reached in my waistcoat pocket, pulled out my grandfather's silver timepiece and noticed its hands began to wildly spin backwards. Wendell took out his compass, and its needle spun both clockwise and counterclockwise.

I clutched my spell book and shoved it into my satchel, as I felt like we had temporarily lost our sense of gravity in our chamber, and everything became weightless. I closed my eyes and held my breath until I was almost ready to pass out. Something inside of me was telling me we made a big mistake. Suddenly, I felt the warm soft breath of my friend dusting my forehead, smelling like the meat pie he had eaten earlier for breakfast.

"John, open your eyes," Wendell said weakly. "Wake up."

"I'm not asleep," I said getting off my knees to a standing position, "but I think I was dreaming, while I was still awake, if that makes any sense."

"Open the door," Wendell begged me, tugging at my shirtsleeve.

A bit skittish at first, the two of us timorously opened the wooden door of the broom closet a tiny little crack.

"We're in a classroom!" Wendell exclaimed.

"Shush! They'll hear us. We cannot give ourselves away."

We peered through the opening and a class was in session. The professor, who had a distinct French accent, was parading up and down the aisles, reciting mysterious words, which sounded like sorcery from an ancient tome. The book had an eerie glow and was so transparent that Wendell and I were able to see right through it like glass. The students seemed vaguely familiar, but at the same time quite different.

"Wendell, that really tall boy in the back—do you see him?"

"The older one who looks like he could be the teacher's assistant? Yes, what about him?"

"Doesn't he remind you of ..." I stopped short. He looked a lot like how I'd pictured Arthur when he was much younger. The resemblance was so uncanny that it was hard not to stare.

"What about their teacher? Listen to that funny accent! Do you suspect he could be Jules Verne? He looks a lot like a picture in the book I have of his back home," Wendell said.

"Boys and girls, what you are about to experience is magic in the making, a first in the history of this course, a ground breaking opportunity to witness..."

Abruptly, the professor stopped dead in his tracks as he caught one of his youngest students performing a coin trick for one of his fellow classmates. He snatched the coin from the boy's hand, pocketed it, then took his own wand and slapped the errant child on the bridge of his nose.

"Erik Weisz! Shame on you! You know you're not supposed to be entertaining your friends in class."

"That's Houdini, sir," the boy corrected him as tears filled his eyes, and he rubbed his nose in pain.

"Houdini? I don't care what you want to call yourself, Erik, you must pay attention!"

Inside our closet, Wendell bumped into a mop.

"Quiet!" I whispered, emphatically. "They'll hear us!"

*   *   *

I didn't want us to be discovered, so I took it upon myself to create an exit point. I caught hold of Wendell's arm, pulled out my grandfather's timepiece along with my designated coin and thrust us back into the present.

"Ouch!" He struggled against the machinery that had him tethered to my old suitcase. "If that didn't make me a bit sore in the head, and I know it wasn't the brandy."

He stretched his legs letting out a huge yawn. I rubbed my eyes and felt like I had just woken from a long nap. Then I pointed at Wendell and made pantomime gestures with my fingers that he needed to pick out debris stuck in his hair. He wasn't entirely sure what I was indicating, so he rushed over to my mirror.

I laughed, "Didn't I warn you that sometimes when you travel in time you might bring back a souvenir?"

"Spiders?" he called out.

Wendell shrugged and brushed the insects off his shoulder.

"Sundry objects, odd memories—sometimes both," I replied, "that's typical of time travel in the past or the future."

Wendell began picking off pieces of straw, remnants from the fact that we'd been hiding in a broom closet.

"What did you think?" I asked, "We were troublemakers back then just like we are now. Don't you agree?"

Wendell unfastened the remaining pieces of his time travel apparatus and inspected them one last time before closing them inside the suitcase.

"You're saying I can take this with me?"

I gave him a nod as he grabbed his coat and hat, and I prayed that he understood that discretion was always necessary. Of course, Wendell wouldn't listen.

*   *   *

124

Intersection at Mid-Heaven

"Laughter is not at all a bad beginning for a friendship, and it is far the best ending for one."

Unfortunately that quote from Oscar Wilde was far from how Whit's and my relationship turned out. As the semester progressed, tensions mounted between us. He began to suspect that I knew that he tampered with the ether and universal balance by unwittingly delving into my spell book. It was supposed to be off limits to those that hadn't been admitted to such places as the Underground University or similar institutions.

Exams were nigh, and as I failed to achieve respectable grades, Whit and I indulged in an illogical clash of wills and sentiment.

"*Ars gratia artis,*" I quipped, quoting Latin and giddy with exhaustion to the point of absurdity.

"Life imitates Art far more than Art imitates Life," Whit replied, continuing to quote Wilde. "All art is quite useless. It is the spectator, not life, that art really mirrors, and John, my friend; you did not do your homework. Let's discuss the overtones hinted between Lord Henry and Basil towards Dorian."

"Let's not," I replied trying not to fall asleep from intolerable boredom. "Are you so blinded by desire that you cannot foresee the pain and trouble that are bound to follow?"

"John, you're steering this conversation far away from *The Picture of Dorian Gray.* I dare say that something else is on your mind."

"Arguably," I said. "Your defense of Sibyl Vane's character, although entirely laudable, has seemed to be way too much of a personal affront."

Whit ran his fingers through his incorrigible curls and was becoming more frustrated by the minute. I was bandying about inane comments and was still one sheet to the wind from last night's bender. Although Whit couldn't make heads or tails of my nonsense, he tried to anyway.

"Pardon me? Dorian shattered that poor girl's aspirations for a better life. He was a vainglorious and shallow, aristocratic boor, and that was his ultimate downfall. I would've wished Wilde had given her longer presence in the story, and it's a pity that Lord Harry and Basil mocked women and looked upon marriage with distain, but what's wrong with being sympathetic?"

"Whit, you're taking this reference too literally. I'm referring to Isabelle, the girl you met at the Bookworm Society soirée. Does she also call you Prince Charming as Sibyl Vane called Dorian?"

"You don't have a very high opinion of her, because you're jealous. Heavens, I'm in love with her," Whit replied, waxing poetically. "Perhaps you have a problem with women? Have you ever been consumed by affection? Sometimes you are as heartless as a piano without its player."

Someone pointed the finger at me once again.

"If one hears bad music, it is one's duty to drown it in conversation," I quoted from Wilde. "You should exercise restraint. 'Lest love be lost with heartbreak in hand.' Wasn't there a famous poet who also said that?"

"Indubitably, that sounds like a *John Patrick Scott*ism, to me," Whit replied, scratching his head in disbelief, readjusting his spectacles and taking a glance at his timepiece.

"Seriously, this ill-humored jousting match has to cease. You'll never be prepared for your examinations. We're here to discuss character development, not my personal matters, and if anyone should be ostracized for his indiscretions, you should be looking in the mirror. Some of the company you keep is much to be desired."

"Wendell?" I interrupted.

"A bad influence if you desire that scholarship. A prolonged brannigan until dawn is not going to help you pass your classes."

"Wasn't it Stevenson who said, 'Dull men travail, whilst noblemen drowse. Peasants sip ale, whilst kings carouse?' What makes you think we put a torch to the town?"

"It smells like gin on your shirt. That's why!" he declared.

I straightened up in my seat, pulled down my waistcoat, and began to unroll and fasten my cuffs after hearing Whit's sobering comment. One of my shirt buttons must have popped off. I'd have to find an unmatched spare and sew it on.

He began to sift through his papers. "You need to pay attention to details, otherwise... What's this?" he asked holding up a piece of parchment inscribed with a chart.

"Oh, I enjoy dallying with astrology," I replied. "Ancient metaphysicians felt that by plotting the positions of where the planets aligned at the time of your birth, they could determine your destiny. I wasn't sure how much to believe until someone drafted my planetary positions and interpreted mine. It was amazing what a complete stranger could tell about my character by looking at what appeared to be symbols on a celestial map."

"Is that so? What information would you need to determine that?"

"Your date of birth, where you were born, and the exact time," I replied.

Whit smoothed back the curls falling in his eyes, straightened his tie and leaned over whispering, "Given that, are you saying you could predict my future?"

"It's not as simple as that, but it could indicate if you were traveling in the wrong direction."

Intrigued, Whit continued with questions. "Suppose I had similar information on Isabelle. Would you be able to surmise a promising future between the two of us?"

"Whit, I am by no means an expert, but yes, I suppose I could assess a potential for long-term compatibility between the two of you, but you might not always like what you hear. Are you willing to accept that?"

"I'll take that risk," he replied.

"Do you know her birthday?"

"In fact, I do, it's March 5th," Whit said with a smile, "I bought her a bouquet of lilies for the occasion."

"Charming," I grumbled sarcastically.

I was still upset after fulfilling my obligation playing her nonsensical tunes at the Bookworm Society's fête. Afterwards, I was late for my appointment with Professor Niecks. Such recklessness could forfeit my chance for consideration at the Royal College of Music in London. Meanwhile, my best friend, Wendell, had been awarded a grant and apprenticeship to work at the *London Review*—a perfect opportunity to advance his professional writing career and interest in politics. He begged me to join him so we could be flat mates. If I lost my opportunity, I'd have to remain in Edinburgh. It was apparent, or at least to me, that I could trace such misfortune back to that party with Whit and Isabelle to blame.

His heart palpitated with excitement. "She's from Glasgow, originally. The time? I think she said she might have been born at dawn. Does it matter?" Whit asked enthusiastically. "I was born July 7th, same year at two in the morning."

"All right," I said. I pulled out an odd metallic contraption, not much bigger than the size of my hand, consisting of mechanical disks connected by gears. Then I inserted another gadget resembling a compass in between rotaries. It had tiny engraved markings, so small you needed a magnifying glass, showing planets and angles.

"What's that?" Whit inquired.

"It's a planetary calculator. With it I can plot those positions," I muttered while figuring things out.

"Fascinating. Where did you get that?"

"Don't ask," I replied, thinking that I probably shouldn't have been showing an uninitiated soul such an object of the arcane arts, but I ignored the warning and began to scribble down my calculations.

"Hmmm," I responded shaking my head.

"What does it mean?" Whit asked a bit worried.

"You fate does not seem to be intertwined."

"What makes you say that?" he asked.

"Your Mars, squaring her Venus, and with the position of your Neptune and Moon, my friend, I think you have been hopelessly deceived," I said with blunt accuracy.

I examined her chart in further detail and came up with the following conclusion:

"She appears to be attracted by older men, those with money and power." I looked at poor Whit, as he failed to illustrate those qualities. "Uranus conjunct Mars at thirteen degrees Scorpio in the Eighth House—even if matters worked out between you, I don't see the two of you growing old together."

129

"I beg your pardon?"

"She might be fated to have a short and tragic life."

When I answered Whit's question, much to his disliking, he quickly forgot about our study agreement, gathered his books and rushed out of the library. Although I was no expert and could have misinterpreted my findings, he was quite upset, and left me high and dry to continue my exam preparations on my own. Regretfully, I should've kept my observations to myself while refraining from being so direct, knowing full well that it would adversely affect him. Thus, with my human frailties of booziness and brashness, cynicism and envy would stab me in the heart. My foolhardy shortcomings ruined our friendship, fraternity and solidarity, unless I had a chance to beg for his forgiveness.

* * *

Prisoner of War

It wouldn't be long until Wendell's and my friendship ran off into two different directions. Wendell left Edinburgh and started his internship in London working for a newspaper. Meanwhile, I remained stuck in the mud in Edinburgh and had to wade through my studies with the intentions of procuring a scholarship so I could join him. The Royal College of Music near Albert Hall in the South Kensington section of London was my first choice and anything less of an option was going to be a disappointment. Several months after his departure, I received a letter.

* * *

Dear John,

I wish I could convince you to leave Edinburgh. Gone are the good times we spent at the University. We must rekindle that flame. Surely, another London school would be glad to welcome you. My engagement has ended with the *London Review*. Taking that into account, I made the decision to drop the rest of my studies in medical school, remain here and seek employment elsewhere. Ideally, I'd like to position myself as a royal biographer, as opposed to a legal copy clerk, which is what I had to settle for. You know me. I'm always one to chase after sensationalism, and working in a law office is way too boring.

My flat is adequate, but its location is superb, as it's a stone's throw from the British Museum. There are several fabulous bookstores in the neighborhood, an amazing shop if you are into collecting rare and ancient coins and a few good public houses and local theaters. It keeps my brain adequately nourished. My only complaint is that my landlady, a fussy old dowager, has a useless little dog with an ear-piercing bark. I'd love to whack that mutt across the room with a croquet mallet. Other than that insipid terrier, my living quarters are fine.

My good man, our friendship exists on the commonality that we are both free thinkers in this Victorian age where open minds are encouraged to thrive amongst artistic circles. Seize the moment, and bask in its revelry! You must keep an eye out for the works of an evocative metaphysical poet, who was educated at Trinity College in Cambridge, named Aleister Crowley. Expect a package with some of his writings.

Regarding affairs of the heart, as much as I try to pursue her, your landlady's niece, Miss Farr, always seems an arm's length away. A woman of that caliber has the advantage of being wooed by richer and more famous patrons than myself. Ah—to have the luxury of capturing a Muse. Next go around, I guess, if you know what I mean. Dear friend, have you managed to capture a young lady's affection? Certainly your music provides the ambrosia of love sonnets. You're probably spending too much time with your friend, Whit, and gossip will spread.

John, I hope you are weaning yourself once in awhile from your piano studies and can find yourself in good social company, and write, for God's sake, and if not for the aim of publication, then simply to stay in touch. I know you have the rare good fortune of having talent in that area.

Mackenzie

*   *   *

Despite any setbacks my goal was to attain a scholarship and join him. I should've been undaunted by performing in another piano recital. This upcoming competition, however, would have dignitaries from both London and top European institutions as judges compared to the smaller, local venues I'd been used to, thus I practiced day and night in preparation for this event.

During that time, I'd wake in the middle of the night with segments of my upcoming concert drowning out my dreams. I'd sneak down to the kitchen to fix a pot of hot tea, wrapping myself in extra warm scarves since the dying embers in my fireplace scarcely did anything. Then, I'd sit at my piano silently playing this piece, with my fingers flying in the air inches above the actual keys, not to wake up the rest of the sleeping household, but sometimes humming softly to myself at least to emit some sort of musical sounds. My wrists and fingers were sore from hours of practicing for days on end, so allowing them to paint the air with imagined melody was a welcome substitute. Alas, my fate was going to ride on my success.

When that important day arrived, I was so nervous and excited that I was barely able to eat the special breakfast that Lydia had prepared. She invited Vicar Chauncey, Margaret Truesby, and a few others from the local lady's needlepoint social circle to bid me well. Unbeknownst to me, she had taken one of my threadbare overcoats and shown it to her tailor, who had fashioned a brand new, charcoal gray greatcoat from its measurements. Vicar Chauncey, whom I barely knew, presented me with an impressive ebony and silver-topped walking stick, and Mrs. Truesby, fairly wealthy after her husband had passed in an unfortunate accident, presented to me a long silk opera scarf so that with my new top hat, I looked like a true gentleman.

Top pianists, from not only from my university but also from other schools, were all after the few coveted scholarships. My nemesis, Archibald Latimer, was far from perfect in technique, but there was a special charm about him that I didn't seem to be blessed with.

"Mr. Latimer, what piece are you going to play?"

"Beethoven's Sonata Hammerklavier Opus 106."

While I waited for my turn backstage, a wellspring of memories began to take me to another place.

        *   *   *

"Edward, restrain her!" the doctor shouted as my father gripped my mother by the hair and arched her over his knee as she thrashed about in hysteria. "Does this happen often?"

"Too often, I'm afraid," my father replied, ripping her dress at the shoulders.

She was kicking and frantically trying to escape.

"I'm afraid I have no choice," the doctor said as he prepared a syringe and plunged a needle into her arm. "I'll leave you the syrup. It contains laudanum, a slightly weaker version of the morphine I just gave her. Insist she take that if these episodes happen again. What I cannot understand is why she gets into such fits of hysteria? Could she be that frail or weak tempered? I was hoping not to have to resort to anything this strong."

As the drug took effect, Mother slumped into Father's arms. He lowered her down on the bed, covered her with a blanket and motioned to the doctor to follow him out into the hallway.

"Mr. Scott, I'd hate to send her off to an asylum. How long has this been going on?" the doctor asked.

"She's not going away. I know exactly what the problem is," he whispered not to wake her up. "If anyone's being sent away…" His words trailed off. "Doctor, thank you for your time. It was kind of you for coming at such a late hour."

He saw him out the door. Now it was my turn.

"John, come at once," my father, shouted.

133

I hid under my bed, as I knew this wasn't going to be good. Why did someone always have to come in and spoil my fun? I distinctly remember running upstairs to my room taking my borrowed treasure, that being my father's top hat, and parading in front of a mirror while the adult-sized chapeau fell over my forehead stopping just short of my nose. As I danced and pantomimed, I snatched one of my mother's cleaning rags, creating a makeshift cravat and also reached for a nearby broomstick to be my gentleman's cane, as I pretended I was a member of the aristocracy or visiting dignitary.

"John, where are you?"

I wrapped myself up in one of my blankets, still wearing that silly hat and curled myself up into the tiniest ball that I could. Perhaps, I would look like a giant pile of dust, and I'd be completely overlooked.

The single burning lamp in my room rimmed a dark silhouette. Claws dug into my scalp. My fantasy was cut short, and my magical hat was whisked away.

"*Yeeeow!*" I screamed as I slid across the cold, wooden floor being pulled by my thick, wild hair. Then, Father caught hold of my shoulders thrusting me against the side of my bed. A stinging slap seared my face.

"Stop upsetting your mother! She cannot handle it!"

My father shouted so loud my ears hurt.

"I didn't do anything!" I cried out in protest.

"If she's upset, you obviously did!"

"My brother did it!"

"You're saying that your brother did it? He said you did, and your sister is agreeing with him."

"They both lied!"

Putting an unbreakable grip on my shoulder and making certain I had no grounds for argument, he swept me off my feet and dragged me downstairs plunking me atop my piano bench.

"Play!" he demanded.

"Play?" I asked, meekly.

"Play as if your life depended on it!" he yelled.

The sheet music that was out was one of Mozart's piano concertos. It was extremely difficult, and I suspected my father was a bit overconfident regarding my talent. I could barely read it with tears in my eyes, and I had no idea why he was demanding that I start playing, but I did, anyway. He got up and poured himself whisky, sat back down and stared back at me.

"Faster!" he replied.

"But, this is the proper tempo," I argued.

"I said *faster!*" he demanded.

Despite the fact that I knew I was playing the piece incorrectly, I followed his orders. Father poured himself another shot and watched me intently. When I finished the piece, I turned in my chair towards him and thought to myself, "What's next?"

"Again," he shouted. "Even faster!"

"Faster?"

"Shut up and play!"

I played the piece, but it was so off kilter. My fingers hardly kept up with the notes going out of control. Just as I was nearing the end, he seized me by my suspenders and forced me to my feet.

"Bow!" he demanded.

"But, I'm not finished yet."

"Yes, you are."

I gave him a half-hearted bow and held on to the piano for balance.

"Why did you upset your mother?" he asked.

"I didn't do it. My brother did."

"You're the oldest, John. You're expected to know better."

"Father, I'm telling you, I knew she'd be making biscuits, but I didn't put that mouse in her flour!"

"It doesn't matter!"

With that he slammed the piano lid on my fingers and stormed out of the room.

I screamed.

"John Patrick Scott?" the head judge called out.

It was my turn. I snapped to my senses. My pants were too long and too large. Suspenders barely held them up, and I tripped as I walked out to the center of the stage. A row of five judges sat there all dressed in black. Others were in the audience, but with the blinding lights, I was unable to make them out.

"What piece are you going to play?" one of the judges asked.

"Beethoven's Sonata Number 17," I enunciated clearly despite the fact that my vocal cords creaked.

"Come here," the head judge called out. He handed me sheet music. "Play this, instead."

"Sir?" I replied looking it over.

Beethoven's Sonata Hammerklavier Opus 106? That was considered one of the most difficult piano pieces to memorize and play in concert.

"That's what Archibald just played," I responded.

"That's correct. Are you saying that you can't read music?"

"No, sir. I can, but…"

"I'd like to see your interpretation of this piece," the judge said.

"Sir, I practiced mine for weeks. I've never played this one."

The door opened in the back of the auditorium. It was difficult to discern his features from the glare of the stage lights, but one of my classmates, a violinist, entered and gave me thumbs up for good luck. I couldn't speak for him, but I was a tad under the influence from last night's toast to my upcoming success and needed all the luck I could get.

"Mr. Scott, are you going to honor our request?"

Time stood still as I sat down, putting my new, unfamiliar sheet music in place. Cool fires of passion streamed from my flying fingers into the keys. Deep inside my soul a little boy was screaming.

*   *   *

136

Dear Wendell,

I'd love to join you, but I had been caught unawares when requested to play Beethoven's Sonata Hammerklavier Opus 106, which cost me the scholarship I expected. My performance was less than stellar, and the judges favored Latimer, instead. To remain at the University of Edinburgh, I began tutoring in my spare time. One of my female students has taken a liking towards me, but I confess that I'm a bit more saturnine compared to you in regards to women.

Since my erstwhile companion, Whit, helped contribute to the loss of those scholarships, I cannot consider relocation to London or anywhere else for that matter. There is much strife between us, and many a nasty letter has gone back and forth. I cannot fathom why he thinks I'm responsible for his sweetheart's sudden demise. She was the victim of a tragic drowning during a picnic where she tumbled out of a canoe and attempts to rescue her failed. He claims I caused it by my mere prediction of an astrological event, which is nonsense. I only hope one day we can make amends and forgive ourselves for our false accusations, but that day has not yet come. Therefore, please continue to share your stories, and at least my spirit will be with you.

Yours most devoted,
John Patrick Scott

*   *   *

Compound Fractures

Edinburgh, July 1901: Despite the fact I was no longer dependent on an elaborate time machine set up, I wanted to reconstruct what I had successfully done before and surprise Arthur by making him one similar to Wendell's. I was starting to make headway when I saw a key turn in my door. Mortified, I sprang to my feet, still attached to the rig I constructed, which in turn toppled over with bits and pieces bouncing all over the floor. I barricaded my door with all my strength to keep the unexpected intruder from entering.

"John, you received several letters," Lydia shouted from the other side of my door, "They seem to have all come from out of town."

"Please, Mrs. Campbell, I told you never to enter without knocking first!"

Sweat broke out all over my forehead.

"I knew you'd be so excited! So, I brought you tea and cakes."

I had to come up with some sort of lie and do so, quickly.

"Leave everything outside. I'm not dressed," I called out, pulling off straps and wires.

"Very well, don't let it get cold," she said and left.

God forbid, she thought I was mad. I looked at the disaster in my room and couldn't believe the mess. I opened my door a crack, poked my head out to make sure the coast was clear, and slid the silver tea setting inside my room and locked the door once again. My landlady always meant well, but sometimes her busybody behavior drove me insane, and I had a lot of secrets I needed to keep away from the inquisitive mundane. There were nether realms and strange universes to explore, which only the privileged few were allowed to travel, and the mystical world of alchemical archeology was not one where you would take your neighbors on a Sunday afternoon picnic.

Three letters—there was one from Arthur, one from Wendell, and one from Germany, by its postmark. Perhaps, this was news about a scholarship?

"Aren't you going to open those up?"

A voice came from behind. It was unmistakably Finn's.

"I will, but first things first," I answered tripping over equipment. Nervous, I quickly hid anything suspicious.

"Not curious in the least?"

"Sherlock, would you stop?" I cried out.

He was amusing myself by being stuck like glue to my backside—a ridiculous game he would always play making himself

138

completely invisible unless I was able to outpace him. Meanwhile, I was spinning around in circles never able to catch a glimpse.

"Why do you do this to me every time, Finn? Why?"

"Playing cat and mouse with you is quite entertaining," he replied.

"Maybe for you, but..."

"Open your mail," he said, finally stepping out so I could see him.

* * *

Dearest John,

Pity you've had to remain in Auld Reeky. I'm now at *Lloyd's Weekly Newspaper,* which has kept me busy, although my superiors always seem to keep the more interesting assignments for their senior staff, which is unfortunate. However, that does give me ample time to pursue my own interests, which include detecting the various metaphysical organizations about town. Edinburgh is fairly quiet compared to activity here. Absolutely anything connected with members of the Golden Dawn piques my thirst for knowledge. Often it seems to be more of a round robin of power-hungry opportunists all claiming spiritual authority. Between my interest in politics and the occult, I'm on perpetual holiday, and yes, of course, the chance of engaging with Miss Florence Farr is a constant whim of fancy.

If, perchance, you do get that scholarship to that London music school, make haste and contact me immediately by telegram. I cannot begin to describe the delightful time you'd have if we can continue both of our educational journeys within the same vicinity.

Oh yes, regarding that time travel device you gave me? Lots of good fun, but I'll have to elaborate on that later.

Keep your chin up and pray for the best, since you are more talented and smarter than you can possibly imagine.

Mackenzie

* * *

Straightaway, I eagerly opened the second letter. Without a doubt, its handwriting indicated that it came from Arthur. Despite the

139

fact that we'd been communicating at midnight on a continuing basis, it was always reassuring to receive physical a confirmation.

*   *   *

Dear John,

I apologize for the brevity, but time is something I don't seem to have much of these days. William Gillette has been portraying Sherlock for the stage with critical acclaim. I only wish I could interest someone to produce something similar with *Brigadier Gerard*. However, I'm probably becoming a bore telling you how much I've tired of our fond detective. I don't understand why the public keeps crying for more.

You've been a godsend writing those stories since my well has run dry. Perhaps as time passes, I'll be able to see things from a different perspective and come up with new ones. I really didn't want to bring Sherlock back from the dead for *The Strand*, but your help has been invaluable. Meanwhile, Greenhough has not indicated a new publication date. I'll edit your submissions and keep them on file until things are more definite.

Keep up the good work as well as our sessions at midnight. Best wishes on your examinations. Let me know if any of those scholarships pan out. I'll need a new address for our written correspondence.

Arthur

*   *   *

Slightly disappointed that there wasn't a London return address, I hoped that I saved the best letter for last. My continued education was going to depend on receiving another scholarship, and so far my local options had fallen through. My grades weren't quite up to snuff in my academic subjects after my misunderstanding with Whit. I was partially to blame. I spent more time either chasing after an elusive girl from the future, or memories from my past, or with my music rather than with my studies for Professor McKnight's class.

Whit refused to talk after being booted from his flat for misconduct. Also, there was that tragedy regarding that poor girl, Isabelle, which I can only surmise had something to do with the ill-fated love potion he concocted. I have to confess if it weren't for Finn allowing me to access the Secret Library, I would've never had the means to recover pertinent details. There had been a warning inscribed in that spell book, and Whit was too much of a half-wit not to notice.

*   *   *

Herr Scott,

It's our honor and pleasure to extend our invitation to give you the exciting opportunity to further your education with us at the Conservatory of Music in Stuttgart, Germany. Our conservatory is proud to have a staff of distinguished and world-renowned professors, who welcome your presence. Should you choose to accept our offer, please inform us immediately of your decision, so arrangements can be made for your transportation and lodging, which are included in your scholarship.

Sincerely,

Professor Friedrich Faustus Schmidt, Deputy-in-Chief

*   *   *

Late August 1901

That last letter pointed the way for my next quest. Shortly before I left Edinburgh, I wrote Arthur a series of letters assuming that while in transit it would be difficult to maintain normal correspondence. Needless to say, we still had our meetings at midnight.

Dear Arthur,

No doubt, it's for the best that Wendell and I established a distance. Since he left for London, I've sobered considerably and have become a much wiser man having refrained from our wild bouts of bacchanalia. My creative spirit has returned in leaps and bounds, and my scholarship to the Conservatory is testimony. I guess each of us has a true heaven and hell within, and I was most fortunate to have made the right choice, but I only wish that I could apply that redemption to some of my other friendships.

Wendell writes me all the time, trying to convince me to drop my studies and move there, even if it means reapplying to another music school and forfeiting my scholarship in Stuttgart. That's preposterous, of course. Alas, the poor man still has his heart set on the lovely Miss Farr. She's elusive, yet captivating.

Wendell also tells me all sorts of rumors about Aleister Crowley. He's wanted to take the teachings of the Golden Dawn and other esoteric disciplines to a whole new level and considers himself a poet and self-proclaimed prophet. If you can manage to sift your way through his tower of babel, you might benefit from bits and pieces of his fictional works and poetry. My concern is that your Spiritualist circles are not exempt from a similar shortcoming. In my own journey to find the truth, my compass needs to point north. Perhaps, I should collect my own pocketful of lodestones—that, a good guide and a trustworthy roadmap!

Have you had the opportunity to meet face-to-face with the great Harry Houdini? If so, what's your assessment of his magical prowess? He's probably the only human on earth that has the wherewithal to outwit someone as clever as Doctor Bell.

Yours most devoted,

John Patrick Scott
P.S. Yesterday, I mailed you a package with your latest manuscript. It was quite apparent that your interests lay elsewhere besides Holmes. Though my writing experience is no match compared to yours, it's been a healthy, but pleasurable challenge. However, I do think you will find my rewrites satisfactory. I suspect you'll enjoy the reference I made to the wizened old book collector. Poor old Dalrymple was my inspiration for that character, but the rest is hush-hush for now.

Please note: There will also be a second package in the mail. I'm sending you a gift, but it's a surprise. Promise me you won't use it without confirming its arrival, but also it's imperative that you read the enclosed instructions thoroughly, several times, if necessary. Ask me any questions, and don't be shy about it.

*   *   *

By and large, Arthur's accounts would keep him out of town, but as an otherworldly traveler, Arthur said we had the ability to meet wherever our hearts desired if we chose our sessions outside of our physical bodies. He did, however, manage to make one last trip in-person to Scotland before I left to continue my education in Germany, and I was looking forward to our reunion.

Dusk approached. I walked over the George IV Bridge and looked over the yawning city as the sunlight faded. The castle grounds were shrouded in cloud cover and trees showed barely more details than silhouettes. The town was bathed in tranquility with an occasional hoof hitting cobblestones in the distance. Contrary to its nickname, Auld Reekie's air was fresh and sweet. We were to meet by Greyfriars Church, not too far from campus.

Haunting wisps of clouds began to emerge in the sky as it turned a slightly darker shade of midnight blue. The smell of the wet masonry blanketed the streets. Underground chambers below the streets of Edinburgh would soon awaken the city's phantoms from their diurnal sleep. Arthur checked his watch and returned it to his waistcoat pocket. I followed his lead as he found an establishment, which only a local would know, in an out-of-the way back alley. By now the evening mist was so thick that we were lucky to see beyond three paces. When we arrived at a public house, a gentleman welcomed us. He showed us to a table in the back, returning with two brandies.

"How does your wife kiss you with that thing?" I asked in jest, referring of course to his distinguished moustache.

143

"It gives me character. Can't be a man without one. How come you don't have one?" Arthur replied, defending his pride while throwing a jab at me at the same time.

"Can't grow one," I said, embarrassed. "I've tried, but enough of the small talk. Arthur, I'm still having unusual dreams, the newest of which places me in the role of a warrior in feudal Japan. I used my secret knowledge of the occult and social position for personal gain— fueled by jealousy, rage and revenge. That was wrong, and I paid the price dearly. Could I have been that man in a past incarnation? For the most part my daily routine consists of my music, my studies, and some writing, but nothing of that sort."

"Is this the first time it's occurred?" he asked.

"Yes, the first. Doctor Doyle, what's your diagnosis?"

"John, I'm not a medical practitioner any more, and in no way could you compare me to someone like Sigmund Freud, but in my professional opinion, you'll probably have to change your diet to include more vegetables, not just roots and potatoes."

We both laughed in unison. A typical Scottish diet helped brave the winter chill, but in other respects left much to be desired.

"Arthur, I'm assuming you're fine with the additions on *The Adventure of the Empty House*, since I never heard another word from you regarding that manuscript. But the original title you came up with didn't strike the right chords, and I changed it with my own discretion."

He nodded, acknowledging what I said while lighting his pipe. I reached for my drink to prepare for what I was about to say next.

"By the way, Arthur, I wrote my own original detective story. It's nowhere near as brilliant as Sherlock Holmes but you will enjoy it."

I pulled a few rolled up papers out of my coat pocket bound with a thin red string, but Arthur's strong hands took them forcefully, almost ripping them. He put on his reading glasses and skimmed through them, then shoved them into his coat pocket.

"That's my only copy!" I called out.

"What were you planning on doing with it?" Arthur asked.

"Read it to you, and then if you liked it I would've sent you your own copy. Maybe you could speak to your publisher and..."

Arthur cut me off mid-sentence. "I can't let you do that. We have an agreement. John, I'm sure you're aware that I've had to burn all our letters including those stories you've been writing for me."

I couldn't believe what he was saying.

"How could you?" I cried. "If you didn't consider them important, then why have we been wasting our time?"

"I told you they had to be secret, " he explained, "and no one in the world was ever to know about them. I pay you handsomely for your ghostwriting. Is it not enough?"

Arthur stared straight into my eyes.

"It's been quite satisfactory," I said, bitterly upset.

"At the moment, my mind is focused on otherworldly things. This will be my deepest and darkest secret that no one except us, not even your friend, Wendell, will know about. The public should never know that I no longer could create Holmes."

There was more privileged information between us, and this barely scratched the surface.

"Is there no chance that you can help me publish them with my own name credited?" I asked.

"My friend, please don't disappoint me. You know the answer to that."

*   *   *

I tried my best to forget about that altercation. Our friendship was too valuable to toss aside. Thus, I continued our ghostwriting arrangement and did my best to remain levelheaded despite my mounting frustration that he had the ways and means to promote my own creative efforts. Meanwhile, I had to prepare to take my first steps off the shores of Scotland. I started throwing or giving away anything that wasn't absolutely necessary and was delighted when I discovered a few loose floorboards under the rug and stones near the fireplace, which could've been removed to hide a few alchemical texts and arcane books that were too much to travel with. I also went to great lengths to brush up on my German, spoken with a distinctive Scottish brogue, which would have to disappear over the course of time.

Finally I had the chance to play that prank on Doctor Lorraine Smith that I had wanted to do for some time. He was one of Doctor Bell's medical colleagues from the university, and when I first commenced those telekinetic practices with Arthur, I desired to make him my test subject. One day I passed by him as he was handing a few coins to a newspaper vendor. The moment he took his paper, I caused it to slip and fall to the ground. The doctor thought nothing of it, assuming it was mere happenstance. However, when he reached over to pick it up, it was as if I had slathered his fingers in butterfat. Not only did he let go of the newspaper letting it fall once again, but he also fumbled with his umbrella, which rolled right out of his hands, dropping to the pavement below. He gathered both, this time tucking them tightly under his arm. But lo and behold, I *willed* a gust of wind causing his hat fly to off his head landing in a nearby trash bin. He lost his balance and nearly fell as he spun on his heels trying to retrieve it. He looked like a clown and three ladies nearby along with a local police officer broke into hysterics, as he became a public laughingstock. I could've continued this comedy of errors, but I didn't have the heart to torture the poor chap any further. He finally looked around and wondered who was the puppeteer, and why he felt like a marionette. I released my hold on him and went my merry way, secretly satisfied with that achievement.

What I didn't anticipate was that the tables would turn. Sarah Elizabeth Chandler, that incorrigible young woman with incomparable persistence who had been stalking me all semester, had her designs on me. I was beside myself as to why I ignited such irrational behavior. One minute she'd insult me. In another, she'd give the impression that she was upset because I rebuffed her affections. Mutual acquaintances were also perplexed as to what to make of it. Counselors at school concentrated on academic matters, of which this was not the case, and I didn't want to approach my nosy landlady for advice although she had a bit more experience than I in understanding the female mind.

One afternoon I was minding my own business and shopping in Old Town for necessities that I'd need to take with me for an extended stay in Germany. Pears glycerin soap and lavender oil were particular favorites in my daily grooming ritual, and I was unsure if they'd be available abroad. So I was inside a shop searching for such toiletries when I felt an encroaching presence.

"Since when does a gentleman wear such a lady's scent?"

I turned around, and it was none other than Miss Chandler. I finally summoned the courage to confront her.

"I fail to understand why you've been following me, and today's not the only instance. You've been trailing me for the past few months. Do you have a problem?" I asked, somewhat indignant at this point.

"You really don't remember a bloody thing, do you?" she asked, putting me on the spot. "The time when you rescued me from a swarm of bees at the school picnic? And what about the instance when I broke my leg and you carried me all the way to the infirmary? The presents...the stolen kisses in the library...my tenth birthday party...the poems and private piano performances—none of that rings a bell?"

"You have me mistaken for someone else," I replied, completely clueless. I think it would've been obvious if I had fallen for her back in the days of my youth, but then again, so many recollections from that period were lost in a fog.

With that last remark she untied a box she'd been carrying from a local bakeshop. Lifting its lid, she clutched a hunk of my curls and yanked me face-first into a generous slice of chocolate cake that was inside. Shocked and surprised, I jerked back up, covered with sticky frosting and becoming the laughingstock of all who witnessed the event. The storeowner rushed over to the washbasin and handed me a towel.

Before I had the chance to ask the meaning of it, Sarah made a quick exit. Even after rounds of inquiries neither the proprietor nor his customers knew what possessed her to do that.

I gave Lydia my last farewells, assuring her that I was man enough to take charge of my own affairs, and that I'd survive quite well on my own. Shortly before my departure, I took out my grandfather's silver pocket watch and began to deliberately dangle it back and forth, but stopped. This was all I needed now to catapult across time, and there was so much more to explore. Wendell and Arthur now had the remnants and reconstructions of the old inventions, but could I trust them to stay out of trouble?

* * *

Forward Advance

My first footsteps upon German soil were lonely ones. Attending classes spoken entirely in a language other than my own was overwhelming, and since I was there by the grace of God and a scholarship, I made it a point to cram in as much of the German language as I could in my spare time. Native-born students grossly outnumbered the foreigners attending the Conservatory.

Students were expected to eat their meals within designated hours at a cafeteria-style communal dining hall located in a separate building, which posed its challenges during inclement weather, as one had to brave more ice and snow than back in Scotland. It was more like an institutional mess hall where we got in line, had an attendant dish out whatever we decided from their pre-set menu, and found a seat at a long table. I generally ate alone.

The dining room had pervasive dampness that penetrated right through your clothes no matter what time of year. Many of the students called it The Catacombs. It reminded me more of a centuries-old wine cellar where one was supposed to hide from invading troops and impending danger. Rumors were rampant about despondent students who had committed suicide, and their skeletons

148

were buried in the walls. Wind rushed down the corridors making eerie *whooo* sounds. It was functional, but not that conducive to being social, and if anything, contributed towards an increasing sense of isolation.

The students were convinced that the dormitory building had been a converted prison or asylum. Most school officials assumed the place had been a former monastery. Accommodations were Spartan-like, depressing dark rooms with a single small window. They didn't have much more than a lamp and a cot, and they didn't even have a closet. The rooms lined up alongside each other with lavatories and communal washrooms located down the hall. For the most part I lived out of the steamer trunks I brought with me from Scotland, and I wound up picking up an old coat stand at a second-hand shop where I'd hang my coats and jackets. I didn't even own a desk and had to create a makeshift one by stacking and rearranging boxes, trunks and whatever else I could find.

Most important, of course, were my studies, and we did not have pianos inside our dormitories. Therefore, in contrast to having the privacy of playing on an old upright piano inside my flat like I had at Mrs. Campbell's boarding house, I practiced all instrumental work on campus. Then I turned into a bookworm, either holed up in my room or the library for anything regarding history, theory or academics. Had this been back in Edinburgh, I would've been out and about with friends carousing through Old Town.

Between Arthur and Wendell always sending new material, after a while I began to possess a substantial personal metaphysical library. So often I took the time to perform additional psychical experiments than what I did with Arthur. Finn often warned me that rushing into these too quickly could open my psyche to either hidden memories or open channels into hermetical realms that I might not be prepared to handle. The mere act of accessing the Secret Library or traveling through time was like doing back flips and somersaults with one's rationality. Not that Finn was purposely trying to dissuade me, but he wouldn't have been doing his job properly had he not

149

advised me. Madness plagued some of the greatest poets and philosophers throughout history. Everyone possessed personal demons, which were eager to leap out of the shadows, and no one was exempt. In fact, it was often the brightest of souls who were the most foolhardy. The Devil rode the same horse as the ego.

*   *   *

A Glimpse of Things to Come

London, 1903: The clock struck six, and the meeting hall was packed earlier, but the throng dissipated as the afternoon stretched long and wearily into the early evening. H. G. Wells was busy acknowledging goodbyes to various friends and associates as the London Fabian Society meeting came to a close. In the back of the auditorium Arthur Conan Doyle pushed past the exiting crowd to meet up with Wells. He was so excited that he could barely contain himself.

"Bertie, I am convinced that I'm on to something— a huge discovery, one that will completely redefine our perceptions of reality. Once we can scientifically prove there is life after death the basic tenets of both chemistry and physics will never be the same. What do you think?" Doyle asked.

Skeptical, Wells wanted to give Doyle the benefit of the doubt. He skimmed over the Spiritualist pamphlet, shrugged his shoulders and slipped it back towards Doyle.

"To be honest, Arthur, you're way ahead of yourself and apparently don't know me very well at all. My books may kindle your imagination, but I've also had my concerns and views on the socio-political directions that Britain is taking. Too many countries have been building up their war machines, and I foresee that turning into a confederacy of doom and disaster. To say it bluntly, I'd say that I'm more concerned about preventing people from dying needlessly rather than being worried about what happens to their spirits after they're dead."

"Quite a few prominent and respectable people are members of the Society of Psychical Research. Many of them are scientists, as

150

well as, members of Parliament," Doyle argued in his defense, presenting more pieces of evidence to support his claim. "Out of this impressive group most of them believe in the existence of life after death."

Wells ignored the pamphlets. He reached into his smooth leather carrying case and took out a few carbon-copied manuscript pages.

"Just because something is in print, doesn't make it true," Wells said.

Arthur interjected, "To quote Sherlock in *The Bascombe Valley Mystery*, 'There is nothing more deceptive than an obvious fact.'"

"We all know that Sherlock Holmes doesn't exist, although there are many who beg to differ because they'd like to believe he really resides on Baker Street. But Arthur," Wells said looking around to make sure no one was within earshot, "I was under the impression that you stopped by to discuss that *other book*! What did you find out?"

"Oh, *that one*...the *red one*," Arthur said with reservation as he leaned in closer. "I still haven't been able to get my hands on it, but I know it exists. In fact, there are several of them."

"Now, is it true that you said that you have a friend who possesses one of them?"

"He's shown it to me. However he's never allowed me to examine it. If you asked me to step into Sherlock Holmes' shoes, I'd venture to say he might not even have it anymore, because it's no longer a pertinent matter in any of our conversations. Mine, yes, but his, not at all."

"How frequent are you in touch with this gentleman?"

"Often enough," Doyle said without disclosing any details as to the psychic connections he had on a regular basis.

"I have to admit that I'm disappointed." Wells sighed. "I want to make sure we're not wasting our time chasing after an elusive book that doesn't really exist."

"I assure you that it does," Doyle interjected. "I've also written Harry Houdini about it. He's expressed interest in exploring its supernatural properties."

"I'm not entirely convinced that I'd go so far as to believe it's magical or anything like that," Wells replied with a slight laugh. "I'm more inclined to say that there's a scientific explanation to everything. Phenomena such as radioactivity and x-rays have been equally enigmatic, but ultimately they've been demystified."

"Then I'd like to know the answers," Arthur said interrupting him.

But Wells was getting impatient and redirected their conversation. "On a personal note, my interests have little to do with the occult and the arcane. They focus more on convincing society to toss aside Victorian morality and to indulge in a sexual revolution as part of a socialistic transformation. This article isn't in print yet, but my publisher has already given his commitment. Please be my guest and take this copy," he said handing over the manuscript.

Arthur donned his reading glasses and skimmed through the first three pages.

"Are you condoning taking on multiple partners?" he asked.

"Advocating it, in fact. I find nothing wrong with affairs outside of wedlock."

"From a doctor's point of view—" Arthur shook his head in defense, "perhaps, we should change the subject. So, that's your main focus, not that of exploring the marriage of new technologies with the budding science of psychology? I'm assuming you've read Freud?

"Oh course, I try to keep up with modern times," Wells replied, "but are you indicating that the suppression of what is so natural to the human species can only lead to an illness of the mind? By the way, your relationship with that woman…"

"Jean?"

"Whatever her name is, Arthur. Rumor has it that you've been with her for several years now while you wife is still ailing with consumption. Being the healthy sportsman that you are, I cannot possibly imagine that you've been faithful and chaste for all this time in order to protect your virtue. I know you're close to your mother. I'm surprised she accepts your situation so graciously."

Arthur strained to mask his emotions. "Think what you will. Now, this liberation of sexual mores— this doesn't have anything to do with the Fabian society, does it?"

"The Fabian Society defends socialistic principles and ideologies leading towards a modern utopia. Although they're generally open-minded, I have many members who disagree with me and take the stand that they are downright offended. Sticking to my principles has cost me posts of authority within their organization," Wells replied.

"Really?" Arthur was surprised that Wells was losing favor.

"I'm afraid so," Wells said. "Regretfully, there's been a price to pay for my candid outspokenness. One last thing, I'd hold your tongue if I were you if you want Sherlock Holmes to be the keystone of your literary legacy."

"I dream of quite the opposite," Arthur replied with confidence. "I'd much rather my readers know me for my historical works or my beliefs on life beyond death."

"I'd amend your main focus if you value your purse," Wells advised him with a slight hint of warning.

Arthur looked at Wells straight in the eye.

Wells concluded, "Consider your reputation, as well, my friend."

*　　*　　*

Demon Est Deus Inversus
—"The Devil is the reverse of God," William Butler Yeats

Stuttgart, 1904: The front window was dirty. I was barely able to make out any details while peering through it from the outside, but when I entered the repair shop a bell tinkled announcing my arrival. Inside, the tiny foyer was packed with old clocks, many dusty, in need of polishing or restoration, and some were mere

153

skeletons and thrown about parts. Some had pendulums, others chimed, or had annoying cuckoos, and yes, there were grandfather clocks.

"*Guten morgen. Ist jemand da hinten?*" My Scottish accent still overshadowed my German.

"Coming!" An elderly man's voice called from the back room replying in German-accented English.

The proprietor emerged as a mole-like man, hunched over with wrinkled clothes. He had three hairs on the top of his head, but a dust ruffle of gray and black curls hanging low from the bottom of his ears that rested on his shoulders. I unfastened my grandfather's silvery pocket watch from its chain and placed it on his glass counter top.

"It's not running properly," I said.

Articulating details to a master craftsman was as futile as having an intelligent conversation about music criticism with my relatives. My timepiece had been running fast. Since I used it for time travel, it was imperative that it was dependable.

"Let's take a look," the venerable *uhrmacher* said as he pulled a sleight of hand, and the timepiece disappeared from my grasp.

He popped open its compartments one by one for a quick inspection. When my father first gave me that watch, I struggled like a fool trying to pop open the front crystal to change the time. My clumsy fingers, which worked miracles on a musical instrument but were so inept on this mechanical wonder, fumbled as I kept pushing groves when I should have been pulling them the other way.

"You'll have to leave it with me," he said.

"You don't suppose you have a spare one you could lend me, erstwhile?"

"I'd be glad to sell you one," he suggested. "The case in front of you has a wide selection of beautiful watches for sale—some new, some used, some that my customers left for repair, never picked up and have been here for years. Take a look."

My eye line went straight towards a gorgeous specimen with astronomical engravings. "Can you show me that one?"

A miniature sun and moon that would travel from left to right along the course of the day graced the top of its face.

"How much?" I was afraid to ask.

"It's a bit steep."

He turned the price tag over, and a pit formed in my stomach. I sighed with resignation, shrugged my shoulders and handed it back to the shopkeeper, disappointed.

"Unfortunately, not on an assistant professor's budget. How long will it take to get mine repaired?"

"Estimate three weeks. Everyone in Stuttgart had his or her timepiece run down at the same time. Never seen anything like it in my life. Lots of repairs, and I'm running behind. Let me know if you reconsider."

I handed him a deposit and left his shop without the watch of my dreams merely holding a receipt. Was there a way I could earn extra funds to satisfy my indulgence, or anything else for that matter? I had to stop doing local concerts for free. What about Arthur? He had plenty of publishing contacts. Could he get any of my own stories or amateur photographs published? His father and uncle were famous illustrators, and there was no doubt that he had considerable influence with many people.

Initially, I asked around the university, but the semester had already started and positions had been filled. Meanwhile, my *conversations* with Arthur faded in and out, and the ether was not transmitting our thoughts. Since I suspected he was traveling, I wasn't sure where to send a telegram. When I went into town and inquired about work, I would either come up dry, or encounter conflicts with my commitments at the Conservatory. Having exhausted nearly every option, I had to make do. Meanwhile, without my timepiece, I'd be grounded from time travel.

Shortly thereafter, I woke from a nightmare so horrific that I was doubled over with severe stomach pains. Finn began to explain how to wake myself up while I was still dreaming to create a diversion or turn of events.

He told me that Aristotle once mentioned, "When one is asleep, there is something in consciousness which declares that what then presents itself is but a dream." Essentially, if I didn't like how the story was going, it was up to me to take charge and rewrite the ending. Also, I had the power to use that knowledge to affect my waking life and soon I'd be called to put that to the test.

Several weeks passed. Obligations at the Conservatory took precedence despite the fact that I felt naked each day that went by without my grandfather's timepiece. When I returned to the repair shop to pick it up, it was closing time. Quickly, I paid my balance and retrieved my keepsake while avoiding looking at that amazing gold watch the shopkeeper had shown me the last time.

The winter sky had already turned dark. Hunger asserted itself, causing me to take a slight detour towards a cheese shop before heading back to the Conservatory. This one came highly recommended, despite the fact that a little voice in my ear clamored for my attention, warning me to wait and go another day, as danger would lie ahead. Like an imbecile, I disobeyed that sound advice and ventured forth, allowing my appetite to lead the way. While I continued along the winding back streets towards my destination, a drunken rogue blocked my path. I should've followed my hunch.

"Your money, if you value your life," he commanded as he brandished a knife in front of me.

I emptied my pockets to demonstrate that he picked the wrong victim. I paid the last of my hard-earned marks to the watch repairman, earlier.

"Ah, let's see that silvery thing!"

It was obvious who had the upper hand, but why had I studied all this magic if I couldn't defend myself using the same powers of persuasion? I'd be damned if he was going to steal my

156

grandfather's timepiece! What could be a better time to demonstrate my mastery?

I inhaled with my breath being so forcibly controlled that it hurt. Then I took my watch from my waistcoat pocket, as I hadn't looped its chain through my buttonhole yet, and held it in front of my face allowing my fingers to let it swing back and forth like a pendulum. He gazed at it like a cat.

My assailant began squirming as if some mischievous child had dropped a hairy caterpillar down his britches. The urge to dance in place and relieve what could not be scratched had overtaken him. Thus, my spell was working. He growled and shuddered, while he let his fingers fly loose, scratching all over his body as swiftly as I would play the Minute Waltz.

"What in the Devil are you doing to me?" he cried in anguish. "You might as well put a pistol to my head and put me out of my misery. Now!"

Did I dare let him get away?

"You really don't want to take my watch, do you?" I sneered with satisfaction.

His lips trembled. His knees quivered. His eyes glazed over as if I had stolen his breath away. Finally, he choked up a response.

"No, sir. Not interested in the least."

I eyed the pathetic man. I couldn't resist torturing him for a few moments longer.

"If you aren't interested in taking my watch, don't you have better things to do this evening?"

"I'd like to be going, but my legs won't move."

He was straining, held fast by supernatural forces. When I finally released him from his invisible binds, he flew forward scrambling and stumbling then ran off into the darkness.

Finn followed me down the street. Although I feared he would scold me, much to my surprise, he spoke in support of my actions.

"So Finn, are you going to tell me that I'm heartless as a piano without its player?"

"No, on the contrary, just the flip side of the coin. Well done, John. Well done, indeed."

*   *   *

Favorite Son
May 1905

Ma'am,

I am down in Southsea on holiday. Had a chance to play cricket. Many thanks for your birthday letter. My speech before the Prince of Wales and four hundred members of the medical community was most successful and by far, one of the wittiest discourses I've ever given. Ultimately, I made uncanny comparisons between the art of medicine, law and the fine craft of literature.

Herewith are some of those highlights: "Gentleman, without desiring to expand upon the whole field of literature, there is perhaps one little section in which I'd like to shed some light. References have been made to writers of fiction using terminology from the legal profession. The conclusion is such that the law of the novelist is even stranger than those common laws with which we are familiar. One aphorism stated, that if a man dies intestate his property goes to the nearest villain."

"But if the law of the novelist is strange, I think you'll admit that his medicine is equally so. Authors dwell on certain peculiar afflictions, yet others are of no use to us. The list of such debilities is surprisingly short, and our cures are strangely simple. First, of course, is the curse of consumption, the ultimate blow to all heroes and heroines as they waste away into nothingness unless we can find a complete cure in the second to the last chapter. The treatment, of course, consists in bringing back the noble man or heroine who has been so wrongly misunderstood in Chapter V. The symptoms of this disease vary. The most prominent one is extreme decline, combined with an almost empyreal beauty."

"Bruises and broken bones are a bore. Mosquito bites and bee stings are not significant although mind you, I prefer to avoid them. You can only go so far with those maladies from the morning after, and discussing the plague is overbearing. No need to bluster and wail until eternity. Another disease that is useful for the writer is having fits, and then there is that mysterious infirmity, which is best known as brain fever. As to small disorders, they are too inconsequential. Revered authors resist complaints about mumps, or from sore throats. If we are to use diseases as literary contrivances, then we might as well pick the most severe cases with full awareness that in all things considered, we respect and are kindly disposed to the medical profession."

The speech was well received, and all felt it was in good taste.

Hope to see you soon.

Your loving son,

Arthur

*   *   *

It was 1:00 a.m. Stuttgart was one hour ahead of London. I was sleepy, but determined to make my arrangements work with Arthur. Before I left Edinburgh, I shipped him a portable time machine in an old suitcase, almost identical to the one I constructed for Wendell. Now, with Arthur, my long-held secret that I guarded with my life was out in the open, and he'd also have the ability to surpass the barriers of time.

He promised me that he hadn't tried to operate the time machine on his own, which I hoped was God's honest truth. He also said that he'd wait until the opportune time whereby we could experiment together even if it meant that a protracted period would pass before we could do it. Perhaps, he had his initial trepidations, but I took his word for it. Our arrangement was to attempt to travel in time together even if it had to be on the astral plane, since it was physically impossible be in the same room at the same time like Wendell and I had in previous attempts. Accomplishing such a feat would've marked a milestone in our psychical progress. Arthur had a set of detailed instructions, albeit in my abominable handwriting, which I insisted he follow to the letter until he had mastered time travel successfully on his own. While he was going through the painstaking procedure of assembling the various components, I explained a few other vital issues to him.

"Arthur, first of all, when you travel to either the past or the future, you might not wind up as a man."

"Really?"

That woke him up and caught his attention.

"Absolutely, and it's not my doing. I have no control over that matter, but it was only fair that I tell you ahead of time."

"Anything else I should be aware of?"

"Quite a few things. Most likely events will be presented out of order. I can't explain as to why, except that I was told that things would be revealed as we needed to know them."

I was conveying to Arthur what I knew from experience despite the fact that I still had so much to learn.

"Have you contacted Wells about your success with this venture?" he asked.

"No. I've been keeping it a secret."

"What on earth for? I would think he'd be thrilled that someone took his idea and put it into effect."

I sighed. I really wasn't up for an argument. Personally, I didn't know H.G. Wells like Arthur did. He was one of my favorite authors, but I rarely had opportunities to hobnob in those circles. For a second, I was on the defense and felt jealous. Both Wells and Arthur had the ways and means to commercialize time travel, which could wreak havoc with entire fabric of the universe. As it stood, I had taken great risks by sharing my discoveries with Wendell and Arthur.

While Arthur continued hooking up his time travel apparatus, Finn poked at my shoulder from behind. He gave me a thumbs-up and pointed to another man standing behind Arthur's table indicating that he was Arthur's *guide* or time travel *escort*. He was a queer looking fellow with funny clothes reminding me of a character from *The Pirates of Penzance*.

"How come I couldn't see anyone when I tried these projects with Wendell?" I asked, whispering so Arthur couldn't overhear us.

Finn shook his head. "Don't worry about that. Just concentrate on what you're doing."

"John, is there someone else with you?" Arthur asked. "I thought this was to be conducted in private."

"No, there isn't," I said shooing Finn away. "Sorry, Arthur, my thoughts ran away from me for a second. The best I could describe how the time machine works is in terms of optics. When you hold up a letter in front of a mirror, the handwriting appears backwards, right?"

"Agreed."

"Then imagine that effect reflected off several slowly rotating mirrors that bounce about continuing to jumble how things look," I explained.

Arthur stopped and scratched his head.

161

"Has Watson baffled Holmes this time around?" I laughed. "I guess I'm doing a miserable job explaining this. Oh well, regardless, the point I'm trying to make is that once we penetrate the barriers of time, strange and implausible events can and will probably occur. Try to be as observant and objective as possible even if none of this makes sense. Most likely, you'll feel like you're an actor in an unprecedented role, which you are expected to play seamlessly, only because you've done it before. This is because we're not only treading upon virgin territory through time travel, but we are delving into the frontiers of reincarnation."

"Ah!" Arthur exclaimed. "That explains a few things."

It was most refreshing that for once, roles were reversed, and now I was the professor, and Arthur was my student.

"Good," I replied, "I hoped it would. This is not a random exploration of events that occurred before. We are going to be discovering *who* we were before we were born, and that's why you need that *buccaneer* standing right there beside you."

Arthur's was bewildered. He had no idea what I was referring to.

"Finn, did I just make an idiotic statement?"

Finn whispered in my ear, "He can't see him, but that's all right. Just carry on like you hadn't mentioned it."

Momentarily distracted, I ignored Finn and turned my attention back to Arthur. "Never mind. But let me add that there's a possibility we might not like each other. In fact, we might be enemies. That happens sometimes."

"Most unfortunate," Arthur said, "but I'll take that into account."

I observed that Arthur seemed to be making headway but was still bogged down.

"Almost done?" I asked.

"I hope so," he replied, getting frustrated.

"It'll get easier with practice, trust me. See, I don't even need all the props any more," I said showing off my grandfather's silver pocket watch.

"Can I make a request as to where we'll be going?" he asked.

I was worried this part was coming and was embarrassed to give him my answer.

"Arthur," I said, hesitating, "Unfortunately, I haven't quite gotten a handle on that yet."

I could sense his anxiety.

"John, are you saying that we are going to make a blind leap and land wherever this contraption takes us?"

"More or less," I sheepishly admitted.

"That's about as reassuring as disembarking from a hot air balloon without a parachute," Arthur said. "I'm rather disappointed, not to mention concerned at this point."

Desperately, I wanted him to feel at ease and not have a change of heart.

"Was there a particular place or era you had in mind?" I asked.

"I was hoping for ancient China," he replied with undertones of dissatisfaction.

Funny that he mentioned that. Wendell seemed drawn there, too.

"Curious, why China?" I asked.

"I've been doing a lot of research about a special object that seems to have originated from there," he replied, somewhat guarded and evasive.

"You're referring to that red book, am I correct?" I asked, putting him on the spot.

"Yes, I guess I can't hide anything from you," Arthur confessed. "You have to admit, it's been a continuous source of intrigue."

"Besides the book, I've also been drawn towards China. But I really can't guarantee we'll wind up there. Arthur, you wouldn't happen to have an item imported from China around the house you can use as an anchoring object?"

"I can't think of anything off the top of my head. Why?"

"Neither can I," I said looking around my flat. "In theory, and let me emphasize that this is strictly speculation, it would seem that if we could ground ourselves utilizing an actual object that came from China, that maybe we could have some success in landing there."

Arthur agreed that idea was logical.

"In the meantime, we'll have to make do with willfully concentrating on where we'd like to go. I'm sorry I didn't think of that earlier. We'll have to trust our luck."

Arthur finished his preparations and began to drop the mystery pellets into canisters to make steam. I settled into a comfortable chair, braced my elbow against a sturdy table and began the hypnotic pendulum-like motions with my timepiece. Then I stopped, placed it tight against the middle of my forehead and squinted to concentrate. We had to connect in order to make this remotely conducted venture successful. Not only did I have the challenge of honing my ability to slip past the tethers of the first years of the 20th century, but also I had the responsibility of

164

maintaining ethereal contact with someone who wasn't even in the same location to start with.

Arthur and I agreed to make sure we were in possession of an indisputably sourced object to secure an etheric bridge between us even if we fell short of preparing a possible link to a specific place and time. Therefore, we agreed to exchange copies of photographs, both of which had a handwritten signature with our names on them. He placed my photo in the upper front pocket of his jacket. In my case, I purchased a locket and cut out his head from a larger photo placing it inside. Thus, if we were ever in doubt of still being connected, on the physical plane we could refer back to those images and ground ourselves, if necessary.

Then we commenced our operation. Once I realized that I was no longer in my dormitory, I felt like I was slowly tumbling in a dark, endless void full of echoes of faint voices accompanied by the cadence of *chū-daiko* drums. *Boom, boom, boom*—the resonance was marked with a consistent beat. *Boom*—my chest cavity vibrated and felt the contact of a mallet as it struck the drum's taut, leathery hide. I couldn't say the same for Arthur, but we had separated, similar to what I'd experienced with Wendell when we traveled together to the future. This, I hoped, was temporary. The more I tested the waters, the more I was beginning to come up with various theories and speculations about whether or not one always transformed into a former personality during time travel, or if it were possible to appear as one's current self. In that effect, I guess both Arthur and I were about to find out.

After a short while, I felt the uneven surfaces of small pebbles under my feet, which felt heavier and more solid as the sensations gradually traveled through my ankles, into my lower legs and then up my thighs. I felt like I was slipping into a costume, but in this case, it not only consisted of my clothes, but flesh and muscles, armor and two swords at my side. For a brief second, I lost my equilibrium and tripped, falling onto the ground, but quickly pulling myself up.

"Tomoo!"

I turned around, as I knew *my* name was being called.

"Hurry, return to the courtyard! You need to clean up for inspection!"

Someone rushed by so fast that I could hardly see his face, which was covered by a large straw hat shaped like a truncated cone. All around was the hubbub of folk in an excited village. A brightly painted temple was to my right, adorned with statuary. Vendors had stalls lined up in rows outside selling everything from religious trinkets to savory *yakitori*, or grilled chicken on sticks. Colorful banners with strange writing swished about like sea foam, but in stark contrast to these festive displays, my clothes were filthy, and there was blood on my hands.

Instinctively, I headed towards the palace. It was an unmistakable fortress of the most unusual architecture—sloping, curved stone walls shaped like an accordion on its end and surrounded by a moat. A wooden bridge was lowered, and I walked across. On the other side was a puddle on the ground. What did I look like? I was eager to see my reflection. Black, thick hair pulled back, cotton pantaloons with excess folds of cloth gathered up for the ease of running. The voluminous flat and wide squared-off sleeves of my jacket were similarly bound—worn over of clothing underneath, crossed left over right, left over right—wrapped, like a folded package with small badge-like *mons* or symbols identifying me as part of a clan. Others wore the same. If I was right concerning my knowledge of history, I suspected that I landed in Japan during the 17th century.

"Finn," I called out, "is this where I'm supposed to be? Where's Arthur? Please don't tell me that everything backfired and I wound up in Japan when Arthur traveled to China, but years earlier."

I tried to sift through the confusion and get past my fear that something went terribly wrong. Strange, unheard of sounds were everywhere, including a clanging warning bell, which I failed to heed from the watchtower up above. Someone nabbed me by the elbow and pulled me out of the way in the nick of time as a gang of men in silken robes charged in on horses. They also had adornments with similar emblems such as I had, but much more ornate and stylized. My thoughts were jumbled. Was that Finn? Part of me said that it was, but it didn't look like him. Yet, my attention was split between being upset that I still did not have complete control at being able to choose my time destination, and the fact that I was about to be trampled.

"Lord Seizo was forced to retreat," one of the men said. "That's a victory for our side, but only a temporary one. We must build up our forces and plan for a counterattack if we are to seize the Yamamoto and Urakawa territories."

A man with an unnaturally high forehead, shaved to make it so, replied, "His advisors are quite crafty with their military strategy. They've been known to use unethical methods of combat."

"Can you explain?" a third man asked. His hair was a bit different and worn loose, but might've fallen into disarray during battle. He was sitting on a white horse with a black mane.

The other two lead horsemen had peculiar hair resembling paintbrushes tied in knots on the top of their heads. In comparison, I had a head full of choppy, thick black hair, tied back and resembling their horses' tails. In fact, all of us had thick, straight, black hair. I had perceived people and scenes like this before, but this time I was living and breathing it, rather than catching a fleeting glimpse as an observer. Meanwhile, I still felt ethereally light, but weight

167

accumulated, especially in my toes, feet and ankles and my hands with each passing second. The men before me looked like high-ranking officials.

"It's rumored that Seizo has hired spies from Iga," the man on the solid black horse said.

"*Shinobi ne!*" the man on the brown one exclaimed in horror. "Let Buddha protect our souls!"

"He has no scruples when it comes to seizing power," the lead man on the black stallion piped in.

"*Ah, honto*," the third man on the white horse with the black mane agreed, "we must surely take that into consideration."

Their conversation would've continued had they not spotted me on the ground trying to listen in. They were speaking in a language, which I had only seconds to comprehend, and besides, I was an assistant music professor, not an expert in ancient combat. Although I was no stranger to the odd and the unusual having made jaunts to the future, understanding all of this was testing my limits, and I still had one major question unanswered: "Where was Arthur?"

"You! Soldier! Where is Takeda-san and his honorable son now?" the lead horseman asked.

I spun on my heels looking all around, realizing after a moment he was referring to me. I guess I was a soldier.

"*Watashi* (Me)?" I asked, pointing to myself and surprised to spit a different language out of my mouth.

"*Hai!* Yes, you!" he replied, "Have you seen where our lords have gone?"

I shook my head. How else was I going to react? Was I supposed to have known them?

The lead man's horse impatiently kicked up dirt. Scared, I jumped back a few steps.

"Why is your head not shaved properly?" he asked.

"Look at his armor! It's too big for him. He must have been recruited at the last minute because our lords needed more troops," the man on the white horse said. "That's why he has a full head of hair. He's not a real samurai. He's a sentry—a simple guard!"

"Young man, you're useless!" the lead man shouted, then coughed and spit on the ground right beside me. He signaled to his partners to follow and rode off.

"Finn," I called out, "Where's Arthur?"

Finn was nowhere to be seen, although that didn't mean he wasn't around. There was also the possibility I had seen him, but hadn't recognized him. If he had shown up in his familiar guise, and had I truly been the person I was supposed to be back then, I would've thought him to be as strange as a man from the moon wearing a three-piece suit and a bowler hat. Regardless, it meant that I was supposed to figure a few things out on my own. I continued walking through a large wooden gateway into an inner courtyard. Some people were dressed like me, which I was beginning to suspect was in some sort of soldier's uniform, and others were bedecked in finery. My attire was simpler and more utilitarian in contrast.

Another young man, who was clothed similar to me, took ahold of my sleeve.

"Ashikaga-san, look at you! Clean up that blood and change your clothes. Your sword will rust! Don't waste any more time! Our masters plan an inspection. Besides, that armor isn't yours. You'll get in trouble if you keep it."

Before I could get further explanations, he sped off. I was getting concerned as I had yet to find Arthur. Once more, I followed my inner voice to simple quarters, which I suspected to be my flat. It

169

had a peculiar entrance made of a lightweight wood and rice paper sliding door, but first I removed my shoes, crude straw sandals to be exact, and left them outside before entering.

The soft, cushioned floor consisted of panels of woven straw mats. I removed my sword from a carefully wrapped belt by my hips. Next, I unfastened what I suspected was a type of protective armor although it was nothing like anything I had seen before. Then I began to remove several layers of robes down to funny underwear that seemed to be made from one long strip of carefully wrapped cloth. I poured a pitcher of water into a basin, took a towel, and began to wipe off the dirt and blood. Dried blades of grass had to be picked out from my hair, which I combed back into place. This routine seemed so familiar, yet completely foreign at the same time. I looked in a mirror. Strangely enough, I had some features in common when I had previously traveled in time back to China—the black hair, the shape of my eyes, the tone of my skin, but in comparison there were other characteristics that were distinctly different such as the shape of my nose and thicker eyebrows. I also wore contrasting attire.

Next it was time to clean my sword from battle, removing the blood so its steel wouldn't rust. My sword was my soul, a metaphor of purification and unconquerable will. Afterwards, I went to the temple and gave my offerings. Lord Seizo, one of our master's fiercest rivals, had fifty of our soldiers killed. Six of them were my friends. Life was so transient.

At sunset, the other foot soldiers, or *samurai*, were celebrating our minor victory. My friend, Kentaro, invited me to join them. He was born in the samurai class and enjoyed the privileges of a higher-ranking soldier. In most cases I'd be excluded from such festivities because I was from a lower class of warrior, but he was my friend and wanted company. As his guest I was allowed to participate. Warm clear liquor, called *saké*, was being passed around in an earthenware jar. Doll-like women served us hot rice balls and slivers of fish. They scurried in and out, disappearing unless called. Celebrations were well underway, but soon to be interrupted.

Our masters' personal bodyguards stormed in first followed by a small team of servants. Then came the dreaded duo, the *daimyo*, Lord Toshiro Takeda, and his vicious, gargantuan son, Masahiro, a giant compared to the rest of us, which made him that much more feared around the castle. His features looked strangely familiar—a moustache, sleepy eyes, large boned and muscular. Deep inside my soul, I recognized him as Arthur.

Lord Takeda was untouchable. He governed our locale and was a vassal to the Shogun, or supreme military ruler of Japan. He was also my employer, and I had sworn my life over to him in service and protection. When he entered the courtyard, we all bowed, and licked the gravel with our tongues if we had to. He gallantly went over and helped himself to our *saké*, then spilled the rest of the jar on the ground.

"He could've been more careful," Kentaro said.

"Shush! He'll hear you," I whispered.

"He has no respect for any of us, Tomoo, and his manners leave much to be desired," my comrade replied.

"Shut up!" I warned him. "He's been known to cut a man's head off and put it on a spike so the whole town can see just to prove a point. He's ruthless. Don't test his patience."

"He will also bury a man up to his head and invite the local farmers to stone him to death," the soldier behind us added.

Filled with saké, Lord Takeda paraded around our eating area and began clearing our plates with the swish of his sword, sending them tumbling to the ground. Dishes broke wherever they fell.

"His enemies all want him dead. There are those within his own court who have the same sentiments," Kentaro complained.

Lord Takeda stepped over the broken plates and stumbled off to chase after whores. His son, Masahiro, remained behind and inspected the aftermath.

"What are you waiting for?" he commanded to the soldier sitting on my left, "Clean it up!"

"*Hai! Sugu desu!* (Yes, right away!)" He replied, bowing once again. Then he sprinted off to find a broom.

Somewhat sympathetic to our plight, Masahiro ordered one of his assistants to fetch us another jug of saké to replace the one his father had destroyed.

"If I had been born the *daimyo's* son," I said under my breath, "at least I'd get some privileges and respect."

Masahiro-san was the only man immune from the wrath of his father. Servants waited on him hand and foot.

"At least he is kinder," I said to my friend, still keeping my voice low.

"Don't be so sure of that," Kentaro replied, "Blood runs deep in that family."

"His father kicks dirt in our faces during inspections and yells loudly in our ears so we're annoyed. He has his pick of the courtesans, and assumes he has his choice of local village women, even if they are already taken as wives. No one escapes his evil eye," I explained while comparing the two.

My friend poked me in the ribs while Masahiro's back was turned indicating that I better be quiet.

"If someone deposes Lord Takeda, his son will take over. Things will be better," I said.

Kentaro-san slapped me on the shoulder. "You're a fool. Keep those comments to yourself."

Meanwhile, my thoughts strangled me. I hated the father. I was envious of his son. I went out of my way, giving the two of them special favors with no reward, such as a higher rank or salary. The *daimyo* the most despicable man who walked the face of the earth.

* * *

I had witnessed enough and consciously willed myself out of the courtyard by rubbing my thumb and forefinger on my locket. I felt a brief rush of wind, as if I was being swept off my feet, but quickly regained balance and resumed my grounding in the present century. Thank God, that wise action brought Arthur back with me. When we returned to our old selves, I began brushing off my shirtsleeves as if trying to remove centuries of filth I had picked up from an old antique shop. Right away Arthur noticed my scowl.

"I didn't expect that we wouldn't like each other," I said. I was reluctant to be up front and felt guilty.

"Didn't you warn me to that effect?" Arthur asked.

"Warning about it and actually experiencing it is another thing altogether. That's the first time it's happened."

"I'm sure it will be better next time," Arthur said trying to uplift my spirits. "Besides, I think I simply fell asleep. There's no proof that we traveled back in time."

"Sometimes there is," I said cutting in. "It's rather unpredictable, but often I bring back evidence like coins, pieces of clothing, twigs, or odd little things that seem inconsequential but in fact, confirm that I traveled to either the past or the future."

Wendell brought back spiders once. I didn't want to mention that.

"You've also gone to the future?" Arthur asked.

173

"I have, but I wouldn't recommend it. There are too many contingencies, and it's very complicated. It's much better to investigate situations that have already happened. I don't think we can change anything, but we certainly can learn from our mistakes."

Arthur was skeptical, but reacted with a calm assessment. "It's unfortunate that we wound up with such enmity, even if this was merely an elaborate dream that both of us managed to share. Think of this as a first-time trial and error. Edison made many attempts before inventing his famous light bulb."

Something felt odd in my pants pocket. I reached inside and pulled out pieces of gravel, evidence that I brought something back from another time and place.

"John, it's over and done with—long gone in the past. On our next attempt we'll aim for China and prepare properly beforehand. Besides, how could it possibly ruin our friendship now?"

* * *

Side Show

Germany, 1905: A carnival came to town. Posters advertised for a few local laborers, and I figured I could get my hands dirty just once to put a little change in my pocket. The atmosphere was filled with barker's cries, the sound of steam-powered calliopes, the tantalizing aromas of sweet treats and other culinary delights flooding the senses at a dizzying pace. There were exotic lions and tigers—animals from all corners of the earth. Besides, Arthur was always talking about Houdini, and his performance was the feature attraction.

While sweeping the fair grounds, I became party to the most unusual, yet propitious series of events. One of the most beautiful women I had ever seen chaperoned a group of children toward the side attractions. Her beauty had me spellbound while her children were mesmerized by one of the stage magicians performing a card trick. Despite my better judgment, I was so enchanted by the moment, that I followed her.

The children were getting out of hand chasing after every distraction. This must've opened the window of opportunity for petty thieves to maneuver into position with well-rehearsed choreography. These hooligans homed in on this earth-bound angel, waiting to strike, but my aim was to thwart their plans. With impeccable timing, my right hand slowly shifted and eased up the shaft of my broom into a weapons-ready position. I felt strength and inert power emanating through my arm transforming me into a ready and willing warrior. The leader of the gang began to make his move, and I stepped in to make mine.

Instinctively, I held my broom at a right angle, shielding my face as I lifted it up, circled it over my head and then blocked his incoming club, which he aimed right at me. The impact of the two weapons striking together dissipated the force of his blow, and I was able to snatch his club with my left hand. Then I performed an underhanded rotation of my broom, striking the ruffian on the bony part of his temple with its shaft and then quickly jabbed him with a thrust of the bristles straight in his eyes causing him to fall to the ground.

The rest of his clan, realizing that I was a force to be reckoned with, abandoned their comrade and took off in all directions. As he scrambled to his feet, I confiscated his club and held it over his head in one last retaliating threat. Terrified, he dropped her purse and took flight. The coins fell out, and the children laughed and ran after them. I bent down, returned her purse, and then I straightened my suspenders and hat.

"How did you do that?" she cried almost fainting in my arms from all the excitement as her brood huddled around my knees.

"I have absolutely no idea, but it was brilliant and served its purpose, I guess."

For a brief moment, my thoughts ran away from me, replaced by visions of flying swords and silk, the clink of clashing steel and war cries in a language I had never known.

The lady choked back tears, "Are you sure you aren't adept at fencing, but just modest? Your skill could've rivaled that of my husband's, and he trains with a master instructor on a regular basis." I shook my head.

Her purse only had a coin or two remaining. "I'd love to give you something for your brave effort, but..."

"That was the least I could do given the circumstances. I cannot accept anything," I interjected.

"A proper hero must be rewarded for..." Before she was able to say another word she slipped in a soft spot of mud, soiling her pristine dress.

"Are you all right?" I asked helping her up to her feet and getting even dirtier in the process.

"Quite all right, just embarrassed. I'd consider going home, but the children would be heartbroken." She examined her muddied frock with dismay.

"Perhaps if I escort you to your seats, I could position myself to hide it. That could work, although I don't think that's appropriate conduct," I offered cordially.

"I admire your chivalry, not quite what I would expect from an ordinary stagehand."

"Ma'am, this is not my usual occupation. I'm an assistant professor at the Conservatory of Music in Stuttgart working on an advanced degree and also training to be a concert pianist," I admitted, bashfully.

She saw the finely crafted chain from my grandfather's pocket watch dangling from my waistcoat pocket, betraying the fact that I was not a common laborer.

"Appearances can be deceiving," she said as she readjusted her hat and tried to tidy up. "It's a coincidence we met. I've been trying to find a qualified piano teacher. Would you be available to come by the house in your spare time for instruction? I will pay you handsomely."

"That would be agreeable," I replied, trying to hold back my excitement.

Agreeable? That would be exactly what I needed to help finance my studies. I was fortunate she was able to see the gentleman behind my filthy appearance. I was not properly dressed, and probably had a smear of dirt running down my face.

"How can I contact you?" she asked, as I was beginning to leave.

I pulled one of my calling cards out of my pocket and handed her one. It had an address, but since I did not have a private phone, I listed the Conservatory's number on it instead. She tore a shred of paper off her program guide to write me a note as to how I could contact her, but neither of us had a writing instrument.

"Thank you, again for your kindness." She looked at my card. "I'll contact you for certain. I promise."

I looked at my watch knowing I had to return to my duties, so I bade her goodbye. Three days later a telegram arrived.

*   *   *

Professor Scott,

It is my sincerest thanks once again to commend you for your gentlemanly act of bravado at the carnival last weekend. Since I mentioned that I've been seeking a music instructor for the household, I'd like to propose the following offer. Our family owns a comfortable estate in the Bavarian countryside, not far from Munich. My ancestry is German and my husband's is French, so I've insisted that we reside there since I miss my homeland.

We take pride to entertain our guests sparing no expense and would be more than pleased to provide you with our finest hospitality if you agreed to spend weekends with us there. Naturally, we would cover all your travel costs from the Conservatory. In return, we'd like beginner's music lessons for my three children, aged seven, five, and three. I am not expecting much for the three year old except mere entertainment and humor.

I also desire lessons and have had considerable instruction already. Therefore, my lessons would be way more advanced, but I'm more than confident you could handle that. If my husband, Francois, were willing, I'd request you oblige him, but I doubt if he'd take you up on that offer. If we have out of town guests or relatives, we might make special requests of your talents, whether it's for private instruction or entertaining at an evening party. Otherwise, we have delightful gardens, and you will have a lot of time on your own. I think you'll find this offer quite suitable. In turn, my husband will generously help finance your education. Please inform us of your decision as soon as possible, as we would love to see you this weekend.

> Sincerely,
> Sophia Poincare

*   *   *

The Sherlock Holmes Suite

Early summer 1905: It had been a trying week at the Conservatory. Much of it was spent grading exams and fretting over my own, since I was both a professor-in-training and a music student at the same time. But the arrival of a first-class train ticket in the mail was an auspicious omen, and I kept clutching my invitation like a love note. When I looked up the Poincare family name I was surprised that my ladyship and benefactress omitted her aristocratic title. Perhaps she wanted to spare me the shock. Their estate was an hour and a half outside of Munich. I tried to relax during the long ride, but couldn't.

Throughout my stay in Germany, I'd faithfully conduct my *midnight conversations* with Arthur Conan Doyle. This was our secret code name for our clairvoyant and telepathic sessions that we performed *per diem* for several years. Following up with the postal service was always recommended, so to pass the time I composed a long overdue letter.

Dear Arthur,

I'm writing you as I'm gleefully passing the time riding the train from the Conservatory to the Bavarian countryside. Since it's been impossible to dismiss the fact that I've been ghostwriting all of those Sherlock Holmes stories for the past few years, I've been inspired to take those thoughts one-step further. I was bursting with ideas about a composition called the *Sherlock Holmes Suite* where I could actually translate the adventures of the great detective into music. A clarinet would signify Sherlock, accompanied by an oboe, and a French horn would represent Watson. The string section would represent Lestrade and the others at Scotland Yard will be bassoons with tubas. The criminal under the suspicion would be portrayed by the piano, created especially so I could play it. A flute would play the nervous wife of the victim, and the victim would be a base and cello with a second piano accompaniment, but also booming percussion. Snare drums would represent a shifty suspect. What do you think? After all, others have taken *dramatis personae* and created musical scores. If you're still writing for the stage with J. M. Barrie this can be a fresh concept.

Unfortunately in the realm of courtship, I've failed to make significant strides. It's not like I haven't put forth a sincere effort, but luck does not like to bless me with suitable or available prospects. This past winter, I had met a young woman named Lenora. Mutual friends introduced us after she performed at a recital since I've always had a soft spot in my heart for a well-trained soprano. In turn, she was equally smitten by my musical acumen. We had a brief long-distance courtship, although I knew it would never end in marriage.

She kept her affairs secretive at first, only telling me that she worked as a nurse and was not a professional songstress. I was willing to accept that, as she was utterly charming, but after a few engagements I discovered that this mysterious hospital where she worked was a place of nightmares—Berlin's Hertzberger Insane Asylum! That discovery marked the beginning of the end. She'd never be accepting of my preternatural exploits, which were unconventional to say the least, and probably less accommodating to my ventures in time travel. On the other hand, Lenora had a compassion, which I could've never possessed for those much less fortunate than either of us. I'm confident she'll find a more compatible suitor who also lives a lot closer.

By the way, I have to thank the great Harry Houdini for introducing me to the Poincares. Mind you, I never had the chance to meet him in person, but I did sneak into his dressing room. He was performing with a traveling show. I needed extra cash and applied to work as a grounds man. Yours truly saved a damsel in distress and the rest is history. I'll keep you apprised as to how my first weekend teaching piano works out.

Please confirm receipt of the last Sherlock manuscript. I'd like to assume that it was a mere oversight and that nothing had been lost in the mail, instead.

Yours most devoted,
John Patrick Scott

*   *   *

I don't know what possessed me to tell my driver to let me off at the gate marking the beginning of the drive. Perhaps it was because the weather couldn't have been more suitable, and a healthy, brisk walk to the house would've been the perfect compliment after a long train ride. But the uphill steps and footpaths leading to the main house tediously crawled through the estate grounds, so I was already winded before the day began. My host had created a majestic sprawling mountainside retreat by engineering a plateau large enough to accommodate his three-story abode with its adjoining wings and gardens along with nearby quarters for his working staff. Further downhill was dotted with additional cottages that I also suspected housed his employees. Beyond that was the nearest hamlet, far more typical of other Bavarian towns, with its art gallery of illustrated houses nestled in the valley near the train station. With a tatty suitcase in my hand, I was a dwarf next to the imposing entryway doors of artfully crafted bronze with bas-reliefs of classical hunting scenes. I rang the bell and the butler escorted me straightaway to my room, where I could drop off my bags.

My hosts were out and had been delayed, but he offered to have one of the other servants give me a grand tour of the house and grounds if I was so inclined. After a splash of water to the face, I accepted his proposal.

"When Monsieur Poincare designed his palace he requested photos from all over Europe and was inspired by only the finest landscape art," my escort said.

A sizeable number of grounds keepers were busy at work trimming serpentine hedges and conical bushes defying natural forms.

"By the way, never use the word *imitate* around either one of them, especially our lordship. In fact, he'll insist that his taste is eclectic, combining various artistic styles. If giving him your praiseworthy opinion, I'd suggest saying something to the effect that it rivals the taste of the royal family, which at the moment seems predisposed to a gaudy overuse of gold leaf and Italian Rococo. Both the lord and the lady like to think they are completely original and always one-step above the upper crust, especially the Hohenzollerns. They'd like to think it's nonpareil with the Sanssoucci Palace in Potsdam."

I nodded, even if only pretending that I understood and continued to follow him out back.

"Here is the rose garden where our hosts enjoy their tea with guests. You must take the pleasure of smelling their fragrance. These roses were imported for that very reason," he explained as I trotted to keep the pace.

Cozy, poetic hideaways branched off where one could disappear to read a book, reflect upon one's thoughts or sneak off to engage in a lover's tryst with no lack of privacy. Beyond the well-manicured gardens the arrangement of foliage became denser and tumbled out into virgin forest. As we headed back to the house, my guide asked me if I desired refreshment. I was left alone in the rose garden for a few moments after being served lemonade touched with the essence of rosewater along with an assortment of biscuits. A circle of red rose petals had been artfully placed around the perimeter of the sterling silver serving tray. I picked one up and sniffed, becoming so invigorated that I got a second wind.

In short, the Poincare estate was an unrestrained picturesque feast for the senses. However, with the exception of a handful of requisite ancestral portraits and a painting in his drawing room where Francois was depicted as Zeus, his wife, Sophia as Hera, and his three children as Cupids, the one odd thing I noticed was that there was a noteworthy lack of women featured in his art collection. Otherwise, the Poincares had acquired an impressive and enviable assortment of 18th century clocks, Chinoiserie, Neoclassical sculpture in both bronze and marble, Art Nouveau Bohemian glassware and curiously enough, fossils and artifacts from archeological excavations.

Besides Milady's personal attendant and the kitchen help, the Poincare household staff also seemed predominantly male. Servants' quarters were scattered throughout the grounds along with other utilitarian buildings. We skipped a tour of the stables since I had finally run out of steam. But the crown jewel of my tour was when we returned to the main house and I was introduced to *Pierre Pierrot*, their amazing grand pianoforte.

"Pierre?" I asked the butler, "and why Pierrot, a reference to a mime, of which one associates with silence? I'd venture to say that music is nothing but the opposite."

"Yes, my master is a man of many contradictions. However, he believes that his pianoforte has a soul like a living, breathing human being. Out of reverence and respect he gave this instrument a name after his late father, so I'm told," he said while pointing to a portrait on the room's far wall. "Now he feels that the lingering spirit of his father can only speak through song, but that's one of many rumors mulling about. This house is full of secrets."

182

"Do you mind if I test it out?" I asked. "After all, I am the piano instructor. I'd like to retrieve some sheet music from my room first, however. Excuse me a moment."

The Poincare house was a fraction of the size of lavish residences such as Schloss Ludwigsburg, not far from Stuttgart, but it was still larger than anything I'd been used to. I immediately lost my sense of direction. The butler insisted on accompanying me over to the proper staircase explaining it was commonplace for all first-time visitors to get confused. After finding my room, I rummaged through my suitcase for some blank sheet music then headed back downstairs where the butler led me back to the drawing room.

"Secrets?" I thought to myself, "This house is full of secrets and so am I."

Keeping in mind the butler's ear-tingling comment, I approached *Pierre Pierrot*, the grand pianoforte with caution. This one-of-a-kind extraordinary masterpiece, adorned with meticulously hand-painted pastoral scenes on both its interior and exterior white cabinetry, was enough to render one speechless.

"Good afternoon to you, Monsieur *Pierrot*," I whispered softly as I bowed to the pianoforte that was rumored to be more than met the eye. "I beg your permission to play you. I'm considered quite good, you know."

I sat down making myself comfortable on the piano bench and said with a compliment, "I seriously hope we'll become good friends, sir, as I've been summoned all the way from Stuttgart to give your owners lessons. They desire to unlock your secrets, and so do I."

Heaven only knows what impelled me towards that uncharacteristic behavior, but I continued with my *let's pretend* conversation. I'm sure I looked as silly to others as when I'd also converse with Finn, but despite my well-trained sixth sense I was unable to fully acquaint myself with the so-called spirit lying within. There was no doubt, however, that it was a visual work of art. I was in absolute heaven allowing my fingers to dance upon *Pierre*, as this

183

excellent instrument was one much finer than anything I had ever played. Thus I lost track of time and got carried away, caught up in the miraculous magic of what music could do to the mind, body and soul. But the spell of the moment was broken the moment the heavy front doors to the mansion opened.

Hard, echoing sounds of riding boots marched onto the marble floors. In came a tall and gallant gentleman, about six foot one, wearing a showy, Neo-Napoleonic-style military uniform jacket in bright red with gold braid trim and white gloves, which he took off in a ritualized manner and handed off to one of his attendants. His lordship had a regal bearing with posture so erect that it was unnatural. Prominently featured, his large distinguished moustache was waxed and curled upwards on the ends. He was beardless; showing off chiseled features—a strong masculine jawline with a slight cleft chin. Otherwise he had medium-to-dark brown hair precisely coifed, pomaded and parted down the center, manicured brows and keen eyes the color of strong tea.

With a military gait one step shy of a goose step, the lord of the house advanced towards me. First he looked me up and down as if performing a peculiar inspection, and then he extended his hand to shake mine.

"Welcome to *Schloss Poincare*, Professor Scott," he said indicating that his stately home was his palace.

"Your lordship, it's my pleasure."

"Please, skip the formalities. Call me Francois. Have you found the accommodations to your liking?"

"They're quite suitable," I replied, trying to be as understated as possible. *Odd they're dispensing with formalities. Francois?*

"Fantastic! And *Pierre*? I'm assuming the piano's in tune?"

"I've had the pleasure of playing it for the last hour or so."

"Splendid! And your trip, was it comfortable?"

"Sir...your lordship...you didn't have to put me in first class."

"Ah, ah, ah..." he said shaking his finger and scolding me like a child. "Baron? Duke? I detest titles and told you to call me Francois. No 'Sirs' or any other other salutations from you. For heaven's sake, you're also an important fellow. You're the revered piano professor."

"Very well, then...Francois."

"So, how does the Scotsman fare at a round of golf?"

I began to blush. "Not very well, I'm afraid."

He stepped closer and put his arm around my shoulder as if he wanted to say something so his staff couldn't overhear. "Professor...do you hunt?"

"Hunt?"

"Shoot game—birds, deer? Ever try falconry?"

"Heavens no," I replied.

"I guess you're not the sporting type?"

"I'm not exactly sure what that would that have to do with piano instruction."

"It doesn't," he said as he leaned over and whispered in my ear. "But I'll be sure to teach you. By now, I suspect you've noticed the frescoes painted on the walls and ceilings throughout the house with hunting scenes to cater to my passions."

With that he gave my shoulder a firm manly squeeze. Then he snapped his fingers and shouted out to one of his attendants, "Wolfgang, run me a bath!"

The he turned back to me, and what he said next was utterly startling.

"Professor, why don't you join me?"

"I beg your pardon?"

He shook his head and laughed, "It's not what you think. Please, come upstairs while I prepare. The rest, I assure you, will be private."

I breathed a sigh of relief and followed him upstairs to his room. He excused himself, slipped behind an Oriental screen and returned wearing an embroidered silk robe that was beyond the

185

conventions of men's apparel. With a few too many frills and flowers, I would've sworn it had been stolen from his wife. When he stopped to comb his moustache in a mirror nearby my eyes glared with disapproval. His robe fell open a tad too much and was indiscreetly tied right above his navel. Assessing my discomfort, Francois wrapped it around his waist a bit tighter. Then he dipped his toes into an elaborate Rococo-style marble bathtub with a spout that looked like a drunken Cupid regurgitating. He said that he would've had the statuette piss into the bathtub, but he didn't want such ideas to suggest things to the children.

"Professor Scott, I hope you brought proper dinner attire?"

My heart sank. I wasn't used to dining amongst nobility. All I had brought were two three-piece wool suits more apropos for teaching duties.

"Formal attire?" I asked.

He nodded. "No worry, my valet will get your measurements. I'll make sure you have the right clothing for next weekend. Besides, we weren't expecting any dinner guests outside of the immediate family. There's no need to be embarrassed."

"But, sir...Francois, I mean...I own tails for performances. I apologize, but it was a complete oversight."

"There's no need to drag extra clothes along for the weekend," he interjected. "Since you're going to be a regular visitor, you might as well leave a set of clothes or two here in your room and make yourself at home. Consider yourself a new addition to the Poincare family."

"You're way too kind," I replied fanning the sweat off my neck with my sheet music.

Then he departed for his chambers. It took a moment to catch my breath, as my heart was beating rapidly. When was Madame Sophia going to arrive? I was becoming nervous in the presence of her husband.

Thus, I gathered my pen and ink and the rest of my composition and headed off to my room. A refreshing nap would be in store, if my patrons expected me to entertain them after dinner. What was I thinking? I had formal attire back at the dormitory, but order a suit for me? Perhaps I didn't deserve such a blessing, but giving music lessons to the Poincare family would be my financial salvation.

*   *   *

Storming the Bastille

Early summer, 1905: My commuter train had been delayed in Munich. When I arrived in Bavaria several hours late, not thrilled at having to explain myself, I barely had time to catch my breath before the drama began to unfold.

"Tonight we are hosting a special party, and Franz, my valet, has your costume," Monsieur Poincare said. "I expect that you'll do a splendid job, as usual, entertaining."

"No one informed me about costumes. Dinner attire won't do?" I asked. My hosts had gone to great lengths to have several custom-made suits on hand, but costumes?

"My tailor already had your measurements when I ordered your formal wear. Sophia's attendant will help you with your wig, as I don't expect you to figure that out," he said before he was called away.

Fresh flowers made the entire mansion smell like their incredible rose garden. For once, I stepped into someone else's time machine, because the entire Poincare household from the décor down the servants' outfits looked like an opera production set in Vienna around 1780 or from the Palace of Versailles. Even *Pierre Pierrot*, their grand pianoforte, was adorned with an appropriate candelabra and ornamentation. Despite my protests, Francois said that I was no exception and had to play along with the fanfare. Since the Poincares knew that I was also an accomplished amateur photographer, they expected me to take the family portraits. I was not thrilled with the prospect of dragging their heavy camera, with its equally cumbersome tripod and emulsion-coated glass plates, around their gardens while dressed, as Mozart.

A caravan of limousines and carriages arrived with guests all the way from France with everyone already dressed for the occasion. Even the children wore powdered wigs looking like porcelain doll figurines from Dresden. My velvet coat of deep sky blue and ivory, trimmed with heavy braid, was stiff, awkward and uncomfortable. Matching it was a detestable lacey shirt with ruffles. I kept reminding myself to grin and bear it. Perhaps after enough whisky, I'd be jolly enough to fit right in and enjoy the merriment.

Amidst the chaos, I managed to sneak off to my master's two-story private library, known as his *grande bibliothèque*, which was large enough to double as a ballroom. For such a world traveler and consummate collector, I couldn't believe that my master could keep accounts of all the titles on the shelves. Thus I felt at liberty to *borrow* one or two books on occasion. There were books about explorers, archeology, chemistry, and others written in ancient tongues no longer spoken.

The only access to its upper floor was by a system of sliding ladders, precarious at best, but designed on purpose to keep children and the faint-of-heart away. I cursed the terrible costume dress shoes they designed for my fat, flat feet, as they were inappropriate and unsuitable for climbing. My other alternative was to kick them off and climb up the ladders in my despicable baby blue stockings, which were also slippery.

This time I brought my infamous spell book; the same one, which had once accidentally fallen into my old friend Whit's hands with disastrous, results. I always wondered where my master's family had accumulated all their material wealth. Although it was possible that it could've been strictly from provenance of birth, I suspected otherwise. Maybe he knew the real secret of alchemy and of turning lead into gold.

What I was convinced of, however, was that anyone who possessed such a magnificent library must also have a few hidden portals. Books provided the most readily accessible forms of portals to the other library—the Secret Library, the one only available to those who had passed a certain level of spiritual achievement. That privilege was actually open to anyone, but to be more specific, that meant anyone who dared to open the vaults of memories to their past in order to realign themselves with their true destiny, for those brave souls who dared to commence the hero's quest or their own personal odyssey. But without getting into a lengthy discourse since I've already gone into detail about this in earlier diaries, the Secret Library, although not synonymous with time travel, contained information from the beginning of time, which I can only say must've been an extraordinarily long time. Within this exalted realm were records of every event and every person throughout history. The most interesting accounts were those that had been unwritten, lost or destroyed on purpose.

One of the basic tenets of physics applied to the Secret Library. In the sense that matter could never be destroyed, neither could the documentation of such historical records. When an event happened, an account of it existed somewhere. If a mere thought had been initiated, there was a record of that, as well. The Secret Library could be described as *God's Grand Diary*. Whether it was perceived in an anthropomorphic context or not, it was rather daunting that nothing escaped a *universal all-seeing eye* or *camera* that captured all cogitations, actions and events connected to humankind. If information wasn't readily available on the physical level, there was always a record of it somewhere hidden on the astral plane where a select group of qualified and closely observed individuals could retrieve it.

To access this special place one needed a guide or docent, but someone equivalent to Finn who'd most likely monitor activities and make sure his or her intentions were noble. Often a magician such as myself was only permitted limited access. Obstacles and traps were set up to prevent seekers from inappropriately prying into others' affairs. That was a perpetually frustrating restriction, as far as I was concerned, because often that prevented me from finding out the full story on people who were directly affecting my life. However, as I was saying before, one of the easiest ways to gain access to such an incredible repository was by discovering a psychical entryway inside of a book. Thus, I was eager to discover not only a portal in Francois's *grande* library, but also have the opportunity to transcribe notes from some of these amazing texts. After taking my pick, I smuggled a few of his rare tomes on a temporary loan and snuck off to my room. In the midst of making copious notes, a soft, barely audible knock sounded on my door. Surprised, I looked up and shoved the contraband into my lap. The lady of the manor made an unexpected appearance. Her painted face was paler than a ghost and whiter than snow.

"Professor Scott, my husband requests your presence. He's engaged in an argument with a group of gentleman. It's beyond my comprehension but it's about Mozart versus Haydn. Would you please oblige them?"

She curiously looked at my hand-made journal, the ink, my pen; a few mechanical drawing aids lay out on my desk. "May I ask what you're doing?"

"In my spare time, I've been ghostwriting for a friend," I said. There were secrets I wished to remain hidden.

"Ghostwriting? Perhaps you should write about the ghosts in these walls. Many a night I've had to console a distraught child."

"This manor is haunted? Should I be concerned?"

"I'm sure you've sensed that portrait on the wall staring at you in the drawing room. There's a reason why my husband named our pianoforte after his father, but that shouldn't dissuade you from playing it," she explained in a nervous tone.

She turned to go. "One last thing. Professor Scott, your wig is crooked."

She closed my door, leaving as quietly as she came. Summarily, I removed my hand, which hid the title of my spell book from view, *The Spell Book of Charms and Incantations*, by J.P. Scott. That book had caused trouble once, and I swore that it would never happen again. I'd have to make it a policy that no one was to enter my room without knocking. Ghosts in pianos? A haunted mansion? Portals in a library? The Poincare estate was full of mysteries, but there was a lot on my plate and a busy agenda ahead. I checked the time on my grandfather's old silver timepiece, the one that was miraculously spared from a recent robbery. Then I put it back in my pocket, straightened my ridiculous coiffure and headed downstairs.

*　　*　　*

Cheshire's Smile

With money in my pocket I retraced my footsteps back to the old watch craftsman's shop in the heart of Stuttgart to see if he still had that incredible gold timepiece. It had been a while, but if that one wasn't available he might have something comparable. Normally my sense of direction was keen. All I would have to do is close my eyes, and my personal North Star would navigate me to my intended destination, but today's journey proved to be an exception.

At least three times I circled the block where I knew it had to be, but when I arrived at the same spot every time, it simply wasn't there. In fact, it wasn't as if another business moved in and had taken over its place. The problem was that the address never existed! Before I gave up the search, I approached a few of the local shopkeepers to see if they remembered or had ever heard of that watchmaker, but none were able to offer assistance. Finally, my hunger took over, and my new quest was to search for supper.

When I entered a nearby cheese shop, it was like Aladdin's cave of cheese. The air was rich with smells ranging from mild to pungent. The proprietor was busy with several ladies ahead of me. So I browsed up and down the aisles, softly speaking to my stomach that it had to be patient. Creamy amberts from France were laced with blue veins. Anthotyro or *flower cheese* had its herbal aroma. There was soft and runny Bath cheese, mentioned by Admiral Lord Nelson in his diaries. However, one particular wheel of Swiss caught my attention. I made my way to the barrel where it made its home,

191

where my sight affixed on the intricate details of its interlacing holes and crevices.

Then, as my imagination stretched way out of proportion, I was less than a half-inch tall crawling through its hidden recesses. I speculated about dragons, snakes, illusionary creatures hiding and living in secret grottoes within this hunk of cheese, or better yet—pirate treasure—as my thoughts ran away on a tangent. But something else was out of place besides suddenly becoming the size of a Lilliputian. I couldn't believe my eyes when I saw a book sticking out of a wall of aging milk curds. I plucked it out. It smelled quite strange, but could I have expected otherwise? Instantly, I flipped it open to the first page written in the King's English.

"Let me tell you the tale of a meek and shy lad, but one who possessed amazing powers in his dreams."

But the odd thing was that when I turned to the next page and then to the one after that the rest of the book was blank. Its title was *Shokunin, The Thief of Tales*. So far this odd red book had turned up several times. The first time was when I was inadvertently initiated into a Masonic order on a train. Professor Mockingbird had given a copy to me on that fateful ride to boarding school, and somehow it turned up once again when I had seen it with a Chinese scribe in a dream. But in that case, he created a scroll, which I suspect eventually got cut up into pages and bound. Regardless of that theory, this book was haunting me!

Could this piece of pockmarked cheese also be an entryway to the Secret Library? I needed to find a reliable portal since I was no longer within walking distance to Ding's bookstore in Edinburgh. Could this have been the new alternative? No, it was more likely that I was suffering from brain fever, one of those romanticized maladies that Arthur had talked about when he had discussed the art of writing. I'd be mad to think there would be a child's book of fairy tales inside a slice of cheese. How absurd!

"Can I help you?" the cheese monger asked.

But I didn't quite catch what he said, because I was still lost in my thoughts. With the aid of another portal, I could find out what was really going on with Arthur, Houdini, Wendell or whomever. Access to the Secret Library? It would allow me to procure anything I needed to know instead of feeling like I was so isolated and in another country. Of course Arthur and I had our tête à têtes, but what I could gather astrally during those sessions was on a need-to-know basis. And this peculiar book? God knows for what reason, but Arthur was obsessed with it, and I left my copy back in the University of Edinburgh library. If I got my hands on another one perhaps I could finally figure out what was so special about it. Thoughts churned like butter.

"Sir, did you want to buy that?" the cheese seller asked, once again.

I snapped out of my trance, still holding that generous hunk of seasoned and aged milk curds, which I finally passed over to him.

"Wrap it up for supper," I told him. "It would go well with a fine, full-bodied bottle of wine."

*   *   *

The Dance of the Seven Veils
Dresden, Germany, December 9, 1905:

It was opening night for the world's debut of *Salome*, an operatic adaptation by Richard Strauss from the stage play by Oscar Wilde. Giovanni Serrano, one of the other foreign students from the Conservatory, insisted that we travel there to witness that monumental event at the Court Opera House. Celebrations were held afterward from upper crust private clubs to *ratskeller* pubs depending upon one's social status.

Instead of one of those classier establishments converted from the basement of an old Romanesque church, our pub had rotted, uneven floorboards and looked like an old escape route from a medieval prison. Steep stone steps below the street's surface led down to its entryway. Familiar faces from previous musical competitions filled the festive atmosphere, but the air weighed heavy with apprehensions and suspicions of enemies lurking amongst our peers. In such circumstances, a wise gentleman would be on his guard and restrain his tongue, especially when beer and bacchanalia were involved. Unfortunately, I lacked such discipline.

"This was one of the most boring operas," I said while yawning. "I would've fallen asleep if I hadn't seen the play and knew what to expect. The only action came at the ending."

I took a swig of beer, dribbling it all over my chin. "This interpretation of *Salome* sounded too Wagnerian."

I could hear, not far away, another group of concertgoers were having a similar argument.

"But, consider the subject matter. This is no *Die Fledermaus* with light-hearted waltzes. That's what I want to think of when I hear Strauss," said Otto Wolf, a tall, thin university-age student—*aced the Bremen competitions last year. Humiliated our entire music department.*

"Usually, there tends to be more gaiety in Strauss's music, but it's based on a biblical story. You can't change the ending," Dieter Becker added. *Superb player—Enviable finger work; slaughtered Giovanni in a contest last spring.*

The night was still young and the spirit of bravado flowed through my veins. Bold and foolish, I barged in on their dialogue.

"Otto, I couldn't help but overhear your conversation with Dieter. *Die Fledermaus* was by Johann, not Richard Strauss...such a common misconception..." I interjected with unabashed vanity, "But in regards to *Salome*, I'm used to more peaks and valleys of dramatic intent and narrative. Compare it to *The Barber of Seville*. Perhaps that's a poor example, because that's a comedy. At least that pacing carries the audience through to the conclusion. Even *La Bohème*—to use a tragedy as an example—that was a love story, and it was apparent throughout."

Our banter went back and forth until a fearsome baritone interrupted it.

"It's apparent that none of you are opera *aficionados* and that's that!" said Heinrich Schmitz, a brawny Teutonic young man, full of muscles and freckles with strawberry blonde hair cropped in a severe military cut. *While he was plucking strings, his family was pulling strings! By the size of him, he was also one not to be argued with.* "I think Strauss should be spending his time with ventures more suited for his talents," I said all too pompously.

Giovanni pulled me aside. "Johann, perhaps you couldn't follow all of the German lyrics. I suspect a lot of us here thought that *Salome* was rather brilliant."

I hiccoughed slightly. "Giovanni, don't tell me you're siding with them?"

One of the men in their party began whistling a few bars from Siegfried's heavy-handed funeral march from *Götterdämmerung*.

I began to sing the overture to prove my point. "If you take the overture from the *Mastersingers of Nuremberg*, for example..."

In response, Otto Wolf and Dieter Becker started whistling from the final act of *La Bohème*. One of the others from the crowd joined the ear-splitting cacophony whistling his version of the overture to *The Barber of Seville*. My friend, Giovanni, was the only admirable tenor amongst us. He began to sing *La Donna è Mobile* from *Il Rigoletto*. With all of the commotion this pub was beginning to sound like a raucous aviary.

"It's easier for a man to hit those high notes by whistling," Dieter said in his defense and resumed the song. The highest notes were way off key, but that's what made his interpretation even funnier. Clutching his chest in feigned agony, he pretended to play the role of the lovelorn heroine dying of consumption.

Meanwhile, Heinrich, quite drunk, stripped off his waistcoat. He removed his tie, swirled it around in circles and began swaying at the hips trying to convince us that he was Salome re-enacting her famous dance of seven veils. I mimicked all of the instruments from

195

the overture of *Tannhauser* while wildly gesticulating my hands like a conductor and turning into a one-man orchestra. A large crowd gathered in the room, and anyone who wasn't performing was applauding. Giovanni laughed so hard that he spilled his beer and had to run off and get another.

All was good fun until Heinrich became boozed up and jealous that I was stealing his captive audience. A firm grip landed on my shoulder.

"So who is the young fool who looks like Medusa?" Heinrich called out.

Because of my hair, I have always been the one everyone loved to pick on. Heinrich reached over and began raking his hands through my untamable coiffure.

"Pardon me?" I asked while taking a step backwards.

One of his fingers got caught in a tangle. He tore at it to get it out. "Let me hear you whistle that in harmony," he demanded, throwing down his gauntlet.

I shook my head and continued my mimic of all the instruments using my own version *con anima* of humming and singing.

Heinrich challenged me once again. "I want to hear you whistle!"

I shook my head once again. "I can't whistle. Forget it."

Heinrich looked around the room and called out, "Gentleman, this poor fellow can't whistle. Did you hear that?"

A crescendo of snickering began to rise in the background chorus. Warning signs rang out in my head bellowing like bassoons and tubas. Several men began to mock me using peculiar hand signals. I had no idea what they meant.

With his powerful thumb and forefinger, Heinrich traced around the contour of my chin and upper lip, taking a moment to scratch here and there to see if he could detect any whiskers.

"Where is your beard?" he asked.

"Can't grow one," I said, timorously as he continued to fondle my smooth, hairless face.

"This man says he can't grow a beard," he announced, embarrassing me. Once again, he seized a clump of my curly locks. "Does anyone have a scissors and glue? I have a brilliant idea!" Oh horrors! He was a head taller than I. When he yanked me up, I tripped over my own two feet and continued stumbling into the lap of one of his classmates. Then he reached over and clutched my waistcoat drawing me in closer. I was no physical match for this brute. All of a sudden his gaze fixated on my pocket watch chain.

"*Fraulein*, what time is it?" he asked.

Taken off guard, I had no idea what he was insinuating, but my first instinct was that he might want to steal my grandfather's timepiece. A ruffian in my recent past had already tried to make off with it unsuccessfully, and I used baneful and questionable enchantment in my defense. But that was in a dark alley. We were all alone, and I was never going to see that bloke again. This time was entirely different. These boys were all competitive colleagues in the music profession. Word could get around and rumors spread quickly. I couldn't disclose in public that I was a secret practitioner of magic.

"You can't have it!" I said defiantly.

Heinrich only pretended to take my timepiece. Instead, he slapped me hard under my chin. Giovanni returned at just the right time.

"Johann, he thinks you're a sissy and wants to start a fight. We must leave. Now!"

"What's this nonsense about whistling?" I asked.

Giovanni's eyes grew wide, amazed that I hadn't picked up on the innuendo. I broke free from his grasp, took three huge gulps from *his* glass of beer and went back into the welcome arms of trouble.

"Fool! Your hair is on fire!" the big bully said referring, once again, to my crazy red mop. "This'll cool you off!"

197

As I tried to duck the beer he poured on top my head, he also scraped the hard heel of his boot alongside my shin and stomped on my foot.

"Put up your dukes!" he called out with a challenge. "Show me you're a man. Prove me wrong."

Waving my hand with a signal of defeat, I began walking away, but Heinrich wasn't going to let me go so easily.

"What other choice do you have but to defend your honor?" Giovanni asked.

"But I don't know how to fight," I confided to him.

"What do you mean you don't know how to fight?" he asked, bewildered. "Get out there and stand up for yourself."

Giovanni pushed me back into the fray. I didn't know if I was the reluctant hero or the recalcitrant buffoon. I tried to curl my fingers into a solid fist, but everyone stared at me as I placed my thumb out to the side. It was obvious that I was inexperienced and terrified. How could I play the piano if I injured my hands?

"Who are you calling *Fraulein?*" I said, spitting a mouthful of beer at Heinrich.

When Heinrich caught hold of my collar, I reached over and grabbed the closest mug from one of his comrade's lips and threw beer in his face. That failed to stop the pinwheel of hard knuckles and fists flying in my direction. Giovanni was helpless in trying to stop the frenzy and wound up on the floor beside me. Finally, the pub's proprietor had to break up the melee, and we were all thrown out. Not wanting to continue the brawl into the street, Giovanni hailed a cab so we could make a quick escape.

"Why did he belittle me because I couldn't whistle?" I asked.

"You really can't whistle, can you?"

"No, but that won't hurt my musical career," I retorted.

"But it could ruin your reputation."

"How?" I asked.

"An *urning* supposedly cannot whistle," he replied.

"A what?"

"That's German slang for an invert."

I raised my eyebrow, still clueless. Giovanni kept dropping hints until I finally got the point.

"A sod, perhaps Uranian, or what you Scotsmen call a confirmed bachelor, perhaps?" he suggested.

"And because I couldn't grow a beard and failed to whistle I gave him the mistaken impression that I might make overtures of affection towards him or one of his friends?"

"Most likely," Giovanni concluded.

I rubbed my sore eye and injured shoulder and was silent for the rest of the ride.

*   *   *

The Gentle Rude Awakening

"You missed Olivier's piano lesson, Professor Scott," Madame Poincare whispered in a liquid voice. Her creamy, poetic face, smelling of roses, hovered inches from my icy cheeks. Abruptly I roused from my dream.

She pulled back as I flinched. "Pears glycerin soap and lavender oil?" she asked sniffing my sheets.

"You have a keen nose," I replied, rubbing my eyes.

"Surprising that a gentleman like you prefers a more feminine scent. Why that choice?" she asked.

"For its calming properties, but my colleagues give me strange looks back at the Conservatory," I said with slight humor, and yawned.

She covered her mouth, politely hiding laughter. I might've looked like a hardy Scotsman on the exterior, but suddenly I revealed a softer side.

"And why did you oversleep?" she asked.

"Too much brandy last night, I guess. Your husband is quite a host."

She was about to pull off my bedclothes when I clutched my sheets even tighter, hiding my thin nightshirt underneath.

"Isn't it rather inappropriate that a lady, such as yourself, would enter a gentleman's room unannounced? What if I were naked under these sheets?"

I made up that remark in haste glancing around my bedroom to make sure there was no incriminating evidence lying about. Thank heavens! My spell book had been put back inside my suitcase, and there weren't any books sitting out that had been taken without permission from her husband's library.

Inches away her breathy whispers blew like a gentle wind across my face.

"To answer your question, Professor, after all I am the lady of the house. I take my privileges when people I've hired miss their appointments."

Yes, I had drunk too much brandy and was still slightly screwed. Her husband and I had discussed Greek philosophy until way past the midnight hour. And that dream—I think it was about my old friend, Wendell, traipsing across the sands of ancient Egypt. Its memory was fading quickly.

"Tea will be waiting for you downstairs, Professor." Her final words were angelic chords. She placed an extra blanket on me as if I were her own child, but not without tangling one of her fingers in one of my wave-like curls.

Grabbing the warm blanket, I drew it over my head. Then I smiled, languishing for a few moments more before starting my day.

* * *

Why was my attention absent? I had played these melodies dozens of times and had committed them to memory. My brain was like a child distracted by the promise of sweets when piled before him was a slice of greasy ham and lumpy mashed potatoes. Suddenly my thoughts scribbled nonsense—in verse, sonnets, no less! Up until now, I had channeled all of my passions into my music. But now they burst forth like a new beginning. No wonder my fingers skipped the notes! My skin tingled all over. I was awake and alive.

Guests poured in through the front doors throughout the day and night, scurrying about like the chorus members in a grand opera sans costumes. When the clock struck midnight I retired from the festivities. I gathered up my sheet music and prepared to turn in when Francois snuck in.

"Come Professor, join me for a nightcap. Let's do it in the *small* reading library."

Lucky was the man who had more than one library. His larger private library, *le grande bibliothèque*, was off limits to everyone. I had stumbled upon it by accident and was surprised it was generally unlocked. Often, I wondered if Francois spied on me, and if there were special peepholes behind some of the eerie portraits that graced its walls. Without question the Poincare children avoided the room with the fear of retribution.

He led me into *le petite bibliothèque*, which looked like the perfect séance room, but in fact was where he enjoyed intimate discussions and games of cards with handpicked company. At its center was an impressive card table made of inlaid wood with gilt vines at its base, surrounded by maroon silken damask chairs. The room itself was octagonal, with a domed ceiling painted with three-dimensional *trompe-l'oeil* architectural renderings. Besides the bookshelves lining its beveled walls, there were wooden panels with recesses displaying classical white marble statues— curiously all male and oddly effeminate if solo, or wrestling naked if in a pair.

I was already giddy from exhaustion by the time he removed a decanter of rare, aged brandy from a cabinet and poured two glasses.

"Cheers to a wise choice," he said raising his glass.

"What sort of choice?" I asked, perplexed.

"My wife has a good nose for sniffing out my kind. Kismet does the rest."

Not having a clue as to what he meant, I took a cautious sip.

"How am I like you, Francois? All I can visualize are the differences."

201

He winked. I got nervous.

"Seekers tend to find each other," he replied, savoring the spirits.

Had we attended the Underground University together as children? Could he have been affiliated with those men on the train back in 1898? Perhaps he was connected with one of those occult societies that Wendell had investigated. My mind was swimming with speculations. He reached over and slapped me on the back, pulling me out of my reverie.

"Professor, I know you've been sneaking into my other library, my *sanctum sanctorum*...the one no one's supposed to know about," he said whispering in my ear.

Suddenly I got a chill.

"Don't worry about it," he assured me despite my growing uneasiness. "I have an unwritten rule about trespassers. If you can manage to get past my invisible guardians, then you deserve to help yourself to any of the reading material as a reward."

He laughed when he saw the look of horror on my face. "Professor, only a fellow initiate of high order and good character is allowed to pass. That silver ring on your finger and the smaller one dangling from your watch chain were dead giveaways. That's why I've never been concerned about any of the children sneaking inside. They'd be terrified. The room is magically protected."

"As in charmed, bewitched or enchanted?" I asked.

"If that's the way you wish to put it," he replied.

"So, is that how you judge that we have something in common?"

"That and something else," he replied, biting his lip and carefully choosing his words.

Once again I felt ill at ease. He reached over to fetch a delicately carved scrimshaw keepsake box and pulled out a stash of opium with a smoking pipe.

"Have you ever kissed the evil dragon?" he asked.

I shook my head, a bit scared and aware of its dangers, but captivated nonetheless.

He placed a small black sticky ball of the poison in his pipe and lit it, taking a few puffs. Then he beckoned me to put aside my inhibitions and give it a whirl. I barely sucked in its perfume-like smoke before I doubled over coughing.

"That won't do. You're supposed to hold it in as long as you can," he advised me. "Try another."

This time he rose from his seat. Standing from behind he placed one hand on my shoulder and handed me the smoking pipe with the other. As I closed my eyes, I felt both his hands firmly knead my shoulders. Without reservations, Francois took the license to continue a very stimulating massage from my upper back down my spine. I was caught up in euphoric bliss and unable to resist.

"Pleasant, isn't it?" he asked, leaning down and whispering as his breath tickled my ear.

Speechless, I was somewhere between heaven and nirvana.

*   *   *

Shooting Straight

Early spring, 1906: By and large Monsieur ignored the Madame for more grandiose pursuits that he deemed ill suited for the weaker sex. Being a daredevil at heart, he fearlessly insisted on living life to its fullest and having the financial means to do it helped immensely. Only his imagination posed limitations when it came to which pastime to indulge in. Many hours were spent playing polo, private fencing lessons or motoring expeditions. Rumors were rampant that he was also involved in riskier sports such as hot air balloons and newfangled flying machines.

In contrast, poor Sophia was woefully deprived of such excitement. It had been a rare but propitious event when we met at that circus. More often than not she was confined to the house where she would read, dabble with art, and play melancholy melodies on *Pierre Pierrot* for hours on end, fighting the devils of boredom. What I failed to realize was that when she hired me, she also had ulterior motives. She craved adult adoration and companionship. Now since I was coming over nearly every weekend she took that opportunity to satisfy her needs and desires.

My naiveté and inexperience with women proved to be my folly. I failed to be aware of her coy and well-choreographed advances, as her Victorian sense of wooing was ladylike and restrained. She asked me constantly to join her for cards and other games. Even with the children present, she'd take those moments to brush by me *accidentally* or touch my hand, dropping little hints of wanting more physical contact. When she discovered that I was also a writer, she was eager to show me poetry she composed and urged me to turn them into songs. She tried to capture my attention even if it meant invading my privacy. What I feared was that the great god Pan was being awakened. Something long-hidden inside of me was being let loose and would be kissing my virginity good-bye.

It was Saturday afternoon. I was busy working on a new Sherlock story for Arthur when I heard the ominous sound of a key inserted into my locked door. Summarily, I gathered my notes and shoved them into my suitcase. If my door was closed all visitors were expected to knock first and announce themselves.

"Who dares to pass?" I shouted. The door slowly creaked open.

"Shush," she said. She tiptoed in and locked the door behind.

"Are you all right?" I asked.

She slipped her delicate shawl off her shoulders, and it fell to the floor as she came closer. With the poise of an arabesque, she swooped down, grabbed hold of my chin and locked her lips onto mine. Stunned, I nearly fell out of my chair.

Hours later I awoke, aware that it was almost sundown and that I was alone and half naked. Dinner was about to be served and the household knew that I was never late for a meal. I never could get used to their strange regimen. Their habits were conventional and unexpected. They always dressed for dinner, that was *de rigueur*, but when it was only the immediate family they shared the table with their children, whom they adored like the dickens.

I scrambled to get dressed, forgetting that it was supposed to be formal wear. I also kept tripping over my shoes and couldn't quite get my tie straight. My hair was still out of place, but with no time left there wasn't much I could do about it. Everyone had been impatiently waiting for me, especially the children, who were beginning to act up.

"Ah, Professor, *wie geht es ihnen?*"

Francois inquired how I was feeling. He often switched from German to French then back to English without warning.

"A bit tired, but better now," I replied as I took my seat. "How was your afternoon?"

"Splendid, thank you. I spent my time with some old hunting friends, purchased a new rifle and lost at three rounds of cards, but the brandy was superb and the company congenial. That's all that mattered."

He continued to humor himself as the servants began to serve our soup. His youngest had to be disciplined when he tossed a baguette at an older sibling. I ate in silence, taking it all in.

"So Professor, how did you spend your time?"

I choked on my soup and reached for a glass of water.

"My afternoon was plebian compared to yours," I replied. "Unless I was giving piano lessons, I spent it alone in my room reviewing student essays." Perhaps that fabrication would bore him enough to change the subject.

"And my lovely wife, what kept you occupied this afternoon?" he asked.

205

"Oh, I sent the invitations for our next soiree. Otherwise, when the children were taking their naps, I enjoyed a stroll outside. It was a marvelous day."

She was a better liar than I was, but as long as he bought our story that was all that mattered. The main course was served with its momentary distractions.

"Professor Scott, I need to test out my new rifle," Francois announced.

While he masticated his filet mignon, I thought my heart would stop. He knew, didn't he? He was going to use me for target practice!

"Why don't you join me hunting tomorrow? I like to leave at the break of dawn, so prepare to get up earlier than usual."

I was mortified. How could I gracefully get out of this?

"I'm afraid I'm not familiar with the sport. I might be more of a hindrance than an asset," I replied.

"Nonsense. Are you telling me that you've never shot a rifle or fired a gun?"

"I'm afraid not. I never really had to for any reason that I know of. Most of my leisure time was spent playing music."

"Then tomorrow I'll break your virginity," he proudly laughed. "In fact, you'll enjoy it so much that you'll beg me to take you out hunting every weekend."

He seemed rather smug with his opinions. I shot a glance at Madame Sophia, and she just rolled her eyes. She was used to such pomposity. I guess I wasn't, but his comment about breaking my virginity? Could he have been psychic and have known what transpired between his wife and me? I finished my meal, but excused myself before dessert.

"Leaving so soon?" Francois asked.

"You did say the crack of dawn, didn't you?"

"I certainly did, but I was hoping you'd join me for a brandy and a game of cards before night's end."

"Regretfully, I must decline. It's been a long day," I said as I began to leave.

"Tomorrow then, bright and early," he concluded.

*   *   *

The cooking staff had packed us a picnic basket to take along, and after a quick cup of tea in the kitchen, Francois and I rushed over to the stables.

"Professor, silly of me, but I forgot to ask if you could ride."

"I'm certainly no equestrian, but my skills are adequate," I said telling the truth. "But a stubborn horse could get me in trouble."

He motioned to one of his grooms to find me an older, more docile mare and saddle her up. Meanwhile, he picked a feisty black stallion.

"This is Lucifer, my favorite and fastest. Trained him myself," he boasted.

Once the horses were saddled and packed, we took off. I had never really seen the full expanse of his estate, but I guessed I was about to find out. Not being the outdoorsy type, I rarely ventured beyond the gardens. It had been years since I had gone for a ride, so my attention was more attuned to staying on my horse than paying attention to where we were going. I also knew I'd be quite sore between the legs for days afterwards. Finally he gestured to dismount and tie up the horses nearby.

He took out one of the rifles from a leather casing, kissed it and said, "It's a brand new 1905 Model, Mannlicher-Schönauer, a consummate work of art—single action and very powerful."

I had never seen anyone refer to a weapon like an object of desire.

"Put it in your hands," he said thrusting it into mine. "Feel its strength."

Reluctant about this whole affair, I nervously awaited further instructions.

"Come over here," he instructed and pointed towards a large boulder. "I like to position against this rock to steady myself."

"Why is that necessary?" I asked.

"First of all, these rifles weigh close to four kilos and are fairly bulky. I know you said that you were unfamiliar with guns, but the recoil is close to that of a twelve gauge shotgun, which means it's got some kick."

"Kick?" I asked.

Francois laughed, "Have you ever been kicked by a horse?"

I shook my head.

"Perhaps been on the receiving end of a good strong punch?"

I nodded, albeit worried.

"When a rifle fires, the operator receives some of the impact from the blast. That's probably the best way of describing it, and why I like to brace myself against this large rock. It helps so I don't miss my target."

All of this new information was a lot for me to take in so early in the morning. Francois took my rifle out of its case and

208

handed it over to me. I was scared to grasp it at first, but he assured me it wasn't loaded, yet.

"Mannlichers are bolt-action rifles that hold five rounds in a non-removable internal magazine that's loaded from the top—an ingenious design," he explained. "Why don't we test yours out?"

I began to shiver.

"How can you possibly be cold?" Francois asked.

"I'm not. Just scared of the gun and what it can do. I've never killed a living thing, and it would be my bad luck that I might do something stupid like shoot myself instead," I said, feeling awkward and handing it back to him.

"Nonsense," he laughed, "I'll show you every safety precaution in the book. As long as you're with an expert like me, there's nothing to fear."

I only wished I had his confidence, but he assured me everything would be fine, and we'd actually have an enjoyable time together. He handed me some ammunition, which I summarily dropped to the ground. Francois shook his head and showed me how it was done on his rifle.

"Now it's your turn," he said.

I recoiled in horror.

"It shouldn't be a traumatic experience." With that he confiscated it and loaded my rifle himself. "You can't always depend on me doing all of your work for you. What if we were suddenly called to war? What would you do then?"

War? That struck a strange chord. I had an eerie premonition of something that would happen in the near future. That was much more daunting than killing some poor creature for supper.

He came over and crouched behind me. "Let me demonstrate how to do this once again," he said, straining to be patient.

"Flip this metal piece up, take the bullets and press them right inside—one, two, three, four and five. It's a chamber round. So you're going to push forward with this latch and flick it down. When you aim and fire it, there's going to be a big kick. It's a similar effect as a pistol. The trigger and the magazine assemblies remain stationery, but the upper half of the weapon recoils back. After you fire the first round, lift this up, pull back, and it ejects the empty shell casing. Then pull back and load another. There will be four more times you can do this. *Boom, boom, boom, boom!*"

He unloaded the bullets. "Now it's your turn."

After a few tries I did my best to copy him.

"Come, now let's do some serious hunting."

Then there was the tiring wait.

"Oh look, a deer," he pointed out and quickly fired but missed. "Now it's your turn."

"You just missed," I said. "And about that kick, I saw you jolt even though it appeared you had firmly braced yourself beforehand."

"That's all part of the sport. You'll get used to it. If it makes you feel better, I'll stand right beside you so you can't fall over."

"Perhaps that's best," I said.

My first attempt was a dry run without ammunition.

"Are you ready for the kill?" he asked with an oddly seductive tone.

He watched as I loaded the bullets, one by one, into the magazine. Another long wait, then birds flew overhead. Something rustled over in the bushes that might've been a squirrel, but I couldn't see a thing. I shrugged my shoulders and was anxious while nothing particular happened.

"Come," he beckoned, "this always brings me good luck." He pulled out his opium pipe.

"Wouldn't that cloud our judgment?" I asked.

"I find it brings out one's clarity," he said handing it to me, "*Après vous*, I insist."

He lit a match. Although hesitant at first, I took a long deep puff. Then he took his share and quickly snuffed it out. He gave me a moment to get back to my senses and then repositioned himself. Once again we waited for what seemed like forever, but this time it was different.

"John, over there…a rabbit. Take aim."

I held my breath. He assured me that he was right beside me.

"Fire when ready," he said whispering words of encouragement.

Silly me, I was so nervous that when I pulled the trigger I closed my eyes. This threw me off balance from the unexpected kick, which in turn thrust me backwards and right into his arms. Shocked, I stared up at the canopy of trees overhead feeling ridiculous and foolish while my head spun under the influence of opium. But that was nothing compared to what happened next. After Francois placed the rifle aside, he began to stroke my hair. I was stunned but didn't resist. Part of me really enjoyed what he was doing. The other part of me considered it utterly shocking.

He let his fingers dance down my face and then trace a trail down my neck. I closed my eyes and opened myself up to a whole new world of welcoming sensations. He tickled me with his meticulously manicured moustache as he lowered his head to reach my lips. I tasted the opium on his tongue. We both drew in a deep

211

breath together and pulled in closer. A warm hand caressed my inner thigh. As we rolled over into a pile of leaves, our thoughts went to another place. We plunged into the realm of the senses, of touch and exploring a forbidden togetherness. For a *second time* by virginity had been challenged. We forgot all about the hunting expedition until our stomachs reminded us that we were supposed to be finding supper.

Francois poured me a glass of wine and took out a loaf of bread and a hunk of cheese and began dividing it up with a knife. I stared off into the distance, still slightly anesthetized from the drug but satisfied.

"Eat, regain your strength," he said with gentle encouragement placing a loving but firm hand on my shoulder. Then he reached over and kissed me on the forehead.

"We'll have to do this again, won't we?" he said with a sly, confident smile. "But keep it a secret. No one should ever find out, especially Sophia. She'd lose her nerve."

I nodded, but my thoughts were sprinting off in diverse directions. I was desperately trying to accept that I actually enjoyed our little encounter and wholeheartedly agreed that we'd have to keep this matter quiet. However, Francois had absolutely no idea what I had done with his wife the day before.

*   *   *

The Other Woman

"Professor Scott, I know it's a long ride, but there's a classical music event in Ludwigsburg this weekend. Do you care to join me?"

I wasn't an overly tall fellow, but I towered over Maria, my piano student. Yet, what she lacked in size was surpassed by audacity, which was most likely necessary for a woman who was not only outnumbered by men at the Conservatory but also in the professional arena.

"That was quite a forward statement coming from a lady, much less a student," I replied, still not yet accepting her offer and taken aback by her strawberry blonde hair. Ever since Miss Chandler hounded me back in Edinburgh, redheaded women gave me the willies and I tended to avoid them.

"You're my favorite teacher, sir, and I'd rather not go alone." The sheet music she'd been clutching in her arms began tumbling to the floor. I bent over to help her pick it up, but as we both stood back upright we collided and bumped our noggins together. A barrette in her hair got caught in mine, and we started laughing, as we disentangled each other.

"Are you all right?" I asked. "I didn't expect this to turn into such an incident."

"Neither did I, Professor Scott, but you still didn't give me your answer."

"Oh, yes…that," I said, still hesitant.

"You're a brilliant professor," she explained, "Quite a handsome one, too."

If I hadn't turned bright red before, I knew I had now.

"Why thank you…Maria…"

I couldn't remember her surname, but she was quick to finish my sentence.

"Maria von Braun, sir."

"Why of course, as you were saying?"

"Did I upset you?"

Underneath, she was a giddy schoolgirl hiding her first crush. The blush on her cheeks began to rival her strawberry blonde hair. I was no less nervous over this unexpected encounter, as I had so little experience with women.

"I guess I'm so used to socializing in the company of gentleman that I wasn't expecting it." I paused to pull down my waistcoat and straighten my tie. "I'd be honored. Where did you say it was being held?"

"I didn't. It'll be at the Waldhorn am Schloss. Mozart and Goethe have dined there. Even Casanova!"

"That place is expensive. I suppose I should eat supper first unless they expect us to order it there."

"Professor Scott, come over to my place for an early supper. I'm a marvelous cook."

"Won't your parents get the wrong idea if you invite me over?"

I wanted to assume that she lived with her family like most unmarried ladies and was also surprised that she hadn't brought up the issue of a chaperone, yet.

"There's no family, sir. I live alone."

"I'm so sorry for your loss," I said giving my condolences.

"Oh no, sir. They're not dead. They live in Leipzig. I stay here by myself to attend the Conservatory."

This young lady was full of surprises, and I'd be damned if someone else accused me of being as heartless as a piano without its player.

"I'm sorry, I just assumed that. I wasn't expecting to be entertained by a single lady. You really shouldn't do this. Please, let me take you out."

"I've been told that my *Wiener schnitzel* and *strudel* could compete against the best of chefs," she said with confidence. My insides chimed like gastric glockenspiels. Both of us laughed.

"I guess my stomach answered for me," I remarked, now completely embarrassed beyond recourse. "Certainly sounds delicious. I don't know what to say, except—yes. It would be an honor, Fraulein."

On the night of the concert I decided to bring her a single, long-stemmed red rose despite my uneasiness that it might give her the wrong impression. After all, I was the teacher and she was my student. There also must've been at least fifteen years between us. But if my colleagues at the Conservatory thought that we were courting, perhaps that would dispel any suspicions about my so-called confirmed bachelorhood. Ever since my encounters with Francois Poincare, I had my concerns. But between her red hair and mine, the two of us looked like candidates for *The Redheaded League*, one of Arthur's Sherlock stories.

The evening went according to plan. The excitement and enthusiasm were undeniable, more on par with that of a grande opera premier rather than a far smaller intimate affair in an upscale restaurant. But it happened that Waldhorn am Schloss got its name because it was across the avenue from one of the royal residences, and members of the nobility were in attendance in their own special section. For a moment I felt jealous that I wasn't one of the entertainers. On a whim, I ordered a bottle of champagne to be brought to our table.

Just as the bubbles of delight danced on my brain and the liquid gold of the grape whispered that the world was all right, the members of the orchestra came out and took their seats. That veil of smug assurance dissipated. Heinrich Schmitz! The master of ceremonies announced that the pianist had taken ill at the last minute, and Schmitz would replace him, instead. My heart stopped.

215

Heinrich Schmitz, that enviable musical prodigy who humiliated and assaulted me in Dresden after the *Salome* premier—resentment had been festering since. Perhaps he was correct in assuming my predisposition towards men and was more aware of it than I was at the time, but he didn't have to make a public spectacle of it. He also didn't have to ridicule me about my hair. He walked to the center of the stage, bowed and scanned the audience spotting and acknowledging me with a wicked wink and a smile.

"Do you know him?" Maria asked, noticing his gesture.

"I've seen him before at competitions," I said, keeping my response short.

The performance got underway, but I was preoccupied with thoughts as to how I could get even. There was no doubt he deserved some form of retaliation.

Back when I was in Edinburgh I had played a trick on Doctor Lorraine Smith, one of the medical professors at the university. For months I was plotting where I could use telekinesis in a way that he couldn't help but notice. My psychical skills had become even better over time; thereby I took it upon myself to use a little bit of dirty magic. Throughout his performance, he missed cues and struck wrong notes. Other musicians noticed, as well as the audience. Maria had no clue that I was the igniting spark, but Schmitz, who had no knowledge that magic, was involved, kept looking at me sensing an invisible connection. He was unaware that I was the puppet master pulling at his strings the entire time.

For the final *coup de grâce*, when he got up to bow I had him trip over his shoelaces. Even more satisfying was his final fearful glance in my direction. That voice inside him revealed that I was behind all of his slip-ups. That was my virtuoso performance and far more entertaining than his.

*   *   *

Splints, Splices and Stitches

London, November 1906

Dear John,

My apologies about a delinquent correspondence, but I've been proposing to the Egyptian Antiquities Service to cover their explorations for various London journals, and it's been a more daunting undertaking than expected. Despite all my world travels, I've managed to retain my flat near the British Museum, even if it has meant giving my landlady with that obstinate dog several months rent in advance. When back in London, I spend as much free time as I can spare in the museum's library as well as seeing their recent acquisitions of ancient ruins. It never ceases to amaze me that the ancient Egyptians developed a cult and religion around the notion and existence of an afterlife. That, and the worship of cats. Perhaps I should summon one of those powerful god-like entities to do away with the dowager's insipid mutt. Time permitting, one of these days I will have to learn how to translate hieroglyphics.

I've been way too involved with my assignments to consider settling down and finding a wife, but that, by no means, indicates that I haven't been a man about town. Have you any good news to share? Being in a stable academic environment is much more conducive to settling down. I, on the other hand, could be booking the next steamship halfway across the world given the opportunity.

I hope you've been able to find sufficient excitement in Germany well beyond your university studies. The photos you've sent me of the Bavarian countryside where you've been working weekends are stunning. You're a man of many talents.

Mackenzie

*   *   *

After he sealed the envelope, Wendell took a brisk walk to his local post office to mail the note. It was all too tempting to drop by the British Museum afterwards and admission was free. Mysteriously drawn to the Egyptian wing, he glared at a group of tourists gathered in front of a sealed entrance to a plain and simple

217

tomb, nowhere near as impressive as the Rosetta Stone, one of the major museum attractions. A photographer was struggling to set up his cumbersome camera, blocking the exhibit. He kept scurrying back and forth, hiding under a dark cloth to focus his ground glass, but he never seemed quite satisfied with the results.

"Do you need assistance?" Wendell asked, poking his head under the gentleman's black cloth. "One of my best friends is dabbling with photography, and I've always wanted to take it up."

Startled, the photographer jumped, almost knocking the whole kit and caboodle to the floor.

"Mackenzie's my name," Wendell said, reaching over to catch the man's tumbling tripod in his left hand while extending his right to greet him.

"Oh my, I'm Horus," the photographer replied, clutching the rest of his gear and giving as brief of an introduction as possible.

Wendell noticed the brass nameplate affixed to his wooden camera. "*Horus C. Aetas?*" The cogs and wheels of reason clicked in Wendell's busy brain. It was ironic that someone with the name of the Egyptian god of war would be connected with that section of the British Museum.

"If you don't mind holding the potassium flash so I can light the display, I'd appreciate it," he said handing Wendell the flash unit. "Be careful, though. Could blow your arm off if there's an accident."

Wendell was glad he could oblige. As the photographer prepared for his shot, the commotion of the two men discouraged inquisitive onlookers, who scattered to less crowded nooks of the museum. It took over an hour to set up for three different exposures, and by the time they were through, both men were exhausted. The photographer shook Wendell's hand vigorously and asked him, besides pay, what he could do in return.

After a moment of contemplation, Wendell suggested, "I hear there are secret archives within the museum that only insiders know about, much less access. Have you heard of these, by any chance?"

"Indeed I have," the photographer replied. "In fact, you're in luck, as I happen to be carrying an extra key."

"A key?"

Handing Wendell his spare, he said, "However, it's not for what you would think."

"How's that so?"

"Head into the King's Library, not to be confused with the round reading room in the Great Court. Look for the statuette, the bust of Plato. All the statuettes of the Greek scholars tend to look alike, but you need to find that particular one. Right at its base, is a keyhole, which no one ever notices, but this key is to be inserted into that hole.

"It's imperative to time everything precisely when the museum is closing to the general public but is still open for one more hour for the staff—no earlier and no later. Beware, and make sure the marble bust is the one of Plato, not Plutarch or Socrates, and God forbid, if it's one of the Romans. Heaven knows what will happen. I've been told that those sculptures also bear keyholes to other passages, and some will send you off in the wrong direction on purpose, so pay very careful attention.

"Then, if you made the right choice and did everything correct according to the instructions, one of the bookcase panels should open up, and you will have less than sixty seconds to run from that statuette and through that portal."

"Less than sixty seconds? That's a huge room. Why, it must be at least ten meters wide and well over thirty meters in length. Suppose one of the sliding doors opens on the complete opposite side of the room?" Wendell asked, surprised.

"Then you better skedaddle," the photographer explained, "otherwise you'll miss your chance, and the museum guards will promptly escort you out."

Wendell twirled the cryptic key in his hand. It looked as intriguing as the story behind it. What sorts of treasures or secrets were behind that door? His imagination came up with all sorts of possibilities but his thoughts went astray, being reminded of a tidbit I shared with him a long time ago. On the day when I first met my old friend, Whit, he disappeared down a passage behind a shelf in the University of Edinburgh Library. When he re-emerged from wherever he had disappeared, he admonished me saying, "Beware of strange books. You never know where they'll take you."

Perhaps Wendell needed to revisit that warning now.

* * *

For Old Time's Sake

Late October 1907: Everyone was overwhelmed with grief when Arthur's wife passed away in the spring of '06. She had been ailing of consumption, and as a doctor, he tried every possible cure to no avail. She surprised all of us by fighting a tough battle for fourteen years, which was much longer than anticipated. It was understandable that he needed time to grieve and spend with family, so he and I took some time off afterwards from our psychical meetings.

On September 18th the following year, Arthur finally got married to his longtime lady friend, Jean Leckie. Both friends and enemies spawned all sorts of stories when Arthur remarried so soon after the tragedy of his first wife's death. Their wedding was held in London, and even George Edalji, whom Arthur lobbied to get an acquittal in a widely publicized murder case, attended their reception. Their honeymoon itinerary included a stop in Constantinople before heading back to London and then on to their new home in Crowborough.

Normally, I wouldn't have been vacationing in Turkey, but I had become quite close with Francois and Sophia Poincare who had also planned a trip there. Thus, I took advantage of that rare opportunity, so Arthur and I could finally have a drink together after all these years. My only hesitation was that I knew that Arthur would provoke me about that elusive red book again. Little did he know that I no longer had it.

Since I had put on a wee bit of weight, he would've walked right past me in the hotel lobby if it hadn't been for my telltale red hair. He was more inclined to remember me as a struggling university student who often skipped meals, because I couldn't afford them.

"John, you look quite different!" Arthur exclaimed, "Your hair? It suits you well."

"More tamed now, don't you think?" I said, pointing out that now all that remained was a heavy crop of waves on top, but the sides had been shaved much shorter to emulate a more professional and *professorial* look. Beethoven's wild locks were no longer in vogue.

Arthur briefly introduced me to his new bride, who wanted to go off shopping while the two of us caught up on conversation. He was curious as to how I convinced the Poincares to take me along since I'd probably not be giving anyone piano lessons while on vacation.

"This holiday I'm serving more or less as the Poincare's nanny," I said.

Arthur was amused as I explained my situation further.

"I doubt if I'd ever make a suitable father. My real friendships are with their parents, whom I find as excellent company. Besides, it was a chance to travel to a place I've never been. That was tough to pass up."

"Taking advantage of the Turkish baths while you're here in town, John?"

"Why should I be interested?" I feigned ignorance and hoped that Arthur hadn't picked up on my aura or anything else giving away the escapades I had with Francois Poincare, which had to be under lock and key.

He lit his pipe, took a few puffs and replied, "Sorry I asked."

I scratched my head changing the subject. "Your new wife is charming, by the way."

221

"Why thank you, John. I dare say I didn't do too badly by picking her out of the crowd."

"Arthur, what inspired you to go to Turkey on your honeymoon?" I asked.

"Why not? I'm always up for a good adventure," he said, laughing.

"And you're settled in now since you've tied the knot?" I asked.

"It was only a matter of time with Touie, my former wife. Poor dear."

"But Arthur, wasn't it rather risky to associate with Miss Leckie? You're such a public figure, and many knew you were still married at the time."

Arthur interjected, "Still married—yes, but my mother approved, and that was the most important part."

"I guess, but..." I took a sip of my beer and didn't want to pass judgment. Both trusted friends and critics argued that he had committed a serious faux pas on moral grounds.

"Yes, it was a risk, but it was worth it. I don't know what I would've done if I lost her to another suitor." He quickly changed the subject. "So, tell me about Germany and the Conservatory—your friends—any lady friends at all?"

"Arthur, I've led a busy life. I teach part-time. I'm still studying. There are concerts I participate in. Plus, travel to Bavaria to tutor..."

"No women?"

"Not really. I have one lady student who has expressed a liking towards me, but we're no more than friends."

Arthur was persistent about this subject. Sophia was always on my mind and so was her husband, but I didn't dare mention a word to him or anyone else for that matter. It was a complex situation and my conscience deal with, not his. He relit his pipe and was disappointed, but perked up when we exchanged gifts. I brought rough drafts of Sherlock manuscripts I'd been working on, which was another activity keeping me busy. I also gave him a finely crafted set of his and hers beer steins as a wedding present. Arthur handed me a large, but lightweight box. I shook it and examined its wrapping paper, unsure what to think.

"John, aren't you going to open it?"

"What's going to pop out?" I asked, a bit leery. Arthur wasn't known for too many practical jokes, but with Wendell it was another story and anything could be expected. I opened the box to discover a red felt fez he must have purchased locally.

"What am I going to do with that?" I said, laughing.

"Wear it, of course. What else did you expect to do with it?"

Playing along with the absurdity of the moment, I pretended to take my large mug of beer and pour it into the fez.

"John, what on earth are you doing?" he asked, pulling the hat away.

"Well, since I've been in Germany I've had to get used to drinking more beer. It looked like a large-sized tankard and might do the trick.

Arthur was flummoxed. I stopped before finally acting out on it and explained it was only a joke. Then I put it on, looking absolutely ridiculous, and Arthur ordered more drinks.

"Cheers to the happy husband!" I called out raising my glass.

Arthur confessed, "Jean gives me unimaginable joy. If I don't behave myself, before you know it, John, I might gain a reputation for turning my Sherlock stories into romance novels!"

That was doubtful.

*   *   *

The Sins of Omission

November 1907: Much was happening within a relatively short span of time. Arthur continued his involvement with the London theatrical scene but finally gave up on politics in Scotland. I guess he had to draw the line somewhere. Thus with all his travels and busy schedule, it was easier for Arthur and me to continue our communication by *flying on the astral wind or* contacting each other on the *ether* each evening.

* * *

Ma'am,

All well and jolly. The publishing community has been *Sherlock Holmesing* me when I would rather put him to bed and do some solid work again. Greenhough is overjoyed to get installments of *Sir Nigel* for the *Strand Magazine*. I only wish that my influence in other circles would be as well received as my literary accomplishments, but alas, some feel otherwise.

Your loving son, Arthur

* * *

Arthur sealed the letter and then reached for his pipe. The clock outside struck midnight in London and one in Stuttgart. Street traffic had already whittled down to a murmur. Concurrently, I poured brandy and closed my eyes.

"Your tobacco smells like black cherry infused with rum," I deduced with my nose twitching as if the aroma was present in my own room. "It also appears you've finished writing a letter to your mother."

"You're good," he replied, acknowledging my clairvoyant accuracy.

He strained a few seconds to test his telepathic acumen and fine-tune his concentration. "Time for a shave, perhaps?"

I scratched the stubble on my chin, which would never grow much thicker.

"Touché! Surprising how accurate we're becoming with constant practice," I said out loud. He was in England and I in Germany. Many countries separated us, but only by distance and not in spirit. On another plane, we were in the same room.

"Should I try identifying some of the objects on the table in front of you?" I asked. Our paranormal experiments were getting rather entertaining.

"No, John, I have a much more important matter to discuss. It's late, and I'm sure you're as tired as I am now. It's my friend, Bertie."

"H.G. Wells?"

"We've had our differences all along, but I do respect him as a writer, and he's gotten himself in a real pickle this time. John, I suppose you've heard that he's rather outspoken with women's emancipation and free love, and by all means, he's a man of his word. He's not been faithful to his wife, and apparently has committed a bit of an ... indiscretion."

"What do you expect me to do?"

"The young lady will arrive in one month's time. Meanwhile I need you to make arrangements. Sending her to Germany and away from the London social scene will dispel any suspicions. After she has the child, she can return home and none will be the wiser."

I was quiet for a moment and upset. Wells was one of my favorite authors. Now, Arthur was confessing that he was morally bankrupt.

"Arthur, that's a tall order to ask. I don't know anyone who could keep her, and she cannot stay with me in the men's dormitory. I wouldn't even know where to start."

"You are very resourceful. After all, you managed to secure accommodations in Stuttgart all by yourself, and that's impressive for a young man who has never lived outside of Scotland."

"I had assistance from the Conservatory. That was quite different."

"Nonetheless, I'm confident you'll come up with something suitable. No one must know the identity of the father. The girl must be hidden away, promptly, as if she never existed."

"Arthur, you're not asking me to do anything against the law, are you?"

"Not in the least. I would never suggest anything like that."

"That's reassuring." I sighed with relief. "However, you've really put me in an uncomfortable position. Suppose I decline?"

"Your failure to comply will forfeit our *arrangement*."

"Our writing arrangement? Is that a threat? I'm depending on that income, Arthur."

"There are others who will be agreeable. Previously, Bertie Robinson assisted me, and I'm sure he'll be pleased to collaborate again. I'll follow up this conversation with a telegram to assure you that what I conveyed wasn't a figment of your imagination. It'll be worded differently, however. The telegram will state that my niece wishes to study at your music school in Germany, and I've requested your assistance. That'll be your confirmation. Am I clear?"

"And you're blackmailing me if I refuse to cooperate?" I asked.

"John, expect that telegram tomorrow. Good night for now and pleasant dreams."

*   *   *

Berlin, December 1907

Back in July, my department supervisor wanted me to revise our long-standing syllabus. We were painfully aware that the need for re-examination and revisions were long overdue. I was busy on that project when one of my colleagues in the music department caught my attention.

"John, there's a telephone call for you in the director's office. It sounds urgent."

"Did anyone give you a name?" I asked.

"No, but it's a woman. She sounds hysterical."

Sophia? Was she in trouble? Aunt Maggie? She would've sent a telegram if there were salient news from Auld Reeky. I hurried into the office to answer it and asked the director's secretary if she could leave so I could have some privacy.

"*Guten tag*...Hello?"

"Oh Johann, *Gott sei dank ich fand sie*! (Thank God, I found you!)"

"*Verlandsamen*. Slow down. Speak in English if you can."

Her voice sounded familiar, but I couldn't quite place it.

226

"Johann, it was dreadful..." There was fear in her voice and heavy breathing.

"Who is this?" I asked.

"Lenora, your old friend."

She was a compassionate woman and a talented songstress. I had courted her several years ago, but our divergent interests failed to make us a perfect match.

"One of my patients...oh no..." She broke down crying. "Johann, he kept saying, 'Away, Away; in five minutes there will be a corpse. There is a child murderer in the neighborhood. Deliver this note to the police. I have killed children in Belforter, Preinzlauer and Hensendorfer Streets.' The police called him the German *Jack the Ripper*. He also tried to kill some of my associates and me."

"Who said this? Are you all right?"

"Paul Minow came to the hospital as an outpatient for fits of epilepsy. Local police found a note with that statement at one of the crime scenes. He lured young girls into alleyways and stabbed them repeatedly with scissors! Eventually, he confessed. It was so terrible. I know it's been so long since we last spoke, but you've always been so sympathetic. I didn't know who to turn to."

She resumed crying. All of this news came as a shock. It took me a moment to come up with a suggestion.

"Listen, why don't you take a break and visit me in Stuttgart? I'm slated to do a piano concert this weekend. The least I can do is offer you a bit of music and sympathy. Consider me as a friend if you will."

"I'm at the end of my nerves," she replied, calming down somewhat, "and I probably should take some time off."

"I'll pay for your room. Better yet, I'll treat you to dinner after my performance and even reimburse your train ticket. How can you refuse?"

"I guess I can't," she said, still weeping. "Johann, you're way too kind."

227

"Always a Scottish gentleman, I suspect. I can't bear to hear a lady crying."

"How can you afford that?"

"Private lessons on the side, but that should be neither here nor there. Lenora, you were lucky you weren't one of those poor victims."

We had a pleasant reunion, albeit not under the best of circumstances. I gave a splendid performance, which she enjoyed thoroughly, and our sumptuous dinner at the Hotel Marquardt was superb. When I escorted her back to her hotel, she thanked me profusely and swore that if I ever needed a helping hand she'd be at my disposal.

A few months later, I took Lenora up on that offer and sent her a telegram. The psychiatric hospital where she worked was still swimming in chaos. Meanwhile, I was beside myself as to what to do with a pregnant girl who'd be traveling from England with no friends or relatives in Germany. Lenora wasn't in any position to take my ward under her wing, but she said she'd make a few inquiries and get back to me within three days.

Some Supreme Being up in the heavens must've listened to my pleas. She gave me the name and address of Frau Adelheid Fuhrmann, apologizing that I'd have to escort the girl to Switzerland if I were to avail myself of her assistance. Frau Fuhrmann was to be contacted a week before "Arthur's niece" was due to arrive, and from there she'd handle the final matters.

*　　*　　*

The train's whistle pierced my ears as it arrived on time and pulled into the station. Steam from its engines merged with my breath from the cold chilly air. Anxiously pacing the platform for the past hour, I shoved my hands inside my pockets and pulled up my overcoat collar, wrapping my scarf a bit tighter, trying to stay warm.

Arthur had given the girl my photograph, and I was sure he included a vivid description, being the competent writer that he was known to be. Other than looking for a pregnant young girl who might

228

be hiding her secret under a heavy woolen coat, I was in the dark. Minutes passed, and I began to get concerned. Was my information incorrect? Maybe there was a change of heart or a switch in plans? Finally I heard a soft youthful voice call out my name. I looked up, and saw a soft-featured lass with long brown hair pulled back and with faint freckles dusting her face. I found it disgusting that Wells was close to thirty-nine, and she looked barely seventeen. I picked up her luggage, said nothing more and escorted her from that platform to transfer to the train we had to take to Switzerland.

Throughout the ride both the girl and I were eerily silent. What were we supposed to do? Entertain each other with small talk? This was a hush-hush affair. I was like a smuggler, party to an act where I was going to make this girl disappear from the public eye. The scenery along our route was breathtaking, but I must've dozed off, as I did my best to distance myself from the situation. When we arrived, I immediately hailed a cab, and handed our driver the address of our intended destination.

We were met by a large, imposing woman waiting at the entrance, standing there with arms crossed boldly over her chest. She wore a short-sleeved dress exposing her fleshy arms, which seemed impervious to the cold. Her silver hair was pulled back in a tight, severe chignon.

I tipped my hat, intruding myself. "Frau Fuhrmann, Lenora highly recommended you." She cut me short and shuttled the two of inside from the bitter weather.

Few words were exchanged. I was given papers to fill out, and Frau Fuhrmann avoided as much eye contact as possible. She was obviously doing me a favor, merely on our mutual friend's recommendation. The atmosphere was as somber as a funeral. After I filled out the last of the forms, one of her associates led the girl away to her room. Part of me felt like I had signed off on this poor girl's death sentence.

"She won't be staying here long," Frau Fuhrmann advised me. "Shortly, we plan on transferring her to Neu Isenberg. There's a

Jewish home for troubled girls like her there run by Bertha Pappenheim, if anyone should care to inquire. From the nature of this matter, I suspect they won't."

"Frau Fuhrmann, the least I could do is relieve you of some of your expenses."

I stuffed a wad of marks in her hand, payment from last week's piano lessons at the Poincare estate. How I only wished I could've known what she was thinking and strongly wondered if she suspected I was the father of the child.

"I am indebted to you for your generosity," I said.

"I called for a driver. He's waiting for you outside," she curtly replied.

I leaned over and bowed, while clasping both my hands together in traditional Chinese style. My unfamiliar salutation perplexed Frau Fuhrmann, and I was equally surprised myself. I couldn't begin to assess where this completely uncharacteristic gesture had come from. It was as if I was a stranger who had jumped out of one storybook into another from a completely different and unique time.

However, when I came to my senses and bid her one last goodbye, I couldn't help but think to myself, *"What did Arthur get me into, and why?"*

* * *

Auld Lang Syne

December 31, 1907: Ever since Wendell and I left Edinburgh, maintaining contact had been a challenge and strictly through written correspondence. Of course that wasn't to say that every so often I'd access the Secret Library and spy on him. But that's beside the point. Good will and affection amongst friends was always best in person—on the physical plane, more or less. However, several months ago he sent a note saying that he'd be returning to London from an assignment in Greece and wanted to meet in Berlin for New Years. I was hesitant to return to Berlin after being backed into a corner for that favor for Wells and Arthur. But

Wendell insisted on meeting there rather than Stuttgart so I gave in. After all, it had been close to seven years since we'd seen each other. He insisted that we celebrate our reunion at a raucous nightclub, but it wasn't quite what I expected.

"I can't believe you dragged me to a burlesque show!" I said, a bit tipsy. Wendell caught me staggering as we walked back towards his hotel.

"You didn't enjoy yourself?" he asked. "I don't want to hear that you only appreciated the music, if you know what I mean." He poked me in the ribs to see if I took the hint.

"Not quite my inclination," I replied.

"At least I didn't make you camp out on another park bench, eh?"

He had to remind me of that, didn't he? I was in no mood to relive occasions in the past when he had exiled me from a shared room while he indulged in his sexual conquests. Spending a sobering night in jail after a Soho bender was not my cup of tea, either. He laughed, saying that he had his fill of raven-haired Mediterranean beauties and for the moment he'd spare me that embarrassment. I hoped he had grown up over the years.

"I guess you prefer the more refined and genteel sort?" he asked.

"You're probably right," I replied, not wanting to continue this conversation.

The two of us stumbled into his hotel lobby. We already decided that since it was New Years we were going to toast the town together. I'd stay overnight, sleep off the whisky and catch a train back to the Conservatory at some point the following afternoon.

"The night's still young," Wendell said as he told the lift operator which floor we were going to, "Why don't I order a bottle of champagne to be brought to the room? I still can't believe you don't want to check out another place."

"You know what," I said, pulling my friend out of the lift and back into the lobby, "I could use a little food in my stomach.

Why don't we pick up something here in the hotel's dining area? Besides, with all distractions in that cabaret, we really didn't get much of a chance to chat."

"Agreed," he said. "Something in the belly might be in order."

Straightaway, Wendell wanted to discuss current affairs and all the subjects that I avoided—German politics and how our rulers were so desperate to catch up with the rest of the world. I, on the other hand, only wished that the world simply revolved around music—that, and the anomalous universe.

Meanwhile, Wendell had been traveling all over the world on assignment. The more exploits that he shared, the more I became jealous that he was getting such opportunities. How I vied for equivalent offers! In comparison, my career had been crawling along with pace of the tortoise rather than the hare. My psychical arrangement with Arthur still remained a secret, and I didn't dare breathe a word about the recent developments over at the Poincare household. Not even to my best friend.

Briefly, he spoke about the photographer he met at the British Museum two years ago when I inquired about the mysterious note he sent. Although I had my suspicions, he skirted around the issue when I questioned him as to whether or not he used his time machine to travel into the future. I warned him not to.

"Speaking of that subject," Wendell said, "I managed to tote an extra *suitcase* along."

"You brought your time machine all the way from London?"

He nodded and checked to make sure no one was listening.

"Let's make a little trip together for old time's sake. What do you say?"

I shrugged my shoulders. After all, it had been a while. Thus, I hailed our waiter and ordered strong tea with dessert and an extra pot to be sent within a half hour up to our room. Being more sober for time travel was advisable.

232

"Let's go back to ancient China," Wendell suggested as he pulled out the same old tatty suitcase I had given him back in Auld Reeky. "I keep on having outlandish dreams that I must've lived there in the past...and with you, no less!"

Besides Arthur, now Wendell was infatuated with going to China. That damned book! Everyone wanted it, and when I had it I couldn't wait to get rid of it.

Nervous at that mere thought, I had a different idea in mind. "Actually, I'd like to go back again to the time when we attended the Underground University," I suggested. "So much of my childhood past still remains a mystery. I'm just beginning to piece everything together."

"John, now I'm getting concerned. Didn't you say that you had little control of as to where this machine would take you?"

"For some reason I do have a relative amount of control going back in time to an earlier point in my present lifetime. Otherwise you are correct. It's a roll of the dice. All I can say is that once I wanted to go to ancient China and wound up in Japan. Hey, wasn't our school motto, *Clavem ad futurum ex clues in praeterito fuit*? The keys to the future lie in clues from the past? Maybe we'll be able to help each other remember what really happened back then. But I still can't figure out why you seem to recall more about the time we spent there than I can."

"If you want I'll disclose my theory," he said.

A knock on the door interrupted his train of thought. I volunteered to get the extra tea we ordered so the steward wouldn't barge in as Wendell set up his time travel apparatus. Alerting the hotel management that two drunken Scotsman were up to mischief on New Year's Eve was to be avoided at all costs. With the tea and the meal we began to get to snap to sobriety, although not entirely.

"So please share this brilliant speculation of yours," I said, begging Wendell for long sought-after answers while helping him assemble his time machine. I was lucky that I no longer needed such an elaborate set-up to do the job.

"Remember graduation day at the Underground University?"

"Somewhat. I recall being relieved that there'd be no more grueling homework, but I also knew I was going to miss the place. Otherwise, so much of it is vague. Why?"

"At first I thought these were all rumors devised on purpose to scare the students, but now I think there was some truth in them. Had you ever heard the one about drugging the students so they'd forget all the magic they had ever learned?" Wendell asked.

"Yes, but that was ridiculous," I said, laughing.

"I wouldn't pass that one off so lightly. You said that for years you've had a hard time remembering those experiences, correct?"

"That's true, but what's the point?"

"Try to refresh your memory about our graduation dinner."

"I was starving. That, I remember, because I was cramming for all those examinations and so busy that I didn't have time to eat. Why? I still don't understand?"

"Think back. What about the dessert we were served?"

"Chocolate cake, but you didn't seem to like yours. So I ate your portion as well as mine. So what?"

"John, it had a disturbing aftertaste. There was an odd ingredient in it. I'm not sure what it was, but apparently it didn't seem to bother you."

"I was famished. I guess it didn't."

"John, I think it contained an elixir so we'd forget all of our magic, but only the magic and obviously not our academic studies. Then for some unknown reason our task was to rediscover that magic again. Otherwise, we'd simply mingle and blend back into the mundane world like everyone else with our memories wiped clean of those amazing experiences. That's what those rumors were all about, although nobody believed them or wanted to believe them at the time. I'm not saying that my recollections are perfect, because they're not, but I think that's why I can remember more than you at any given time. I only ate a few small bites of that cake. You, on the other hand, ate two large portions."

Was that the reason why I was the butt of a joke regarding Sarah Elizabeth Chandler and an incident involving being shoved face-first into a slice of chocolate cake? Could she have been telling the truth, and I had truly forgotten everything that transpired between us? I wanted to take pause and reflect on Wendell's statement, but it was late and despite any efforts to sober up I was still under the influence. Besides, we made a commitment for time travel, and it was either get started or spend all night arguing as to whether he was really serious or not.

"John, you did bring your timepiece, correct?"

I rubbed my eyes, then reached into my waistcoat pocket and held it out for inspection. "Never without it."

*　　*　　*

It was a balmy and lazy summer afternoon circa 1888, somewhere in the Scottish countryside. I was sitting on a rock, and when I looked into the lake's surface, I saw a lad close to nine staring back at me. My shirt was unbuttoned, exposing a bare chest, and the cuffs of my pants were rolled up so I could dip my toes in the water and cool them off. Then a rock flew over my shoulder striking the water that dissipated my impromptu scrying mirror.

"Wendell!" I cried out in a high-pitched, pre-pubescent tone.

"Who else?" he laughed in an equally funny voice as he joined me, took another rock out of his pocket and threw it in. "Lost in your thoughts?"

"As always, I guess."

"Is this your secret place?" he asked removing the rest of the stones and tossing them aside.

"It's peaceful, especially in the summer. Often I need somewhere to escape from the teachers and the other students. It can get so hectic at times."

"I agree. They really expect us to learn an awful lot of complicated spells in a very short period of time, don't they?"

235

"I don't know how I manage to keep up with all of it. Listen; since you've gone to all the trouble to find my special hiding spot, stay for a while. Do you have anything else right now that's urgent?" He began unlacing his shoes. "Here's your answer."

The two of us stripped off the rest of our clothes and went swimming. Wendell, being the constant teaser, dove under the water and surprised me from behind when he surfaced.

"For God's sakes! I thought it was the Loch Ness monster!" I was panting hard and then dunked him under in retaliation.

"Hey, what if there were strange creatures under there?" he asked. "Perhaps we should invent an undersea vessel to see what really exists?"

"Like Jules Verne and Captain Nemo?"

"Yeah, something of the sort."

The afternoon's tomfoolery seemed to rally on with harmless abandon, but suddenly I started having thoughts concerning sex. My parents never talked about it much, and it was the Victorian moral interpretation that masturbation caused diseases of the mind, body and spirit and therefore was not considered a viable option for a boy or a man. At one point while skinny-dipping, I began to get silly. I'm not sure what possessed me but I began to pull at and touch Wendell's pee-pee during our rambunctious water play.

"What's with that?" Wendell scolded me as he slapped my hand.

"Oh, I thought it was a little fish swimming around down there, and I'd try to catch it with my bare hands," I said jokingly.

"My parents said that our brains would rot away if God caught us touching ourselves!"

"That's ridiculous, but if it upsets you that much I'll respect your wishes." I said in defense, "I was just playing. Remember that."

"Do that once more, and I will never speak to you."

I must've broken the spell of the moment and had put the fun of our afternoon to an abrupt end. He began heading towards shore, and I followed.

"Boys aren't allowed to touch little girls, either, or did your folks also fail to teach you that?"

"What about a kiss?" I asked as I leaned over and gave him a peck on the cheek like a young lad wooing a girl. Wendell smacked me right on the face. "Bloody hell! Did the Devil prompt you on that one, too?"

"Can I not express my affection as if to a cousin, or an aunt or an uncle?" I asked.

I didn't realize that I had crossed the line and was so naive.

"Friends don't do that to friends," Wendell yelled. "No one taught you that, either?"

I shook my head. Maybe it was because I'd been separated from my parents at such a young age. Since I didn't see my aunt and uncle very often, they weren't much of a strong influence in shaping my moral fiber.

"I guess you have a lot to learn, then," Wendell said with bitter undertones. He put his hand on my shoulder to assure me that we were still friends but implied that I was never to repeat those actions.

That was my cue to squeeze his hand. It was best to stop there and return back to our Berlin hotel room. That's when having the ability to actively step into a dream-like state and alter the outcome came in very handy. That same skill applied to time travel. Otherwise, it was too easy to get caught up and get lost. Being able to objectively step back and realize that you were in a different time from the present was a huge benefit.

This was also an instance with another person proving that trips back to the past weren't always pleasant. Arthur and I also had our trying moments when we went to feudal Japan, but regardless I was still keeping my time travels with Arthur a secret from Wendell.

Tired, he looked at the clock, loosened his tie and began preparing for bed. That's when I spotted him take a quick swig of whisky from a small flask hidden in his jacket pocket.

"I'm not sure if I want you sharing my room tonight," he said. "Maybe I should make you sleep in the tub."

"Under no circumstances," I protested. "That's ridiculous."

Carefully, I took my precious timepiece out of my waistcoat pocket and put it back into my suitcase. It was undeniable that we were still apprehensive. I hoped that once we slept off the drink, by tomorrow we would have forgotten everything. I hoped.

*   *   *

1908

Dear John,

Or should I start calling you Johann? Over at the *Strand*, Greenhough keeps after me for more story ideas. It's impossible to assuage his demands, because my mind is constantly divided. Thus, I am deep in writing Sherlock and will need your continued assistance. It's so much easier once you lay down the groundwork and let me put on the finishing touches. Then I don't have the bothersome task of creating something from scratch.

Our written correspondence has also sparked ideas. One of your unusual dreams inspired me to write *The Adventure of the Bruce-Partington Plans*, which is about a plot to steal plans for a submarine. It was also a good excuse to bring back Sherlock's brother, Mycroft, after introducing him in *The Adventure of the Greek Interpreter*. One of these days, I might also develop the idea of a German spy on British soil.

Much to my dismay, my efforts to reach out to Wells continue to fall short. Being much more of a pragmatist, he insists that there's always a sociological or political explanation for the cause and effect of nearly everything. Recently, he's speculated on the perfect society in works like *A Modern Utopia*. Every time I turn around he's had another book or essay hot off the presses. That's not without saying that he's also attempted to revolutionize the Fabian Society, as he sees fit, finding that even those colleagues have been too rigid in their outlook.

The two of us remain quite the opposite in opinions, and it's almost as if he's my nemesis, my personal Moriarty. Perhaps there's a story in that, and knowing you, John, you'll probably say that our enmity stemmed from some other existence in the far off past. Nonetheless, Wells seems content to remain a skeptic, and his good friend, William James, also seems to be of influence. Many of his views seem to stem from his scientific background with biological and evolutional explanations saying that, "The species is still as a whole unawakened, still sunken in the delusion of permanent separateness of the individual and of the faces and nations."

Whatever I do, I can't seem to convince him about the possibility of considering unseen, otherworldly forces at play. Still, I plan on continuing to invite him to some of my Spiritualist lectures. When Sir Oliver Lodge and other scientists are at the helm he might find them more convincing. I think he also forgets that I, too, came from a scientific educational background.

Arthur

* * *

Moving towards the latter part of the year, Sophia invited me to join the children and her in Berlin one weekend instead of coming to Bavaria for piano lessons. She planned a surprise and wouldn't reveal anything until after I arrived, except that I should plan to stay overnight. Otherwise, I was anxious with speculations.

"So what's the special occasion?" I asked as I approached her on the platform at the Central Train Station. The children were already running off in all directions. Once we rounded up her brood, I took her bags. How I wanted to lean over and kiss her, to express my affections, but I couldn't. Not with the children present.

"Aren't you going to drop a hint?"

"Give me your hands," she said.

"Pardon me?"

"You heard what I said. Give me your hands," she softly demanded.

As soon as I put the luggage down she slipped off her silk scarf, grasped my hands and tied them behind my back. I was bemused. When I tried to break free, I couldn't. One of the children pointed at me and started laughing.

"That's your hint," she whispered in my ear. "Now guess."

"Aren't you going to untie me first?" I asked.

"Not until you figure out the answer," she laughed; enjoying that now I became the brunt of a joke and our little spectacle was beginning to draw attention.

"You're going to have to give me a better clue, or I'm afraid we won't be going anywhere," I called out.

Every second that passed was torture, and somehow Sophia delighted at that prospect. Obviously I didn't, and it started opening up a portal of memories that were vague, but unpleasant. The last thing I needed was to jump back into another piece of my sordid past. I played along with the tease, but my sense of humor was waning. Meanwhile, the children started skipping around me, playing games. A book fell to the floor from Olivier's pocket.

"You're reading a copy of *The Time Machine*?" I asked.

"Professor Scott, I want to learn how to travel in time like that man did," the boy replied.

"Perhaps I'll show you how," I said trying to entice him to do my bidding and untie those knots. But Olivier passed off my remark as nonsense. How could I, his weekend music professor, have possibly shown him how to travel in time? Thus he picked up the book, shoved it into his back pocket and ignored my plea, continuing to ridicule me like his younger brother and sister.

Sophia finally pulled five tickets from her purse. She held them far enough away where I couldn't quite read everything, but close enough where I could make out the large print that said Circus Busch and today's date.

Think. Try to concentrate. We initially met at a circus...but being tied up? Wait a minute. Houdini was featured at that circus where we first met.

"Are we seeing Houdini?" I asked.

"He's playing over at a fabulous stage over by Präsidentenstrasse," she said, wondering why it took me so long to figure that out. "Why don't you hail us a cab?"

According to the playbill, Houdini had been a busy man and traveled a lot that year. At the end of March, he had performed his Weed Tire Grip Chain Escape at Hammerstein's Ballroom in New York. Shortly after that he jumped from Boston's Harvard Bridge wearing handcuffs. He also published a book about the history of magic, *The Unmasking of Robert-Houdin*. For the first time in front of a Berlin audience, Houdini was about to introduce his most daring stunt yet.

"It is now time to go beyond mere handcuff tricks!" Houdini announced. "Failure means a drowning death, and now I will perform the Milk Can Trick!"

Several assistants surrounded him as be began to step inside a milk can.

"Now, I want everyone in the audience to count how long it takes me to get out. If you dare, try holding your breath to see if you can hold it as long as it takes for me to escape. I bet you can't do it!"

He squatted down. Liquid gushed out of the can and onto the stage floor and the lid was sealed. Sophia and I looked at the children. We all held our breath and tried to mimic Houdini. When we thought all hope was lost, the magician reappeared, giving a grand bow to a cheering audience. Houdini always insisted that it was refined skill and not supernatural prowess that helped him do it. When I returned back to Stuttgart, I wrote Arthur to tell him all about it.

*　　*　　*

Strange News from Another Star

1909: One afternoon, upon Wendell's request, I visited an occult bookstore in Berlin. That city still rekindled resentment about that favor I had done for Arthur. Yet, bygones needed to remain in the past, and that shouldn't have been a deterrent.

But I couldn't help noticing the shopkeeper's eyes grow wide, as he watched me count my change. He was staring at the silver engraved ring, the one I had involuntarily received during that commuter train incident back in 1898. Before leaving, I mentioned that I was looking for a copy of the *Posthumous Writings and Poems of Hermann Lauscher*, written by an up and coming author, Hermann Hesse. Our conversation ended with him saying that he'd contact me should it come in.

Little did I know that a week later, while honing my ability to master the German language by reading a translation of Sherlock Holmes in the town library, I would be joined by an unexpected companion. It happened that I received the upsetting news that I had been turned down for a teaching position at London's Royal College of Music. While taking a break from my book, I was agonizing over drafting a letter in my defense stating that I was clearly the best man for the job, but as much as I tried I couldn't word it to my satisfaction. That's when my attention was pulled aside.

"If you hate a person, you hate something in him that is part of yourself. What isn't part of ourselves doesn't disturb us."

I looked up and saw a thin, bespectacled man who sat down across from me.

"Well, it's true, isn't it?" he said, speaking in a crisp German accent. "Do you need some help composing that letter? I'm a writer. Perhaps, I can be of assistance."

I withdrew the sheet of paper with my fourth unfinished draft as soon as I realized I had been under observation. Besides, I was quite confident of my own writing abilities. It seemed highly suspicious that this uninvited person would make such an offer.

Then the stranger placed the same slip of paper with my contact information that I gave the bookshop owner a few weeks before in front of me. He reached back into his jacket pocket, pulled out a book and inscribed something inside.

"I think you inquired about this," he said, while handing me that book.

He extended his hand to shake mine, but I wasn't sure how to react.

"Hesse," he said in a brief introduction.

I was honored and humbled at the same time.

"Yes, and I hear you're seeking certain hard to find books on metaphysics and spirituality. I might be able to enlighten you on that subject."

I felt like I'd been tracked down.

"That ring," he said pointing the silver engraved one that never left that particular finger, "where did you get it?"

I held my tongue.

"Come, it's a pleasant day outside," he said. "Let's take a walk."

*   *   *

That was my introduction into the H.G.A. Society, the secret gentleman's consortium, which met once a month in Munich. I'd break a sacred oath if I revealed what its initials meant, but its members consisted of some of the most brilliant minds from all over Europe. These elite members embodied the *zeitgeist*, the spirit of the times, bringing forth transformation in the birth of the new 20th century. Some were socialists, and others were scientists, artists and intellectuals. That was how I had the pleasure of exercising my discursive faculties with such greats as Jung, Freud, Rudolf Steiner, Hesse, Charles Proteus Steinmetz, Wilhelm Reich, and Einstein, amongst others. Magical minds would come from all over to our private location in Munich.

There were also some equally brilliant but lesser known members such as Theodore Reuss, who I knew had connections with esoteric circles. Wendell had to be an initiate, by now, or at least involved in one of the scions of Golden Dawn, since so many illustrious writers were in their midst, such as Rohmer, Machen and Yeats, and of course, he had his unrequited infatuation with Florence

Farr. I was particularly interested in learning more about Brodie-Innes, who was believed to be one of Dion Fortune's students and had founded the Amen-Ra Chapter of the Golden Dawn in Edinburgh. There were other guilds or alliances in existence, ones that had memberships that included women—brave, bright women like Marie Curie, Edith Garrud, Annie Besant, Annie Horniman and many more although I was not connected directly with them. It wouldn't have surprised me that between his Freemasonry and Spiritualist associations back in England that Arthur was already associated with a similarly elite circle. Often his name was brought up. However, his rash and unbridled outspokenness about the controversial fringes of Spiritualism had the potential of marring his reputation, and I feared that all my support on his behalf would prove useless.

To access the Society meeting rooms, one had to utilize a roundabout means. The building's facade was unremarkable and easy to overlook. Members had to bribe the doorman outside with a whisper and a gift, giving him the password told beforehand which changed all the time. Then we were led down a passage to the back of the building where we had to find a staircase on our own leading to what appeared to be an oversized dumbwaiter. That, in turn, would function as a private lift to take us over to another floor with a specific coat closet. Next to that was another corridor heading over to a flight of stairs that would connect only between two floors and not by the normal lift that stopped only at the public floors.

Trust me, it was a lot to learn. Once, I tried approaching our private meeting room, forgetting that I needed the initial escort and wound up in the maid's quarters of an alternate suite. Not only did I have to backtrack my way to the initial entrance and go through my steps all over again, but I also intruded upon one of the female house servants in a state of undress, by accident. She was alarmed, and I was embarrassed, plus the whole incident caused me to be late for an important meeting.

Heinz, the Society's private butler, opened the tall cherry wood doors to our parlor without a sound. He was unmistakably tall, noticeably bald on top with dark hair of what remained and always dressed in tails. As he entered, his soft footsteps were overshadowed with the clinking of teacups against his serving tray. He set it down and glided towards the windows to air out the room from the aroma of cigars. If only I could've tapped his mind for the stories about the society and its notable members over the years. Few knew little of his past, but we were assured that our secrets were always safe, and our attendance would never be publicized.

I preferred to be like a fly on the wall, observing everyone from a distance while minding my own affairs, but it was impossible to be completely invisible. Gustav Mahler donated a stately grand pianoforte that proudly resided in the main library room. Since my talents were widely known, I'd often get requests to play.

"Bravo! Bravo!" Doctor Jung commenced a round of applause.

I just finished a passionate interpretation of Chopin's *Fantasie Impromptu* while the others settled down. It was comforting that at least I didn't feel like an organ grinder's monkey providing mere entertainment for pennies. Here, I was appreciated.

"Professor Scott, you've outdone yourself again. Hesse, do you mind passing the cream?" Doctor Jung asked as he poured himself another cup of tea. "Einstein, one day you should join him. I've heard you are quite good on a violin."

I didn't realize that Einstein also had musical talent. I merely thought that the only thing we shared was our unruly hair. Enlightening conversations made their rounds.

"I think we've gotten off on the wrong track concerning our American counterpart, Edgar Cayce," Steiner said, while wiping stray pastry crumbs off his upper lip. "He's made significant progress in the spiritual path through the use of dreams. Einstein, don't you agree?"

Einstein nodded in the corner, putting philosophy books back in their proper shelves. Freud sank back into his comfortable rich leather chair digging the tips of his shoes into the sumptuous jewel-toned Persian carpeting, reminiscent of his own study in Vienna. He casually stroked the cool porcelain surface of a rare, oversized Chinese vase with his thumb and forefinger. I perched erectly on the edge of a hand-carved piano bench, atop a soft velvet cushion, tired from a long day. An opulent oil painting of Goethe on the wall winked at me, reminding me of the story of *Faust*. This, in turn, rekindled bittersweet memories of my old and former friend, Whit, when he tutored me for my exam on *The Picture of Dorian Gray*. Portraits of other illustrious predecessors graced the walls— Nietzsche, Kant, Hegel and Schopenhauer, not to mention Mozart, Chopin, Brahms, and Beethoven.

"Professor Scott, what do you think?" Doctor Jung asked, urging me to snap out of my reverie and join the discussion.

I winked back at the painting on the wall, changed seats and moved in closer. Everyone's banter became blended into one harmonic chord as I tried to eavesdrop on the entire crowd at once. However, I was the lowly music professor-in-training swimming in a savage sea of highly educated intellectuals with a cacophony of questions and convoluted answers. If we were discussing music theory, perhaps I could hold my ground. In contrast, I could only envy the genius of my comrades in the sitting room. My mind flew dizzily like a honeybee from flower to flower sipping drops of nectar from a variety of conversations.

"Crowley, what do you think of him?" Reuss posed to the group.

"A madman in desperate need for psychoanalysis," bellowed Freud, "not to mention that he despises women. I'd love to know more about his relationship with his mother. Professor Scott, what's your opinion?"

"Never heard of him," I replied, hiding the fact that Wendell had sent me quite a few copies of his published works.

"I raise the motion that he is banned from our meetings," Jung called out.

"When was he invited?" Freud asked.

"Since Herr Reuss welcomed him with open arms and without our consensus," Jung complained, bitterly.

"And Conan Doyle, did he ever join the ranks of the Golden Dawn?" Reuss interjected.

"I believe he hasn't," I replied in confidence, "Too much political bickering for his taste. He rose in the ranks of a traditional Masonic order, instead, but after a time I suspect he lost interest."

"Do you know him?" Einstein asked.

"Yes, we've met once or twice," I replied, understating our relationship.

"I think he's too obsessed with his mother," Freud said.

"A son's devotion to his mother doesn't necessarily mean he has a mental abnormality," I said harshly, but I realized that I could be treading in dangerous waters. I was no intellectual match for Doctor Freud.

"Perhaps you're jealous. What's your relationship with your mother?" Freud cut in to challenge my remark.

"Gentlemen, gentlemen," Hesse interrupted, "I didn't travel to Munich only to engage in petty arguments."

Finneas must have snuck in when I wasn't paying attention. Visible only to me and none else, he placed a reassuring hand on my shoulder.

"Finn, I feel so insignificant in comparison to these men," I lamented.

"Soon enough you'll be a published writer. I foresee great things."

"Now, you're predicting my future? Is there anything else you wish to tell me?"

"Let's see, the impending war, the…"

"War?"

It was as if Finn had seized my vocal chords, and my cries were silenced. I reached for my tea to clear my throat.

"I'm afraid I've revealed too much already. Cheerio!"

Finn made a quick exit. Meanwhile, I excused myself, abandoned my tea and poured myself a brandy, deciding to sit alone in a far corner while everyone else's discussions whirled around me. Hesse walked over and broke my moment of introspection.

"Professor, what do you wish to accomplish in your lifetime?"

I was unprepared to share my innermost thoughts, although it appeared that he wished to divulge something.

"I'd like to be known as an accomplished concert pianist and composer, but I'd also like to be known as a writer, and I don't talk about that very much."

Mahler and a few other notables were also members of our society. Part of me felt so disheartened in comparison to the others that I almost hoped I'd never run into them. So far, I hadn't.

Hesse replied, confidently, "I live in my dreams—that's what you sense. Other people live in dreams, but not in their own. That's the difference."

*   *   *

Buried Warriors

Vienna, 1909: I was burning the midnight oil and catching up with notes in my diary. There were too many stories with way too little time to tell them. After all, I was still pursuing my advanced degree while working as an assistant professor at the Conservatory. Three weekends per month, I traveled to the countryside giving private piano lessons, and on the remaining one I attended H.G.A. Society meetings in Munich. Midnights (or technically one hour past that) were dedicated to Arthur, and more often than not a good night's sleep was interrupted by dreams of the strangest kind. Not to mention that I still took my trips in time travel whenever there was a moment to spare.

Bizarre changes began to occur as a result of my otherworldly pursuits. A whole new world was unveiled, and that might've explained why there were always caveats posed to those who dared to embark upon the esoteric path. Unpredictable results were to be expected, and those surprises were often far more challenging than one could've possibly imagined. On numerous occasions, images from my dreams created what I called a *silent meridian* or a fine, nearly imperceptible separation between my subconscious and my waking reality. Transitions were blurred and frequently revealed overlapping elements pulled from different points in time.

As my time travel excursions persisted, it became even more difficult to distinguish whether or not I had actually traveled, or only imagined that I did unless I gathered physical proof by obtaining *souvenirs* that I brought back with me. However, that didn't always happen. Besides, with my hectic schedule, it was easier to willfully make these travels through the realm of sleep, whereby I could accomplish the two actions, simultaneously.

When it came to time travel, there was also the issue of where to go and what to investigate. The problem was that outside of journeys within my present sphere, I never learned the trick of being able to control my destination. Conversely, finding out information in the Secret Library was a different game altogether except that often I'd only have limited access, despite the fact that I knew, in theory, that the ability of finding out whatever I desired existed. It was almost as if someone else made that decision for me, and Finn insisted that he had nothing to do with it.

A while back I confessed to Arthur that I had visions of being in Japan in a previous lifetime. Then, we traveled there together via a remotely conducted experiment with unanticipated results. Inasmuch as there was a lot more to discover on my own— details about my family and upbringing, my education, specifics about my childhood that weren't related to anything he and I had done together, the questions were endless. Thus, I began to have an obsession with the Far East as unexplored territory.

Back in 1900, Freud published *Die Traumedutung, The Interpretation of Dreams*. Given that and my long history of strange dreams, I knew that he was the expert that I needed. When the Poincare family took a holiday on one of my normally scheduled weekends, I traveled to Vienna for an appointment with Doctor Freud, instead. It was exciting to make any excuse to go there, since the city had such a colorful history, especially with music.

Bergasse 19 was on the second floor of a building flanked by Kornmehl's butcher shop on one side and a grocery on the other. I entered the doors facing the street, went down a walkway and up a flight of stairs to face a door saying Prof. Dr. Freud, 3-4. I was shown in, and the first thing I marveled at was his impressive private collection of authentic antiquities worthy of a museum.

"Doctor, I have sinned," I said, still mesmerized by all his artifacts.

"This is not a confessional, Mr. Scott. This is psychoanalysis. All of us are guilty of something one way or another," he said as he lit his cigar.

"Please, if you don't mind while I am in the room," I interrupted, gasping from the smoke.

The doctor, disappointed that I wanted to stifle his moment of enjoyment, snuffed his stogie in the nearest ashtray and walked over to the window behind his desk and opened it to air out the room. He returned to his desk noticing that my shirt fit a little bit tighter than usual and the buttons were strained on my waistcoat to keep it closed.

"One of my music students likes to keep me amply supplied with fresh pastries. I guess those lean days as a student at the University of Edinburgh are a thing of the past," I explained while trying to make myself comfortable despite wearing clothes that were uncomfortably too small. I picked up a button, which had popped off my waistcoat on to the floor and pocketed it.

"The clock is ticking," Doctor Freud replied, hinting that I should use our valuable time for discussing matters other than German cuisine.

"I'm sorry, I'm quite nervous."

"Don't expect miracles right away," the doctor replied. "Often it takes years to establish a breakthrough. Some patients never get cured."

"Doctor, what if issues are left in the balance, like you've run up a certain amount of debt by the time you die?"

"Then you've lived a life unfulfilled and with unresolved anxieties."

"There should be a source, a point of return for the soul," I elaborated.

Doctor Freud, slightly agitated from being deprived of his cigar, began rearranging some of the papers on top his desk.

"Maybe you should be consulting with Doctor Jung, instead," he responded. "He seems more inclined to believe in esoteric concepts, and lately he and I have had vast differences of opinions."

"You also have specific views on the importance of dreams," I interrupted.

"In a very different context," he replied. "The root of one's anxieties stems primarily from one's upbringing, and finds its genesis in one's parental relationships. Conversely, Jung digs deeper into a universal presence tied with myths, dreams and soul memories within a broader context. I cannot agree with those theories. However, you traveled quite a distance to be here. John, what's been bothering you?"

"Are you just going to prompt me with a bunch of questions?"

"We'll use a technique, which I like to call free association. What you need to do is to lie down, relax and let your thoughts flow. That shouldn't be too difficult."

He gestured for me to avail myself of his couch, then got up from his desk and took a seat directly behind me where I was unable to see him.

"For years, since I was a child, I felt like there was a giant storybook dancing in my head, willing to open its pages and share its strange tales whenever it felt like it, as if it had a mind of its own."

"That's an interesting way of describing it, John, but why are you finding that upsetting?"

"I find this disturbing, because whatever is buried deep in my head dissolves into real events that are happening today. If I had control of the matter that would be one thing, but in many cases I take on a more passive role, and the results happen to me. I'd prefer to have the power to step in and change my surroundings."

"Don't you think that's exaggerating it a bit? I suspect Jung has suggested you read too many myths and fairy tales," Freud mentioned as he cracked his knuckles and drained his teacup.

"Doctor, do you believe in life after death?"

Unable to hold back from his habit any longer, the doctor lit up another cigar and puffed on it voraciously before answering.

"In the unconscious every one of us is convinced of his own immortality, and death doesn't exist there. Neither does the concept of time work in chronological order. I also have my own thoughts that when people say that they fear death, that they actually fear other things such as guilt, unresolved conflicts, abandonment or even sexual insecurities. Those fearing death created religions. Not to denounce your friend, Arthur, and his belief in Spiritualism, but personally, I feel that beliefs in reincarnation are a result of people's denial of the finality of death."

"All right, you're a skeptic. I suspected as much. Then, I guess it would be hard for you to imagine if I did something terribly wrong during this lifetime that it could come back to haunt me later."

I paused to gather my thoughts, which were darting all over the place. I retrieved my journal from my jacket pocket and began to read what I had dreamed, as if it were just a story.

*   *   *

Doctor, the details were very clear. I was a young boy, around the age of ten, maybe twelve. I had long, straight black hair, not as long as a girl's but much longer than I have now, and I tied it back. I wore short, loose cotton pants and a *happi* coat, or a short cotton jacket that was wrapped with a soft, fabric belt. In my hand was a hard stick, which was more like a short staff, but to me it was a make-believe sword. I held it in a defensive stance against anyone who dared to challenge me. This dream took place in a place far away and in another time, in feudal Japan.

My young sister was crying. A delicate porcelain doll, with finely painted features dressed in soft silk robes lay shattered in many pieces on the ground.

Father stormed into our garden. "*Nan desu ka?* What is this?" he shouted, demanding answers.

Furious, he turned to me assuming I was entirely at fault.

"You are the oldest. You should know better," he called out as he slapped me across the face.

"It's not fair. Mother gives Mosu special treatment," I protested, angrily.

Father raised his arm wanting to lash out once again at whomever was responsible. Mother safeguarded my little brother, holding him close by her side.

"I was protecting Akemi. He was hurting her!" I cried out pointing at the real culprit. My little sister ran behind me, clutching my short jacket.

Mother screamed, "Mosu would never do anything to hurt anyone!"

She denied any of his wrong doings, but I knew he was responsible. I believed Akemi. She was telling the truth, and he wasn't. In fact, he was always dishonest.

"The *oni*, the demons made him lie," I shouted out loud.

253

It was as if he couldn't help it, and they willfully acted through him, like a puppet. I was willing to stand firm on that prospect.

"Somebody's lying," Father said.

He looked at me, then Mosu, then Akemi, and then back to me again. Then he seized the stick I held in my hand, as if that would have helped in a feeble defense and snapped it in two.

"That's enough. We're sending you away!"

"Where?" I asked. I was still obstinate, but now becoming scared.

"If you like protecting people so much, you can defend Lord Takeda and his family and train to be in his guard. *Ippo, sotowo suimin no inu!* Meanwhile, sleep outside with the dog!" he barked.

As soon as my back was turned, he kicked me on my bum, causing me to stumble and roll face first to the ground. Then he stormed into the house and returned holding a bundle of my belongings, which he tossed in a pile beside me. He made several trips back and forth taking my favorite books, toys, or anything of importance and not only threw them down on the gravel below, but stomped on top of them, as well.

That night, I cuddled up with our dog outside in the backyard. All I could think of was that my brother should've been the one to be sent away, and that he should've been sleeping with the dog, instead.

But to train with the samurai? There was an honor and thrill about that, nonetheless. It was something that the son of a merchant could only dream of. The moon shined brightly. The dog scratched his fleas and snored. Was I going to leave my friends? What about my school? Was I going to learn the family trade, or would that go by the wayside? Life as I knew it would end the next full moon.

*   *   *

"Doctor, in this dream my mother defended my brother at all costs even at the expense of the entire family. The irony is that it's not all that different from what I experienced in my childhood."

Freud cleared his throat and replied with a slight smile. "If I recall correctly, in one of Conan Doyle's stories, *The Red Headed League*, Sherlock said that his case presented a three pipe problem, and that he begged that no one speak to him for fifty minutes."

With that Doctor Freud, reached for his cigar. "Do you mind?" he asked, knowing that I wasn't fond of tobacco smoke. "In this case I think I have a three cigar problem, so to speak."

"As long as I don't have to sit and wait for fifty minutes until you reach a conclusion," I replied, resigned that my lungs would pay the price. I was also hoping this was all a joke and that he actually wasn't going to be smoking three whole cigars. It was bad enough that he was smoking one.

He lit his cigar and began puffing away. "John, you're a complicated man. It appears to me that you have some unresolved issues or repressed feelings concerning your father. Are you frequently in touch with him?"

I shook my head. My father left years ago, and my uncle hadn't been much of a substitute. The most influential men in my life had been my mentors, like Arthur, or my teachers.

He continued, "What I find particularly interesting in what you described was the appearance of the stick. You used it in your defense and to also protect your sister. To me, this symbolized power, assertiveness and even masculinity.

"However, your father confiscated it from you and destroyed it by breaking it in two—using your specific words, or dividing it. One can analyze that with a variety of meanings, but if you want to take to even another level, you could interpret it along the lines of breaking your will. John, do you care to add anything to that?"

*   *   *

Munich, 1909

Freud and I coordinated our next appointment with one of the weekends he'd be in Munich for one of our society meetings.

"What seems to be the reason you are here today?" he asked.

"Dreams," I replied, "the interpretation of dreams, both unorthodox and rather frequent. My mind seems to be still fixated on Japan. Japan is outside the realm of the British Empire; its history hasn't been the primary focus of a typical Scotsman's education," I laughed, but with serious undertones.

I opened my journal and began reciting it like a bedtime story. Similar to beginning a new scene in a film, the dream opened up to a warrior training session in an outdoor courtyard. The main practice had finished, and I stayed behind with Monk Wei, my private tutor. Repeatedly, I was attempting a technique, but I was getting tired and frustrated that I couldn't outsmart the master.

One last time, I charged with full force as the air whistled through my *shinai*, or bamboo practice sword, and my *sensei*, or teacher stepped aside avoiding its strike. This time, not only did he evade my attack, but also before I was cognizant of his defense technique, he grabbed the hilt of my weapon, confiscated it, and at the same time sent me tumbling into the dirt. Consequently, I found myself sitting on my bum, scratching my head and having no idea whatsoever how I had gotten there. It was as if he had performed magic, and I had been tricked!

"What happened?" I asked, somewhat dizzy from the somersault.

"Remember the principle about using your enemy's force against them?" he asked.

"Yes, but?"

"That's exactly what I demonstrated. You applied force and power by rushing towards me. I just assisted you in tumbling forwards using that same motion," he laughed, "but it looks like you've had enough for the day. Tomorrow then?"

I turned around and gave him a customary bow out of respect.

"*Ashita.* (Tomorrow) *Hai!* (Yes)," I said as I ran off.

"Doctor, in previous dreams, there was a misunderstanding, and my parents sent me away. I don't think I was the direct reason behind it, but I was blamed, anyway, and really had no choice in the matter. Also, I've strongly suspected that these images connect with something I've been going through now. Did any of that make sense?"

"Possibly," Freud replied.

"My father acted on his word, and more or less sold me over into servitude with the *daimyo's* army. Their rigorous training consisted of using a staff, spears, learning archery, how to ride a horse in combat, and of course, the epitome of this training involved sword fighting. What I didn't expect was to become a low-ranking foot soldier, more or less a security guard, always on the line to give up my life for the whims and fancies of my employers. The most revered soldiers were born as samurai. In contrast, I was an acquisition, a hired hand. Men of that status were looked down upon. We ranked one notch above prisoners of war who switched loyalties.

"The world and the stars revolved around Lord Takeda and his son. The father was unscrupulous. Often, I would stand guard outside meetings where he would be conducting business, and I could overhear everyone's conversations. He would deliberately cheat poor, unsuspecting fools, and then would laugh over *saké* afterwards. Other times, I'd witness him in reprehensible displays of public drunkenness, gambling, striking and hurting women where I'd be forced to turn the other way and not pass judgment. So many times I'd wonder if the situation would be better if his son, Masahiro, was in charge, instead.

"Doctor, it appears that in these dreams I was contending with repressed issues of anger and wanting to have revenge, but if these dreams are mere symbols for something in my mind that I'm experiencing now, why would they all be taking place in Japan? Wouldn't you think that I should be having dreams in the present time period, instead?"

Doctor Freud scratched his head, as bemused as I was.

"Doctor Jung ventures into realms I don't believe in, and this certainly seems to be one of them. Your needs will be better served if you consult with him, instead."

*　　*　　*

The Door of Many Colors

Summoned or not, the god will come

That was inscribed above Doctor Jung's front door. No sooner was I was about to knock than one of his house servants had already opened it. This was my first time meeting the doctor at his office in Zurich. Doctor Jung adjusted his glasses and perched on the edge of his seat.

"Thank you for seeing me on such short notice. It's my dreams." I coughed and cleared my throat.

My secret, which I couldn't tell the doctor, was that often I was having difficulty distinguishing between my dreams and my trips in time travel. Sometimes I projected either into the past or the future without being entirely sure by which means I had traveled there. Often there were only thinly veiled transitions between either these dreams or these consciously planned trips where I found myself, often unwillingly, with one foot on terra firma and the other in a netherworld of unimaginable proportions. That's what was tearing apart my sanity.

I whipped out my diary, my journal of personal recollections, from my jacket pocket and attempted to solidify all of the phantoms swimming around in my head.

Doctor Jung handed me a handkerchief to wipe the sweat off my neck and collar.

"Can I offer you any refreshment?" he asked.

I loosened my tie while fanning myself with a newspaper I snatched from a nearby table.

"Water, thank you," I replied as I began smoothing down my sweat-dampened hair. I adjusted my socks and tightened my shoelaces and told him my story.

"My dream took place at some point in the future in the same Edinburgh pub, the Deacon Brodie, where I had first met my mentor, Arthur Conan Doyle. He had died...in the dream, of course, because he's certainly not dead now. I was also married in this dream, believe it or not. So...in the dream, while finishing up lunch, I rearranged the single red rose I purchased for my wife's birthday next to the bowler hat she had given me for mine.

"Throughout, I kept thinking about Arthur. He had always sworn that he would transcend the inconvenience of death and return to walk amongst the living. Our encounter at this very spot forged a paranormal partnership lasting nearly three decades, and now I wondered if it was going to span beyond the grave. On my end, I had made a few transgressions. There was a karmic debt to be paid, and I wasn't sure if there was time to make amends before it was too late. When I pulled out my watch from my waistcoat pocket, I realized that I needed to head back to the university and teach my class on music theory. So, I paid for my meal and headed outside.

"The Royal Mile was bustling with activity, but I still couldn't get used to the fact that now there were increasing numbers of motor cars on the street. When I sidestepped on to Lawnmarket Street, all of a sudden a gust of wind took hold of me. My newspaper flew in every direction. The rose I bought for my wife was tossed high up the in air and danced like a bandleader's baton, and my hat became a spinning wheel skipping over the cobblestones down the street.

"Foolishly, I ran after it like a hound on a trail. On that fateful day of March 5, 1931, I stepped through the revolving door of time. Honestly, I didn't know what hit me. The head of my music department wrote a complimentary obituary for me saying that I had been a talented, perhaps undervalued, and very likeable person. Another colleague wrote a eulogy praising that I was a distinguished pianist who had won a high reputation in musical centers both on the continent of Europe and in my homeland of Scotland. 'As a teacher, the revered Professor Scott possessed the gift of clarity, patience and enthusiasm, and as a man of great personal charm and kindness, (my) untimely death was mourned by a wide circle of friends and admirers.'

"All I knew was that when I emerged on the other side and was finally able to comprehend what was going on, I learned that I was of the female gender and back in college again, but this time it was a vastly different type of university in a far off century."

I paused and took another sip of water.

"Doctor Jung, I saw my own death as I projected into the future. Am I wrong to believe that at one point everyone realizes in one way or another that they are seeking the answers to the absurdities of life, and the events that happen are their trials and errors leading up to that?"

"John, William Blake once said, 'If the doors of perception were cleansed every thing would appear to man as it is, Infinite.'"

Both of our statements raised a lot of questions.

"Doctor, I know this sounds strange, but I'm also worried about what might happen if I continue to disclose these narratives. What if this diary were a talisman and by sharing these accounts its magic will be released—almost like a contagion. I cannot guarantee what will happen or how it will affect you. Others will also feel its influence."

This confession did nothing to dispel my restlessness.

"I'll take that into account," the doctor said, finishing up his notes and not at all concerned. "Nonetheless, it was such a pleasure. I hope our session was of help."

"Likewise, Doctor," I replied, but he stopped me before I slipped out the door.

"That's quite a story, John," he concluded with a smile.

Quite a story? He hadn't heard the beginning of it yet.

*   *   *

260

The Space in-Between
Early 1909: The most extraordinary thing happened. It was as if locations moved like transparent sliding doors that opened and shut and then reappeared somewhere else. In fact, it was so perplexing that I scheduled a meeting with Doctor Jung in order to make sense of it.

"I was shopping in Stuttgart, picking up a few items I needed around my flat when out of the corner of my eye I spotted a watch repair shop. Instinctively I was drawn towards it, not even fully conscious of where I was. I opened the door, stepped inside, and the next thing you know, I realized that it was the same shop where I had my heirloom timepiece repaired several years earlier."

I got up and began nervously pacing the room. The doctor looked up from his notebook and calmly observed my shift in behavior.

"What was so strange was that the last time I made a conscious effort to return to this particular shop…it wasn't there."

I became very quiet all of a sudden.

"Plain and simple—the shop wasn't there. It disappeared. I scouted the neighborhood and made a few inquiries with proprietors nearby to see if they'd ever heard of it. The first place I approached was an upholstery repair shop.

"'Sir, I'm looking for an *uhrmacher*, an elderly watchmaker who repaired my *time machine* a few years ago.'"

Suddenly, I realized I made a slip in front of Doctor Jung. Time machine? I meant to say timepiece. I pretended that none was the wiser and carried on.

"'Sorry, there hasn't been a watchmaker's shop or a repair shop on this street, and I've been here for longer than I can remember,' the man replied.

"Determined to get to the bottom of this I scratched my head and went next door. Perhaps I had the two places confused, but that proprietor had never heard of the *uhrmacher*, either. The general consensus was that none of the shopkeepers had ever known that watch and clock repair shop to have ever existed and suspected that I must've been confused and traveled to the wrong neighborhood by accident. Behind my back I suspected they thought I had gone mad."

"And you never found out what happened?" the doctor asked.

"Never, and yet, the man clearly repaired my watch when it wasn't running properly. My finances also reflected that I paid for those repairs. Even more amazing was when I stumbled upon the shop for a second time, its address matched up with the original one. This was not my imagination."

"I'm not saying that it was, but let's try this" Jung said. "Close your eyes. Try not to think too hard, but what are your first thoughts?"

I took in a deep breath and gave myself a moment.

"Alright, I know this sounds insane," I said, trying to put my visions into words, "but a dimension opened up that I only had access to on certain occasions. At other times access would be denied or simply unavailable. The ability to enter that world vanished, or it simultaneously existed alongside whatever I perceived as being ordinary and real."

"Did you feel any unusual sensations when you entered this shop? Like vertigo or a headache?" he asked.

"Nothing conclusive. Why?"

Jung shook his head. "I was trying to scientifically analyze your experience as best as I could, but I'm finding this as much of an enigma as you are."

"It really makes one think there are invisible layers to everything that we perceive as reality, but every so often they make themselves visible in our consciousness. The concept of that is a bit frightening," I said.

"John, didn't I hear you say at one of our H.G.A. Society meetings that you've been conducting psychical experiments of various sorts over the years? You've also practiced astral projection, am I correct? Theoretically, you're disengaging an invisible layer or body that surrounds you at all times in order to be two places at once. Even you have told me that you've had a certain amount of success verifying items or details of locations during these psychic activities."

"Yes, Doctor, but what are you leading to?"

"Consider the possibility that an inanimate object or even a location can also exist on various planes simultaneously."

I took a deep breath and tried to follow his rationale. That would certainly be one explanation as to how time travel was possible. Once again, I thought about the conversation I had with Arthur years earlier during one of my first visits to his estate in Windlesham. I complained about a missing book that had disappeared and reappeared without warning, and he laughed it off saying that he witnessed phenomena like that all the time, especially when his wife's hats were always winding up in odd places.

The doctor got up, went over to a shelf and retrieved a carved wooden box. Inside of it he kept a collection of tarot cards, ancient symbols of human existence. He skimmed through the deck to find one in particular. Then he pulled it out and placed it on a table in front of me.

"What's the first thing that comes to mind when you see this card?"

The specific card he was referring to was Temperance. It showed an image of a figure that had one foot on dry land and one in the water.

"The figure is in balance, as if nothing is unusual," I added.

He nodded.

I scratched my chin. "How can it make sense that this watch repairman and his shop existed at one point in time, disappeared for a while, and then returned years later back in the same spot?"

Doctor Jung reached over and took an orange from a bowl of fruit. Taking his pen he placed a mark on it.

"This shows where the original shop was located," he said.

Then he placed the nib of his pen right next to it. "John, try looking at the situation in reverse. Consider the idea that maybe his mysterious shop was there the entire time, but you just sidestepped its location."

"But, I had witnesses who said their shops had been there for years, and they never heard of the place!" I argued in my defense.

"What if those other merchants also existed in their particular locations, but they also sidestepped the spot you initially discovered?"

At that very moment, everything that I believed about the universe turned upside down.

"John, think of the possibility of experiencing an overlap allowing you to be two places at once. You were in a remarkable position, like the person in the card, where one foot was on dry land and the other simultaneously in the water. Man is full of dualities."

As soon as he said that, I pinched myself so hard that I flinched.

The doctor laughed. "What was that all about?"

"Just making sure that I was really here discussing this and not dreaming about it." I was half joking, but also halfway serious.

*   *   *

The Force of Destiny Overture

Like minds attracted others like magnets. That's certainly how I felt when a simple inquiry in a Berlin bookstore led to a chain of events whereby Hermann Hesse and I managed to find each other. He also lived in Bad Cannstatt, a small town not far from Stuttgart. Hesse's writing career was beginning to get a strong foothold, and although I read some of his works, I never dreamed that I'd have the chance to meet him face-to-face.

Many pivotal developments happened over the next few years. On a prosaic level the world of music opened its arms to me. I earned my Ph.D. and was promoted from being an assistant professor to full status at the Conservatory. Throughout Germany I stunned audiences with praiseworthy performances, and in Switzerland,

France, in Krakow, Budapest, Salzburg, and one of my favorite places, Vienna.

However, despite all my advancements in the musical realm, the most serendipitous people and circumstances occurred outside of the Conservatory. With the exception of my *special studies* at the Underground University as a child, this was the first time in my adult life where I felt like I wasn't alone, singled out, or so different that I questioned my own unorthodox views on life. The H.G.A. Society was a unique organisation. One couldn't join it willfully. As far-fetched as this sounded, it was almost as if a qualified person displayed an *astral insignia badge*. This would be one that was invisible to the naked eye of the mundane population, but could be perceived by others attuned to such higher vibrations. Then those, who were up to snuff, were sought out and invited to join this elite fellowship. I was extremely lucky to have been so fortunate.

On the other side of the world, Arthur was celebrating the birth of his first son with his new wife, Jean. We continued performing psychical tests, although I pulled back my reins concerning joint time traveling after our first unpleasant encounter. I suggested concentrating on individual time travel excursions for the time being, and I was always open to sharing those results. Also, I really wanted to know whether or not Arthur kept the fact that he owned a working time machine a secret. Often I wondered if he had told Wells and the two of them partnered together to experiment with it.

Regarding Wells, he recently published *Tono Bungay* and *The History of Mr. Polly*. He also set up and became the first president of the Royal College of Science Association. Arthur sent me an except from Wells' novel, *In the Days of the Comet*, where utopia came to pass as a result of mood-changing gases emanating from the comet's tail affecting human behavior. He also sent me a copy of a short story that Wells wrote about a super intelligent ant species. Additionally, there were rumors that Wells had another child out of wedlock, but they were just rumors. As usual, they didn't seem to agree on anything.

Meanwhile, Harry Houdini attended a flying exhibition in Hamburg, Germany, and purchased a French Voisin biplane, thus starting his fascination with aviation. Arthur sent me a clipping from the 1909 London Daily Mirror stating that Parisian police threatened to summon Houdini for being improperly dressed and jumping into the Seine while handcuffed. Supposedly that stunt had also been filmed.

By 1910, I was spending nearly all of my weekends either in Munich or in the Bavarian countryside. Throughout this time, I also took full advantage of meeting with Doctor Jung in person. Conversations were always invigorating, and there was never a lack of insights to share.

I continued to lead a double life when it came to the Poincares. Neither Francois nor Sophia knew what was going on with me behind closed doors, and my intention was for it to remain that way. From outward appearances, I was merely their hired music instructor sent there to give private lessons and to entertain other guests when apropos. That's not without saying that there weren't close calls.

Regarding my friend, Wendell, we did our best to stay in touch despite both of our hectic schedules. He was still based in London although writing assignments had him gallivanting all over the globe.

*   *   *

Dearest John,

First of all, thank you for all of the metaphysical material you've shipped from Germany. On the London home front, although the original members of the Golden Dawn have scattered, I've kept an eye on their scions. Dion Fortune (aka Mary Violet Firth) has embraced occult doctrines incorporating the viewpoints of both Freud and Jung. Supposedly she also has an association with Brodie-Innes, the chap from Edinburgh you've asked me to inquire about.

I've also heard that Sax Rohmer (aka Arthur Henry Sarsfield Ward) knows Houdini. Although McGregor Mathers has faded into obscurity, several others have been forming their own opinions, Aleister Crowley being the most outspoken and predominant. Mind you, my friend, I am not directly involved in these circles, although I'm sure you'd believe otherwise. I am strictly a journalist with an objective eye fascinated by all of their goings-on.

The British Museum has also offered another highlight in my life. There is a lady named Claire who works as a catalogue assistant that I've taken a liking to. She's been more than helpful with all of my Egyptian research. The rest I won't bore you with, because I know you hate when I talk about women and sex.

You'll have to rely on Sir Arthur's generosity and widespread influence for introductions and referrals for publishing fiction. My co-workers are strictly involved in the publishing of non-fiction. I can attempt to submit any material you might have on music criticism or technical issues on photography. Unfortunately, photography intended as fine art is not suitable, and it's so obvious that you've demonstrated much talent in that area. What about your old friend Whit from Edinburgh? Are you still in touch?

Much of what I write is in the realm of business enterprise. To think, that I was so bold as to introduce myself as a writer and editor from David Balfour's publishing office to Bram Stoker and George Bernard Shaw when we saw them at the Avenue Theatre! For a quick second, I swore they'd believe me. Alas, my literary career is not as glamorous as my wit, candor and imagination.

We've not seen each other in such a long time that I fear I might run out of ink or stationery before all my thoughts are finished.

Mackenzie

*   *   *

I was way behind in grading my students' papers and nodding off in a corner over at the teachers' administrative offices when I thought I could retreat into a few minutes of repose. But the last thing I expected was to have a handful of my colleagues interrupt my nap embroiled in a political debate. Professor Schneider, one of the more outspoken members of the *Klavierleher* or piano teaching staff, Eisenmann, a *Geigenleher* from the strings department, Reisinger, also a piano instructor and Professor Schwab, from vocals and choir, insisted on engaging me in their arguments.

"Now that Bismarck has united Germany and strong alliances have been made with Austria-Hungary, our leaders are promoting expansion of their empire," Schneider said while pouring me a cup of tea.

He plopped a *buchtein* sweet roll on a plate and requested that I take it. Juggling the roll and tea along with my papers, I abruptly opened my eyes as an unwilling participant to avoid an avalanche.

"That redheaded female student of yours that's always following you around dropped these off. She said they were for you, but from the looks of it there's plenty to share."

"Fraulein von Braun?" I asked.

"Yes. She's also in one of my classes," Reisinger interjected, "but she never brings me sweets. I think she's fond of you. Is there a possibility that the two of you might get serious?"

"Perhaps, but right now we're just good friends. I'm afraid my true affections pine away towards a lady who's already taken." I laughed it off, but realized that I might be opening myself up to a conversation that was better off avoided. The last thing I wanted was for someone to say, once again, that I was as heartless as a piano without its player.

"Well, I wouldn't let a good one, who is available, get away," Schwab, said. "True love is a rare blessing. It doesn't show up on your doorstep very often."

Everyone's conversation steered away from affairs of the heart to the pertinent affairs of state.

"Frankly, in regards to politics, I'd just like to close my eyes, listen to music and forget all these squabbles ever existed," I said, but my comments were ignored.

Schneider added, "Unfortunately, the German imperial family seems to be no exception in wanting to catch up with the others, especially the British who have spearheaded the colonial imperialistic game. I don't understand how these rulers think that this is part of their birthright. Has there been anyone throughout history who was kind or fair? Off the top of my head I can't think of anyone."

"That's why there's been sentiments towards the Red Berlin movement with Karl Marx and Friedrich Engels," Eisenmann explained. "The *Communist Manifesto* has been gaining in popularity. To hell with those imperialistic royal bastards! The power and the profits need to trickle down to the working classes! What do you think, Professor Scott? You come from a different background than us."

"I'm finding it interesting that one of our prominent, outspoken and well-respected British writers, H.G. Wells, has been active in the Fabian Society, which has socialist leanings. He's also written quite a few books on political speculations. He tends to tackle the issues from a more scientific point of view, basing his concerns about mankind's potential annihilation via weapons of mass destruction and perverted uses of technology. However, I don't think he's concerned about a raid from a well-trained cavalry."

"Professor Scott," Schneider said, "I think you underestimate the German mind. Since Medieval times we've always taken pride in wielding larger shields and longer swords. Even our architecture inspires one to make a grand entrance, but we're not all flash and fanfare. Let me remind you, that we've always been fascinated by technology and have also sought to outdo others in that arena. Perhaps your head has been so wrapped up around music that you

269

haven't kept up with the times. After all, Carl Benz did invent the first commercial automobile and Count Ferdinand von Zeppelin created our superior airships. It was others that improved upon it and perhaps marketed it more successfully. Germans are clearly an inventive race."

Eisenmann insisted on adding his opinion. "I'm convinced that egos will eventually collide and Germany will declare war as an excuse to expand its empire and power."

"War? Are you certain?" Schwab asked.

"There's always been a bone of contention against British imperialism," Reisinger chimed in.

"I don't see it as any other alternative considering how all these rulers have behaved in the past," Eisenmann replied.

While my companions all had to put in their two pence, our department head, Professor de Lange, entered and ended our discussion at once.

"War and politics? Unless you're elaborating on military themes in masterpieces such as Tchaikovsky's *War of 1812* or von Suppé's *Light Cavalry Overture*, it's back to work—all of you!" he shouted, shoving a few of my partners aside.

* * *

Summer 1910   Windlesham, Crowborough
John,

Sincere thanks for the good work on *The Adventure of the Devil's Foot*. Greenhough keeps lighting a fire under my tail and can't get enough of Holmes, so it will be up to you to fulfill that request while I'm off chasing ghosts. Sherlock reminds me of an unwanted houseguest who keeps knocking at my door, but I'm obligated to invite him in and be hospitable, anyway. The mere thought of each story request kindles such a lack of enthusiasm.

I made a few final edits to guarantee my personal signature since you have your own distinctive way of wording things, but overall it's quite satisfactory. Send me your thoughts for upcoming themes, and I'll let you know what I think of them. Meanwhile, I've been busy writing for theater. National mourning for the death of King Edward upstaged *The House of Temperly*. That, plus its boxing theme didn't have much feminine appeal. However, the theatrical version of *The Speckled Band* has been well received. It's always been one of my favorite Sherlock Holmes stories, but it's been difficult to deal with live snakes.

Arthur

*   *   *

Since Doctor Jung was in town for a society meeting, he and I met in his hotel room at the Hotel Torbräu, the oldest hotel in Munich, which had been around since the time of Columbus. It was a well-preserved gem in the heart of town and a stone's throw away from the famous Rathaus-Glockenspiel in the Marienplatz. The concierge downstairs boasted that Mozart had lived nearby back in the late 18th century.

"*Willkommen*," Doctor Jung greeted me and motioned for me to get comfortable.

I busily began winding my timepiece. I couldn't help but notice that despite his cheery manner the doctor looked disturbed. "Doctor, is there something wrong?"

He took a moment to put his thoughts into words. "Didn't you warn me a while back that peculiar things might happen after you read from your diary?"

I nodded.

"Last night at supper my wife got chatty about a luncheon she attended earlier. My attention was diverted with a rush of memories. Out of nowhere I began to recall when I was a young boy that I was convinced I had two personalities and often felt like I lived in different worlds. Naturally, I was born Swiss, but part of me also

271

felt like I had lived in the 18th century somewhere else. My parents, especially my father who was a member of the clergy, could neither accept my opinions, nor could they answer my questions on that matter. As I got older, I experienced other inexplicable occurrences where I kept imagining that I was different people from various times in history," Jung said.

His confession brought to mind that Wendell also reported remarkable reactions when he brought up the topic of dreams and visions taking place in ancient China.

"John, I am so sorry. Here I'm taking up all of your time talking about myself. What seems to be your issue today?"

"That's all right, Doctor. Recently, I felt like I was experiencing a dream, which took place in both the past and the future, if that makes any sense. Since I've been on a crusade to recall as much as possible about my childhood, I felt this was a milestone. However, I can attest to the fact that this incident never actually happened, which you will realize in a moment. I was close to nine years old and was playing with my younger brother outdoors by a pond. It was winter, and the pond was iced over. The two of us were throwing small sticks and stones towards the pond to see if the ice would break, but they would bounce and slide, so we assumed that the ice had frozen solid. We both dared each other to venture out onto the ice, but since I was the older, I volunteered to go first.

"I stepped out on to the ice carefully, testing my weight one foot at a time with each step being scarier than the next while my brother continued to shout challenges at me from shore. Then, as I waved my arms up and down to signal that it was safe, I began to hear that terrifying sound of the ice cracking below.

"Beneath me, fissures quickly spread like spider webs. My brother screamed hysterically. Then, time slowed down, similar to the experience when you are seated in a cinema and the film gets caught in the projector. As the film comes to grinding halt, the hot lamp inside the projector burns the film so that what you see on the screen is a frozen still image with a hole, getting wider and wider until it finally fades to black. In my case, the ice gave way beneath me, and I plunged into the freezing pond. I cried and frantically tried to crawl my way out but succumbed to the cold and sank as my numb body fell below the water's surface."

"Did you die in your dream?" Doctor Jung asked.

"Surprisingly, I didn't, but I'm not sure if I'd be sitting in your office telling you this if I did. I entered a state of hibernation. I could surmise that Hindu fakirs or people like Harry Houdini consciously achieve a similar state in order to survive when they are buried alive or locked in chains underwater for an inordinate amount of time. I closed my eyes, and yes, I did feel like I was going to die."

"Were you scared?" Jung asked.

"Not at all, which is hard to believe, and that's what makes this experience that much more amazing. Also, I can assure you that I would never have taken on such a dare. I might have done some crazy things when I was a lad, but nothing like that.

"Then, after being submerged under the water, convinced that I was dead, when I opened my eyes, I was no longer a child, but a grown man. I was dressed in a dark business suit and sitting in a stately, exclusive private club somewhere in London!"

"That's quite a transition," Jung remarked, "Did that look like anything familiar?"

"Not at all," I replied, "In fact, I appeared a few years older than I am now, and so I suspect it was at some point in the near future."

I reached for a glass of water and loosened my tie. Doctor Jung was writing so fast that he scarcely kept up with me.

"Have you ever suspected that you've had a precognitive dream?" Jung asked.

"This is not the first time I've dreamed about an event in the future. But there's no way of judging whether or not any of these particular dreams could come to pass."

"This multiple layer symbolism is interesting, however," the doctor commented.

"There's more," I explained, scratching my head, trying to bring more thoughts to the surface. "This new location had a palatial room, very ornate—ivory in color, very high ceilings, tall Greek Corinthian floor-to-ceiling columns, windows curved on top with deep red velvet curtains. Rich dark-blue Persian rugs adorned the floors, and there were oversized porcelain Chinese vases filled with ferns at the foot of every column, white linen table cloths—oh yes, and the wait staff was formally dressed, very top notch."

"John, do you recall what you were doing there?"

"In my dream, I seemed to be affiliated with the British government, but my involvement had nothing whatsoever to do with music or performing, which was most unusual. My fluency in the German language was a major factor. The men who accompanied me were also British government officials, but I wasn't quite sure what their business was or their reason for being there except that it was for a serious matter. Also for some reason, I felt like the Germans were our enemies. Can you make any conclusions from this?"

"Sounds like you're describing a scene from a film," he said.

I got up to stretch my legs, walked over to the window and looked out on to the street. Normal people seemed to be scurrying about their business focused on their daily routines. What I experienced was far from normal.

"Details of our conversation weren't evident, but minute visual images were crystal clear. Our first waiter poured us all glasses of Cabernet for those who desired red and Riesling for those who preferred white wine. Another waiter entered carrying a large white oval porcelain tray with fresh warm rolls, which he served each one of us with a pair of silver tongs.

"A third waiter arrived with a silver tray, covered with a lid, carrying a roast. My distorted reflection appeared on its curved surface when he removed it. Within seconds I was no longer in that dining room, but I passed through that mirrored image and out the other side.

"Everything was out of focus, at first, similar to a camera when you haven't adjusted your lens, or that first feeling when you've woken up after too much to drink the night before and your consciousness hasn't quite caught up with you. When images became clearer, I found myself in yet, another unexpected location. However, that's when I realized that I had woken up, and I was back in my bedroom."

I closed my journal, returned it back to my coat pocket and reached for my glass of water.

"What's your diagnosis, sir?"

Doctor Jung scratched his chin and placed his notebook down.

"Let's hope it's not a medical condition causing these visions," he replied, "It might be a good time to conduct a physical evaluation. Have you formed any conclusions?"

Instead of answering him directly, I digressed slightly. "Doctor, have you ever felt like you created a painting, but without a specific plan? Imagine going up to a canvas and sketching out an idea, but as soon as you take out your paints and start the project you decide to go back to some designs you had in mind earlier. You add some images that you had planned for your next project, but decide to put them in this one, instead.

"Then, you allow the paint to dry. Weeks, perhaps months later, you decide to go back to the older concepts and elaborate on those details, taking out your thinnest brushes. This allows you to focus on those particulars, as if viewing them under a magnifying glass."

"John, if I recall correctly, artists in the Renaissance set down a monochromatic foundation on their canvases and then glazed over that with layers of oils. It was called the *Verdaccio* technique of underpainting. Leonardo da Vinci used multiple layers of paint along with another process called *sfumato*, which translates to vanished or evaporated, blurring boundaries and edges making them nearly undetectable. Both of these in combination produced that translucent, otherworldly and haunting effect on Mona Lisa's face. However, from what you described, I can't see how this would be any different to composing a piece of music. Transitions must appear seamless between movements."

"Precisely," I said. "You put that into words better than I did. Often, I can start out with clear objective, but in the process of fine tuning, it might turn out very different than I had originally expected, because it's a constant process of taking apart sections, examining them and toggling back and forth before finally moving forward."

"Why, then, are you bringing this up?" Doctor Jung asked.

"Doctor," I replied, "my life is an unfinished symphony.

*   *   *

Winter 1910

My good friend, John,
Jean gave birth to our second son, Adrian. Now we have two boys plus the children from my first marriage. Kingsley, my oldest, is at Eton. I think he wants to study medicine like his father.

You are proving to be a man of many talents. The photographs you sent me of the German countryside now hang on the wall of my study. However, I'm especially proud that you have taken a leap of faith and tried to write a few books on music theory. Although they aren't short stories about Sherlock, so what? Be persistent, and I know you'll also get your music published and recorded so it could be played on that new-fangled Edison contraption you're so sold on.

Although several countries separate us at the moment, I insist that our relationship go beyond the one I had with Robert Louis Stevenson, which regrettably was only through letters. I was planning to visit him in Samoa while extending my American tour in

1894, but unfortunately he never made it through the year. Once I tried to convene with his spirit through a medium, but our séance had no discernible results. Continue to contact me at our normal hour.

Arthur

*   *   *

Early 1911

Dear Wendell,

You're becoming quite the adventurer having recently returned from India and soon you will sail to the New World. I'm in complete agreement with you that we shouldn't have surrendered those thirteen colonies. I wish I could stow away in your steamer trunk, but I still have my obligations at the Conservatory. Hopefully, the arrival of this letter finds propitious timing and does not reside in the company of your landlady for months on end.

Tell me more about Crowley, the controversial poet and writer you've been following. I cannot understand why publishers are boycotting his work, and you've had to forward submissions as his proxy. The situation seems rather complicated and sinister to me. It sounds like you've had no problem procuring suitable work on your own as a writer. Otherwise, how would you have the freedom for such travel?

One must admit these have been interesting times. Besides paying our respects at our monarch's funeral, in Germany, Mahler's 8th Symphony premiered in Munich with over a thousand musicians and the first zeppelin launched with passengers. Both you and I and everyone we knew were on the edge of our seats when Halley's Comet made a close call. We all thought the world was coming to an end.

You must promise me you'll continue your correspondence. In turn, I'll give you my solemn vow that I'll read any metaphysical publications that you send me even if I fall short of understanding

277

them. Finally, didn't you say that you received a mysterious key from a man while helping him photograph an Egyptian artifact at the British Museum, and that it was helping you uncover all sorts of remarkable information?

Yours most devoted,

John Patrick Scott

*   *   *

The Case of the Ardent Traveler
August 1911

Dear John,

Back from the longest motor trip that I think I'll ever take. Jean and I participated in the Prince Henry of Prussia Cup. The Brits won. Ironically the prize was a carved ivory statue of a lady inscribed, Peace. Unfortunately, I think our opponents, the Germans, had the complete opposite on their minds.

Fifty British and fifty German drivers went on a grand motor tour starting in Homburg on July 4th. We traveled to Cologne on the 5th, Munster on the 6th, Bremerhaven on the 7th, took a steamer abroad and went to our country after that, including a round in Auld Reeky. Each British driver had a German military officer escort. Our man, Count Carmer, Rittmeister of the Breslau Cuirassiers, was a bit standoffish at first, but proved to be quite a gentleman. There was quite a bit of dissent when it was discovered that there was a gross imbalance as to the ranks of the observers. The Brits had sent high-ranking officers to accompany the German team, but apparently the Germans reciprocated with mere captains and lieutenants.

Meanwhile, rumors were afoot that the whole affair was a strategic diversion. Prince Henry was not only the sponsor of the race but also head of the Prussian naval forces, and during our motor tour a controversial naval offensive occurred over in Morocco. Many fear that the Germans wish to wage war and expand their territories. I've always been sympathetic towards them, but now I'm seriously beginning to have second thoughts. Being in this race allowed me a prime vantage point to spy on them. Unfortunately, I do think they plan to initiate war.

This, of course, brings my concern straight over to you. Have you overheard any conversations on your end, and what about the newspapers? Certainly, you have access to more journals and magazines than I would from England, including those that would be slightly more radical in thought. Should war break out, have you considered your options? I know that politics has never been your game, but it's vital you become aware of your surroundings. The world does not consist entirely of art and music. Now since I'm back home, I've been writing again. Recent scientific discoveries have piqued my interest in paleontology. Expect some thought-provoking stories as a result. Take care of yourself and keep your eyes open.

Arthur

*   *   *

I bravely plunged head first into some of the arcane texts that Wendell sent. So much of it was disguised beyond recognition to dissuade those who really have no bloody business poking their noses where they didn't belong. Dangerous forces could be unleashed, and I certainly didn't want to be on my hands and knees begging for some priest to come over to my flat to perform an exorcism!

Yet, my morbid curiosity made it impossible to stay away from them. Often, I'd want to slap my hands and put them away, even throw them out. So instead, I took out my tarot cards and fingered through the deck. My gaze honed in on the Magician. That's what I wanted in my life—the ability to bend, manipulate and control my reality. How come I wasn't automatically privileged with the good fortune that seemed to come so easily to others? What was magic for, anyway?

In comparison to Arthur or Wendell's exploits, my travels traversed other worlds, either along the corridors of time or in the astral realm. Thus, on my pre-determined evening, at the proper hour, I put sandalwood incense in a brazier, lit white candles, and sat within a circle inscribed with sigils and esoteric symbols, waiting to align myself with spirits unknown. What I didn't realize was that by conducting such a ritual, which would also include all ceremonies that I performed in the past and planned to do in the future, that it would have its indelible imprint. Finn had warned me about this many times and constantly insisted on giving me pre-astral flight lectures. There was no such thing as insignificance in the metaphysicality of the universe, and nothing escaped that *all-seeing eye* that recorded everything to be stored in the Secret Library.

Without the security of trained and experienced teachers like I had at the Underground University, solo explorations into the world of magic were always risky. In that sense, I guess I was one of the blessed. By the time I was aware that I had a guide from the higher planes that had been assigned to me (referring to Finn), I already had mentors and teachers within a school setting, who were a bit more accessible (and believable) looking out for my welfare. After all, it has been and still is difficult to reconcile that after all these years that I am an adult and still have an *invisible friend* who gives me advice. Often he tells me what and what not to do, and leads me off into impalpable and improbable dimensions. What's even more difficult to comprehend is that everyone else has a guide similar to him (or at least in function), forever present like a shadow that won't go away even in the dark. The irony is that I don't think I've ever been as grateful for his friendship as I should've been.

Another issue that I'd been contending with was regarding my faulty recollections of childhood experiences. I had to become an ethereal archeologist and unearth such memories. But I was not alone. I knew that Arthur had similar experiences although Wendell seemed to be more adept at accessing such buried information. I wasn't exactly sure as to why except that he told me a ridiculous story about chocolate cake that had been tainted on purpose. He always seemed less surprised about events from our youth, with the exception of that recent incident where I was trying to cope with sexual awakenings. I highly suspected he did a fine job of putting those thoughts out of his mind and suppressing them.

Often I'd try to take a step back and reflect upon what was really happening my life. What was going on with my friends and others who I cared about? Why did I seem to make progress in some areas and in others I'd be stopped? Throw the issue of time travel into the mix, and a whole new world opened up. Possibilities were limitless. Link magic, metaphysics and reincarnation to concept of time travel, and it was easy to convince oneself that he or she was immortal. Thus, it was easy to deceive oneself that taking personal responsibility was pointless, and that one always had a second chance.

*   *   *

Another Lost World

In 1912, Arthur published his novel, *The Lost World*. Professor Challenger was a far cry from Sherlock, and yet the public embraced the diversion. Something in the back of my mind wondered if Arthur's inspiration had come as a result of solo runs with the time machine I gave him. After all, the concept of explorers encountering dinosaurs and a civilization frozen in the past certainly had the earmarks of time travel. If the success of his novel was a direct result of one of his personal ventures, then I owed him my hearty congratulations.

In the interim, Arthur had written a few letters mentioning that he still wanted to go back to explore ancient China coming up with all sorts of new excuses as to why. He even went so far as mailing a small, imported silk-covered jewelry box that I could use as a link for our next time experiment. He wasn't fooling me. I knew that he was still engrossed with finding that legendary book, which at this point was starting to get me worried stiff. If it supposedly had the power of creating stories out of thin air, then it might put me, as his ghostwriter, out of a much-needed job, but I suspected he had motives far beyond that. It almost made me regret that I hadn't taken full advantage of it when I had it in my hands, but then again, I had received it under such bizarre and exceptional circumstances that I honestly didn't know what to make of it. We were both bewildered as to how we wound up in Japan, instead, except that Finn explained that it meant there was a lesson to be learned that would be relevant now.

Arthur seemed to have a playful, mischievous streak inside him this evening during our astral meeting. He materialized in the chair opposite of me. Immediately thereafter, he knocked an object off my table.

"Arthur, what did you do that for?" I asked, a bit puzzled while thinking about the pranks I played years ago on Doctor Lorraine Smith and Heinrich Schmitz.

"Much of it has been trial and error, but you'd be surprised what some of the members of my Psychical Research Society group and I have been doing," he replied.

"It appears that way," I said while beginning to get annoyed. "Since you're in such an adventurous mode this evening, do you want to take another stab at time travel?"

"I'm game although still skeptical about the results we had previously," Arthur replied. "But I don't think I have all the components for the time machine to operate. I'm certain that I don't have any of those pellets to make the steam."

"You won't need them," I assured him. "Do you have two mirrors handy?"

"I think I can arrange something like that," he said looking around in his study at two decorative brass-rimmed mirrors hung on his wall.

"Take them and position them so that one is in front of you and one is behind you. Put your chair in the middle and sit comfortably so you can see that optical illusion where your reflection, both in front and behind, multiplies itself into infinity," I explained. "That will create a vortex, a focal point, or a tunnel where we can project into the past. There's no time to explain the theory behind it. But if you want to do this, please do as I say."

He removed both mirrors from his wall as per my instructions, and I followed suit in my own flat. All the while, of course, we were communicating telepathically on the astral plane, and on the physical plane were in two different locations.

"Arthur, give me your hand, your astral hand, of course."

He pulled his chair over, rearranged the mirrors and sat back down extending his right hand towards my left. Then I placed my left astral hand on top of his.

"Can I assume you're wearing your pocket watch?" I asked.

"But of course, why do you ask?"

"Take your left hand and clasp it tight," I instructed, "We'll use it as a reference point for maintaining a bond between us."

I took out my timepiece and Arthur did the same. Then, while concentrating on the hands of my timepiece going backwards, the reflecting mirrors created a powerful vortex. We were sucked in with such force that it was like being swept down a drain. The room spun and rapidly disappeared. My reflection in the mirror no longer looked like a redheaded Scotsman. Instead, my hair turned black and straight, pulled back like a horse's tail, and I had dark black wisps of a moustache shadowing my upper lip with the beginnings of a soft, dark beard on my chin. My starched white cotton dress shirt and navy blue pinstriped waistcoat melted away into a soft silk kimono, and my hard leather shoes transformed into straw sandals worn with soft cloth socks. It looked like our plans had been botched again, because this looked like Japan, not China, and Arthur disappeared.

My feet became more solid and heavier on the ground, and it was then that I realized that I was wearing weighty and cumbersome armor over those softer undergarments. At the time I was performing guard duty outside a room where the daimyo's son, Masahiro Takeda, was having a business meeting. Considering the fact that it was easy to overhear everyone's conversations on the other side of those very thin, rice paper walls, it really didn't sound like anyone was conducting business any more. Meanwhile, one of my friends and fellow soldiers approached.

"Ashikaga-san, how long have you been standing guard?"

"This so-called meeting has been going on for hours."

"You missed supper."

"I'm starving, but I can't leave this post. If I did I'd be whipped, or used to test out someone's sword," I replied.

My friend went over to a fountain and came back with a ladle filled with cold, refreshing water. He held it up to my lips and offered me a drink.

"Here, take a few sips, you must be parched."

"*Domo*, Katsu-san," I said, "You're very kind."

"Maybe you should ask Yoko to bring you some rice and fruit. She likes you very much," my friend suggested.

"Yoko-san? The farmer's daughter?"

"She'd make you a fine wife. Maybe you should consider her as a prospect," Katsu said.

I laughed, but not too loud as to attract attention from those inside.

"That's funny. Several people have also told me that. Is there a contest or conspiracy going on behind my back? I couldn't picture myself with a farmer's daughter, and I have my sights on someone else. Yoko would want a very simple life. I have much greater ambitions."

"Besides serving Lord Takeda, what sort of ambitions?"

"Well, for one, I'd like to learn to play the flute." Then I pulled out a small bamboo flute that I had in a casing camouflaged as an extra weapon.

My friend laughed, but was surprised that I had hidden it so well. I immediately put my hand over his mouth so no one could hear that I had company.

"That's clever. Can you play it?" he asked.

"Not very well, but I'm trying to get Monk Wei to teach me."

"You still spend time with that crazy monk?"

"He's not crazy. He's very wise and talented," I said. "He also coaches me with my staff and sword training."

"There are stories that Monk Wei talks with spirits—ghosts haunting graveyards—commands them to do his bidding. Is that true?" Katsu asked.

"Don't know. Being around the dead scares me, but maybe those ghosts endow his music with magic and special powers of transcendence. Remember, they are linked with our ancestors. Maybe they can impart their knowledge from the past."

Katsu-san tugged my sleeve. "What purpose would a flute serve?"

"None whatsoever," I replied. "Except that I enjoy it. What's wrong with that?"

"Nothing I guess, but to me it all seems like such a waste of time...and scary...if ghosts are connected to his melodies. Do you desire anything more practical?"

"Yes, I'd like to write," I said.

"You can read and write?"

"My father owned a print shop, so I had to learn in order to help him out, but I'd like to learn more. My education was cut short when my parents sent me over here to work and train."

"Maybe you should ask Masahiro-san if he could arrange for you to find a teacher. He's obviously well educated."

"Don't be silly! Why would he want me to get smarter than I already am? As far as he's concerned, I'm only cut out to be a *dōshin*, his low-ranking security guard," I replied, a bit upset that my friend would suggest such absurd ideas.

"I never learned to read and write," Katsu replied. "My parents sent me over here at a very young age."

"You mean they sold you into servitude like they did to me?"

"Yes, if you put it that way, but I was a lot younger than you when I arrived. I was only six. I think you were at least twelve."

"You can't read at all?" I asked.

285

"A few words here and there, important words and simple instructions, but I cannot pick up a book and read a story. Things like that have to be read to me."

"That's too bad," I said. "However, you're a much better swordsman than I am."

"That's because I've had longer to train than you have, but I don't see that as something to be envious of," my friend replied.

"It might save your life in battle one day," I said. "But you better go. We're not supposed to be talking to each other."

"Before I do, can you play your flute for me?" he asked.

"Someone will hear us. I could get in trouble."

"Then play it softly," he said.

When I blew into it trying to keep the volume down, a loud shrill sound came out instead. My friend ran off just in time before the doors to the meeting room opened. Masahiro-san, who was a big and heavy man, stumbled out, quite drunk, and stepped on my foot. I bit my lip hard to keep from crying out. Behind him were his clients and a group of ladies as their escorts. All were very drunk, telling jokes and carrying on loudly.

"Where was that music coming from?" he asked with a booming voice.

I tried to hide my flute behind my back since I didn't have enough time to put it back in its secret casing. He caught wind that I was keeping something from him so he kicked me hard in the shins and then reached behind me as I doubled over and pulled out the flute.

"Since when did I hire a musician instead of a body guard?" he bellowed and belched.

I shook my head as he took my flute and broke it in two over his knee. Then he tossed the ruined pieces aside. I stood there in shock, silent.

This was a good time to make an exit back to the present. I gave a firm squeeze on to my timepiece to ground myself. Then I held onto Arthur's hand, albeit astrally, and willed my consciousness away from 17th century Japan and leapt forward into the time of King George V. Arthur remained seated in his chair, a bit sleepy from the late hour, but still intact. I reached for my brandy to clear my throat.

"I guess I had another strange dream," Arthur said rubbing his eyes with a long, drawn out yawn. "Are you sure this time machine is working properly?"

"I'm convinced we made a jump," I stated as I reached into my trousers. Splinters had become embedded under my skin from that shattered flute—keepsakes and a testimonial that we'd been there and hadn't fallen asleep or made everything up. In a macabre sort of way, it was comparable to claiming we were passengers on the Titanic. Whether or not we survived the tragedy was immaterial. We were still able to bring back the tickets we purchased as proof.

Arthur was disappointed. "Once again, I don't seem to appear in the best light. You, however, continue to find these excursions rather entertaining. Have you considered the possibility of writing those thoughts down and turning them into a story? It would certainly be unique."

"Would you assist me in submitting them to your publishers if I did?" I asked, returning back to a forbidden topic.

The mood took a turn for the worse. Arthur mumbled to himself. "*No! Goddammit, if Bertie had only kept his mouth shut...If only he...*"

"Pardon me?" I asked cutting in, barely able to make it out. "Were you saying something to me?"

Arthur shook his head. "Oh no, it's nothing."

"Are you sure? By the look on your face, it seemed fairly important."

Arthur was agitated. "I just remembered something entirely unrelated that had nothing to do with you whatsoever. Forget I even said anything."

I suspected that comment wasn't intended for my ears, but what was he thinking? That I'd turn an incident like that into

287

something he'd get credit for? Tension had been mounting between us for a while. He'd been leading me around like an obedient little dog for years. Without giving me the answer I so desperately wanted, he struggled with another yawn, signaling that we should call it a night. I finished my brandy and was fiercely determined to get him to change his mind.

*   *   *

My Valley of Fear

1914: Francois and I spent the week in Prague. He had set up a meeting with several influential officials interested in having me perform in a series of prestigious concerts, but decadence and debauchery took precedence. After an all-night bender we overslept and foolishly missed our appointment. When he begged his contacts to reschedule, they informed us that the people we had to meet with had already left town. Unfortunately our first impression was a not a favorable one. I was sorely disappointed and took off to find solace in a local pub. After a round of inquiries as to my whereabouts, Francois caught up with me and also got soused. I broke down like a young child and wept in his arms that night. He kept reassuring me that there'd be other opportunities, and the least we could do was to enjoy the rest of the trip instead of being miserable over it. At the end of the week, we returned to his manor rather melancholic in spite of futile efforts to cheer me up.

Sophia and Francois had me as their marionette and pulled my strings as they saw fit. She eventually confessed to me that they hadn't bedded together in years. I suspected something was afoot when I first discovered they slept in separate bedrooms. He did his minimal to fulfill his fatherly duties, and beyond that his interest had always been with men. My presence was the perfect cover up. It kept him away from the lowbrow street hustlers and assured that his reputation in society would stay intact. Who would've expected the piano instructor to be the paid harlot on staff? For the madam, my role was pretty much the same. Admittedly, I came to enjoy our entanglements. If I hadn't, I wouldn't have played along despite my dependency upon their generosity, which helped round off financing my education where my scholarships stopped short. Yet, all parties experienced both the drawbacks as well as the benefits. Although the Prague incident was a complete debacle, Sophia charmed the right people to get me a series of bookings in Vienna, for which I'll be forever in her debt.

My challenge was to ensure that neither my lord nor lady knew what the other was up to, which put me in the unenviable position of constantly covering up affairs while telling white lies and struggling to remember what I had said and to whom. Thus, I was constantly looking over my shoulder especially in regards to Francois. I knew that he dabbled in the mystical arts and had all sorts of ways and means at his fingertips of finding out information, if so inclined.

The problem was that I had no idea as to whether or not Francois was capable of accessing the Secret Library. The conversation never came up, and Finn never dropped any hints one way or another. Then again, it also occurred to me that perhaps he knew all about what was going on between his wife and I already and didn't care.

But my masquerade extended beyond the gates of their manor. There was a young student at the Conservatory who was quite fond of me. Considering the fact that only one woman had ever stolen my heart, my association with this student provided my alibi to hide my leanings towards the same sex. Without a doubt, my colleagues were thrown off track, and that's exactly what I wanted to accomplish. If word had spread about my real attractions, there could be serious repercussions. My position at the Conservatory would be in jeopardy, and I'd never make headway on the concert stage. One false step and all my career aspirations would shatter if I were to be blackmailed out of spite or malice. It was terrible that I was deceptively motivating poor Maria to believe that our mock courtship might lead to something serious. Everyone had their own little compartment with their own particular story. My task was to keep everything straight and pray that it all didn't fall apart. Meanwhile, I continued to consult with Doctor Jung to make sure my head was screwed on tight.

* * *

Seven of Swords In A Sea of Court Cards

Munich, February 1914: Because of my insistence on making one last excursion in time travel before leaving town, I was delayed back in Stuttgart and had to take a later train than anticipated. There was a chance I might get to meet Stravinsky over at the Society, who was living in Switzerland but would be visiting Munich on business. I was eager to share my enthusiasm for his ballet, *The Rite of Spring*. Therefore, I took extra pains to dress for the occasion.

With the money I was earning from the Poincare family giving piano lessons and the hush-hush ghostwriting arrangement I had with Arthur, I splurged on some finery after years of lean times and frugality. Perhaps I chose fashionable Chinoiserie, because I was inspired on a subconscious level by my time travels back to the Far East. Stunning carved jade and cinnabar cuff links added a crowning touch to my freshly pressed shirt, custom-made, as I was beginning to outgrow my old clothes. The lady, who did a splendid job of fattening me up ever so slightly, had purchased an expensive piece of silk, which she took to a tailor to fashion into a unique tie, and today I would also be breaking in my new waistcoat of paisley Oriental silk. This unorthodox, rather flashy attire was going to have me stand out from the crowd. Therefore, I was going to have to summon the confidence to look dandy and dapper and wear it with pride. After all, I was no longer simply, John Patrick Scott, the mere musicology professor. Now, I was also the Time Traveler Professor.

My folly, however, was despite the fact that I went to great pains to pick out my wardrobe that I dressed quickly, assuming that nothing was out of place, and I failed to glance in the mirror before leaving my flat. When I received a few stares along the way, I suspected that others were jealous. Upon my arrival, Heinz tried to put a firm grip on my shoulder preventing me from entering our meeting room. However, with stubborn persistence, I broke free and opened the tall, imposing wooden doors while trying not to draw attention to my belated arrival, which was impossible.

Doctor Freud placed his cigar aside and covered his mouth, holding back a guffaw. Doctor Jung refrained from a similar outburst of laughter. I looked around the room with nervous anticipation, but couldn't spot Stravinsky anywhere. Apparently, I was the only musician present that day, but by some of the others' reactions, I might have walked in looking like a circus clown. Heinz caught up with me, ushered me back out into the hallway, and insisted without further ado that I head forthwith to the lavatory.

What I encountered was quite a surprise. I had disobeyed Finn's request to refrain from "poking my noggin into the future" because I felt there were some unresolved issues that warranted a second look. However, while traversing through the 23rd century, Miss Lleullne was dressing up for a night on the town, and the memento I brought back with me upon my return was the effect of painted cherry red lips from her cosmetics. Since I failed, in haste, to notice such a queer countenance before leaving my flat, I must have been entertaining everyone throughout my train ride with all sorts of perverse thoughts until confronted with this looking glass.

Therefore, I rubbed off the greasepaint as best I could, leaving a slight crimson stain in its wake and rejoined my comrades in the other room. Once again, heads turned my way, but the reactions died down, and the members resumed their conversations, which were soon to be upstage by someone else's entrance.

Our sanctuary doors opened once again, and this time Heinz escorted an odd looking man wearing a happenstance bow tie. He had a bald, shaved head as round as a full moon, ominous, intense eyes and was wearing a baggy, wool gray coat and carrying a large well-worn briefcase. Hushed conversations buzzed about. He shot me an unnerving glance as he crossed the room, enough to make me sweat, as I swore I had seen his photo before from one of the many books that Wendell was always sending. My sixth sense set off alarms. My chest tightened with a panic I hadn't felt in years.

"Oh, that's that egotistical mountain climber Reuss has been talking about," Steiner whispered into Jung's ear.

"He's a libertine, a pompous poet, and probably the wickedest man on the face of the earth," Jung replied.

"I thought we had a previous discussion that he wasn't permitted in here," Freud confided.

Reuss stood up and motioned to Aleister Crowley to sit in the chair beside him. All eyes warily gazed upon both of them.

"He's also an advocate of heroin, known to perform bizarre rituals involving sexual intercourse, and has one hell of a temper. You would never want to wind up on his bad side," Jung added.

Steiner interjected, "I've read some of his poetry, and it was quite invigorating. He studied at Cambridge, after all. You cannot discount that."

"However, I heard that while at Cambridge, he performed same-sex relations with Herbert Charles Pollitt, president of the Cambridge University Footlights Dramatic Club," Jung added with intensified fervor.

"Is that so?" Steiner asked.

"I also heard that while he was still at student there, he was sent to St. Petersburg posing under the false pretense that he was attempting to learn the Russian language, but instead was acting as a British intelligence agent," Jung explained with agitation.

"Really?" Freud replied, laughing quietly.

"You don't find that disturbing?" Jung asked.

"Actually, I find it somewhat amusing," Freud responded with a wry smile.

Meanwhile, I tried to capture snippets of everyone's reactions, which were, for the most part, not very favorable. Crowley had a colorful personality where his fearsome reputation preceded him, and I suspected that he thoroughly enjoyed it when rumors were blown to extremes. Freud, Jung and Steiner were particularly upset.

Einstein and Hesse stayed out of it for the most part. Every so often Crowley would make eye contact with me. I'd quickly break the spell by scratching my nose, rubbing my eye or looking away trying to not make it apparent that I was also observing him. However, each time our eyes would lock, I felt more irritable by the minute.

Jung crossed his hands over his chest. "He's also into some cockamamie Egyptian mumbo jumbo, something about an angel dictating some *Book of the Law* while spending the night inside the Great Pyramid, and then there was also that incident about finding a particular tablet in the British Museum. It's all rubbish."

"We're finally beginning to agree on things, again," Freud replied and sat back in his chair, lighting up.

As the clock struck four, our consortium adjourned until next month. Everyone flowed out of the gathering room. Crowley began to exit with Reuss, striking his briefcase quite hard, as if deliberately, along my side. Unable to ignore the event, I bent over rubbing the painful spot, but somehow also got bumped, causing me to lose my balance. A bizarre feeling came over me, like I had been cursed or bewitched, which was ridiculous, but then again, considering his reputation anything was fair game.

Once everyone left, I stayed behind to peruse the society's coveted private library. I opened the glass door to one of the bookcases and noticed it was unlocked. I didn't have the luxury of staying several more hours and besides, Heinz would have never have permitted me to remain, so I donned my coat, which had deep generous side pockets and placed several rare manuscripts inside them, *borrowing* them for the time being.

I went straightaway to a tiny little hole-in-the-wall cafe in the vicinity of the train station. Few knew of it. I chose it, not only for their delectable wares, but I was hoping for privacy. While rummaging through my contraband, once again I felt the queerest sensation in my solar plexus. Chalking it up to slight indigestion, I dismissed it at first, but it persisted and was impossible to ignore. In the opposite corner, I spotted Reus and his guest, Crowley, engaged in conversation. They must've snuck in while I was unaware. I stuffed my absconded goods back into my overcoat pocket and picked up my newspaper, peering over the edge to eavesdrop the best I could.

Crowley got up and headed for the lavatory. Meanwhile, Reuss settled the bill and left ahead of him. When Crowley re-emerged, he retrieved his hat and coat, but this time took a different route. He passed by my table and brushed beside me on purpose.

"No one is innocent. Everyone's got a secret," he said, continuing to walk towards the door.

Intrigued, I followed him out.

       *   *   *

Parallax

Munich, March 1914: I entered Doctor Jung's hotel room and spared no time getting to the point.

"I had another dream that took place in the near future. In this dream I was still myself, but I was no longer living in Stuttgart. I was living in London, where I'd like to be ideally, but in this case not exactly doing the usual."

Doctor Jung was busy writing notes and documenting our session. He raised his eyebrows, slid his wire-rimmed glasses off his nose and cleaned off a smudge with his handkerchief.

"John, I seem to recall that this is not the first dream where you found yourself in a situation where you were doing something outside of your normal realm."

"Correct, and in this case, similar to another dream I had before, England was at war with Germany. That's absurd!"

The handcrafted clock on the wall suddenly seemed to tick louder. Both of us heard a policeman's whistle down below on the street and the sound of children laughing.

"I was working for the London War Office, and God knows how I wound up there! My role was to observe, and I don't know what the bloody hell that was supposed to mean, but I was being paid to stare at and even photograph people of notable interest in London.

294

"I was talking a brisk walk not far from Westminster Abbey and heading toward the Thames wearing a heavy charcoal gray and black tweed overcoat. It was a fairly old coat in good shape, but my favorite coat, since it had two very deep pockets, which were perfect to hide a book or a parcel. In addition to that coat, I was wearing black leather gloves, a black bowler hat and was carrying a black umbrella."

"Those are a lot of details to recall. Are your dreams always that vivid?" the doctor asked.

"Always," I replied, "I guess that makes me unique. Well, as I was saying—in this dream, I had been sent out to observe any unusual activities. At first, everything was humdrum. Then I noticed a man in a tan overcoat. It must've been at least three sizes bigger than necessary. Otherwise, I would've walked right by him not paying much attention. No one in his right mind would have worn such an ill-fitting garment. Something told me that he wasn't from London, Scotland or Wales, but he didn't seem German, either. Since we never exchanged words, I never had the opportunity to detect an accent. Why? I had no idea, but he started following me. I didn't like being the mouse hunted by the cat."

Doctor Jung continued taking notes.

"You swear you had never seen this man before?"

"Not now, and not in the dream."

I began to nervously fiddle with my watch chain. "It was as if I had or knew something that he wanted although he never directly confronted me or asked me for it, and for the life of me, I sure as bloody hell didn't know what it was. It was all so strange—so strange. Perhaps, I was missing the boat by not knowing his identity or what he wanted, but I never found out.

"Then, in my dream, I sent a telegram the following day to my friend, Sir Arthur Conan Doyle, asking him about a prisoner he encountered on the Front."

"The Front?"

295

"Something to do with the war," I loosened my collar, nervous that I was sharing predictions that I wasn't supposed to, "I did say there was a war going on, didn't I?"

"Yes, you did. Go on."

"Well, I requested a comprehensive description of that prisoner. When he wired back, all of the details seemed to fit that particular stranger I had just seen. The synchronicity was too uncanny."

"John, I strongly feel there's no such thing as coincidence," Doctor Jung interjected.

"Yes, doctor, that's why I'm sharing this with you, and please, this must be confidential!"

"Of course, continue."

"Words kept popping up in my head—in the dream—words, which said, 'Keys—you have the keys.' What keys? That's what I'd like to know. Then, I woke up."

"Let's examine this." Doctor Jung put his memo book back in his desk. "You had no clue who this person was, yet he kept on following you when it was your duty to follow and observe others. This was essentially a role reversal. Then, he kept on mentioning that you had special keys. Did I miss anything?"

"No, you summarized it, well."

"Can you attribute the notion of keys as a symbol or the ability to unlock answers?"

I paused. "The fact that I had a dream about the future, could this have been a key?"

"Possibly," Jung said.

"Could he have come from the future?"

Doctor Jung put down his writing pad and sat back in his chair. "Don't let your imagination get the better of you," he smiled, raising his brow.

I donned my coat, retrieved my hat and umbrella and began walking towards the door.

"You're ending our session early?" Doctor Jung asked, somewhat surprised.

"Something is bothering me and I can't quite put a finger on it, but thank you for your time," I replied in haste, continuing to head outside.

God knew what I wanted to confess to Doctor Jung and couldn't. I had taken documents from the H.G.A. Society and gave some to Arthur and also to Wendell. That was against house rules. There were other issues, too, including that unforeseen encounter with Crowley, which continued beyond our meeting. But I wasn't going to disclose that, either.

Outdoors, I picked up my gait, breathing in the fresh air to clear my head. I wanted to assume that this man—the man in my dream was from the future, but that was preposterous, like something from one of Wells' novels. Too much was happening, and I kept thinking that a phantom was on my trail. After all, I was imaginative, and I wanted to be a published writer, but I thought I was going to be helping Arthur ghostwrite his stories, not turn my own life into a sensational piece of fiction. Why was I picturing some man from the future? Perhaps, I knew the secret of how he could return to his distant world, and that's why he was following me.

My nerves were getting the better of me, and I needed something other than a drink to calm them down. I ducked into an alley, leaned against the side of a building and closed my eyes finally remembering more. At one point in that dream I sat down on a park bench, pulled a book from my coat pocket and began to read. My pursuer took some crumbs out of his pocket and began feeding pigeons, stalling for time. We were both watching each other.

Even more extraordinary was the title of the book I was reading. It was called, *Time Travel in Theory and Practice*. When I paged through the book, I saw that it was published in 1927. However, there was a newspaper left behind on the bench next to me with headlines reflecting current events. Printed on its front page was the date indicating that it was 1917, ten years earlier, and yet, in real

297

life outside of my dream, I knew that it was only 1914. What I couldn't understand was why I had a dream that took place three years into the future with supporting evidence to prove it, and yet something from even further into the future appeared within that dream with no explanation as to how I obtained it. Then, to make matters even more complicated, I must have been so upset about being spied upon that I inadvertently left that time travel book behind on that park bench when I returned to my office. As soon as I realized the book was missing, I rushed back to that park. But it had disappeared, and I suspected that my stalker had taken it and left.

*　　*　　*

Events occurred at the wrong place, at the wrong time and in the wrong year. Such an occurrence could fray the threads of time. Therefore, I had a "three pipe problem". I reached into my coat pocket and pulled out a pipe and a pouch of tobacco Arthur had given me as a present. He claimed that once a gentleman smoked he was immune to its nasty smell, but nobody told me that tobacco several years old would become stale and taste terrible. I inhaled my first puff, gagged and spat on the cobblestones below, while dropping my pipe and nearly shattering it. My reflection stared back at me from a puddle on the ground. My whiskers were orange and transparent. I hadn't shaved in days, another symptom of distress, and there were even more silver threads in my hair than there were yesterday. I was beginning to look like an old man when I was barely thirty-five. When I bent over to fetch my pipe, I spotted a shiny metal object and picked it up. My house key must have fallen on to the ground. Was this the key to my dreams Doctor Jung just spoke about?

*　　*　　*

The Proof of Things to Come

Arthur Conan Doyle was wrapping up a Spiritualist lecture he was giving in a London school auditorium when he spotted his friend, H. G. Wells, in the back of the audience.

298

"Ah, Bertie, thanks for taking time out of your busy schedule to come and meet me here. What did you think of the lecture?" Doyle asked while escorting his guest over to a table in the reception area and pulling out two chairs. Behind them a large crowd of enthusiastic spectators were packing up their belongings.

"I'm afraid that I only caught the last twenty minutes," Wells said apologetically, still wearing his dampened overcoat and scarf as he sat down.

"Never mind, at least you came. So, as one man of science to another, isn't it amazing that we are getting steps closer to proving the existence of these phenomena?"

"Phenomena?" Wells replied, pulling out a handkerchief to catch a sneeze.

"We have photographs of mediums spewing out ectoplasm as easily and naturally as you just blew your nose." Doyle smiled confidently and showed him samples he had brought along. "I'm finding it an area of never-ending fascination that the human brain is capable of connecting with the spirit world and creating such miraculous events as slate writing, table tipping, spirit photography, and hearing messages from the dead that can predict the future!"

"Honestly, Arthur, I think the only sound assessment of the future involves rational minds guided by the world's rapid discoveries in technology. With the burgeoning advancement and means to create weapons of mass destruction, I feel mankind, as a whole, must be tuned into analyzing political trends in conjunction with the psychology of nationalism. Therefore, I really don't see the connection of your beliefs with my platform. In respect to your theories, I think you are forgetting to take into account the notion of a group mind, an infectious hive-like mentality, where if enough people want to believe something they are capable of generating their own form of mass hypnosis in order to convince themselves it is real."

Doyle disagreed, but allowed Wells to take center stage.

"Telepathy, clairvoyance, all this nonsense I classify under the term of *border psychology*, which is in vast contrast to classic neuroses that Freud, Jung, or Adler deal with. We all know that prior to Freud popularizing the practice of *free association* that hypnotism was widely used by psychologists as a potential way to understand why these issues occurred and would continue. The problem with that method was that while it might have numbed one's senses or memories or conversely brought thoughts to the surface that were buried for ages, it still didn't cure patients from those shortcomings that prevented them from either functioning normally or experiencing what they had hoped would have been a happy and fulfilled life.

"Even Jung took matters a step further away from the Oedipal complexes of Freud into the realm of a Universal Mind linked with myths and deep-seated symbols of dreams, but according to my knowledge, Jung didn't venture into talking with spirits of the dead. Personally, I think that Spiritualism, despite the fact that it has attracted many well-educated and respected minds, has gone way off on a tangent.

"Therefore, Arthur, I'll continue to take the scientific stand regarding all of your so-called occurrences. Although I cannot completely rule them out as impossible, they're still highly improbable. Didn't your character, Holmes, say something to that effect?"

Doyle sighed in dismay. "I find it rather disconcerting that we are in such disagreement over this issue, and actually, Holmes said, 'When you have eliminated the impossible, whatever remains, however improbable, must be the truth.'"

A volunteer came in from the nearby lunchroom carrying a tray with tea and biscuits. He momentarily interrupted the two gentlemen as he explained that for lack of china teacups, the beverage would be served in clear, glass cups, instead. Meanwhile, the friction between Wells and Doyle continued.

"Not that I'm always in agreement with your friend, Houdini, but I do respect his expertise in his ability to sniff out the charlatans. Such showmanship has a tendency to steal money out of a few pockets."

"Eusapia Palladino, the famous materializing medium, was genuine," Doyle, stated emphatically.

"My concern is that you've lost your sense of objectivity. Everyone loves a good stage performance. I think Houdini himself mentioned that just because something is unexplained it doesn't mean it's supernatural, am I correct?"

"But, I've witnessed so much that suggests otherwise," Doyle objected.

"Unless I have measurable and calculated results from not one, but a wide spectrum of scientific authorities, I beg to differ," Wells replied. "It's too bad we stand in opposite corners." He reached for a biscuit and allowed a few seconds to pass in silence.

"Changing the subject," Doyle said, "I've been so anxious to tell you that I have an acquaintance who's invented a genuine time machine. It looks and works a lot different than what you describe in your story, but it actually functions and that's the most important feat."

"That's preposterous!" Wells exclaimed.

"But you've written about one. Bertie, please tell me that it isn't true that you only pictured that as a fictional invention…"

"Arthur, you'd think I was mad if I proclaimed that we'll be invaded by Martians and slaughtered by heat rays."

"Well— perhaps if," Doyle hesitated.

"Perhaps, not, and I'd venture to stake my reputation on that," Wells replied. "I might publish some articles here and there about my views on the political impact of a utopian society or possible threats from expanding imperialism, but the invasions by beings from other planets are purely make believe. Please don't tell me you now fear bizarre and unethical vivisection-like experiments like those in Doctor Moreau, or threats by invisible terrorists?" Wells said, putting Doyle on the hot seat.

"In fact, that's about as absurd as the stories of that silly red book you keep pestering me about. I bet that now you'll tell me that you can use this ridiculous time machine and go back in time to find this book that doesn't exist. Am I right?"

Doyle cleared his throat. "Actually I *can* go back in time, and I plan on doing it. I know it exists back in China, but a few centuries ago. I've uncovered way too much from my extensive research to think otherwise. With this working time machine my friend built, I can prove it to you."

Wells shook his head and checked his timepiece. "Arthur, I told my driver to be here at 5:00. I suspect he's been patiently waiting for at least a half hour. Good day and good luck," he said shaking his hand in parting.

Dejected, Doyle sat back down at his empty table. He poured a fresh cup of tea, dropping in two lumps of sugar. Slowly they dissolved like ethereal matter, swirling around in a dark sea of pain.

*   *   *

New Feet on Old Ground
Early June 1914: Kings Cross, London

For the past fourteen years I'd been so busy in Germany studying and teaching, as well as traveling to surrounding countries performing that I nearly forgot what my old homeland was like. So I decided to travel back to Edinburgh during the summer hiatus. By the time I landed in London, I was so exhausted that I would've ignored the gentleman in the three-piece banker's suit who materialized next to me on the final train until I realized it was Finn.

"I thought I sensed something out of the ordinary," I said while eyeing Finn up and down.

"Looking forward to Auld Reekie?" Finn asked.

"It's been a long time."

I took a few brief naps interspersed with intermittent glances out the window at the fleeting landscape while reading one of

Hesse's books, *Uterm Rad* or *Beneath the Wheel*. It was about a prodigious student, an ardent intellectual unable to cope with life outside his university when thrown into a completely opposite situation entailing hard work and manual labor. I was almost done with it and curious about the ending.

"Last stop, Edinburgh!"

The whistle screeched its hawkish cry and steam obscured my window. I gathered my belongings, and with hard suitcases banging against my legs and thighs, I headed back to my old home.

The town still smelled the same—perpetually wet streets, horses with motorcars here and there and centuries-old masonry near the castle. I must've been crazy to walk up the steep hill towards the Mound all the way from the station, but there was so much to drink in and remember. Finally, I hailed a cab.

"Uncle Tommy? Aunt Maggie? I'm here!"

A bird's nest snugly found a home where an old stone was missing not far from one of the windows. Their front door hinges needed oiling. *Creeeeak!* It was unlocked. They expected me. Pots boiled on the stove, one of potatoes and turnips and the other simmered with soup. The old upright piano with three broken keys was still in the living room, covered with a fringed embroidered shawl. Porcelain collectible plates hung on the walls. A few had fallen, cracked and had been repaired. Paint was starting to peel from the ceiling. Footsteps announced the approach a dark silhouette, smelling of powder and familiar perfume.

"John," my aunt said while leaning over to kiss me on the forehead, "you've gotten a bit bigger."

No, I hadn't grown taller since I had seen her last, just a bit larger around the middle.

"Good food and German hospitality," I laughed.

"Do you have enough clothes?"

"You can't expect me to be wearing the same old clothes all these years," I replied, still amused.

303

Uncle Tommy came in from the garden, smeared with dirt and holding a sturdy shovel. He gave me a hardy slap on the back.

"*Johann, wie geht es ihnen?*"

"Uncle, since when do you speak German?"

"I don't," he chuckled. "I asked the immigrant butcher down the street and practiced how to say that for weeks. So, how have you been?"

"Tired, it's been a long trip."

"Hungry?" Aunt Maggie interjected.

"Almost too tired to eat," I sighed, "do you mind if I freshen up?"

I hauled my suitcases up to my old bedroom, which was up two steep, narrow sets of stairs. It was like living in an attic since it was the sole room on the top floor. The golden glow of sunset illuminated my window silhouetting spider webs clinging to dried dead flies. I opened it a crack to air the place out. The room probably hadn't been dusted. I took off my jacket, waistcoat, then my tie, and unfastened my collar draping everything over a chair. Then I saw myself in an antiquated brass-rimmed mirror with its silver rubbed away in places, wearing only my undershirt, pants and suspenders.

"The goose has been fattened for dinner," I thought to myself, agreeing that I had put on a bit of weight over the years.

Too tired to draw a bath, I fetched some water and a towel and wiped myself off over a basin. Then I literally sank into my old mattress.

*   *   *

"Drink up, me lad!"

I got my fingers on his flask, took one more swig, grimaced and spit on the ground. Vile stuff that cheap whisky!

"Mister Nigel, I'm going to vomit." I burped. Seven-year-old boys weren't made to drink like fish.

"That's Sir Nigel to you boy!" he said with pompous airs while his tattered coat brushed across my face. "That'll turn you into a knight in shining armor and put hairs on your chest."

"If you insist," I replied skeptically as the landscape around me was spinning. I plucked a few of his hairs off his raggedy coat, grabbed my bag full of schoolbooks, excused myself and got up. Probably shouldn't have befriended the town drunk, but I was embarrassed to admit that I'd enjoy the times he'd sneak me into a pub and allow me to indulge in absinthe.

I went over to the other side of Princes Street Park to be alone. My thoughts conjured up fairies, phantoms and will o' the wisps. While sitting under a spreading shade tree I began randomly plucking extra long blades of grass weaving them, along with Sir Nigel's hairs that I had stuffed in my book bag, into the shape of a little green man. When done, I placed the poppet next to a rock, took some matches from my pocket and lit a votive candle I stole from a church. Then I started to skip around my ceremonial altar in circles, chanting rhymes off the top of my head until I was so dizzy that I almost tripped. By then I felt a touch queasy. So, I dusted myself off and ran back home.

A week later I returned to the same spot. I wrapped the poppet, wet with dew, with a cloth, and placed him in my pocket. Usually, I would find Sir Nigel over by the statue in front of St. Giles, but today when I looked for him he wasn't there. I ducked into the close directly across the street from the church, but he wasn't sleeping in any of those grottoes, either. When I ran out of ideas as to where to find him, I sneaked into McLaughlin's to see if he was inside.

"Aren't you a bit young, son?" the bartender shouted as I entered.

"Have you seen Sir Nigel?" I asked, innocently.

"That old fool? Left town yesterday."

Sir Nigel had always told me that he had no family or money to go anywhere.

"Must've been the luck of the draw," the bartender said. "Was in here three nights ago, completely pissed, but must've picked up enough alms on the street to win a huge bet on a game of cards.

Probably never saw so much money in his life. Cleaned up, bought a new set of clothes and disappeared."

Immediately, I ran out of the pub and back to the park. The remains of my melted votive candle were still there. I scooped up the melted wax and buried it along with the poppet in a tiny burrow I dug with my hands. Then I washed them in a nearby fountain before returning home to celebrate my triumph.

"It worked," I thought to myself, satisfied and smug.

* * *

When I rolled over and kicked my bedclothes to the floor, only my appetite knew what time it was. I was so exhausted that I slept way past midnight and overlooked that it was also past the hour when I'd conduct my astral consultations with Arthur. I put on a fresh shirt with my waistcoat over it and adjusted my tie then went downstairs to light a lamp, then the stove. Auntie had left out a loaf of bread and an apple. Minutes later Uncle Tommy joined me.

I lifted my head up from my hot Cullen skink. "No word?" I asked.

"Sorry, I haven't heard from your family."

My uncle tossed a small pouch on the table in front of me. By its clinking sound, I could tell it contained a bunch of coins.

"Your father left this for you. I was instructed to give it to you once you graduated."

Graduated? I just received my doctorate. I pushed it back towards my uncle.

"I don't want it," I said, wiping the soup off the sides of my mouth as I began to leave the room.

"You're not interested to see what's inside?"

"He never accepted me," I replied, bitterly.

"I never understood you, either, but I loved you regardless and did my best to make sure you stayed clear of trouble," my uncle explained.

It must've been my magic, my wizardry that marked me for eternal damnation. Simple pleasures like love and family eluded me.

Perhaps that was also the reason why I was so drawn to time travel. Was redemption possible, and what was the price I had to pay for stepping upon the mystic's path?

*   *   *

Reconnoiter

     The next morn I was up early and eager to surprise my old landlady, Lydia Campbell, with an unexpected visit. Auntie insisted that I wear the brand new pair of shoes she found in my old closet that had been long forgotten, never worn and hiding there the whole time. The problem was that despite the fact that they still retained their shine, they hadn't been broken in, which I was to regret by the day's end.

     Old Town Edinburgh was a city for walking up and down a lot of steps and many hills. My sense of direction came back although I noticed a few of my favorite stores were gone. One could always plot one's course with churches as landmarks since many of them had been there for hundreds of years.

     I gave three knocks on Mrs. Campbell's front door.

     "Lydia?" I shouted, hearing footsteps after a minute.

     "Who's that? You sound familiar," she called out from behind the door.

     "I am familiar," I replied.

     The door opened inch by inch. Then it swung open.

     "Oh my, gosh, John Patrick Scott. It can't be?" Lydia cried as she rushed towards me to clamp her arms around my middle with a huge, affectionate hug. In her excitement, her shawl fell off her shoulders. I reached down, picked it up and returned it to her, but she took a few steps back and inspected me from head to toe.

     "A wee bit plump?"

     I laughed, "A bit hardier, perhaps."

     Everyone was noticing my size. Since most of these folk knew me from my youth when I was a skinny little thing, I guess that was quite a contrast.

"Perhaps I should forgo offering you your favorite scones and tea," she said.

"But, I haven't eaten breakfast yet."

"Then by all means, John, please do come in and join me."

Lydia was exceptionally chatty, as if she had bottled up over a decade's worth of news and uncorked it all at once. She served sweet raspberry scones, fresh from the oven, which were still warm and smelled divine. A cut glass vase with daisies from her garden sat right next to the breakfast platter. Everything was exactly as I had remembered.

"What brought you back home?" she asked. "It's been such a long time."

Jam squirted on my fingers. She handed me a napkin to wipe it off.

"A change of pace. I had the summer off."

"You must love Germany to have stayed there so long."

"I've made incredible friends, studied with master instructors, and now I have a very satisfying position teaching music."

"Then I guess it was a wise decision. I was sad to see you go when you received that scholarship and left the University of Edinburgh. Have you stayed in touch with any of your old friends or professors?"

"Wendell, of course, or at least the best I can. He could be in India one month, and several months later he'll send me a letter while running off to the Orient."

"Weren't you also close with that lad, Whit?"

"Ah—Whit," I grimaced, "we had a disagreement. It shouldn't have ended that way, but I suspect he's in London by now."

"You should ask around. Perhaps he's still in town. Does he have family here?"

I changed the subject. "Do you still have my old upright piano?"

"Of course. I was hoping that one day you would come back and play it for me."

"I can honor that request."

"My, I'd be delighted. Follow me."

With a youthful spring in her step despite her age, she skipped up the stairs to my old two-room flat on the top floor. Those shoes my aunt gave me were beginning to pinch my feet as I climbed up after her.

"It looks the same, as if I never left." I said, surprised. "You never had another lodger?"

"I've had plenty in this house, but for some reason, no one wanted your room. You didn't put a curse on it, did you?"

I was unsure if she was serious or said this in jest.

"Why should I?" I raised my eyebrows in curiosity.

I began looking around like I was examining objects in an old, abandoned museum. I wondered if my hiding places still existed— the one under the floor boards in that tiny space hidden by her rug, the loose stone near the fireplace in my bedroom, the one in the wall behind the clock. I had hidden some books before I left Scotland and wondered if they were still there.

"John, are you forgetting your promise?"

I smiled and settled atop my old bench, took out my handkerchief to wipe off a thin layer of dust and commenced with the piano version of the *Blue Danube Waltz* while ending with jocular Hungarian rhapsodies. Lydia began tapping her fingers and toes to the light-hearted beats.

"Bravo Maestro, bravo!" she exclaimed with a standing ovation.

I got up, gave a deep graceful bow then carefully closed the piano lid.

"John, how can I convince you to stay and not return to Germany?"

I pulled out my timepiece, leaned over and gave her a parting kiss. "Lydia, you flatter me, but I must be going."

When I started walking towards the stairs to retrieve my jacket and hat she called out, "I'll keep your room the way you like it, but next time you come back return with a wife!"

*   *   *

A trip back to Edinburgh wasn't complete without revisiting the university. I made a beeline for the library, still intrigued about the hidden passageways that my old friend, Whit, would disappear behind. Alas, it had been fourteen years since I had attended school here. None of the staff knew of Whit, anymore. It would've been wise to mend our friendship.

Since I was bitter from not getting either a local scholarship or one to London, I had also cut off correspondence with other folk I knew from school, including the teachers. By now, a new professor had taken over as head the music department. When I spotted an empty classroom, it was too tempting to pass up the opportunity. So, I sat behind a grand piano and began to play. Someone from the department overheard the music and came in to investigate, assuming I was trespassing. Too much time had passed. Sadly, I didn't recognize anyone, and no one recognized me.

For old time's sake, I waited at St. Cuthbert's Cemetery at midnight to meet Arthur back on familiar ground for one of our tête-a-têtes, but this time I was in the flesh. The risk of getting caught was worth the thrill, although I hugged the shadows of the tombstones, avoiding being revealed by scattered gas lamps. Two shots of whisky dispelled my aversion to the moss-covered crypts and broken marble markers by lonely graves, but he was late. I looked at my watch. A police whistle blew in the distance. I made a bad mistake.

A half hour passed. Gradually, a ghostly form began to take shape.

"Arthur?"

I wasn't sure whether to close or open my eyes. I did both. Vapors seemed to rise from the ground like steam, getting denser.

"Arthur?" I called out once again, this time a little bit louder.

I could see his head, his hands, and his feet. He lit his pipe, puffing it three times.

"John, I thought you hated to meet in cemeteries."

"I still do," I replied, shivering with the dampness eating right through me. A large centipede the size of a hefty earthworm crawled on the stone cross beside me.

"Come, it can't bother me, but you need to get out of the cold. Follow me."

We cut through the park, up past the Mound towards Lawnmarket Street. Despite attempts, we hadn't spoken in a while, so I was eager to catch up.

"So, you're back in Edinburgh. What on earth for, and for how long?" he asked.

"Until the start of the new school year. I had some time off. Besides, it's been a very long time. Didn't recognize anyone at the university. Doctors Bell and Lorraine Smith are no longer there."

"Joseph Bell died three years ago. He was a good man. I owe much to him. Actually, Sherlock Holmes owes much to him. He was quite an inspiration."

Arthur paused and requested that I knock on a certain door. I was so swept up in our conversation that I was unaware that we had ducked into a few back alleyways, and I really wanted to pay attention to where we were going. Suddenly I realized we had come here before, but the last time we traveled to this place we both were in our physical forms. Now, I was flesh and bone and blood and Arthur was...ethereal...an astral projection. I wanted to find out as to whether or not he was visible to others.

Seeing that I was still freezing, Arthur asked, "Give him something hot, but with a shot of whisky, can you?"

"Of course, sir," the man said pulling us inside.

Six steps ahead, Arthur found a table and sat down. I followed.

"Can anyone besides that man see you?" I was getting more unstrung by the second. "I'm not going to look insane talking to myself, am I? I also don't want anyone approaching me and starting up something."

"Not in here," he assured me while relighting his pipe. "The rules of reason are meant to be broken."

"Arthur, the last time we met here, I shared with you a dream from the past that I suspected took place in Japan. Since then, we took several trips back in time together, and I discovered that in a past life I must've been a soldier."

"I remember that, well," he replied, knowing that our journey also unearthed a few unpleasant incidents. "Is there a special reason why you're bringing this up now?"

I wasn't sure how to put my thoughts into words. It was a miracle we were still friends after those attempts. Each time it would only get worse, but both of us had this crazy infatuation with time travel. But it also was a kind of self-punishment, where we'd derive pleasure while kindling a growing antagonism between us.

"Arthur, I've never been one to really experience premonitions, but I feel like I'm going to return to a soldier's life. I suppose you'd think that was utter nonsense. Right?"

*   *   *

"All books by Shakespeare, Chaucer, Burns and Cunningham are on sale today," a hoarse voice shouted as a tiny bell rang announcing my entrance.

"Cunningham?" I asked, looking around for Mr. Dalrymple, who must have been rummaging in the back where I couldn't see him.

"No one's ever heard of him. He's my second cousin and owns his own printing press. Loves poetry. Not too bad in my opinion."

"I'll take your word for it," I said while examining a few samples he had on display.

"Looking for anything in particular?"

"I'll know what I want when I find it."

I gave my same old reply, but he must have forgotten it. I spun around. Something caught my attention. At first, I thought it was Finn, but it was only the wind blowing open his front door, so I went over to close it. Dalrymple's Rare Books—the perfect repository for portals to the Library—the Secret Library. Perhaps, I'll be lucky.

He always had so many books, and this was always a trusted location. So, I followed my fingers like a compass, sliding them over embossed leather bindings, hand cut pages and some with tipped-in illustrations. Just as I was beginning to wonder if Ding's shop had lost its magic touch, I noticed a book that had fallen to the floor.

"*Shokunin, The Thief of Tales*?"

"Have you seen this book before?" Ding asked.

I jumped, as I didn't realize he had snuck up from behind.

"Where did you get this?"

"Funny you should ask," he replied with a slight laugh. "A woman brought it in years ago saying that she wanted to trade it in for another storybook. It had been given as a gift to her daughter, but as soon as the young girl received it she couldn't stop crying. Had nightmares and was terrified for weeks. Couldn't understand why? Most of its pages are uncompleted—bare with nothing on them, but supposedly it produced unaccountable effects. The child would use the blank pages as a coloring book and claimed that at night whatever she drew would come into form and chase her around like a specter. But her mother promised she'd remove it from the house and replace it with another. It's been hiding in my bookstore for years."

"Do you mind if I take a look?" I asked.

"Be my guest," Ding said handing it to me. "You've been forewarned."

On its first page it was inscribed, "1900—To my dear Cicely Isabel Fairfield.

Her name sounded familiar.

* * *

313

So, what was the difference between time travel and entering the Secret Library? Often it was difficult to make that distinction. With me, it was even worse, because my dreams frequently transported me elsewhere. Even more mystifying was that everyone who was capable of entering the Library could have an entirely unique perception of it, even if they were all seeking identical information. Wendell confided to me that he entered a secret chamber from within the King's Library at the British Museum.

It was one of those other worlds—a space in-between, that was timeless, most likely without boundaries, and ever changing like a theoretical perpetual motion machine, if there ever was one, or almost like a Mobius strip embracing the concept of infinity—an archive of the gods. Pinning down a simple definition was like the proverb of the three blind men describing an elephant. However, I guess the best way to explain the difference was that time travel entailed a full immersive experience. So far in all of my travels through time I either became a younger version of myself as a child (when it pertained to this lifetime) or I became another person altogether such as Tomoo Ashikaga from the past or Aliskiya Lleullne in the future. Going to the Secret Library was like going on a research expedition, with a slightly detached semblance of objectivity, although it could also become a complete immersion. When that happened, the terminology, conditions and actions often appeared interchangeable.

For some the experience lasts a few seconds, and for others it feels like it's endless. The Secret Library constantly generates and stores information about all existence, except the future. That's where the line has to be drawn between time travel and going into the Library to retrieve information. If something hasn't occurred yet, it can't be found there.

Up to this point I had received snippets of information about feudal Japan from my previous time travel excursions, but major portions of the jigsaw puzzle were still missing. Finn had warned me that many times bad tidings were saved for last after the initial excitement of discovery had worn off.

I took that copy of *Shokunin, the Thief of Tales*, tucked it under my arm and continued browsing up and down the crowded aisles, as usual, to see if anything else in particular would jump out at me, because nothing unusual had started happening yet. After I thought I had exhausted every possibility, I asked, "What's in your basement?"

"Not sure if you want to go down there," Ding said.

"Is there something about the cellar that you're not telling me?" I asked.

"No. I guess I'm being superstitious," Ding replied. "Go ahead, but be careful. It's a trap door entry with a ladder."

"Thanks for the warning," I replied.

"Yell if you need assistance," Ding added.

Going into Ding's cellar was as thrilling as sneaking into a cemetery at midnight. For years I imagined this was his sacred, off-limits retreat, a hidden, dusty den of wonders—a place that turned all away except those who were worthy. Unfortunately, I wasn't watching where I was going. There didn't seem to be any additional lights beyond the one tiny overhead lamp at the foot of the ladder towards the entrance. When I stubbed my toe on a large wooden chest of very old books, it hurt like the Dickens, even while wearing shoes.

"Bloody hell!" I cried out. I pulled of my shoe and began rubbing my aching foot. Finally, I groped over towards a small table lamp, turned it on and pulled out a stool to sit down.

"I guess I'm not going any further," I groaned, still in pain.

I began foraging through the decrepit old trunk reminding myself that a long time ago Ding had mentioned that there were books down here older than the Gutenberg Bible. I didn't believe it, but who was I to argue? Most of these books had brittle pages that were already starting to crumble. Spines were broken and needed repair. A few were missing the front or back covers. Sometimes both.

Just when I was digging down to the bottom, one particular book caught my attention. This one was in better condition than most. It had a black leather cover with a simple bamboo design on the embossed border. In its center was a tipped-in woodcut of a man wearing a ceremonial kimono. He held a scroll clenched between his teeth. His eyes were crossed as if in some sort of trance, and his hands were poised in a magical gesture. He was surrounded by smoke with Japanese writing inscribed off to the side. Without hesitation, I opened it.

Instead of a normal book, I realized that this was one of those false containers or hollowed out books concealing something else from public view. Inside was a small rectangular object, artfully wrapped in silk and secured with a string using intricate knots.

What I discovered was a hand-painted deck of playing cards. They looked like they had been created on a thick, toothy water color paper with hand torn edges, and they were neatly stacked on top of one another. Instinctively, I began shuffling the cards, spreading them face down. I randomly picked up several to see if they'd tell me their own story.

The first card that I turned over showed The Daimyo, the lord of his own domain. The second pictured a younger man, whose title miraculously transformed from the *kanji* or Japanese characters into English, spelling out the words—The Privileged Son. Following that was The Pawn. Embarrassed, I had the funny feeling that it represented me, or Tomoo Ashikaga, which was what I was called back in feudal Japan. In my previous time travels, I was a pawn in regards to everyone controlling my affairs with little free will of my own.

Oddly enough, the next two cards were of women. One lady was plain and simple. She held a basket bearing fruit. This card was called The Farmer's Daughter. The other portrayed a fashionable lady wearing layers of expensive silk robes and coyly hiding behind a fan. She was The Courtesan, but as I examined the card a bit closer I noticed that her kimonos were slightly bunched up in front, as if she was also concealing something else besides her face. The card after that was called The Monk. He had a shaved head, carried a long staff and wore ascetic garb with a sling to carry a large shakuhachi flute like the one I remembered Monk Wei had.

Fascinated, I continued turning over these unusual cards. Many were soldiers with their various ranks indicated by their armor or uniforms. An archer was easily distinguished from a horseman, as was a swordsman or spear bearer. It was particularly disturbing, however, to discover that there was only one pawn in the entire group of samurai.

"It's awfully quiet down there," Dalyrmple shouted from upstairs. "I haven't lost you to the book goblins or anything like that?"

"Not yet," I replied laughing. When I returned my attention back to the remaining cards, my gut reaction was that something or another was wrong. The next four represented the family—The Mother, The Father, and The Brother and Sister cards. This came as no surprise, but what came after did. There was a blank card titled The Child. I twirled it around between my fingers a few times to see if any other images would appear, but it still remained the same. Since I had taken *Shokunin, the Thief of Tales* with me, I sat it down and opened it to an empty page. Then I took the two most disturbing cards in the deck, The Pawn and The Child and placed them on the left blank page. Looking around, I found a bottle of ink and a pen on top a stack of books. I grabbed that, then I closed my eyes and poised my hand holding the pen over the blank right hand page similar to what I had seen mediums do when they practiced automatic writing during séances. If anything extraordinary was going to happen, I wanted to document it.

Taking a few long and controlled deep breaths, Ding's musty basement room vanished. For an indeterminate time, my consciousness wandered into a void, neither here nor there, losing all references of time and location. My only anchors were the pen, the book and the two cards. Then there was a whirring sound—

317

something mechanical and humming. Other atonal sounds I couldn't recognize. The noises persisted for a while and then faded off. After that I lost track of the rhythm of my breathing. I fell back into a deeper state of whatever you wanted to call it—meditation, repose, maybe it was an out-of-the-body experience. I was weightless and floating somewhere in space until I began to fall. The further I fell, the heavier I seemed to become. It didn't seem like it was ever going to end. Finally my feet landed on soft ground. As I took my next breath my new body materialized.

* * *

The entire community was involved in preparations for *Sakura Matsuri*, the Cherry Blossom Festival. It was a time for rejoicing and celebration. Once more I transformed into Tomoo Ashikaga. Despite my surname sounding similar to others who were higher officials, I was a low ranking guard under the employ of the daimyo, Lord Takeda, a local provincial ruler in Mie Prefecture, who was in service to the Tokugawa Shogunate.

I patiently took my post and observed everyone else's excitement as they prepared for the dancing and musical extravaganzas later that evening. Extra stalls had been erected in the marketplace. Vendors from the countryside stocked their booths with everything from kites and toys to religious trinkets. Aromas of grilled meats to baked sweets were pervasive. Sounds of preparation filled the courtyard—the clip clop of wooden *geta* skipping like pebbles, jangling iron pots carried from the kitchen, horse hooves hitting the pavement—all created a harmonic. Despite all the excitement, I was bored as a log watching everyone else having all the fun. But that was my job to ensure no trouble was afoot, or at least I guessed it was.

"Tomoo!" someone called out in a high-pitched girlish voice.

Quickly, I looked about and saw nothing.

318

"Tomoo!" That mysterious voice called out again. I couldn't see where it was coming from. Unable to leave my post, I continued to stand guard.

"Tooomooo…" This time the person mocked me. Then *plink, plunk*! A few pebbles bounced off my helmet making the funniest sound. I turned like a teased cat. Where were these coming from?

"Look up silly boy!"

A stunning young lady called down to me with a voice like sparrows. Her hair was artfully pinned up with hand-carved combs of tortoiseshell and ivory, and she was wearing a delicate blue kimono covered with images of cherry blossoms commemorating the holiday. I took a few steps backwards and nearly lost my footing, overwhelmed by her charm.

"I can arrest you for assaulting one of the lord's guards!" I shouted. It was hard to get completely angry with one who looked like a goddess. My heart felt so light that I thought it would fly away.

"Don't you recognize me?" she asked.

I scrutinized her carefully, keeping my hands readied on the hilt of my sword in case this was a ruse for an ambush. One could never be too careful. The warlord had enemies, and we were sworn to defend him.

"Am I supposed to?"

She giggled. "You're Tomoo Ashikaga, am I correct?"

I nodded.

"I'm Chiyo. Chiyo Tentaikawa. We played together as children."

Without warning my memories transported me back even further into the past. I was much younger, playing a game of hide-and-seek and finding refuge behind a large tree. There were a bunch of us, sons from all of the local shopkeepers, who had run out to a nearby field. Besides my little sister, whom I was supposed to look after, there was only one other girl. We flirted with each other from our hiding places until I finally gave myself away and was caught by one of the other boys.

Chiyo Tentaikawa. When she was born her parents created for her a special name. They combined the Chinese characters that translated to that of a celestial river of a thousand generations, or one that would go on forever. My recollections of her were that the stars touched her hair. My heart would sing songs of rapture with the nightingale's cry. Back then; even for a lad so young, I swore that one day I'd make her my bride.

My grandfather would always tell me to pick a star in the sky and make a wish. Then that wish would fall as a seed to the ground and blossom into greatness, giving me whatever I desired. He consulted an astrologer, a palm reader and even a destinologist and convinced me that my path was meant for lofty things far beyond that of my father's. Despite the fact that my grandfather was convinced that his incessant offerings to the Shinto spirits were responsible for my destiny, my father thought I was a troublemaker and arranged to have me sent off for the daimyo's guard. Grandfather protested. He argued that this wasn't my true calling, but Father thought that was nonsense. Being in the guard was a very prestigious position to hold in our culture, although it often went hand in hand with an early death. It was expected that we had unquestionable loyalty to our master. But these were considered honorable deaths, meriting an afterlife of recompense and abundance. While I served in his guard, I was ambitious, worked and trained hard, but was often taken for granted.

Fate did not let me fill the shoes of a true samurai warrior. Humble from birth, I did not come from the bloodlines of the warrior classes, but from one of the local village book merchants. My father had essentially sold me into indentured servitude. Whether it was merely to alleviate a tough domestic situation, or whether he had to satisfy a debt or obligation with Takeda-san, the local warlord, I was too young to know or understand at the time, and I'll probably never know the real truth.

My reveries faded and my thoughts returned to the present. I readjusted my conical helmet and tightened my obi.

"You've grown up quite a bit," I said, still surprised that my childhood sweetheart had turned into such a beauty.

"So have you," she replied brushing aside a soft tendril of hair that had fallen across her soft powdered face. "In fact, the only way I really knew it was you was that one of the other guards confirmed my suspicions and told me your name."

"*Ah honto.*" I replied, "Alright, that makes sense."

"Will you be participating in the festivities this evening?" she asked.

"I'll be performing in the battle demonstrations," I said proudly. "For many months I've trained hard in preparation. I can't wait to show off what I've learned. Hopefully that will attract the attention of the daimyo and his son. I've been long overdue for a promotion."

"Then I'll make sure to be there and cheer for you," she replied.

"Come and join me afterwards," I asked.

"I can't," she cried. "I have to do what I'm told. Most likely I'll be expected to escort either the daimyo or his son to their own private affair."

"Not them! How terrible. I stand guard for the son. He's vulgar—gets drunk and beats women. I hope he's never laid a hand upon you!"

Suddenly I took pause, caught up with too many emotions. I could only speculate about Chiyo's feelings. Long ago we had made a promise to each other that someday we would be together as man and wife.

"Chiyo, we have to see each other. When can we do that?" I asked.

"I can sneak out tomorrow," she said. "I've been given the afternoon off. We can meet behind the mountain shrine in private. No one else will know."

"*Kibou Tori?*"

"It's an abandoned temple and shrine. Nearly everyone's forgotten about it, but I guess no one will ever tear it down due to respect for the old burial sites."

"Are you sure?" I asked.

"Positive. I go there all the time when I need to be alone. You said that you were sold into the service of the daimyo. You're not alone. My father was hoping that the daimyo's son or another high-ranking samurai might ask for my hand in marriage. That was the best hope for his most beautiful daughter. None of the merchants' sons came up to his standards. Instead, he sold me off to this…brothel." She hung her head in shame.

I bowed my head, sympathetic to her plight, but painfully well aware that Arthur was the reincarnation of the daimyo's son. "How stupid of me for not realizing you were a courtesan. Had I not been sent away you and I would've had a chance."

"But not now. I only wish I could forgive my father. My beauty is my curse," she confessed while holding back tears.

"*Chiisana Hana!*" some called out from within the house. That meant little flower.

"Who's that?" I asked.

"That's me," Chiyo said looking worried as she looked around to make sure we weren't being watched. "*They* have given us new names."

"Who are *they?*" I asked.

"My masters—new owners. My life is no longer my own. You're not a paying customer. No one can see us. I must go."

Throughout the afternoon all sorts of thoughts raced through my mind about all of the pleasant times Chiyo and I had spent together. Meanwhile visitors poured into town from the countryside. The daimyo and his family were readying themselves for the upcoming excitement. Acting troupes arrived from out of town along with acrobats, jugglers and *Bunraku* puppeteers. Samurai of all ranks circulated nearby to ensure that no mischief was being stirred.

That evening the samurai put on a tournament to entertain and impress the local citizens. I wore practice armor and was to fight an opponent using a *shinai*, or a split bamboo practice sword— obviously not a real one as we were fighting our partners and not real enemies. All it took was one moment's distraction when Chiyo called out my name from the crowd. My opponent caught me off guard, and his shinai crashed down upon my protective helmet hitting it with such force that it cracked in two. I stumbled backwards from the blow, tripped over a stump and fell over with my head striking hard on the ground.

Several of my comrades rushed to my aid. They pulled me off to the side while the physician gave me an eye-opening sip of saké.

"You're sitting out the next round," he commanded. "I won't hear otherwise."

"But I must impress the daimyo!" I protested.

"You're lucky you didn't have your brains bashed out," he warned me. "No more war play for you this evening. If this weren't *Sakura Matsuri*, I'd be ordering you straight to bed. You can watch the festivities from the sidelines." He gathered his implements and left me alone.

I was still woozy and couldn't quite focus my eyes, but I was able to discern the clip clop of wooden geta approaching in haste.

"Tomoo, are you alright?"

"Chiyo?" I asked. It was still hard to focus. She reached out and cradled my head in her arms.

"Are you hurt badly?"

"I guess not. Otherwise the doctor wouldn't have picked up and left."

"I want to stay with you," she cried.

"You better not. Everyone's watching. Please, run off. Lord Takeda could have you imprisoned, or killed."

"Tomorrow then? Promise you'll meet me?"

"I will," I replied, rubbing my sore head. She looked around anxiously, hoping no one had noticed the two of us together and then she ran off.

Time seemed to flash forward to the following day. I was willing to toss aside all reservations to meet Chiyo up at that abandoned temple as planned. When I climbed up the rugged hillside and finally found her I was surprised that she was wearing plain, unsightly clothes almost looking like a beggar. Her hair was down and tied back, which was a vast contrast to the elaborately coifed arrangement I had seen before.

"I didn't want to get noticed or followed," she explained. "The silken robes I usually wear are way too colorful and would attract attention. If anyone sees me they'll think I'm a simple peasant and never suspect I'm one of the Takeda family's favorite courtesans."

"You service both the daimyo and his son?" I asked, incensed.

She nodded. "Let's not discuss that. Let's enjoy each other's company while we can."

I was furious, but she took my hand and led me to her secret hiding place. When we reached a shady patch of trees she laid out a blanket and insisted that we sit down and rest.

"Here, I like to sort out my thoughts and write poetry," she said with enthusiasm.

Without a chance to explain any further, I couldn't contain my urges any longer and I leapt right on top of her. Upset that I was unable to express a more romantic gesture, Chiyo slapped me and wanted to throw me off, probably more out of surprise than anything else. But she finally surrendered, because she also wanted this long-awaited moment as much as I did. We were taken to a space in-between, somewhere between the clouds and the rainbows—*sans souci*—without a care in the universe and only the overwhelming passions between us.

The film of my life skipped forward in fast motion. We continued to sneak away meeting whenever possible. One day, however, when I found Chiyo in her usual place she was crying and covered with cuts and bruises.

"What happened?" I asked, shocked and appalled.

"I don't want to talk about it," Chiyo said turning her back, as if that would hide her wounds from view.

I gently touched her shoulder and turned her back around. "You must tell me who did this to you. Was it the daimyo or his son?"

"It was the boorish father. He deserves to know the meaning of suffering," she said bitterly.

Softly, I began to caress her face. I lowered my mouth to meet hers, longing for a kiss, but I tasted blood from a cut on her lips.

"There's more to this," she said, hesitating to see my reaction. "I'm with child, and it's yours. Spirits have called out telling me so in my dreams. If either the daimyo or his son find out, they'll slit my throat."

I swallowed hard, didn't know what to say.

"I'll protect you," I finally said, "and your honor."

"How? They'll kill you, too, especially when they discover you're the father."

"We can disguise ourselves and run away...to a fishing village in the southernmost island of Japan. It'll be too much trouble for anyone to hunt for us there. Then we'll get married," I suggested. "Or we could head up north to Edo. I could get a job in a print shop similar to my father's. You'll cut your hair. We'll blend in with the crowds. It's a populous city."

"Tomoo, I'm scared. I think you're too confident. There is more danger than you realize. Once Lord Takeda's mind is set he will stop at nothing. It's for that reason that he remains in such a position of power. Everyone fears him," she explained.

"I have an idea," I said. "There are some people outside the village. I've heard that they have the magic to right things that have been wronged."

"That's silly. You're not talking about that crazy shinobi clan for hire? They have no sense of honor or loyalty. They will sell their infernal skills to the highest bidder."

I nodded my head. "Their supernatural powers are surpassed by none. They are blessed by the gods."

"More like the *oni* or demons, I'm certain. You're treading a dangerous path, one you'll regret," she warned me. "Let's head back. Perhaps Monk Wei will have a wise solution."

Days and nights passed as if the earth had quickened its orbit. At Chiyo's request, I approached Monk Wei. His idea was that stowing away in the back of the wagon of a traveling peddler was more apropos. Once we were beyond the local fortifications and passed through all of the security gates we could assume any disguise we desired and start a new life. I wanted to go in another direction. I had heard of so many myths and legends of the shinobi. They were also known as ninja, the hidden shadow warriors.

*　　*　　*

Finally, I re-emerged from the basement carrying a stack of books with the hollowed out one hiding on the bottom and *Shokunin, the Thief of Tales* tucked under my arm.

"You were down there quite a while. Did you fall asleep?" Dalyrmple asked.

"I'm afraid I did," I said stretching the truth. "How much will these cost?" I handed him the stack. He started inspecting the first few.

"*Romeo and Juliet?*" he asked. "This copy's really worn. I have copies in much better condition upstairs. Haven't you read that by now?"

He couldn't understand why I wanted to buy a book that would probably fall apart before I finished reading it.

"Where did you find them?"

"Inside a dirty old trunk—one that I stubbed my toe on, no less. Nearly every book there is in bad condition."

"Most of those are rubbish. I've wanted to toss that trunk for a while now. I guess I can sell you the whole stack for one shilling."

"For those rotting books?" I asked. Maybe Ding was getting back at me for browsing all those years and not buying anything.

Ding took the stack from my hands and began recounting them. "Are you hiding one from me?" He pointed to the one I forgot that I tucked under my arm. I handed it over to him and he began to examine the story that I must've written and illustrated while another part of my consciousness was somewhere else.

"If you're going to start scribbling on my merchandise you're going to have to buy it," he said as he held that odd book open so both of us could witness my handiwork. "For that book alone, since you drew in it, you'll owe me three shillings in addition to the one shilling for the other stack."

I was so disoriented from being drawn back to the present that I felt like a whole bookcase had fallen and struck me on the head. "Oh no, I'm sorry. I'll buy it," I said reaching into my pocket for my wallet and not entirely sure what permanent impact that would make either on my finances or the rest of my universe.

*   *   *

The Thieving Magpie

Dearest John,

Oh bloody hell, I should've listened to you! I know you warned me that I shouldn't be poking my noggin in the future. Well, several years ago I was pigeonholed at my current London paper and bored beyond reason. So, I disobeyed your command and rigged up that time machine you gave me to take a glimpse of things to come. In choosing to travel a few years ahead to the year 1914, our present year, I found myself chasing after a fair lassie from Serbia of all places. This incredible lady sang, wrote poetry and was liberal in expressing her affections, which was her most pleasing quality of all.

Of course, it would be just my luck that others also admired her turning the game of courting into a challenging competition.

I continued my assignment while wooing her on the side, but she had one particularly jealous lover who was a bit of a loose cannon especially when too much booze and guns were involved. Word circulated that he was a political extremist involved with outlaw gangs, many of them known to be disruptive and violent. Perhaps it was his renegade charms that attracted her, but since I have a tendency to get drunk and be an ass, I'm convinced that I must've done something to set him off. Unfortunately I was so sozzled at the time that I can't remember. The idiot's name was Gavrilo Princip. Trust me, John. You'll hear that notorious chap's name once again and not in the best light. June 28th—remember that date for *this* year!

I'm sorry that I can't turn back the clock. If officials knew that I was in any way remotely connected with this, I'd be in front of a firing squad. John, you were smart by telling me to stay away from the future. This is way too much for a man's conscience to bear. My weak heart over women will be the undoing for the entire world. Please destroy this letter after you read it.

Mackenzie

*   *   *

Wendell's letter arrived on the 25th. On the 28th, Gavrilo Princip assassinated the Archduke Franz Ferdinand of Austria-Hungary and his wife, causing a turn of events affecting more people worldwide than ever thought possible. When news rapidly spread of the tragedy, many folk questioned where my loyalty would lie with the King or the Kaiser should the war expand across the continent. I was so fortunate to be back in Edinburgh on holiday. Had I been back in Germany I would've probably been thrown into an internment camp, but I still feared for my friends and associates back there.

Finn had been dropping hints over the past few years that there would be an upcoming war, but I was more inclined to pass it off as nonsense. After all, he was constantly warning me not to even think of traveling into the future, because it could be changed. However, there was a vast difference between the controls I could exercise over my personal fate versus the collective destinies of nations. There was an unavoidable predetermined path that the world had to experience as a whole. Yet, I recalled conversations that I had with both Finn and Doctor Jung that if enough enlightened and evolved individuals could step in and influence others to also get on the right evolutionary path, that shifts could occur in a group consciousness. This would ultimately affect world-changing events and alter the course of history. Unfortunately in 1914 when the *civilized* world went to war, there weren't enough enlightened individuals at that time to affect the necessary change. Deranged megalomaniacs ruled powerful countries. We were all puppets of the damned.

The best way of keeping a firm head on my shoulders was to stay as busy as possible throughout the panic. All of Lydia's lodgers had gone on summer vacation, so I volunteered to help her around the house in exchange for some excellent home-cooked meals. I wasn't the best of handymen, but much better than her. Everywhere I turned, there was always something falling apart, or an object that had to be nailed back together. Over the years she accumulated way too much. One could hardly wade one's way through her cluttered attic, and most of it, I suspected, was beyond repair and should've been thrown out. Regardless, the poor woman was desperate for help, and circumstances found me at her doorstep. She'd let me stay the night in my old, vacant two-room flat instead of returning to my aunt and uncle's house, which was a far distance away, plus hiring a cab was expensive.

A quote from *The Adventure of Charles Augustus Milverton* kept playing over and over in my head. In the story Sherlock said, "I think that there are certain crimes which the law cannot touch, and which therefore, to some extent, justify private revenge." I became obsessed and wanted to know what finally happened to Tomoo

Ashikaga. But now I also had that strange red book back in my possession, the one that I never fully understood but was willing to take great risks to find out what powerful peculiarities it had. After a hard day's work, I'd retire to my room and continue to uncover what really happened back in feudal Japan.

*   *   *

"Sleeping on the job?" Kentaro asked while knocking on my hard helmet to rouse me.

"I wasn't asleep," I replied rubbing my eyes.

"Then what were you doing?" my friend asked as he inspected me closer. "Looks like you nodded off to me."

"No. I was thinking…perhaps imagining that I was somewhere else besides here. I detest this place. I'd like to envision a better world filled with art and music, one not filled with all the wars and fighting and political power mongers always trying to usurp one another, raping and pillaging one town at a time."

"Yoko's been asking for you," Kentaro said, cajoling me out of my bitter mood.

"Yoko?" I asked.

"Don't act like you don't know who she is. That girl who's always following you around—the farmer's daughter."

"Oh her," I sighed, "always offering me fruit and rice balls when I don't want them."

"You should pay more attention to her. She'd make a loyal wife and companion," he suggested.

"My friend, Katsu-san, said the same about her."

"I wish I had a young lady offering me gifts like that, but she has no interest in me. If you knew what was best you'd stay away from that courtesan who's been flirting with you. Being with her will only bring trouble, and that's the last thing you want, Tomoo."

"Chiyo and I have been friends since our childhoods. The bond between us runs deep and strong like roots from an ancient tree," I explained.

"Old trees are still vulnerable. One strike of lightening and a centuries-old tree will fade into history," Kentaro replied. "I think that was from an old Shinto proverb. You are young and have so much life ahead of you. Lord Toshiro Takeda, and his son, Masahiro, will crush you like an ant if they think you are competing with them for the same girl."

"Ants? Trees? These sound like superstitions to me. I am convinced that benevolent spirits will favor us," I said, perhaps with false confidence.

The two of us heard temple drums in the distance.

"Both of us had better run along and get back to work." Kentaro gave me one last warning and ran off.

I finished most of my chores and had time to spare so I went back to that abandoned shrine where Chiyo and I had our trysts. This time, I came alone. I needed time to come up with a plan. Suddenly a rare white raven flew overhead. It circled back towards my direction and landed on a tree stump beside me. As I stared at him, he stared back at me. I thought that animals like this really didn't exist, except in myths and fables. When he hopped closer, he nipped at my nose.

"Ah, here you are, my friend," a strange peasant said who seemed to appear from out of nowhere. I suspected that he had been

331

observing me the whole time from a safe distance. He extended his hand and the bird landed on it as if previously trained.

"I'm impressed," I said.

"You should be," he replied.

"You were spying on me this whole time," I pointed out. "You and your bird."

"This raven is my second set of eyes. He's a magical bird."

"I suspected as much," I said as I stepped closer.

"We've also been keeping an eye on you and your lady friend every time you've gone up to this abandoned shrine."

Before he could utter another word I reached for my sword. How dare he invade our privacy! But my threat didn't go too far. The giant bird cried out and flew off. Then the strange peasant disappeared behind a blinding puff of smoke! How could someone simply vanish? My hunting skills were keen, but his mastery of the art of camouflage must've been better. The bird finally re-emerged, perched on a far off high branch. He silently stared down at me. It was only his telltale color that gave him away. But where was his elusive master?

The next morning I awoke to find that pesky white raven hopping all over my bedroll. He finally forced me to get up after he poked his beak inside my ear.

"It's my day off," I mumbled reaching for a cup of cold sake. "What did you want that couldn't wait until later?"

There was a note tied to the raven's leg. I reached over and carefully removed it.

"It's a map," I thought to myself. Besides that, the only other inscription was, "*Kyō, ni-ji gogo.*" The bird's owner wanted me to meet him at two o'clock that afternoon. I shooed the bird away, figuring I should get some breakfast.

I wondered if I should pursue that invitation. There were so many tales about shinobi clans, and many of them weren't all that favorable. But what other options were there? Being under the daimyo's wing was like being a few notches above a prisoner. I decided to at least check it out, but first tied my long hair up and hid it under a blue and white print cotton kerchief. By the time I donned an old set of training attire, I looked more like a wandering peddler than a warrior. I topped off my disguise with an old straw hat.

After climbing up and down unfamiliar hills, I found a fallen log and sat down. I brought with me a small basket containing food and a small jug of water. I was so thirsty that I drank the entire jug, wiped the sweat off my brow with the kerchief and tucked my hair back inside. After a while, that strange peasant, master of the white raven, reappeared.

"Twenty ryo," he said, cupping his hand as if asking for alms.

"I don't have that kind of money," I protested.

"My friends and I don't work for free," he said as began walking away. "You want the girl to be safe, am I right?"

I nodded my head. "What would you do?"

He laughed, "If I revealed secrets, you'd try to save the money and do the deed yourself."

I bit my lip. About twenty meters out by a clump of bamboo was that odd man with the chopped off, conical basket hat that I'd seen the first time I traveled back to Japan. I thought it was Finn, but dressed apropos for the moment. He was leaping about, gesturing like a wild savage. His words were gibberish, monkey-like chattering and were barely audible, but probably meant that he didn't want me to get involved with the shinobi clan.

I ignored him.

The peasant continued, "Samurai have a rigid code of honor, which you must obey without question. The shinobi don't have such restrictions. We operate outside of those limits. I can smuggle your friend out of town. You could join her later."

"This must be done," I said with my heart beating faster. "Perhaps I can get the payment."

Who was I fooling? That was more than I made in two months. There had to be a solution. The daimyo seemed to have unlimited resources, plus whenever he vanquished an enemy, he'd plunder their estate. There were chests of gold, rich silks, ivory *netsukes*, and exquisite decorative swords merely for show that would never see a battlefield. Some of his most coveted prizes were Portuguese rifles. It would've been impossible to account for every single item he owned, especially the ones he acquired by force. He'd never notice an item or two missing.

The little man smiled. "Tomorrow, show me what you can find, that you're earnest. If you hide it behind the Buddha statue at the Temple of the Weeping Tree my friends and I will get to work."

I agreed, picked up my basket and began to leave when he made one last request.

"I also need a token of your trust." He pulled out a small knife and cut both of our hands. "We're making a blood bond. You are part-ninja now. You cannot run away from us."

I looked at the wound in my hand and drew in my breath.

"It's for your protection as well as mine," he explained forcing the blood from my hand to flow into his. Then like a wounded animal, he licked his hand clean. His cut was shallower than mine. I had to tear off a piece of my bandana to serve as a bandage. By the time my bleeding had stopped, he was gone. In order to pay their commission, I'd have to steal from Lord Takeda. Now I was bound by an oath.

*   *   *

The Final Problem

Shortly after the assassination of the Archduke Ferdinand, Germany declared war on Russia and two days later on France. On August 4th, after Belgium was invaded, Britain finally declared war on Germany. I was looking forward to meeting Wendell in Edinburgh. He was on his way to visit his parents in Glasgow, but once war erupted, newspapers needed extra journalists willing to face the risks, and he was called off on assignment.

It was surprising how much enthusiasm my contemporaries on the home front showed regarding their commitment to the cause. My brain, perhaps tarnished from numerous time travels into the past, couldn't help but compare the new recruits to the knights who gallantly served in the Crusades. Young men lined up in the streets and were swept up in a pervasive patriotic fervor, eager to pledge their hearts and souls to an ideal that seemed as remote as stars in the sky.

This, however, was going to be a cross-examination of true convictions mixed with rude awakenings. It was one thing to prove one's manhood and be a role model to one's family and community. It was another to realize you were probably going to die for King and country. Besides, there were so many debates as to how and why the war started. Arthur took a stand and warned others that he saw it coming. H.G. Wells, who was always outspoken with his political commentaries said, "No one living, you know, knew what war was; no one could imagine, with all these new inventions, what horror war might bring. There was no music but a jangling war-song over and over again, and everywhere men enlisting, and in the dancing halls they were drilling."

Part of me wanted to imagine a dialogue between Arthur and Wells going something like this:

Arthur: "So Bertie, despite our long-standing differences we finally agreed on something. We both thought war would break out."

Wells: "Doyle, now you have a solution to finally get rid of Sherlock Holmes. Send him, along with Watson, to the Western

Front and have them blown up in the trenches. He might've avoided Reichenbach Falls, but I doubt if either one of them will survive German artillery fire."

Everyone was going crazy with war panic, and I was no exception if I was coming up with conversations like that even if it was only in my head. Meanwhile, I was stranded in Scotland. By day, I promised Lydia to excavate through the mess in her attic. By nightfall, I became the *ethereal archeologist* and continued to dig up more information by traveling back into the past.

Through dogged determination and persistence I discovered that I, as Tomoo Ashikaga, had stolen quite a treasure trove. The Takeda family had accumulated such a vast collection of antique porcelains, jade and ivory trinkets, guns, spears and knives— that nothing was missed. Much disappeared and wound up in shinobi hands. And since that funny little man and his shinobi clan did the worst of the crimes, I was above suspicion. Yet, it went without saying that I lived in the perpetual shadow of guilt and the fear of being discovered as the instigator behind all of the mishaps. So far, I'd been lucky.

A series of odd events surfaced around the compound. Such abnormalities were, in fact, so finespun and inconspicuous at first that it was nearly impossible to attribute any connection to shinobi wrongdoings and mischief making. Groups of samurai sentries were constantly being distracted by minor upsets. These would range from trivial pranks like having the daimyo's clothes disappear after a bath to subtle acts of sabotage, such as a flood and backup in his *benjo* or W.C. I suspected shinobi representatives had expertly orchestrated all these.

One day I, as Tomoo, awoke to hear clanging bells and banging drums sounding an alarm all over the village. My first thoughts were that a nearby building was on fire since this was also becoming rather commonplace. Was this an ambush from a rival warlord or another subversion? I got dressed as soon as I could,

336

grabbed my swords and joined my fellow comrade-soldiers in the courtyard to see what all the commotion was about.

"He's dead," someone whispered.

"Who's dead?" I asked.

"His mistress found him this morning with his throat slit. There was blood all over the place," someone else mentioned.

"Murdered?"

"He got murdered."

"An enemy, perhaps?"

"Or maybe one of his courtesans who wanted revenge."

"Buddha will take his revenge. The afterlife will offer no solace."

I kept turning my head this way and that trying to piece together the conversations and discern who was sharing them.

"Who got killed?" I asked.

"The daimyo," Kentaro said softly, as he came up from behind and placed a hand on my shoulder.

I blanched. "There's security everywhere all hours of the day and night. One would have to be a magician possessing unfathomable occult powers to get past that. We're not talking about simple herbs and potions where a guard could've been drugged and someone gained entry to the daimyo's private chambers. That's way too easy. Any one of us could've figured that out, although it's against our code of conduct to commit such a crime.

"It must have been an arcane act above and beyond the norm. Scaling the castle walls like a monkey and then disappearing in a puff of smoke," I replied vainly trying to come up with the best answer.

"Well, perhaps that's what someone did," another soldier said sarcastically. "I guess the *machi-bugyō* police haven't inspected your quarters, yet."

"No, they haven't," I replied, taken aback. I was still in shock. I turned back to Kentaro and asked, "Does that mean his son, Masahiro, will take over?"

337

"He already has."

"Maybe life will be easier," I said hoping to lighten up a grave situation.

"That's doubtful. He's already ordered a handful of his own guard to be executed. He's taking no chances that someone will also threaten his life. You were fortunate you weren't included in that bunch."

"That can't be so," I said, shaking my head in disbelief.

Our supervisor galloped in on horseback and officially called the troops to order.

"Men, you have probably heard that our beloved master is dead. Each and every one of you will also be interrogated, and we expect full cooperation. Meanwhile, Masahiro Takeda is our new leader. Pay him your full respect."

He considered all of us suspects. I began to sweat. Were the shinobi behind this murder, and would someone discover a link between us? The daimyo had been as much of a danger to them as he'd been to Chiyo and me. He was always talking about slaughtering each and every one of them, including the women and children, because they often allied with his enemies.

Later on I snuck over to a special spot behind the Buddha at the Temple of the Weeping Tree, where I'd anonymously leave my bounty or messages. I was determined to know the truth about Takeda-san's death. One of the clan members must've anticipated my arrival.

"So it was magic," I said accusing the man, whom I had never seen before. Cautiously, I drew closer.

"If that's what you want to believe," the stranger said, teasing me.

He casually leaned against a pillar, almost blending in with it. I knew all too well that before I had a chance to blink, he could've leapt at me with a drawn sword, or perhaps disappear. Ninja were masterful tricksters. I had to be on my guard.

"Did you turn yourself into a bird and fly over the fortress walls?" I asked, puzzled about the nature of shinobi magic.

The man started dancing and flapping his arms. He mocked me by pretending to be a giant bird. He thought it was comical. I did not.

"If your partners used such enchantment in their plot to kill Takeda-san, then I'm partially responsible. If it weren't for me your clan would've never been involved."

Murdering the daimyo was inexcusable. They didn't have to go as far as that, either to protect Chiyo and me, or to seek revenge from prior transgressions.

"I want to learn your magic," I said.

"You can't," he replied, as he silently and quietly came a bit closer and then poked out from behind a different pillar in the temple.

"Why not?" I asked.

"You're an outsider."

Once again I was not being accepted because of my station in life. I was never able to fully become a samurai, because I was inducted into the lower ranks from the outside. Now I had betrayed Takeda-san's community only to become like a wanderer, rejected and without a family.

"Even if I have to become as devious as you are I *will* learn your magic," I said, with confidence.

"Ha!" The man laughed and began to run off with speed beyond human capacity.

"No, wait! Stay!" I demanded having no idea where he had gone, or how far he had gotten.

"But there is no magic," he said, suddenly nearby again. "We only want stupid fools like you to believe that there is. Then we have control over your minds. Your imagination is a powerful weapon, and we know how to use that against you!"

He slipped behind the pillar. I charged over there, but in the few seconds that it took to catch up to him he had vanished.

339

"Show yourself!" I called out flailing my sword in the air like an imbecile. Maybe I'd get lucky and cut him down, even if it were impossible to see him. Finally, after searching all over the temple grounds, I ran out of steam. I re-sheathed my sword, took a few small coins out of my purse to pay my tithe, and knelt down in front of Buddha's statue.

"There is special magic," I said praying to my god, "and I want your help to learn it." I lit some incense, returned to my prayers, and listened to the wind for answers. Then that peculiar white raven flew into the old temple and landed on Buddha's shoulders. That was my sign.

Rumors stated that a ninja was only loyal to himself. Whether it was for the lure of gold or a matter of life or death, they would even betray their own friends and family. So in order to be one-step ahead I'd have to start thinking like one of them. It would've made tactical sense to avoid risks by sending different delegates to retrieve my secret messages and stolen artifacts. Assuming that my theory was correct, I took that gamble and carefully plotted to leave a series of notes that would eventually allow me to follow their representatives back home.

Often I'd bribe a few of my friends and sneak out of our fortification at night. I'd sleep in a carefully chosen hiding place to see if I could catch a glimpse of one of the shinobi retrieving my messages. This went on for weeks testing my patience and continued until everything backfired.

Suddenly, while in my hiding place, I gasped and choked, unable to breathe. I clutched at a nearly invisible, thin wire garrote that had been looped around my neck, pulling me backwards. I struggled to no avail. My captor loosened the noose's grip after securely tying my hands behind my back. Camouflaged fabric shrouds hid his identity, but when he spoke I was in for another shock. He was a she!

"How dare you spy on us and betray us!"

With unheard of strength for a woman, she threw a sack over my head, dragging me down the steep hillside to her camp. The next thing I realized I was trussed up against wooden poles in the middle of a village clearing. My inquisition followed.

"You've made a blood oath," a venerable man resembling a village elder stated. "Now you dare to rise against us?"

When I mumbled out nonsense, someone removed my gag so I could finally speak.

"No, you misunderstood me. I had no intentions of going against any of you."

"Then why were you trying to trap us?"

"I wanted to find out where you were hiding so I could explain everything. I had requested that the daimyo be indisposed, not deposed. He could've been sent far away, maybe to fight a battle or settle an argument. You weren't supposed to murder him. As much as I clearly despised him, you took this matter much further than I had anticipated. Now I bear the mark of being responsible for unconscionable crimes, which will haunt me for the rest of my life, perhaps beyond. We're all doomed. The gods will seek retribution."

"You shall be punished for your insolence," the elder announced. "Bravery has its time and place, and this was one instance where you were unwise to rise up against us."

"Cut his damned head off!" an innocent, young girl shouted.

I was stunned.

Next, a toothless hag relished the thought of torturing me to death. "No, keep him tied up and let him remain here. The crows will peck his eyes out."

Suggestions for reparation made their rounds, as a strong, tall man whisked me away and threw me into a ramshackle prison joining another captive. When I was tossed inside the cell, I stumbled and fell right on top of the other prisoner waking him up.

"What crime did you commit?" I asked.

"The crime of being different, I guess."

"That doesn't sound too serious."

"According to these shinobi, being an outsider is."

"Then I'm guilty of the same offense," I said, with regret.

"What about you?" the captive asked.

"They caught me spying on them."

The prisoner doubled over laughing. "Ha! A spy spying on a spy! I'd know better than to do something stupid like that."

"Tell me the *real* truth as to why the shinobi have such interest in you," I demanded.

"I'm a bard with magic and stories, or should I say enchanting fables? It's neither here nor there, because they're intertwined."

He pulled a small coin out of his pocket and twirled it around in his fingers making it disappear and reappear through simple sleight of hand. He offered it to me, but as soon as I reached for it he made it vanish. I looked down on the floor to see if it had slipped out of his fingers, yet I never heard it drop. Then the prisoner held out his closed hand. Slowly, he opened his fingers to reveal the missing coin.

"I bet you can't read my mind," I said, challenging him.

"I'd wager the opposite," he smugly replied.

We tried a few rounds. Each time he won the bet, and I lost. I did my best to banish my thoughts, but he took the pictures right out of my head.

"How did you do that?"

"Magic," he replied.

"Not the same as the shinobi use," I said suspecting otherwise.

"No, it's different."

"Then where are you from?" I asked.

"I escaped from Japan posing as a fisherman, accused of a crime I did not commit, but I encountered an unexpected storm and my boat got shipwrecked. Then a *huge* door opened up from inside a giant wave. I thought it was death calling out to me. Much to my surprise I was sucked inside, and I wound up all the way across the sea in China! There, I was also taken prisoner. Because I was so different, others assumed I must be evil or cursed."

The prisoner prattled on with his tall tale.

"There was a Chinese scribe named Jiang. He was the only one in the Emperor's court who could speak my language. He found me fascinating, so I took advantage of his trust and convinced him to help me escape and return to Japan. But I stole from him an unfinished scroll. It was a story he was writing for the heir of the throne. I guess it was my natural inclination to make off with something that wasn't mine, but that action has haunted me ever since."

He continued his monologue. My thoughts spun in circles.

"Wait a minute," I said interrupting him, "Who are you really? I don't even know your name."

"Does it really matter?"

I nodded my head. Of course it did.

"I'm Shokunin. There are others that call me the Thief of Tales," he said proudly. "I have the gift of a golden tongue along with the expert ability to talk my way out of any predicament with my magnificent anecdotes. Even if it means stealing another's dreams or sharing my own, I can conjure yarns out of thin air."

"What a marvelous power to possess. I wished I had it. But why are the shinobi so interested?" I asked, still unable to make the connection.

"Many ninja pose as actors, musicians, singers, dancers or swordsmen in traveling theatrical troupes. That's how they often get inside the fortified walls of their enemies, which are otherwise inaccessible. Everyone loves to be entertained, so it's easy to engage an attack or take revenge upon someone when he is full of saké and his guard is down. Sometimes their goal is to obtain information, and other times it's for far more serious concerns. Remember that ninja are hired as spies by the highest bidder, and a good spy always has a trunk full of disguises.

"Since I always have a tale to tell and I suppose that they're not as creative as I, maybe they're running out of ideas. They've performed the same old shows over and over again. It's not only bad for business, but it's too dangerous to risk being found out that they're only posing as entertainers and have ulterior motives.

"But getting back to why they were interested in me, I know they seek this scroll, but you saw what I did with that coin, earlier. I'm quite adept at hiding it. However, I also suspect that I tend to talk in my sleep. Themes of some of their new performances have seemed strangely familiar, as if they were stolen from my own tales. It's just been impossible to confront them about it. My weakness is that I tell these incredible stories, but I can't write. I never learned how. These narratives? I forget them, especially the dreams."

"You don't remember a thing?" I asked.

"Not much. It's an affliction, a hex or an evil spell I suspect—a glib tongue and a faulty memory. Can't believe I was born with it. How long are they detaining you?"

"Once I prove my innocence, they should release me. They can't get to the daimyo's hidden treasures without me. Greed will prevail," I insisted.

"Help me break out of here," Shokunin said, "and I will reward you justly."

His air of mystery intrigued me. Both of us had to escape, and I needed to find out what was happening with Chiyo. Had arrangements been made for her to leave town? No one would ever give me details. I wanted to know that she was safe and well. After all, she was with child and had to escape before it became obvious to the new daimyo and his cohorts.

Days passed and my anxiety was mounting. There was only so much that my friends could do back at the compound to cover up for my prolonged absence. One day my temper flared. I was tired of waiting.

"Teach me your magic chants—your incantations," I angrily shouted at Shokunin.

In reaction to my outburst, he took that scroll he'd been hiding all this time and struck me hard in the middle of my forehead.

"Just like what everyone else told you, it's all in your mind," he said with an impish look in his eye. Then, he magically materialized outside the holding cell while I still remained behind bars. How did he do that? I couldn't believe my eyes. He wished me good luck and ran off. And he said that there wasn't any magic? He lied!

But suddenly, I understood that I had the uncanny ability to think on my feet. No longer was I the naïve samurai bound by convention, with a limited imagination. Somehow, the magic had transferred, perhaps rubbed off when he slapped me on the forehead. Whether it was genuine or not, it gave me the confidence to talk my way in and out of any situation I desired, much like Shokunin. My mesmerizing stories began to gain favor. Finally, I convinced the shinobi guards to release me from prison so I could also return home.

When I arrived back at the Takeda Castle grounds, I was terrified. What kind of convincing excuse was I going to be able to come up with? But I wasn't the only one who was scared. It turned out that not only did Masahiro prove to be more treacherous than his father, but also as a result of my unexplained absence I was demoted and no longer trusted to be part of his private guard. My new assignment was to oversee the grounds keepers to make sure they were doing their duty! But the gods must have been on my side. Disobedience was paid for in bloodshed. More heads rolled with frequent executions. Somehow I was spared.

Now the risk was even greater in robbing daimyo's coffers to pay off the shinobi, and they threatened blackmail if I didn't comply. All this time, I was also fighting my own private battle. Poor Chiyo was missing, and there wasn't any news as to what happened to her. I lived in a constant state of guilt mixed with the fear of being caught. Were my storytelling powers going to allow me to cheat the demons of death? I was concerned that I'd be put to that test.

I couldn't bear to live with myself a moment longer. My crimes were unpardonable, and my actions were irreparable. Second thoughts? It was way too late for that. I adjusted my kimono, all white, trying to murder my misery. I wasn't supposed to scream. I was supposed to be stoic and resigned to ceremony, but I did scream, loudly and hysterically. This was the only honorable way when there was no other way out. My guts fell into my hands. I dropped my *wakuzashi*, drenched in blood. No, I did this out of shame. And I did it alone, in my room without the mercy of having a trusted comrade end it all with one swift stroke of a steel sharp blade to my neck. A straight horizontal cut across, from left to right, with a sharp pull upwards at the end with the belly meeting the spirit.

Memories flipped backwards like still images from a film, frame by frame. I finished writing my swan song of devotion and death, artfully made on rice paper with a brush and ink. The *kanji* disappeared one by one in reverse order. Then back to internal dialogue—well planned with thoughts of *jushin*, inglorious passions to chase my true love into the afterlife. The ink touched the paper's surface. The brush returned to its inkwell. My blood became black ink. Cryptic pictographs dissolved into my skin, as I tumbled head over heels into a dark whirlpool of impending death and my breathing became more and more shallow. Finn held fast to my hand.

"*Quod ita sit, iam factum est.* It's already happened, hasn't it?" I asked, turning back towards Finn as my brain twisted inside out.

This was the only option: *seppuku* or disembowelment, otherwise known an honorable suicide. What about the promise of seeing Chiyo in the afterlife? She had performed a similar act by slitting her throat. This was the lovers' abomination—the bane of being born in the Land of the Rising Sun. Once again, I tumbled head over heels through the blackness of chaos.

My consciousness finally stepped back from Japan and my attention returned to the present. Finn was patiently waiting beside me, and I tried to stop choking from all the dust and filth in Ding's

346

basement. Then I let out a hardy sneeze, nearly dropping the book that contained the necessary portal.

"Was this what led up to my demise?" I asked Finn, still trying to clear my throat.

"This is just a sample of what happens when you fail to accept my guidance."

I wasn't up for another lecture, so I started to gather my belongings to head upstairs, but Finn stopped me.

"John...there's more."

"More? Tomoo was responsible for the death of Arthur's...I mean, Masahiro's father. Am I going to pay that price now for those wrongdoings then?"

"For starters, if Tomoo Ashikaga had married Yoko, the farmer's daughter, none of this mickle mess would've happened."

"But I, or Tomoo, didn't love her," I protested.

"But she was an honest girl, and one who was dependable. Little do you know, but Chiyo lied to you. You swam against the stream of fate trying to pursue her affections. You knew that going in, and yet you still chased after her."

"I don't understand. We loved each other and trusted each other implicitly."

"I wouldn't be so sure of that. Chiyo was with child..." he confided to me, "but it wasn't yours."

Finn's soft voice trailed off. Misty-eyed, I slowly closed the ominous storybook that led me into the Secret Library and had also allowed me to immerse myself into the experience and travel back in time. Tomoo's tortured soul finally vanished. A troubled man, who was hopelessly in love, died in vain.

*   *   *

It's a Long Way to Tipperary

No one expected the war to escalate, and I was no exception. Talk about town suggested that the conflict would be over before we'd know it—six weeks at the most. My relatives insisted that I go over to my old alma mater, as well as, some of the other local colleges to see if they needed any music professors since we all suspected there would be complications in returning to the Conservatory. No matter where I went, there were no openings despite my impressive credentials.

One evening I was sitting and finishing dinner with my aunt and uncle.

"Any luck finding a position?" Uncle Tommy asked.

Being in a sarcastic mood that evening, I quoted a line that Sherlock Holmes said in *The Man with the Twisted Lip*.

"My mind is like a racing engine, tearing itself to pieces because it is not connected up with the work for which it was built."

Uncle Tommy hadn't read that story and failed to grasp the connotation. My aunt asked if I cared for dessert.

"Perhaps I should join the military and earn the King's shilling," I said, plunging my fork into a slice of pie. I felt dejected and at a loss.

"You're not a soldier. You'll die!" Aunt Maggie protested. "You're not used to that kind of life."

"I'm not going to die, because I'm not a famous pianist, yet," I said, adding levity to an otherwise grim situation.

Realizing that we could've continued arguing until way past bedtime, I excused myself and went outside to take a long walk until my feet were tired, and it began to rain. There was a lot on my mind, and it was incomprehensible that I committed such malfeasance before I was born. In that sense, ignorance truly was bliss, but if there was a lesson to be learned, I still hadn't figured it out.

When I turned around and decided to head back, I came upon The Admiral Benbow, a pub that had been one of the familiar cornerstones of the old neighborhood. Since I still wasn't quite up to returning home, I ducked inside to rest and dry off. It was crowded for a weeknight, and besides the usual there were several card games in progress. After a few shots, I felt lucky, let down my guard and joined in. What I failed to realize was that a team of shrewd opportunists not only started cheating me out of my hard-earned savings, but managed to pick my pocket, as well.

It wasn't until I finally I felt ill, left and vomited in a back alley when I discovered that I had been bamboozled. I looked up, and there was Finn leaning against a lamppost, utterly disgusted and staring at me while I was despondent.

"You could've used your magic," he said.

"Come again?"

He went on with his diatribe. "First of all, you should've been perceptive enough to know what those blokes were after, but I guess the bacchanalian spirits had the better of you. Secondly, with your psychic prowess, I'm surprised you couldn't second-guess them at cards. You have that ability."

"That's beside the point. I haven't developed that skill and didn't realize that I could. My money's gone. I can't borrow anything from Uncle Tommy, and I've been unable to find employment."

Inside of my coat pocket was that mystifying red book that haunted me from time immemorial. It made my dreams materialize into realities and provided a gateway to the unrecorded truths behind history. I clutched that in one hand and my timepiece in the other.

Then I called out to Finn in defiance, "Can't I sidestep this bloody war and hide someplace off in the future until it's over?"

But it seemed like there were certain life lessons one couldn't avoid, and there was no magic in the universe powerful enough to arm-wrestle with the will of the gods. As if I hadn't already drunk from the cup of bad luck, a seagull flew overhead and covered me with splat. It was impossible to return to Stuttgart. Omens seemed to suggest that my days in Edinburgh were also numbered. I wished I had the influence to turn back the entire world's clock so the war wouldn't have started to begin with. Powerless in that respect, I made a tough decision. My mentor, Arthur, previously served his country and became a better man for it. Now, it was my turn to prove that.

349

Acknowledgements

To my agent, Paula Munier, and Steven Emecz and Brian Belanger at MX Publishing who had the insight to believe in this project. Louise Herring-Jones and L.S.L who came to the rescue, Wendy Padob, and J.P. and P.K., who said that my karma was to write. My hat also goes off to teachers Michael Neff, Susan J. Breen, Bill Milling, my History of Cinema professor, and I also dedicate this book posthumously to Dorothy Dobbins who never doubted my creative abilities. My freelance editors John R. Douglas and Karen Heuler, and Alex Franks, for his expertise and knowledge of Victorian literature and life in Edinburgh. Thanks to Clare Button and her associates at the University of Edinburgh library and Professor Peter Nelson in the music department. A special thanks to Charlotte Dickerson and Rachel Foss at the British Library, A.F. Judge, Joyce Hutton and everyone at the Military Intelligence Museum, the staff members at the Imperial War Museum, Librarians Martin Cherry and Susan Snell at the Museum of Freemasonry and the staff at the National Archives in London. Also D. Bennie, Fiona Hooper, Lan Chen, Eric Taxier, Trina King, David Kogelman, James A. Moore, and Sherlockians Dr. Robert Katz and Christopher Zordan. Dr. Masaaki Hatsumi, Professor Mark P. Donnelly, Jesse Barnack, Aldric Giacomoni, Rachel Klingberg, Martin Page and Paul Macdonald for their expertise in martial arts. John Clute, Kenny Lane, the staff at the Rare Book Division at the Library of Congress and Eugene Ossa. My German, Viennese and Czech constituents: Neza Lovse; Max and Julia Bach; Liz Birsztejn; Jitka Kotria; Gaga Paudyal and family; Mandy Hering; Christian Wilhelm and family; the staff at the Stadtarchiv and the Schwules Museum Library in Berlin, the staff at the Stadtarchiv in Kiel, Dorothea Bader, Staatsarchiv Ludwigsburg; Sabine Schrag and Doris Segbehe from Landeshauptstadt Stuttgart Kulturamt Stadtarchiv and Claudia Nebel at the Staatliche Hochschule für Musik-Stuttgart.

www.elizabethcrowens.com

Also from MX Publishing

MX Publishing is the world's largest specialist Sherlock Holmes publisher, with over a hundred titles and fifty authors creating the latest in Sherlock Holmes fiction and non-fiction.

From traditional short stories and novels to travel guides and quiz books, MX Publishing cater for all Holmes fans.

The collection includes leading titles such as *Benedict Cumberbatch In Transition* and *The Norwood Author* which won the 2011 Howlett Award (Sherlock Holmes Book of the Year).

MX Publishing also has one of the largest communities of Holmes fans on Facebook with regular contributions from dozens of authors.

www.mxpublishing.com

351

Also from MX Publishing

Our bestselling books are our short story collections;

'Lost Stories of Sherlock Holmes' , 'The Outstanding
Mysteries of Sherlock Holmes', The Papers of Sherlock
Holmes Volume 1 and 2, 'Untold Adventures of Sherlock
Holmes' (and the sequel 'Studies in Legacy) and 'Sherlock
Holmes in Pursuit', 'The Cotswold Werewolf and Other
Stories of Sherlock Holmes' – and many more......

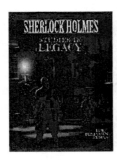  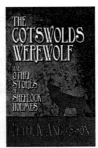

Also from MX Publishing

"Phil Growick's, 'The Secret Journal of Dr Watson', is an adventure which takes place in the latter part of Holmes and Watson's lives. They are entrusted by HM Government (although not officially) and the King no less to undertake a rescue mission to save the Romanovs, Russia's Royal family from a grisly end at the hand of the Bolsheviks. There is a wealth of detail in the story but not so much as would detract us from the enjoyment of the story. Espionage, counter-espionage, the ace of spies himself, double-agents, double-crossers...all these flit across the pages in a realistic and exciting way. All the characters are extremely well-drawn and Mr Growick, most importantly, does not falter with a very good ear for Holmesian dialogue indeed. Highly recommended. A five-star effort."
The Baker Street Society

www.mxpublishing.com

CPSIA information can be obtained
at www.ICGtesting.com
Printed in the USA
FFOW01n1712240416
23459FF